THE WIELDER'S DISCOVERY

Editing by Kelly Hammond, Pickles Editing

Proofreading by @Brittany_Bookworm

Book Cover by Maria Spada

Map by Saga Mackenzie

1st edition, 2024

ISBN: E-Book 979-8-9905423-0-3

ISBN: Paperback 979-8-9905423-1-0

Library of Congress Control Number: 2024916732

To Morgan, for being the first person to help me finish a book

and

To Rachel, for challenging me to write this one.

MISTFELL
NOREINDAR FOREST
BESA
WORGRETH MOUNTAINS
AERDMURE
ARKWOOD
ADENAPORT
ASTRIA
N
S
E
W

PROLOGUE

KAEL BLACKMORE CLOSED THE door to his lab as silently as he could. Wynna was still here, hunched over the microscope, one hand on the notebook next to it ready to scribble her latest observation. Her long, dark hair was pulled back, those eyes he frequently lost himself in hidden from view. Kael smiled at her. How had he gotten so lucky to have a woman like her as his wife, as the mother of their child?

"This is it, isn't it?" He walked toward her and slid his hand onto her back between her shoulders, the strands of her hair brushing against his skin.

She glanced up at him, those eyes sparkling like sapphires as her lips curled into the smile that always weakened his knees. "I really think it is. We should alert the others and get them here to share this. We won't be able to keep it quiet for long."

Kael sighed. "One more moment. I want to bask in this revelation alone with you for one more moment."

He closed his eyes and tipped back his chin, facing the rocky ceiling of the underground laboratory they'd built three years ago. Underground was the only place for him and his partners to conduct their research; it was out of sight and easily hidden. Not that they tried to be secretive about their efforts in the lab. No, they'd received funding and permission to conduct their research from the governors themselves. But no one knew how the public would react to their research or its ramifications, so Kael decided it was best to keep it secretive until they had proven their theories. Or disproven.

Except this morning, Kael did it. He discovered the missing link.

Wynna, ever the diligent mother, balancing their one-year-old on one hand and her passion for research on the other, came over to the lab as quickly as she could after dropping the baby off with her parents. She'd spent the last hour reviewing his work, a second set of eyes to confirm that their discovery was sound, Kael's calculations correct.

Kael had left her to it—she preferred to work in silence and solitude—and used the time to find something to eat from his office off the long hallway that led to the laboratory. He always seemed to forget to nourish his body when his mind whirled as it did today. If it wasn't for Wynna constantly reminding him to eat, he probably would've wasted away into nothingness already.

"This will change everything, Kael," Wynna said reverently, glancing up at him. "For the better. This is how equality begins, with this discovery."

Kael nodded and smiled, rubbing his hand along her back, savoring the softness of her hair. "A better world for our family. And you are the pioneer behind it all."

Wynna stood and moved to the empty wall behind where she had been sitting. "But you were the one with the grand idea that led us here. Show me again." She gestured to the empty wall.

With a wave of his hands, a myriad of numbers, symbols, and letters appeared on the wall, almost like they were etched into the rock, shining as if made from light. The outcome of their work, the final calculations that Wynna had checked, and the code that would bring equality to their world once and for all. Wynna giggled and wrapped her arms around Kael's waist.

"My genius," she whispered and kissed his cheek.

He grinned back and pressed his lips to her forehead. "My jewel."

He savored this moment, breathing in her warm and soothing scent as he held her. "Ok, let's send the signal."

He released her and closed his eyes, straightening his arms down by his sides as he collected his power within him. His mind shifted to send each of their partners a sign to come to the lab, an invisible wisp of power sent from his body to theirs. They would know what it meant. That Kael and Wynna had made the final discovery they had all been working so hard and so long to achieve. He opened his eyes and looked to his wife, his happiness showing on every line of his eyes, every crease of his lips.

"And now we wait."

Margot and Hendl arrived first. Hendl, as usual, was stoic and unexpressive, while Margot, just a few steps behind him, exuded an excitement that mirrored Kael's own. Though they were twins, Margot and Hendl could not have been more dissimilar in personality, but their minds were forever linked in a way that made their intelligence nearly insurmountable.

"You did it, didn't you?" Margot gasped for breath from her rush to get to the lab, her red hair hanging in loose strands around her face and her chest heaving.

They'd arrived so quickly they must've used their aero-witch powers to help push the wind at their backs.

Kael only nodded, settling in to wait for Benedict, their last partner. It was their rule. Everything was done as a team. It was rare for all five of them to be working in the lab at the same time. Despite this, or maybe because of it, they would wait to share their biggest developments until the entire team could be assembled, even if it meant holding the rest in suspense to wait for the last member to complete the circle. Sometimes for hours.

"Last I heard, Benedict was going to meet with the governors to provide an update. He may not come for a while," Margot said. She pushed the loose strands of hair behind her ears, waves of auburn hair falling like flames against the black of her tunic. "The elven governors called the meeting specifically."

"Then I suppose we could pour ourselves a drink while we wait." Kael nodded to Wynna, who popped the bottle of sparkling wine they'd reserved for this occasion.

She poured out five glasses and handed three of them to the witches standing around, reserving one each for herself and Benedict. Kael marveled at the amount of power that stood in this room alone. Not all witches were as gifted as these. And to have all of them working towards the same ambitious goal was truly astounding. He doubted that the discovery could have been made if their team had included anyone with even a drop less power or intelligence than these five.

Their glasses were nearly empty when footsteps reverberated from the hallway leading to the laboratory door. "About time, Benny!" Hendl exclaimed, moving to open the door for their partner.

As soon as the door swung wide in front of him, he collapsed, clutching his neck as if he couldn't breathe. Margot screamed and ran for her brother, but soon found herself collapsed next to him, struggling for air.

Kael looked through the doorway to see armed assailants, swords and daggers cluttering their belts, masks covering their faces. The first few in the group must have also been aeros, to snatch the air from Margot and Hendl's lungs like they had. Kael froze—unable to move, unable to form words, unsure what to do but certain this was all a mistake.

Wynna's scream knocked him out of his trance, a throaty, guttural sound that pierced his heart. This threat was real. His wife was in danger.

And he would do anything—*anything*—to protect those he loved.

1

ANY MINUTE NOW. THAT horn would blare any minute now.

Nova Astor looked around her classroom, the students within it just as anxious as she was to hear the sound announcing the start of summer. The twenty eight-year-old witches, elves, and humans that made up her final period mathematics class had pushed their desks against the walls and were playing games in the center of the room. It was the last day of school. She hadn't dared try to teach them anything.

"Your turn!" a young elf roared over his peers. Nova leaned back in her chair, watching the group, only enough to ensure they didn't get too rowdy. If her prior three years of teaching had taught *her* anything, it was to let kids be kids today.

The elf was pointing at a human child, who happened to be one of her best students this year. The girl, Addy, was quiet but studious, and from what Nova could tell, didn't have many friends in the class, which unfortunately didn't have any other humans on its roll. But maybe this would be an opportunity for the girl to join in some fun.

Addy pursed her lips and shook her head, directing her gaze down to her crossed legs. The kids were playing Truth or Dare, or something very similar to it. Instead of whoever was "it" picking a truth or a dare to do, the classmates picked whether whoever was "it" had to answer a truth or perform a dare. The game was popular among students during lunch or recess breaks.

Nova hated the game. But as long as no one got hurt or was pressured to do anything they didn't want to, she tried not to interfere. She'd just sit here, a fly on the wall, watching the next generation of Astrians have their fun.

The class groaned at Addy's response, giving Nova the impression that she did this often. *Good for you, kid,* she found herself thinking, running a hand through her long black hair.

"Come on, Addy! Live a little!" one student cried.

"Yeah, don't be such a human," another said, earning a laugh from the crowd.

The horn blared, and Nova caught the look of relief on Addy's face. Cheers rang out from the students as they grabbed their bags and ran out the door, some stopping to wave to Nova, all forgetting entirely that Addy had declined to play along.

Addy moved slower though. Nova studied her for a moment before standing to approach her.

"Addy?" Nova asked, stopping next to the girl. Addy's face was blotchy, but her eyes were dry. "Are you excited for summer?"

The girl looked up at Nova, her expression morphing into a joy that Nova suspected was only a mask. "Oh, yes, Miss Astor. Very much."

Nova smiled and bent down to match Addy's height. "Don't let the other kids get you down. You are smart—smarter than all of them combined."

Addy's eyes met hers for a moment before they lowered to the ground, the toe of her shoe twisting into the floor. "But...I'm just a human."

"Just?" Nova sighed, trying to still her heart. "Let me tell you, there's no such thing as *just* a human. Especially when it comes to you.

You might not have witch magic or elven abilities, but there is magic in math. There is magic in science, which I hear you're quite good at too. *That's* the magic in you."

Why were those words always easier to say than to live by? If only she could listen to her own advice. A lump formed in her throat, but she swallowed it down and forced a smile again.

Addy looked up with a grin. A real one this time. "Thanks, Miss Astor. I'm going to miss you next year."

Pressure built behind Nova's eyes, emotion threatening to burst through. The last day of school was always bittersweet, but she hated the good-byes the most. "I'll be right down the hall next year if you ever want to visit." She reached out to squeeze Addy's arm gently. "Now, go, enjoy your summer."

With one last smile, Addy picked up her bag and skipped out of the classroom, leaving Nova alone with her thoughts. Thoughts of magic, thoughts of her own insecurities and inabilities, despite being born a geo-witch...

Not a moment later, someone came bounding into the room with so much excitement exuding from her the desks rattled against the walls. Nova whipped her head toward the door to find a certain geo-witch with bouncing chestnut curls and a slender body just a few inches taller than her own who she happened to know quite well.

"Summer is officially here!" Raelyn Astor said, twirling in the empty space Nova's students had just vacated. Nova laughed, watching her sister's infectious joy. If anything could loosen the grip on her heart that lingered from her conversation with Addy, it was Raelyn.

"Finally." Nova grabbed her bag from the back of her chair and draped it across her back. "Shall we go find Cassie and Bea?"

Raelyn looped her arm through Nova's. "Yes. Time for our celebratory drinks and then tomorrow—"

"Beach!" Nova finished, her smile growing wider. The family's cottage at the beach was her favorite place. There was no better way to start the summer than a trip down there.

"I can't wait," Raelyn said as she started to pull Nova toward the door.

With one last glance over her shoulder at her classroom, Nova crossed the threshold and pulled the door closed behind her, officially leaving this school year behind.

The next morning, Nova awoke to the sun streaming in her window, illuminating the cozy bedroom. Birds tweeted merrily outside. A grin broke out across her face, erasing the dull ache growing in her head.

Perfect.

She'd slept in, just as she had hoped on this first day of summer break. She rolled over, pulling her covers in close, and sighed. Another year down and another summer ahead full of freedom—total freedom to do whatever she wanted. And yet, so far, she had only their beach trip planned.

The shuffle of footsteps on wood and creak of a cabinet opening floated toward her through the closed door. Raelyn. Of course she would be up and ready to go. Whereas Nova preferred to sleep after a night like the one with Bea and Cassie last night, Raelyn could more easily shake off a hangover. Especially when a trip to Adenaport was on the line.

The scent of coffee brewing in the press made its way to her, and her eyes widened further. There was one thing and one thing only that could get her out of bed with any sort of urgency, and that was a steaming mug of coffee.

"Morning, sis," Raelyn said when Nova entered the galley-style kitchen a few moments later. Raelyn's shoulder-length curls were already perfectly styled. How had she managed to get such natural ringlets when Nova's long, sleek hair could barely hold a wave, even if it sat in a braid all night?

Nova grunted in return, the headache strengthening, and reached for the ceramic mug that Raelyn was pouring. Just one sip was all she needed to start feeling alive, the jump start she needed to begin her day. And with any luck it would help counteract that witch wine from last night, too.

She savored that first sip, then smiled as the warmth of the mug radiated through her palms and the brew traveled through her veins. The aroma of chocolate and chicory had a therapeutic quality, which she inhaled as the steam from the mug reached her nose. There was something about her sister's coffee that was superior to all other coffees. Raelyn claimed she did nothing special to it, but Nova was certain that as a geo-witch, Raelyn must use some of her earthly powers to add a certain richness to the coffee beans.

They came from a long line of geos. Their father, Luc, was currently one of the three witch governors. His power was immense, enough to summon an earthquake and fell even the tallest of trees. Raelyn had inherited much of his power, though she rarely used it, likely so as not to show up Nova.

Because Nova had inherited very little power at all.

While most geos could grow a flower from soil as infertile as sand, she was unable to get even a seedling to appear. Where Raelyn could move boulders to form a bridge to cross a river, Nova had trouble getting rocks to skip across the same river's surface. It had always been so—Nova, the elder, watching as Raelyn, one year her junior, surpassed her magic in every way.

She'd long since accepted the fact that she would never be a stand-out witch, that she would never be able to do many of the things her friends and family could do. But acceptance didn't make the anguish go away. Didn't stop the vise that clenched her chest, tighter and tighter every time she tried a new spell...and failed.

It was one of the reasons that the conversation with Addy had rattled her so much yesterday.

Nova was certain her sister knew that she harbored doubt and anxiety about her true standing as a witch if she had no magical abilities to show for it. She was sure that was why Raelyn kept her powers close to her chest, only letting them out for things like this mug of coffee, when the impact would do more good than it would harm. Nova appreciated her sister's compassion, even if it added guilt into the mix of her suppressed feelings.

She set the mug down on the counter of the island that separated the kitchen from the main living area and exhaled. "Much better."

"Ready for the first of what will hopefully be many adventures this summer?" Raelyn asked, clapping her hands.

One of the best perks of being a teacher, and sharing a career with her sister, was the summer breaks. It had been Nova's dream to teach, and since Raelyn had always followed in her footsteps, it made sense that she, too, began instructing young witchlings, elves, and humans a year after her. Nova specialized in non-magical subjects like mathematics, while Raelyn preferred to work in a more physical environment, teaching her pupils how to harness their geo-powers through spell work and charms.

Nova grinned and took another sip. "Yes! I'll be ready to leave in about an hour. I'm mostly packed."

Raelyn turned to the sink to start cleaning up the coffee press and grounds. "Great! The carriage should be here around then. Three whole days at the seaside, just you and me, Nova, can you believe it?"

Their family's seaside cottage was about half a day's journey by carriage from Arkwood, the capital of Astria. It was their "start of the summer" ritual, or at least it had been for the last four years they'd both been teaching. They used the time to decompress, relax, read, and soak in the sun. And usually set some plans into motion for the rest of the summer.

Nova was most looking forward to lying in the sand with a novel and her annual trip to the nearby spa. The humans who ran the spa near the cottage worked wonders and always made sure she left feeling even more relaxed than when she came. If she closed her eyes and tried hard enough, she could almost smell the eucalyptus oil now...

This year, Father and their mother, Raella, would not be joining them as they usually did. "Duty calls," he had told them last week over family dinner. "Besides, you both are old enough to deserve some time away from your old parents."

It would be strange without them there, Father's booming voice filling the halls and the scent of Mother's numerous hair products wafting into their bedrooms. But he was right. They needed some time to be true adults on their own.

Her father had been elected one of Astria's governors just a few months before Nova was born. He'd held the position ever since, alongside two other witches, three elves, and three humans. This regime had been established to build peace among the three races almost half a millennia ago, when Astria had been ravaged with war. Back then, its human citizens, powerless and seemingly weak, were subjected to ridicule, abuse, and even slavery. A group of well-minded elves and witches had finally banded together with the humans to overthrow the monarchy that put witches in power and brought in the nine governors. The governors were to be elected by their race, serving until they decided to leave or were voted out by a majority of the other governors. It had been a good system, as evidenced by the fact that very little war had broken out in the five hundred years since its establishment. But things were not as perfect as they seemed, if the way the students in her classroom treated each other was any indication.

"I'm going to go pack," Raelyn said, drying her hands on the dish towel next to the sink. Of course she had waited until the last minute to pack. *Classic Raelyn*, Nova thought with a chuckle.

She used that as her cue to head back to her room and finish her own packing. Her bag lay open on the floor next to her bed, her armoire doors left cracked from last night. When she had returned from their night out, she'd grabbed a few tunics and dresses and one bathing costume from inside and threw them in the bag, the best one could do after a few drinks. There wasn't much else she would need, but she grabbed the novel she'd fallen asleep holding last night from her bedside table, plus a spare one she'd picked up from the library for this trip. They ended up nestled in with her clothes and the extra pair of sandals she scooped up from next to the armoire.

Just under an hour later, the caffeine from the coffee set in, and her mind cleared, the ache now gone entirely. She could almost keep up with Raelyn's ebullience as they entered the carriage Father had arranged for them. The windows were open to let in the breeze, and the cushions atop the benches inside had been lined with white linen instead of the deep red velvet that they bore in the winter.

"Here we go!" Raelyn squealed, clapping her hands with childlike excitement as she settled into her seat.

Nova laughed, kicked off her sandals, and settled in for the long ride.

Though the road to the seaside was filled with ruts and bumps from the rocky terrain, Raelyn had bewitched the carriage wheels to roll smoothly, regardless of how the earth below them appeared. Nova and Raelyn played their usual games to pass the time but eventually resorted to gossip like they often did.

"I'm so glad the school year is over. The kids this year were...beastly." Nova took a swig from her water skin, her thoughts turning to Addy again. Her legs were resting on the bench seat in front of her, her back against one of the windows. "Please tell me *we* weren't that catty."

Raelyn scoffed and leaned her head against the wall of the carriage. "Definitely not. I had one hydro this year who found out how to make it look like the poor human kids wet their pants and made it a daily ritual! I talked to his parents numerous times, but the little shit never stopped. I'm guessing the apple didn't fall far from the tree."

"You never mentioned that! What the hell is it with these kids?" Nova rolled her eyes. "What happened to the respect and decency we were raised to show for humans? Sure, they don't have powers, but they have intellect, and they are an important part of our society." She quieted her voice, adding, "Besides, powers don't determine anyone's worth."

"Exactly." Raelyn reached across the carriage and squeezed her hand. "Let's just hope I don't have to clean up after kids 'peeing' themselves again next year. I'm so over that." She rolled her eyes before looking out the window. "Oh look! We're here!"

Nova glanced outside, and sure enough, the carriage was pulling up in front of the cottage. Sunlight shone through the panes of glass lining the side of the carriage, and when the driver opened the door for them to disembark, a gentle sea breeze blew into the carriage. She exhaled and allowed a wave of peace to overtake her. The sea. The salt air.

Her happy place.

2

THE COTTAGE HAD BEEN the family getaway for as long as she could remember. Most summers growing up had been spent down here. It provided a great opportunity for Nova and Raelyn as young witchlings to practice their magic outside the city, but it also served as a family retreat and one of the rare times they could have Father to themselves. When they were in Arkwood, he was generally so busy with government business that family moments were few and far between. But here at the seaside, it was just the four of them.

Well, and the staff who helped run the household.

As a governor, Father felt it was his duty to portray equality among the races in everything he did, including in his hiring practices. Humans were excellent for office work and record keeping. Elves, with their exceptional senses and strength, served as the perfect security and reconnaissance teams. And witches of all types had roles to play, too: pyro-witches for keeping the candles and lamps lit; hydro-witches for ensuring places stayed clean and had access to running water; aeros for their ability to regulate temperature within buildings with warm or cool air; and of course, geos for tending to the lands, food, and structures. In fact, the only types of witches he didn't directly hire were healers, because they were all employed at various ministries for heath, and wielders, because there were so few of them anymore.

There were also so many new laws regulating wielder power that they generally kept to themselves in the witch woods that filled the Worgreth Mountains to the west of Arkwood. It was safer for everyone that way.

At the cottage, the Astors employed mostly humans and hydros. Humans ran the day-to-day operations of the house, like cooking and laundry. The hydros were mainly responsible for protecting the house from surges should a mighty storm decide to unleash itself on the cottage. Such events happened often enough that Father kept a hydro on the payroll living in the attic loft year-round just in case, though he rarely showed himself.

The butler approached them down the wide front steps, grinning from ear to ear. He was dressed in the same black suit and white collared shirt he always wore, but his hair was noticeably grayer than it had been the last time they'd seen him. "Miss Raelyn, Miss Nova, welcome home. Always a pleasure to have you here."

"Hi, Mr. Larson," Nova said, brightly. Mr. Larson had been running the cottage since she was about five years old. He treated her and Raelyn like they were his own children, though he didn't have any of his own.

"I've got Chef preparing your favorite supper. Leave your bags with me and go enjoy yourselves."

Raelyn squealed and leapt into his arms. He took a step back to steady himself against her embrace, the grin never leaving his face. "Thank you, Mr. Larson! Oh, it's so good to be back. Come on, Nova, let's check out the beach." She grabbed Nova's hand, and they sprinted off around the back of the cottage with a wave and a smile to Mr. Larson.

The cottage sat directly on the beach, nothing separating the back porch of the cottage from the rolling surf and silky sands save for some wild vegetation. There were no other cottages within sight on either side, even if the closest village was only a mile inland. It was an oasis, a hideaway, a retreat.

Just what Nova was looking for.

"Finally!" she said, as they came to a stop just a few feet from the edge of the surf. She tossed her sandals aside before she buried her toes in the sand, listening to the waves crashing as sunbeams caressed her skin. A seagull cawed overhead, searching for its friends or maybe a crab to feast on. "Remind me, why are we only staying three days this year?"

"That was your idea, not mine!" Raelyn twirled once, her arms outstretched. "Although I must admit that the idea of missing out on a whole summer in Arkwood is less than appealing."

It was true, Arkwood came alive in the summer. Positioned not far from the coast itself, Arkwood may not offer the white sand beaches that Adenaport and its surrounding towns offered just south, but the parks and gardens came alive with blooms of every color, musicians played at many street corners, and festivals seemed to occur every other night, in honor of some heroic governor or one of the three goddesses—Canta, Dalia, and Terra—or sometimes just because.

Their friends would never forgive them if they missed out entirely on summer in Arkwood.

"Let's come back later in the summer then. And invite the girls." Nova tucked a strand of black hair that had blown loose from her braid back behind her ear. She started mentally cataloging all the activities they could plan for a trip here with Cassie and Bea: pampering at the spa, swimming in the ocean, exploring the shops in town. Their friends had never been here before; there was so much to show them. "It's about time we shared this cottage with someone other than Mother and Father."

"That would be so fun!" Raelyn plopped down on the sand and reclined her head back into her hands, her elbows splayed wide. Her thin muslin dress was long, pooling around her knees and leaving her shins exposed to the late afternoon sun. "This is going to be the best summer. Nothing is going to get in our way."

Nova smiled and stared out over the white-tipped ocean waves, praying to Canta that Raelyn would be right.

The next morning, Nova slept in again, her belly full of Chef's special fish dinner that had always been her favorite. The sun was shining brightly, its beams bursting through her window, and the gentle roar of the waves outside beckoned her to join them.

She tied her hair back into a braid, her favorite way to keep the long tresses out of her face, and changed into her bathing costume, throwing a sheer, short, black dress over it as a cover-up. Aiming to spend as much time on the sand as possible, she followed the smell of bacon to the dining room for a quick breakfast, her novel in hand. Despite its lofty title, the dining room wasn't anything as formal as the name suggested. Rather than a large room with a stately table that could be set for twelve like Mother and Father had in Arkwood, the room had a small, circular table with four seats. An elegant buffet along one wall rounded out the furnishings.

Chef had placed a buffet of breakfast dishes and drinks on the table for her and Raelyn to enjoy. Though considered human, Chef was actually half-witch. His father had been a pyro, or so he assumed since he was born with a small amount of pyro power. But he had been raised solely by his human mother in Adenaport, and it had been a surprise when he found, around age ten, that he could light a candle with the snap of his fingers. His powers may be weak, like Nova's, but they came in handy when cooking. Or keeping meals warm for two sisters who slept in too late.

She was helping herself to coffee and a heaping scoop of eggs when Raelyn emerged, arms stretched above her head and still in her pajamas. Her hair had been pulled back into a short ponytail, though a few curls hung loose around her neck.

"Good morning!" she greeted, always the more chipper of the two.

Nova shook her head and pointed toward her full mug. "Not yet."

Raelyn laughed and grabbed a plate, joining Nova at the buffet. "Drink up quick. We have lounging to do."

The brew wasn't quite as good as Raelyn's, but after a few sips, the fog in Nova's mind cleared. She couldn't have pointed a finger at when her coffee addiction truly started, but it must have been sometime in her years of studying to become a teacher. Late nights writing out essays on parchment using a pen geo-enchanted with mineral ink followed by early mornings in class had meant very little sleep. Coffee had been the only cure then, and despite ensuring she slept more now, coffee had become too ritualistic to give up.

"Ok, you can talk to me now," Nova said. She picked up a piece of bacon and took a bite.

"Oh, thank Canta. Nova's back," Raelyn teased, placing her plate at the seat next to Nova. She pulled back the chair and plopped onto it. "What would happen if there were a coffee famine?"

Gasping around a mouthful of bacon, Nova replied, "Don't even joke about that. I'd never wake up."

Raelyn laughed. "Speaking of sleep, that's my plan for once we get to the beach today. A nice, long nap."

"You just woke up," Nova deadpanned.

"Your point?" Raelyn raised an eyebrow and sipped her own coffee. "It's vacation, Nova!"

They finished their breakfast quickly, Mr. Larson coming in at the end to clean up and let them know he'd set up their lounge chairs along the shoreline, a canvas canopy stationed between them to provide shade for both.

"What would we do without you?" Nova grinned at him, as she grabbed her book and headed for the door.

It was an idyllic day: Just the right amount of heat, a gentle sea breeze, clouds blocking the sun at semi-regular intervals to give them a break from its strength. While not a typical geo-witch ability, protecting her skin from the sun's harmful rays was something Nova had mastered. She was even able to protect others, including Raelyn. Her sister had never mastered this ability, but Nova was happy to help, especially since there were few things she could do that Raelyn couldn't do for herself.

They spent the day chatting, reading, and sleeping on the beach. Mr. Larson brought them lunch, so they didn't have to leave their oasis and then retrieved the scraps and dishes an hour later.

"Shall I request a certain dinner for you both tonight?" His eyes twinkled with the usual sparkle Nova would catch when he did something for them.

While the fish dinner last night was their favorite, there was one particular meal where Chef excelled. "Could you ask Chef to make his pasta?" Nova asked. Next to her, Raelyn nodded vigorously as she sipped from the fresh glass of water Mr. Larson had delivered.

"Of course." Mr. Larson smiled and winked, turning to head back to the cottage to deliver the message.

Nova picked up her book to resume reading, her finger slipping between the pages that held the bookmark.

"Want to know another great thing about vacation?" Raelyn asked. Nova let out a small sigh and closed the book again, turning to look at her sister. "Not having to cook or clean. Sleep all day and let others take care of us. The dream." She put her hands behind her head and leaned back against her chair, her elbows splayed wide.

Raelyn had always been a little...spoiled, perhaps was the right word. A byproduct of being the youngest, she somehow found a way to make it endearing. To most people at least.

"You know I do most of the cooking and cleaning at home, right?" Nova kept her tone calm, because in truth she didn't mind doing those things at all. But she couldn't deny the nag in her gut from Raelyn's lack of appreciation.

Raelyn picked up her head and looked back at Nova. "And a damn fine job you do, sis." She flashed a grin, a grin that immediately dissolved that nag in Nova's gut, because who could get mad at Rae, let alone stay mad?

<h1 style="text-align:center">3</h1>

DINNER WAS AS DELICIOUS as expected. Once it was cleaned up and the sun sank behind the horizon, she and Raelyn decided to go for a walk on the beach, another of their favorite pastimes as children. The early summer night air carried a slight chill, but the humidity leftover from the day hung around, keeping them warm enough. Waves continued to crash on the beach, a beam of moonlight highlighting their crests.

Nova inhaled the salty sea air, feeling immediately at peace. This place—this beach—was her favorite place in the entire world. It was full of serenity and nostalgia, happy memories of the four Astors together as a family, building sandcastles by day and chasing the nocturnal crabs in the evenings.

The sand was soft under her feet, a scattering of driftwood and shells lining the high tide mark from a few hours ago. Nova stopped to pick up a shell. "Rae, look at this. Isn't it pretty?"

The shell was a perfectly intact scallop shell, pearlescent and white on the top, its ridges shimmering in the moonlight, and a deep pink on the underside.

Raelyn stopped walking and peered over at the shell. "Oh, it is! Save that one for our collection."

The ever-growing shell collection at the cottage originated when the girls were about five or six years old. It had gotten so big that Mr. Larson had been forced to find an aquarium-sized container for it a few years ago, though admittedly its growth had since slowed.

A loud splash echoed off in the distance. Nova looked up quickly, catching the iridescent tail of a sea dragon entering the water. "Did you see that?"

"I did!" Raelyn replied, her gaze fixed on the horizon. "Maybe it will come back?"

They stopped and watched for a few more moments, but the dragon never reappeared so they continued to walk.

"Remember when we were little," Raelyn said, breaking the silence, "and Father told us that if we went in the water, the sea dragons would eat our toes?"

Nova laughed. "How could I forget? I don't think I went anywhere near the water until I was about ten and realized he had been joking."

Raelyn turned to face Nova, so she was walking backwards, just a few steps ahead. "Whereas I saw it as a challenge and tried my best to lure one in."

"Didn't you want to keep it as a pet at one point? You made a collar for it and everything." The breeze blew a stray lock of her hair into her face. Nova brushed it away, but it blew right back across her cheek. This time, she left it there, despite the tickle that lingered.

"Sure did. I was going to name it Twinkle, because that's how their scales always appear when lights hit them." Raelyn sighed and turned back around. "Oh, to be young again."

They returned to the cottage as darkness was fully setting in. Mr. Larson was waiting for them on the porch, unusual in and of itself because he generally let them be and only appeared when necessary. Nova hadn't expected to see him again until morning. But there was a shift in the air, a new tension that could be cut with a knife. The breeze had stilled, and the ground beneath her feet seemed firmer than sand should. Her body stiffened.

"I just received an urgent raven from your father." Mr. Larson held out a scroll for them to read.

A raven. Not the cheapest way to deliver messages, but certainly the fastest way to do it.

Nova took it, hands trembling. Father wouldn't have bothered them here if it wasn't urgent. Wouldn't have paid the exorbitant fee for a raven if he didn't think his daughters needed this message right away. It wasn't like ravens were even that easy to come by this late in the day when the post offices were closed.

She read the words on the paper, but they didn't make any sense. A male witch she had never heard of had apparently broken out of Mistfell Prison in the cold northern region of the country, far north of Besa, the elves' ancient stronghold. To her knowledge, no one had ever escaped from Mistfell before. If they had they were quickly apprehended by the warden who manned the prison walls and the protective wards that surrounded the fortress. Father was summoning them back to Arkwood immediately, "for their protection".

She handed the note over to Raelyn to read and looked up at Mr. Larson, raising her eyebrows. "Who is Kael Blackmore?"

The look on Mr. Larson's face said everything she needed to know. Kael was someone to be feared, someone powerful, who would stop at nothing to get what he wanted. And if he broke out of Mistfell, there must be something he wanted, badly.

"Shortly after you were born, he was apprehended for dangerous research activities just outside of Arkwood. When he realized he was caught, he blew up the lab, his partners with it. It was quite the story at the time, especially because one of his partners was his wife."

Raelyn gasped, the note falling out of her hand and onto the floor. "That's awful."

"Your father was the one who issued the order to arrest him and send him to Mistfell," Mr. Larson continued, stooping down to pick up the note.

Nova swallowed. "So, we are in danger of retaliation."

"I assume so, yes." His hand shook as he spoke. "I've already readied your carriage and loaded your bags. You should leave as soon as possible to get home. It's unlikely Blackmore would have made it this far south so quickly, but no one really knows the extent of his power. He can't be underestimated."

"But if he's still so far north," Raelyn said, crossing her arms, "why can't we stay for the rest of our trip? There's no way he'd get here within the next two days."

She had a point. Nova looked to Mr. Larson for his response, but in her heart, she knew there was no way he would disobey a direct request from their father.

Mr. Larson straightened his back. "I would love nothing more than for you to stay, but your father—"

"Wants us to come home in the middle of the night, without a guard to protect our carriage?"

Nova winced at her sister's tone. She understood being upset, but for Raelyn to take her frustration out on Mr. Larson was unfair. "Rae, you know our driver is trained in defense. He's a fantastic pyro-witch—"

Raelyn shot her a look of such fury that Nova clamped her mouth shut. But Mr. Larson stepped forward and pulled open the sliding door for them to pass through the house. "These are unprecedented times, Miss Raelyn. Hopefully Blackmore will be caught soon. You and Miss Nova are welcome back when that happens." He spoke with a calm that helped put Nova's heart at ease.

"Thank you, Mr. Larson." She gave him a hug, then crossed the threshold into the house.

"I don't like it," she heard Raelyn say behind her, "but I can see there's nothing I can do about it." Nova turned back to see her giving Mr. Larson a hug of her own.

He released Raelyn then glanced between the two of them. "Be safe." The look in his eyes twisted Nova's insides. It wasn't just their safety he was worried about, but the safety of all Astria's citizens.

It wasn't just fear that was coursing through her veins as she stepped into the carriage. Confusion mixed itself in, too. Her brow furrowed as she took her seat, wondering why she'd never heard of Blackmore. Why his whole story was a surprise.

She and Raelyn settled into the carriage for the overnight journey home. Though exhausted, neither slept, instead trading theories as to why they hadn't heard his name or his story before tonight. And what the research could have been about to cause such an uproar. Whatever it was, the governors must not want anyone else to find out and continue with it.

The speculation seemed to help cool Raelyn off. "Maybe it had something to do with dark magic?" Raelyn theorized. Dark magic was highly dangerous but wasn't something Astrians often had to face. Astria had its crime problems, but with a zero-tolerance policy for unauthorized dark magic, most didn't bother even considering it. Not to mention that all books containing the lore of dark magic were either kept under lock and key at the Atrium or had been destroyed centuries ago.

Nova shook her head. "I don't know. Only a fool would try to attempt that, but what else could be so horrific, so dangerous, that Father would send him to prison?"

"Aside from him killing his whole family? His partners?" Raelyn's voice shook, and not from the rattle of the carriage.

"Mr. Larson made it sound like he only did that once he was caught." Nova leaned her head against the wall of the carriage, her braid falling across her shoulder and onto her chest. "So, what did he get caught doing?"

They arrived back at their Arkwood flat just as the sun was starting to peek over the horizon. The driver unloaded their bags, and they made their way up three flights of stairs to their flat. To Nova's surprise, their father was pacing the living room in front of the L-shaped couch that took up most of the area, clearly waiting for them to ensure they made it safely.

"Father!" Raelyn exclaimed, throwing herself into his arms. Nova dumped her bag on the floor and leaned against the island. She'd never been much of a hugger, at least where her father was concerned, so she simply nodded in his direction.

"Girls. Thank the goddess." He embraced Raelyn, then pulled away, leaving one arm around her back. His dark eyes exuded worry, but something else lurked behind them too that Nova couldn't quite place. Sadness? Determination? Fear? "You both must be exhausted."

Nova *was* exhausted, now that he mentioned it. A yawn escaped her lips. "We couldn't sleep."

He gave Raelyn one more squeeze around her shoulders. "Go rest. I will be here when you wake up, and we will discuss arrangements."

"Arrangements?" Another yawn. She really needed some sleep.

He shook his head. "Sleep. You're safe." And with that he sent them off in opposite directions toward their rooms with a wave of his hand. With another wave, he turned the front door and windows into impenetrable stone, though their appearance didn't change. Nova's heart eased enough that by the time she curled up under her blankets and closed her eyes, sleep overtook her quickly.

4

A FEW HOURS LATER, a thunderous knock on the front door pulled Nova from sleep. Moments later, her mother's voice filled the apartment. "They're here? They're safe?"

"Yes, come in quickly, Rae." Father. Still here, still watching over them.

At the sound of her mother's voice, Nova threw her blankets off and rushed to meet her in the living room, needing the warm comfort only her mother could offer. Delicate arms wrapped around her, her mother's floral scent filling her nose. "Oh, Nova, thank Canta. I'm so relieved you both made it back."

Mother had the same curly hair as Raelyn, but her frame was shorter, stouter. She wasn't perhaps a witch of traditional beauty, but she knew how to stand out and was revered as a governor's wife. Anyone who wanted to be anyone in the Arkwood social scene needed Raella Astor on their side.

"We have so many questions, Mother." Nova's voice was hoarse from sleep. She put a hand to her throat, rubbing the delicate skin there with her thumb.

"I know, I know. Once Raelyn gets up, we will do our best to answer them all. Come, I brought breakfast." She shuffled over to the kitchen counter, where two white boxes emitting a warm, buttery aroma were perched. Father was already there, helping himself to one of the pastries.

Mother didn't cook, never had for their entire childhood. But she had not come empty handed this morning, having stopped at the family's favorite bakery on her way over or, more likely, having asked the baker to drop an order at their penthouse that she could bring with her to their flat.

Nova and Raelyn lived in what was affectionately called the Outcast District of Arkwood, though the name was a complete misnomer. It was the place to be for any young, single witch, and they had felt no shame using their family connections to score an apartment in the most coveted building. But they had grown up in the Business District, which was close to Father's office in the Atrium, the ornate domed building that held all the government offices for Astria. It was about a thirty-minute walk from the penthouse to their flat, but by carriage, the ride was cut in half.

Nova was helping herself to a chocolate croissant when Raelyn emerged. Her mother shrieked and ran to her younger daughter, embracing her in what may have appeared to an outsider to be a hug identical to the one she gave Nova. But deep down, Nova knew Raelyn was her mother's favorite and that there was more behind that hug than met the eye. It used to bother her, much in the same way her lack of magical power did, but she'd gotten over it long ago. And just like with her powers, Raelyn recognized the favoritism their mother displayed and constantly tried to downplay it.

Sure enough, Raelyn pushed her mother away slightly, saying, "Mother, I'm *fine*. Do I smell croissants?"

After helping herself to one, the four of them settled around the tiny dining table off the kitchen. Nova cleared her throat and spoke again. "Ok, what's really going on?"

Mother tapped her heel anxiously on the ground, biting her lip. Father reached a hand to cover hers and squeezed.

"Twenty-five years ago," he began, "Astria suffered one of the worst displays of dark magic in recent memory. Kael Blackmore, his wife, and his associates were conducting research in an underground lab, experimenting with magic they never should have touched. One day, the experiments went too far, and one of his colleagues managed to escape to the Atrium to warn the Governors. We were immediately dispatched to bring them in, but ultimately, we were too late. In his fury and mania, Blackmore killed his wife, their baby, and his in-laws, before then destroying the lab and his other two associates, twin aeros, with it. Six lives lost in the blink of an eye." Father paused, appearing to need to collect himself. A tear slid down Mother's cheek as she stared at her hands.

It was worse than Mr. Larson had described and more horrible than Nova could imagine. Who would kill their own family? What drove someone to do that? Her hands gripped her seat, her knuckles turning white.

Raelyn spoke first. "What were his powers?"

"Wielder," Mother said softly, her eyes round and brimming with tears.

Father nodded. "And he went too far with it. We managed to get him before he could do any more damage and sent him to Mistfell. I'll never forget the meetings I had with the other governors in the aftermath, trying to figure out the best way to keep as much of the incident under wraps as possible. We couldn't risk anyone else getting wind of Blackmore's experiments and picking up where he left off."

"How did it come to that? Isn't research highly regulated?" Nova asked. Father and his fellow governors had an entire team solely devoted to following research, and they were known to pull funding when things went in the wrong direction.

"I'll regret this part until my dying day," he began, hanging his head. Raella squeezed his hand, which was still gripping hers. "I was the one who initially approved the research. But Blackmore didn't follow his plan. He deviated from the approved experiments, and we didn't catch it until it was too late."

"Your father took it so hard," Mother cut in, her voice cracking as a tear slid down her cheek. "He made it his personal mission to find Blackmore quickly and deliver him to Mistfell as a way to right the wrong he felt he had committed by approving the research."

"Father, you couldn't have known," Raelyn said.

He shook his head. "No, but I learned a powerful lesson that day and have been working hard every day since to redeem myself, to make this world a safer place for both of you through efforts like the wielder regulations. But now...he has escaped."

"And he wants revenge." Nova's heart was starting to race, her blood pulsing rapidly in her veins.

"It's very likely. He may also try to pick back up where he left off. He was incredibly passionate about his research."

Nova and Raelyn exchanged glances. She could tell Raelyn wanted to know about the research topic as much as she did, but if their father had spent twenty-five years keeping it confidential, she knew better than to ask. He did not show preference for his family when it came to following the laws.

He continued, "We are all going into protective custody."

"What?!" Nova and Raelyn exclaimed simultaneously. Nova whipped her head around to her father again, her jaw gaping open.

Mother reached for Raelyn's hand. "It's for our safety. Blackmore is dangerous, and he likely knows that targeting us would hurt your father the worst, so we must look out for each other."

Father nodded and clasped his hands in front of him on the table. "It's only until he is caught, which we expect will be soon. We have all our best tracking him, elves, witches, and humans alike. He will not elude us for very long."

"But what does protective custody mean?" Raelyn asked.

How was this going to impact their ability to enjoy their summer, see their friends, explore the city, or even go back to the cottage?

"This building and ours will receive extra security detail," Father began, his voice level and calm, a complete contrast to the turmoil building in Nova's body. "And we will each be given our own personal guard as well. Elves. I've been promised they are highly skilled trackers, concealers, and proven warriors." His eyes flickered toward the door. "They should be here soon."

"So, we can go about our daily lives, as long as our new elf friends come with us?" Nova clarified. This wasn't ideal, but perhaps it wouldn't be so bad. Her heart slowed a bit as she drew in a deep breath.

Father sighed. "For now, yes. If Blackmore is sighted anywhere close to Arkwood, or we receive new intelligence on his motives, that may change."

Nova leaned back in her chair and crossed her arms. "Surely, he'll be caught long before he gets anywhere close. Mistfell is weeks away by carriage and the entire country is looking for him."

"Can we do anything to help?" Raelyn asked before shoveling the last bite of croissant into her mouth, seemingly relieved their summer wouldn't be ruined.

Mother shook her head, but Father spoke. "No, just listen to your guards, remain vigilant, and keep in close contact with us." He paused, then looked directly at Nova, her insides turning to stone under his gaze. "Blackmore operates in fear, but his power shouldn't be underestimated. Leave this to the Mistfell guards and the soldiers who are searching for him."

She frowned. Was her father implying that she would search him out herself? Why would she do such a thing?

Mother's mouth turned up into half a smile as she stood and headed toward the kitchen. "We will stay till the guards arrive. Hopefully in a few days, we'll be laughing about how quickly he was found." She started tidying up the leftover pastries and crumbs on the counter.

Nova didn't buy it though. She could see the fear hiding poorly behind her mother's eyes. Could see her arms trembling just slightly as she stacked the pastry boxes and pushed them to the side.

Nova excused herself to bathe, shuffling toward the bathing room attached to her bedroom. She turned the knob on the faucet, filling the tub with water from the pipe system set up by hydro-witches. She dipped her fingers into the stream and exhaled. It was exactly the right temperature, having been warmed by pyro enchantments.

Wanting nothing more than to sink into the warm water and not emerge until Blackmore was captured, Nova dropped the T-shirt and leggings she'd worn to sleep onto the floor and dipped a toe into the water, followed by the rest of her. The water had a soothing effect on her body, but her mind—that wouldn't settle so easily.

Without any remarkable powers, what could she do to protect herself? She would become insignificant, small, fully dependent on her elf guard and at the mercy of their protection. The full weight of her lack of power had never hit her so monumentally, never seemed as important to survival as it did now. Most of the time, her lack of power was more of a nuisance than something that impacted her life. But now, all that had changed. Oh, what she wouldn't give for the ability to throw a boulder, open a pit of quicksand, or summon an earthquake.

Drawing in a deep breath, she submerged herself in the water, her dark hair floating in swirls around her head, wishing beyond belief that she could cleanse away every fear, every doubt that consumed her mind as she did.

5

WHEN NOVA RE-ENTERED THE living room an hour later, physically refreshed but still emotionally drained, she found its population had doubled. Raelyn and her parents had left the table and were facing a group of four elves, three males and one female, all with characteristically pointed ears, who were crowded around the kitchen island. The eldest male elf, whose light hair was cut so short he appeared bald, was conversing with her father, his black eyes squinting and brow furrowed as if taking every word Father said with much scrutiny.

She instantly tensed, a small fire starting to kindle in her chest. Having a guard *theoretically* had been one thing but seeing them here now—in the flesh—was another entirely.

"Ah, Nova." Father turned toward her with a small smile that did little to calm her. "You'll see our new guards have joined us." He started waving toward each of them in turn. "Esta Larue will be with your sister." He indicated the pretty female, whose dark eyes, tightly formed ponytail, and perfectly made-up face made her look delicate, but the weapons on her belt and the size of her biceps indicated otherwise. "Atlas Martel will watch over your mother." He gestured to the tallest of the males who stood in the back of the group, who gave a small nod in her direction. "Persy Voss will try to keep up with me." He threw a smile at the male he'd just been conversing with, who simply nodded in response. "And that leaves Fynn Voss to guard you."

She looked at Fynn, who was standing just behind Persy. He was tall—more than six inches taller than herself—muscular, and had his blonde hair pulled back into a bun, though not nearly as tightly as Esta. One strand near his forehead had fallen out and was tucked behind his ear. He had dark eyes like the rest of the elves, but where most that she had met had eyes that appeared like midnight flecked with stars, Fynn's had an almost violet tint to them. Maybe it was just a trick of the light, but she wanted to look closer, move closer to find out. And his body—those well-defined muscles nearly begged her hands to run over them. His facial features were highlighted by prominent cheekbones that made her heart flutter, and—

The left side of his mouth ticked up in a half grin, having noticed her appraising him, and he nodded her way. She averted her gaze, her cheeks flaming as her eyes drifted to the floor. Where in Canta's name had her mind been wandering?

"Excellent." Persy clapped his hands together, ignorant of their exchange. "As I said, Governor Astor, your family is in the best of care. I personally selected these warriors and have been overseeing their training. Fynn may be my son, but don't worry; he has proven himself time and time again, and his agility in particular is top of his cohort."

Cohort. So, these elves had been in training, likely at the prestigious Besa Academy, which turned out more warrior elves of the highest caliber than any other institution in Astria. Situated in the elf stronghold, its establishment predated the governors and produced a legacy of notable elven warriors, both male and female. Nova had never met one that had graduated from Besa, but their reputation preceded them. The anxiety sitting heavy on her chest lightened, ever so slightly, at the thought.

"I have no doubt that you've assigned your finest, Persy. You haven't failed me yet." Her father glanced among his wife and daughters. "Each of your guards has been briefed with the rules and is aware of where the other hidden guards are surrounding your building. Should you need to get word of anything to me, or your mother, let Esta and Fynn know, and they will be able to send a message."

Nova nodded in acknowledgement, still trying to divert her full attention back to the room by focusing her eyes on Father instead of her guard. But Raelyn said, "Wait, does this mean constant supervision? Are they living with us? I assumed it was only if we needed to leave the flat that we'd need a guard."

That got her attention. Nova's pulse quickened as her father replied, "Yes. It's for your protection, Raelyn. Blackmore's power is immense. We can't risk that he might find a way to get in here and find you unprotected."

No, no, no. This was not what Nova had imagined either. How was she supposed to enjoy herself, *be* herself, if she was being constantly watched? If there were eyes on her every second of the day like an animal in a cage?

Heat was continuing to build in her body, like a fire slowly catching, being fed more and more fuel, and her mind was a jumbled mess of thoughts she couldn't sift through. She wanted to tell her father he was being ridiculous, that she and Raelyn deserved some privacy, but couldn't form the words.

Her eyes flicked frantically over to Raelyn. She hoped her sister, who was never afraid to stand up to their parents, never at a loss for words, would say something more, but she found Raelyn standing there red-faced and mouth agape. As speechless as Nova.

Father straightened and brought his hands together at his chest. "Now, I must be off. Back to the Atrium, to brief the remaining governors."

Mother extended her arms, moving toward Raelyn first. "And I must be getting back to the penthouse to take care of some arrangements for upcoming functions I need to either cancel or tighten security on. My girls, you are in the best of hands. But please, be smart and stay safe. This will be over soon."

She wrapped her arms around Raelyn tightly, landing a quick kiss on her cheek, before turning to Nova. The hug she received was a little less tight, a little less warm, and her mother skipped the kiss good-bye entirely. But the show of favoritism was overshadowed by the looming sense of dread, of anger that was growing inside her.

Father merely nodded at each of them, his gaze hardening as it landed on Nova. She swallowed, unsure why it left a tingle in her spine, but she forced herself to smile and nod back.

The elder Astors and their new guards left the apartment. Mother turned for one last glimpse at Raelyn, the look on her face pained. It was clearly killing her to leave Raelyn, but Father would never have stood for her remaining behind. He wanted them to act as normally as possible, not letting on to the public that they were living in fear.

Mother exhaled a deep breath, then shut the door behind her and was gone.

That left Nova and Raelyn alone with their new guards in the suddenly very small apartment. Raelyn looked close to tears, while the elves remained stoic and steadfast by the door.

"So," Nova said, trying to break the tension, to ignore her body's urge to flee. "What now?"

Esta snorted, but it was Fynn who answered, "Pretend we aren't here. Orders are to go about your lives as normal until we hear otherwise. We're just here to accompany you."

Nova looked at them incredulously, brushing aside the way the sound of his voice struck her like a chord from a perfectly tuned piano. Raelyn had turned away and was staring out the window, ignoring the situation, but the heat that had started building in Nova the moment she'd met the elves had reached its threshold and exploded out of her as she said, "Does that mean you'll be watching us sleep? Bathe? Get dressed?"

"Don't be ridiculous." Esta rolled her eyes.

Fynn elbowed the female elf, as if to remind her not to talk impolitely to their charges. "She means that of course we will grant you privacy when you need it. We will only enter your bedrooms if requested, for instance, and will set up our cots out here." Nova noticed for the first time their collection of belongings, including two folded up cots pushed to the back of the room.

At that, Raelyn turned back to them and said, "Perfect, I'll be in my bedroom until he's caught then." She turned and strode to her room, slamming the door behind her in a huff and rattling the shelves and art that hung on the adjoining walls.

Nova winced. "Give us a moment," she said to the elves before following her sister. She opened the door slowly and peeked her head through the opening. "Rae?"

Raelyn was lying on her stomach on her bed, her face turned away from the door, looking instead toward the window that overlooked the street below. Nova crossed the threshold, closed the door behind her with a soft click, and sat down next to Raelyn, rubbing her back soothingly.

"I know this is awful and not at all how we expected summer to go. But I'm here. We're in this together." Thank goodness for that at least. Not only could they stay together, but they could also stay in their own home, rather than somewhere else in hiding.

"It's so unfair." Raelyn's voice was muffled slightly by the pillow, but Nova caught the resentment in it. "We've been in the public eyes our whole lives, but we've never needed guards before. I guarantee you none of our friends will have guards. No one will want to be around us if we have to bring those two along everywhere." She flailed her hand toward the door, indicating the elves waiting expectantly beyond.

Nova continued the circular motions on her sister's back. "It won't be long before they find Blackmore, and we can go back to normal. Everyone is looking for him, and no one trusts him enough to hide him or help him."

At least, she hoped that much was true. Father hadn't said as much, but if Blackmore had killed his entire family and his research partners, who could he have left?

Raelyn rolled to her side and looked at Nova, her eyes watering. "We have babysitters. Babysitters, Nova. At least yours is handsome. Mine looks like she wants to flay alive the next person who looks at her wrong."

Nova laughed at that assessment of Esta. It was not incorrect. Esta definitely had the more intimidating demeanor of the two, not that she would dare cross Fynn, either. But apparently, she wasn't the only one who found him attractive...had Raelyn also imagined what those sculpted muscles felt like? Had she also noticed the purple gleam in his eyes?

She shook her head, pushing aside thoughts of the elf that had somehow weaseled into her mind again. "What if we think about them as new friends? Maybe if we get to know them and they get to know us, we can just be like friends hanging out together all summer."

Through a sniffle, Raelyn responded, "I doubt Miss Loaded with Knives is one for enjoying a game night or drinks in the city. Nor is Mr. Perfectly Built."

Yep, Raelyn had definitely noticed the muscles.

Raelyn brushed a curl out of her face. "They're here to work, Nova, not to party. Even if we *did* befriend them."

Nova pulled her hand from Raelyn's back, clenching it into a fist in her lap. It wasn't usually worth arguing with Raelyn when she was in one of her moods, even if Nova disagreed. "No, you're right."

They sat in silence for a few more minutes, until interrupted by the sound of Fynn clearing his throat from the next room. Raelyn sat up, rubbed her hands against her thighs, and laid her head on Nova's shoulder. "Together?"

Nova sighed, inhaling her sister's sweet floral scent. "Always."

They'd been making this promise to each other for as long as Nova could remember. Only a year apart in age, she and Raelyn had always been thick as thieves growing up, and nothing changed once they moved out of the penthouse and into the flat. They shared a profession, they shared hobbies, they shared friends. They also shared their struggles, and there were times in her life where she would not have made it through if it wasn't for Raelyn. Together was their favorite way to be.

After one more deep breath, Raelyn caught her eye and smiled. The two grasped hands and stood up to face their new reality together.

6

NOVA AWOKE THE NEXT morning, hoping it had all been a dream, that she was still at the seaside cottage about to spend another lazy day at the beach. But when she peeked her eyes open and was met with the white walls of the flat instead of the pale green walls of the cottage, she groaned. It *had* been real. There were indeed two elves sleeping on fold-out cots in her now cramped living room, one of them assigned to watch her every move.

She might have decided to lay in bed all day were it not for the smell of coffee that wafted into her room and the grumble of her stomach. Last night, a human woman had delivered a wagon load of food, compliments of their mother. Nova could have sworn her mother expected them to be locked down in the flat all summer with how much she had ordered. Nonetheless, she appreciated the thoughtfulness behind the gesture, especially since it contained a plethora of fruit and vegetables that Raelyn was able to enchant so they didn't spoil too quickly. It hadn't all fit in the kitchen cabinets and so in the end, Fynn had stacked the overflow as neatly as he could in the corner of the kitchen. Her eye twitched each time she spotted the clutter, but she also recognized that the irritation was likely amplified by the general lack of amusement for her current situation.

When she entered the kitchen, she expected to see Raelyn hovering over the coffee pot, but she stopped in her tracks when she found Fynn, pouring coffee from the press into a mug. He looked like he had been up for hours already: his white-blonde hair neatly tucked into a bun, his clothes fresh and clean, no sign of the dark circles like those that tended to dwell under her eyes.

He looked her way as she walked in and handed her the mug. "I heard you stirring so I took it upon myself to get the coffee started. Raelyn let slip last night that you were less than savory without it."

Nova nodded and took the mug without making eye contact. Fynn was being kind. This situation wasn't his fault after all. He was likely just as annoyed to have to watch over her as she was to have him watching over her. Yet here he was, making coffee for her, trying to help her in the part of the day when she was at her worst.

Attractive *and* kind? Maybe she *could* give him a chance. To build a friendship, that is.

Then again, she hadn't had a sip of the coffee yet, so the "Thanks" she grumbled was not as generous as she had intended. Fynn stiffened and turned back to the press, pouring himself a mug as well.

The brew was good, not quite as good as Raelyn's, but it would do. The warmth filled her, floating down through her throat and into her stomach, and she could feel the change in her brain as the caffeine drifted through her veins.

Raelyn hadn't come out of her room yet, but Esta was sitting on the couch with her own coffee, her sharp dirty blonde ponytail still intact and an unfolded piece of paper on her lap. She'd been so quiet that Nova hadn't even noticed her until now, although that may have been more the lack of coffee than anything.

"Good morning," Nova said, her voice still a little scratchy.

"It is in fact not a good morning," Esta replied. "This arrived by raven from Besa overnight, and Persy had it forwarded here as soon as he and Luc read it." She quickly stood and strode over to the kitchen where she threw the paper down on the island in between her and Fynn. It appeared to be a handwritten letter in the common tongue, but with a handwriting style that suggested elvish was the writer's primary language. Most of the elves in Arkwood didn't even understand elvish, let alone speak or write it. It was a forgotten language here in the city, though up north in the Noriendar Forest encircling Besa, the elves still mainly conversed in their ancient tongue.

Fynn picked up the letter and read it, eyes scanning faster than seemed natural. The purple undertone of his eye color was still there.

So not just a trick of the light from yesterday, Nova found herself thinking before quickly shutting the thought out.

"His trail was found, but it appeared to be hours old, and he did a remarkable job of covering his tracks," Fynn said, looking up from the note.

"What does that mean?" she asked, cupping both hands around her mug and leaning against the counter.

"That we were this close," Fynn held up his forefinger and thumb, a small gap of space between them, "to catching him, but he thwarted us and now we have no idea where to look."

"He can't have gone too far, right? He must still be on foot?" She looked between the two elves, unsure who would answer first.

Esta snorted and crossed her arms. "For now. Once he makes it out of Noriendar, it'll be impossible for the elves to contain his magic anymore. As a wielder, he could potentially find a way to jump."

"Jump?"

A voice from behind them startled Nova so much she herself jumped. She turned to find Raelyn standing in her bedroom doorway, tying a dressing gown around her waist. Her curly hair was a mess, completely flat in the back.

Fynn turned to pour a cup of coffee for Raelyn while Esta explained further. "Some wielders can jump, meaning they can transport themselves from place to place over short distances. Like jumping through space and reappearing in a different location."

"That's a thing?" Nova asked. It was news to her, but then again, thanks to Father's regulations, wielders in general were a mystery.

"Yes," Fynn responded, handing Raelyn the mug. "It's rare, but wielders are all different. They harness raw magic and bend it to their will, wield it to do what they want. A few do figure out how to make it fold space, allowing them to jump."

"How is it that elves know this, but we don't?" Nova pressed. How did the elves come to know more about her race than she did?

Esta shrugged and returned to the couch. "It's not our fault that your father's regulations on wielders caused your education to be lacking. Or that the Academy's defensive program has delved into depths of witch magic that would surprise even the governors, I suspect."

Raelyn sank into one of the dining chairs. "So, Blackmore could jump his way here very quickly. Never mind that he started out leagues away." Her voice wavered slightly in a tone Nova recognized as fearful.

"Noriendar is enchanted with ancient elven magic," Esta continued. "It's one of the reasons why Mistfell was located beyond it—so that Noriendar could be a buffer, a guard for the rest of Astria against Mistfell."

"But elves don't have magic," Nova said.

Fynn cast a smirk at the ground, and Esta rolled her eyes. "Spoken like a true witch, though I don't see much power from you either." Esta had known her for less than twenty-four hours and already knew how to throw a punch where it could do the most damage. Nova dropped her gaze to her mug and took a sip to hide the warmth in her cheeks.

"We don't have the same kind of magic as witches, but we aren't without any powers." Fynn paused for a sip of his own coffee. "Noriendar holds the secrets of ancient elves, who battled with the witches for their land and were able to hold their own, even without true magic. The forest itself has its own enchantments now that prevent witches' magic from being cast within its boundaries. They say it was made that way by Dalia herself."

Dalia, the elves' goddess, was sister to Canta, the witches' goddess, and Terra, the humans'.

"As long as he stays within Noriendar, or he's captured before he gets out, then he can't jump?" asked Raelyn, her eyes wide.

Esta nodded, leaning forward, so her forearms rested on her thighs. "Precisely. Glad you caught up. And this is why it's bad news that he wasn't found today. He's making too much progress, getting too close."

Nova set her mug on the counter, running her finger in circles over the rim. "He hasn't even been out for two days. Let's not get too discouraged."

"Hard not to when you're trapped in a box with nothing to do," Raelyn said under her breath, turning her face away from the group.

But Esta's elf ears heard her. "Last I checked you weren't in prison. You can go wherever you want. I just go with you."

Nova glanced up at Fynn, who stood across the kitchen from her. She caught a grin as he took in the sight of Esta and Raelyn: two hard-headed, stubborn females who were forced upon each other. If she got too bored, she and Fynn could just sit and watch them bicker.

She turned back to her sister, attempting to diffuse the tension by changing the subject. "Rae, let's hit the library today. Get some reading material just in case we do end up forced to stay indoors," she suggested. She ran her fingers through her hair and made a mental note to comb it before they went anywhere. How had she not done that when she'd first woken up? She probably looked like a mess right now.

Not the best first impression to be giving the unfortunately attractive elf that was now looking her way and grinning.

"Great idea," Fynn said.

Heat rushed to her face as her heartbeat accelerated. This elf was smiling at her, but she hadn't even brushed her hair this morning. Hadn't even changed out of her pajamas. She would need to remember to get dressed before coming out for coffee tomorrow morning.

"Fine. I'll get ready." Raelyn turned on her heel and headed back to her room. "Oh, and let's grab lunch at the cafe while we're out. You know, in case it's the last time."

With a slam of the door, she disappeared. Nova looked up at Esta, who was still fuming on the couch, and then back to Fynn, who was clearly bemused, and apologized. "I'm sure she'll warm up to you both soon."

Fynn shook his head and stifled a laugh while Esta just glared at her. She took that as her cue to get dressed. She found a fitted but casual dress with ruffled short sleeves and a hem that fell to her ankles. Slipping on some brown sandals, she then fixed her hair, and ran a small amount of kohl above her eyes and onto her lashes so she didn't look like she just rolled out of bed.

She had no idea why she cared so much about her appearance today, but something about the way Fynn had looked at her a minute ago unleashed butterflies in her stomach.

Wait, was she really developing a schoolgirl crush on her body-guard? The absurdity of the thought almost made her laugh out loud, but before she turned to leave, she found herself throwing some rouge on her cheeks too.

Raelyn was sitting on the couch picking at her nails when Nova announced she was ready. Raelyn had fixed the flat spot of her curls and donned a long black tunic, but other than that had done nothing to change her appearance. "You sure you want to go out like that? People will talk."

Without a word, Raelyn stormed back into her room and emerged ten minutes later with a smattering of make-up. She looked more presentable, ever so slightly, but Nova knew it would be enough to keep the gossip mongers at bay.

Growing up as a governor's daughter had its perks but also its downsides. She and Raelyn wanted for very little and had access to privileges that many citizens of Astria would give anything for. But they traded that privilege for a life in the public eye, and Arkwood was known for its gossip. Neither of them had escaped scrutiny growing up. If the rumors were to be believed, Raelyn liked to sleep around, preferably with more than one human at a time. And Nova was a functional alcoholic. In reality, those stories stemmed from one glimpse of Raelyn being her typical bubbly self at an opera opening, chatting with a son of a human governor and her then-boyfriend, who also happened to be human. Nova's rumor started when she was seen tripping on her way out of a bar on her twentieth birthday and letting her nose break her fall. It wasn't far out of the realm of possibility that Arkwood socialites had heard the Astors were under elven protection and were waiting to see how they would react. Canta forbid that they give them something to latch on to by going out in public appearing anything less than normal.

And for Raelyn, a full face of make-up was normal.

The library was a short walk from the flat, but it couldn't end fast enough, given the stares they received as they walked the cobblestone streets. It wasn't uncommon to see elves in this part of town, but these types of elves? With longswords hanging from their guards' uniforms and muscles so large they could have surely ripped the head off anyone who looked at Nova and Raelyn wrong? These types of elves, Besa Academy graduates, weren't normally found in the Outcast District.

"Think we could ask them to ditch the blades next time we go out?" Raelyn whispered. Her arm was linked through Nova's as they walked down the street to the library, the elves just a few paces behind.

A young witchling holding his mother's hand stopped to gawk at the elves. "Unlikely," Nova muttered back.

"She's right."

She whipped her head back and stopped walking, Raelyn turning with her. Esta was scowling at them while Fynn grinned at the child.

"You never know when we'll need these blades. Where you go, they go," Esta said.

Raelyn groaned and spun to face forward again, but Nova let her eyes linger on Fynn, who had clearly made the witchling's day just by acknowledging him. The little boy scurried off with his mother, and Fynn chuckled, his gaze drifting up until it collided with hers. The smile lingered on his face, reviving the butterflies in her stomach, until she broke his stare and turned back to walk with Raelyn again.

7

I T TURNED OUT THAT the library wasn't quite the refuge she was hoping it would be. Fynn watching over her shoulder was distracting—who was he to judge her reading selection? And Raelyn hadn't spoken a single word since their exchange on the street.

Nova looked over the stack of books she was perusing toward her sister. Raelyn's curls were sticking out over a winged chair by one of the windows, while Esta stood silently in the shadows along the wall next to the window.

She didn't realize she sighed audibly until Fynn's voice interrupted her thoughts.

"You know, we understand this isn't an ideal situation."

His tone wasn't demeaning, but compassionate, as if he was extending an olive branch. As if they might well try to be cordial if they were going to be stuck together in a less-than-ideal situation. She glanced at him, and the expression on his face echoed the sentiment. No hard lines, no frown, and a softness in his violet eyes.

"Thank you. I think I'm going to need to be reminded of that." She moved her eyes back to Raelyn. "She'll come around too. She's normally impossible to shut up."

Fynn nodded and moved closer so they could continue the conversation in the hushed tones required in a library. Nova caught a whiff of cedar and briny sea air as the scent from his body engulfed her. She was instantly transported to Adenaport, to the cottage, and her body relaxed slightly.

"I'm not worried about her," he said, dipping his head lower. "Esta is more than capable of handling whatever is thrown her way."

The way he paused after speaking made it seem there were words left unsaid. Was he worried about *her*?

"I'm fine, too. The initial shock of it all has worn off, and now I just need to adapt, move on. Hence, the books." She waved the historical fiction she'd picked up as proof that she was fine.

Fynn raised his eyebrow at her, then reached for the book. His fingertips brushed hers as he took it from her, sending the smallest jolt of energy through her hand and straight to her now-fluttering heart.

What the hell was that?

Thank Canta he was reading the description of the book and didn't notice the shock that surely registered on her face.

"Ah, a novel about a family of wielders at the time of the revolution. Maybe not just pleasure reading, maybe also research?"

She stole the book back, fighting the urge to hit him with it and instead turned toward the end of the aisle where the check-out desk was. Fynn, of course, fell into step right behind her.

Nova checked out the tome, then collected Raelyn (still silent), and the four of them made their way toward the nearby cafe for lunch. Wicker tables and chairs had been set up outside on a stone patio for patrons to enjoy the beautiful summer's day. Fynn and Esta grabbed a table for two within sight of them, but out of ear shot to give them some semblance of privacy. For most of the meal, it turned out that it didn't matter if they could hear anything because Raelyn still wasn't talking, but finally, just as they were finishing up eating, she broke her silence.

"What do you say we give them the slip?"

Her brown eyes beamed with rebellion in a way Nova had gotten used to seeing when they were teenagers. Always the more adventurous one, Raelyn wasn't afraid to bend or flat out break the rules, while Nova, the typical older child, preferred to operate within the boundaries set before her. "Where did this come from? You give us the silent treatment all day and now you want to 'give them the slip'?"

"Come on, Nova." Raelyn's eyes pleaded, and Nova could feel her resolve already starting to falter. "I just need to do something exciting. I promise it'll lift my mood."

Nova sipped her water while Raelyn continued to wear what Nova usually called her "sad puppy face." She shook her head. "Not a good idea. Let's think of something else to do that'll lift your mood." She glanced around for inspiration. "What about a walk to the park?"

But Raelyn would not give in that easily. She never did. "We can go to the restroom and slip out the back of the kitchen. They'll never know. We'll buy ourselves a few hours of freedom before they eventually track us down. Come on, sis." Her brown eyes were wide, pleading in a way Nova always found hard to resist. If there was one thing that could motivate her, it was her sister's happiness.

But that was followed closely by her sister's safety. "No, it's a stupid idea. It's been one day, Rae. And honestly, not even that bad of a day."

"But it could get worse from here. Don't make me grovel, Nova." Raelyn stuck out her bottom lip.

Nova wiped her mouth with her napkin and glanced quickly at the elves. They were both looking down at their food. What would her parents think about an escape? Mother would be desperately worried, and Father would probably yell, might even restrict their ability to leave the flat. She loved her sister, but this just didn't seem worth it.

"Please, Nova?"

She looked back at Raelyn, the little sister she always wanted to please, and the last bit of her resolve crumpled. This time, happiness won over safety. "Fine, but when we get caught, it was all your idea."

Raelyn grinned but tried not to react any more than that so as not to draw attention to them. "I'll meet you in the kitchen in one minute." With that she stood up, walked into the café, and headed towards the restroom. Nova pretended to finish up her water, then got up to join. Her gaze collided with Fynn's, but she casually dismissed him.

"Just going to check on her. She said she wasn't feeling well."

He didn't try to stop her, though his gaze burned into her back the entire way into the restaurant. She didn't feel truly safe until she was around the corner and in the hallway leading to the restrooms and the kitchen. Barely had she made it two steps when Raelyn's hand grabbed her arm and pulled her along the hall and through the swinging doors into the kitchen so quickly she nearly lost her footing.

They flew through the kitchen, avoiding the servers and chefs, most of whom knew them and therefore were accustomed to seeing them come by to visit, but were definitely not accustomed to seeing them flee out the back door. Raelyn, her eyes wild with glee and laughter pouring from her lips, led her through the back door and into the alley behind, which was lined with trash, the stench a mixture of spoiled food, sulfur, and piss. Nova gagged and had to put her free hand over her mouth as they continued to run, her sandals clacking loudly on the uneven cobblestones. Raelyn magicked rocks and old bricks to fling behind them as they went, squealing each time, hoping to deter anyone following them.

At the end of the alley, Raelyn turned left into another alley, then right at the end of that one, and finally they ended up back on Main Street in the throng of the midday crowd. Nova wasn't sure she agreed they were less likely to be discovered in a crowd than they were hidden in an alley, but this was Raelyn's show, and she was just following her sister's lead, so she kept her mouth shut. Her hand clenched Raelyn's, ready to pull her aside at the first hint of danger.

"Where are we going?" she hissed at Raelyn, glancing over her shoulder to see if she spotted Esta or Fynn. It wouldn't be long before they realized their charges had left the cafe and came looking for them.

From the wild look on Raelyn's face, Nova could tell she hadn't gotten that far in her escape plan and had no idea where they were going next. They kept walking swiftly, hand in hand, blending with the crowd on the sidewalk. Nova kept her head bowed, but Raelyn tipped her chin back and continued to laugh.

Someone needed to take charge now. Nova tried to catch her bearings as they walked, and once she oriented herself, she pulled Raelyn to the right.

"In here."

She opened an arched wooden door in the old building next to them. While Arkwood had many newer, taller buildings, such as the one with their parents' penthouse and the one they lived in now, there were still some older buildings, like this one, that stood the test of time, likely because of geo magic holding the place together. She recognized this particular building as one of their favorite dive bars from their late teenage years and even though she hadn't been there in four or five years, she figured its dark, smoky interior was as good a place to hide as any.

Once they were both in and the door was closed behind them, she looked over at the bar, where only three others were sitting. She supposed that's what the daytime crowd probably consisted of in summer, since most people would be at the seaside or enjoying the beautiful weather outdoors. She didn't recognize either of the witches seated on the far side of the bar—the auras around them gave them away as hydros—but approached the side where one hooded person was sitting to order drinks for herself and Raelyn. Her sister trailed behind her, still gripping her hand and grinning excitedly.

"We did it! Just one drink, Nova, and then we'll go home, ok?"

Just then, the hooded figure pulled back his hood and revealed a loose blonde bun and pointed ears. She stopped, Raelyn bumping into her back with a small yelp. A familiar voice trilled in her ears.

"By all means, stay for as many as you'd like."

Fynn. He had found them.

Somehow, he'd not only found them, but gotten there *before* them.

Raelyn finally stopped giggling and clammed up, but Nova spoke for them both. "How? How did you get here so fast?"

Fynn shrugged and sipped the beer that was already in front of him. "We heard your whole plan of escape from our table." He pointed to his ears, reminding them that elves had superior hearing. "Then we followed your scent—" pointing to his nose this time "—and it just so happens there are only two places on this block for witches to hide. So Esta and I split up. Lucky me for picking the winning one and getting to enjoy a drink while I waited."

"But how did you get here so fast?" Raelyn asked.

"Elves aren't necessarily gifted with magic like witches are—" he took another swig of his drink "—but some of us do have some special abilities, other than superior senses. I was gifted with agility. I can run quickly enough I become nearly invisible."

Nova tried to hide her surprise, but the grin that appeared on Fynn's face proved how badly she failed. "And Esta?" she asked, trying to draw his attention away from her awe.

Fynn shrugged. "As far as I can tell, she's just gifted with being extraordinarily bitchy."

Beside Nova, Raelyn barked out a laugh, relaxing at Fynn's words. Either he was a genuinely kind person, or he was also a gifted manipulator. She hoped he wouldn't be around long enough for her to find out which one.

Then again, a small part of her hoped he would be. And that he would turn out to be genuinely kind.

Raelyn pulled herself onto the stool two down from Fynn, leaving the one between them open for Nova. "What are you drinking?"

"I'm a sucker for a good summer ale." Fynn smiled and took another swig.

"Well, if you're going to stalk us into a dive bar, the least you can do is buy us a round."

There was the Raelyn she loved. Nova made a mental note to thank Fynn for bringing her back to life as she sat on the stool between her sister and her guard.

"Thought you'd never ask."

Fynn signaled to the barkeep for two more ales. Once the ales arrived, he held his up for a toast. She and Raelyn joined him, the glasses sounding off with a dull clink. "To a summer of fun...but no more escapades. Unless you invite me."

Raelyn laughed and took a large gulp of her beer. Fynn caught Nova's eye and winked, sending her heart into the same flutter his touch had earlier.

8

After that beer, tensions cooled between Raelyn, Fynn, and Nova.

They never discussed the attempted runaway out loud, but neither did the sisters make a repeat attempt. An unspoken truce arose between the witches and their elven guards. Over the next two days, they spent most of their time in the apartment, playing games or reading, but occasionally they went outside for walks or to visit a shop or cafe. The apartment wasn't large enough to house all four of them comfortably for too long, and Raelyn especially started to get cabin fever.

There was no further news of Blackmore. Their father hadn't been by personally to update them, but he checked in via message every day. They also sent their promised daily updates back to their parents, who had promised that as long as they heard from them directly, their elves need not report in themselves. Maybe it was a sign of trust, or maybe Father just wanted them to think the elves weren't reporting back on them. Either way, she and Raelyn had been happy to oblige with a daily note of their own.

Nova handed one such note to Fynn after dinner one night. "Will one of the other elves guarding the building deliver this?"

He nodded, pocketing the note. "There are one or two others on rotations gifted with agility. I'll find whoever is on tonight, probably Daro."

"Oh, so you aren't the only elf with super special running powers?" She nudged him playfully with her elbow and laughed.

He nudged her back and said, "No, but I am the fastest." Without another word, he vanished out the front door to hand off the note.

"Show off," Nova said under her breath, but inside, those butterflies had returned to her stomach.

Her mother, on the other hand, had been keeping busy making sure that appearances were made at various events and that to the public eye, all was well with the Astors, even with the addition of their new security detail.

Nevertheless, the atmosphere in Arkwood had noticeably shifted the last time Nova and Fynn had ventured out for a walk. Shoppers moved about with more determination, no one stopping to browse the shop windows. Fewer people stopped to chat or engage in small talk along the sidewalks. Most shops put up signs that they would be closing early, to ensure that none of their employees were out past dark. Posters with Blackmore's likeness on them were posted all over the city, along with information about how to report tips or sightings.

"He doesn't look all that terrifying," Nova said, as they studied one such poster on their way home from the market. The hand drawn sketch on the poster showed a middle-aged man with a round face, shaggy hair, and a short beard. There wasn't anything truly identifying about him, if she was being honest. He looked like any other witch that could be walking around Arkwood.

Fynn's hand gripped the hilt of his sword. "Looks can be deceiving."

She hoisted the bag carrying their goods higher onto her shoulder and looked up at him. "Kinda like you?" The corner of her mouth twitched into a smile. "All tough on the outside with your blades and your muscles, but really just a teddy bear on the inside?"

He laughed. "No one has ever accused me of being a teddy bear."

"It suits you." She shrugged and turned to continue walking to the flat, his laugh echoing in her ears, lifting her up like she was walking on air.

On the fifth night of their new regime, Raelyn declared she was going to attend a dinner with their mother. Nova raised her eyebrows in disbelief. This particular dinner was for one of the many charitable organizations that their mother patronaged, and Raelyn usually hated those types of events.

"You really are desperate, aren't you?" Nova was leaning against the doorway to her room wringing her hair in a towel, having just finished taking a bath

"I need social interaction, Nova. In whatever way I can get it." With that, she retreated to her room to change into something more formal.

Nova looked over to where Esta had been lounging on the couch. The elf's mouth was hanging open in disbelief. "I guess that means I need to change too." She trudged over to her bag and started rummaging through it.

Esta and Fynn had each brought a bag of clothes with them, mostly their gray tunics and black leather pants that constituted their guard uniforms. So far, she hadn't seen them wear anything else, so she doubted whether Esta even had anything else to change into. But sure enough, Esta pulled out a dark blue and gold-lined version of the same uniform and slipped into Nova's bathroom to put it on.

Fynn chuckled from the floor by the couch where he had watched the entire exchange. "Guess it's just you and me tonight, Al."

Nova shot him a look of annoyance. Fynn had taken to calling her Al ever since he found out at the dive bar that Nova was short for Alinova. She had never in her life been called Alinova and frequently forgot it was even part of her name. But apparently the fact that she rolled her eyes each time the nickname escaped his lips was enough of a reason for Fynn to make it a thing. That and the fact that Esta seemed inexplicably unnerved whenever she heard it.

He must enjoy getting under both of their skins.

"Don't get too excited. I'm just planning to finish that wielder novel I got from the library, now that we'll have some peace and quiet."

Once Raelyn, looking stunning in a green satin floor-length gown, and Esta, ponytail as tight as ever and looking more serious than usual (if that was possible), left to meet Mother in the carriage waiting on the street, Nova grabbed her book and flopped onto her bed to read. With her door still open, she could see Fynn, now lying on the couch, staring at the ceiling. He had finally let his hair down, and now it cascaded down along the arm of the couch where he rested his head.

What would it be like to run her fingers through that hair? Would it feel like silk? Or more like wool?

She checked on him every few pages, partially to quell the pang in her gut for not entertaining him (which was absurd; he was employed by her father, not a guest in her house) and partially because she enjoyed that flutter in her chest when she laid eyes on him. She had dated a few witches and one human before, but never an elf. They tended to keep to themselves and their own kind and didn't mingle with witches or humans socially. But the idea of getting close to an elf, close enough to consider dating...the hair on her arms began to rise.

An image of Fynn shirtless flashed into her mind. Fynn reaching a hand toward her, running that hand down her spine, that spark she'd felt in the library coursing through her entire body. Fynn leaning in to kiss her...

She shook her head and pushed away the vision quickly. Fynn was not here to be her love interest, nor was he even here to be her friend. They may have reached a point of friendly banter over the last few days, but that was purely because they were forced to be in close proximity to each other at all times. It certainly wasn't because either of them was attracted to the other. Nova reasserted her focus on the novel, even if she did continue to glance at Fynn every few pages.

It was during one of these checks that she discovered Fynn had fallen asleep, right where he lay on the couch, left arm dangling off the side and mouth lolling open slightly. She smiled at the sight, surprised how different it made him appear from his brutish, stoic self when he was awake.

Teddy bear, indeed.

She was sure that even at the slightest movement from her, he would startle and wake—no way was she underestimating his elf hearing again. So, she got up from her bed and went to grab a glass of water from the sink. She certainly wasn't trying to be quiet, but when he didn't wake up from the clink of the glass or the whirl of the faucet, a new idea floated into her head.

An evening out, on her own. She'd always been more of an introvert, finding moments alone refreshing and revitalizing. But the last few days had left few opportunities for alone time. Surely just a short walk through her own neighborhood, one she knew like the back of her hand, which would be bustling with people out for dinner or getting an early start to an evening party, could do no harm. She wasn't usually one to break rules—that was always Raelyn—but the tickling feeling crawling up her neck was telling her to lean into this opportunity, not run from it. Blackmore was still in Noriendar. She was still safe.

Without giving it another moment's thought, she slipped on her sandals and quietly opened the front door to the apartment, sending a silent prayer of thanks to Canta that its hinges didn't squeak in betrayal. Once the door was closed, she paused in the hallway, taking a deep breath. Her heart was racing in excitement, but her brain was clear enough to remember that there were still elven guards surrounding her building. Though she hadn't spotted them, they were there and would notice her instantly if she just waltzed through the front door.

She turned on her heel and instead of heading for the main stairwell, took a smaller one in the back that was used by the cleaners and staff of the building. Though she'd never been down it herself, she knew it emptied onto the alley at the back of the street, which, like the alley she and Raelyn had escaped down earlier this week, would be filled with places she could hide if need be.

As she descended the stairwell, she summoned every drop of power that she could in hopes of camouflaging herself, even just a little. The cover of night would do most of the work for her, but if she could manage to blend more smoothly into her surroundings, she was more likely to elude the guards. Raelyn could camouflage herself so well that she disappeared almost completely into whatever landscape surrounded her. But Nova was only able to take on color schemes and blur her edges slightly.

At the bottom of the staircase, she again paused and looked behind her. The stairwell was silent. Good. Fynn wasn't coming for her yet. She allowed her magic to flow through her body, let the coolness of it wrap around her skin as it softened and changed her appearance. Once she was sure it was as good as it was going to get, she quietly pushed open the door just wide enough for her to slip out.

The summer air hit her skin like a warm blanket, wrapping itself around her and engulfing her. It wasn't the same as strolling the seashore by the cottage—the city air, for one, was nothing compared to the brininess of the sea air—but at this point, she would take what she could get. She grinned to herself and set off down the alley, walking closely to the walls of the buildings, remaining in the shadows. Between the semi darkness that twilight had brought and her weak camouflage spell, she'd wager she could get to Main Street undetected.

Like her escape with Raelyn from the cafe, she didn't have a fully developed plan for where to go next. She wandered the alleys, racking her brain for ideas. Cassie and Bea lived on the other side of the large park that took up much of the center of Arkwood and was only a few blocks from the apartment. And she had been on a few dates last month with a male pyro who lived just a few blocks south. They hadn't been in touch since the start of summer, but maybe surprising him with a visit would be the spark she needed right now.

Ultimately, she decided to stroll through the park. Solitude was what she craved, so it was what she would grant herself. Summer strolls through Arkwood Park were dreamy—the trees and ground were luscious, aided by the help of the geos on staff to tend to them, birds and small mammals came alive, scurrying to find food to store, and fewer people crowded the pathways. As a teenager, strolling these pathways hand in hand with someone was as much of a declaration of love as hormonal teenage witches, elves, and humans could give. The first time she partook in the ritual, with a human she had dated for a year, she had been about fifteen. He had moved out of the city and down to Adenaport after graduation, but they had lost touch long before that anyway.

Nova made it to the park easily, and whims of nostalgia overtook her when she found her favorite path. How many times had she walked this very path with Raelyn, on their way to work or to meet Cassie and Bea? This path also led to her favorite picnic spot from childhood. Mother would pack up a basket full of food, and she, Nova, and Raelyn would play card games or take turns making up stories while they ate. Father was usually at work so it would just be the three of them.

Those picnics were some of the rare moments when Mother's favoritism for Raelyn wasn't as obvious. When Nova almost felt like they were equals in Mother's eyes.

She released her hold on her magic, the camouflage wearing off now that she was out of sight of her building and darkness had truly set in. The pathways were lined every few feet with lamps enchanted by pyro-witches, and the trees were high enough to block much of the city light.

The night was clear, the stars shone brightly, and crickets chirped incessantly. A few couples had spread blankets out for stargazing—one couple cuddled around a small fire, whose distinctly silent burn and lack of any fuel source gave it away as one that was pyro made. She frowned at the simplicity of it, jealous of how so many other people's lives could just go on while hers was stopped in its tracks, all because of one wielder and the grudge he supposedly held against her father for his actions twenty-five years ago. A small part of her that she had been suppressing since Father delivered the news, a part that was furious at the situation, started pushing at the wall she had built to contain it. Pushing to break through somehow. But now was not the time. She did not want to draw attention to herself out in the open, where anyone could recognize her and inform her father that she had eluded Fynn.

Detection was out of the question.

She slipped down a side path that led through a small garden of shrubs. It was one of her favorite places, with benches engulfed by shrubs making one feel completely alone, and not in the middle of Astria's largest city. No one else walked this particular path tonight, allowing her to breathe a little more easily. She had this space to herself. She'd made it this far. Any more time she could be out here alone before Fynn caught up with her was just a bonus.

She approached the first bench and sat, her mind wandering back toward the elf. But barely had she settled into the seat than a hiss echoed from the bushes behind her. She sat up stiffly and started to turn her head to see where the hiss had come from, but her feet began to burn. Lightly at first, but then almost like they were catching fire from the inside out. Pain racking her body, she tried to lift one foot to shake off the burn, but it wouldn't move, like it had been frozen to the ground.

She tried to call for help, but only a hoarse screech erupted from her mouth. She clawed at her throat as the air was ripped from it, her heart hammering in her chest.

What the hell was happening?

A tear slid down her cheek as the pain in her feet raged on, and she struggled to catch her breath.

With no sign of who was doing this to her, she frantically looked around for help, but no one was on the path. No one could see her.

Air—she needed *air*. She dug her fingernails tighter into her throat.

The hissing voice rang out behind her. "Come with me."

9

T HE WORLD AROUND HER fell silent, the erratic drumming of her heart all she could hear. She still couldn't move or see where that voice had come from, still felt the unbearable pain in her feet, but whoever was in that shrub behind her was not someone she cared to meet.

Darkness started to swirl in her vision.

She needed to move—now.

Her feet were still frozen *and* burning, the pain beginning to radiate up her legs, but she tried to stand, her knees too weak to sustain her. After only a moment she collapsed back onto the bench, tears starting to slip down her cheeks in earnest.

She managed to draw one breath, enough for her to remove her hands from her throat, but still couldn't find her voice to cry for help.

Large, icy hands closed around her arms and started pulling her backward. She tried with all the power she could summon to turn the ground to quicksand or mud or even unsteady rocks, but nothing worked.

Tears were falling in torrents now as she tried to writhe free of the grip, but without air, without the ability to move her legs, there was only so much she could do.

This was the end. This stupid adventure was how it ended. Raelyn would never forgive her...

A new set of hands—firm, strong, *warm* hands—landed on her shoulders. They yanked her off the bench, throwing her onto the pathway, not at all gently. Cold lingered on her bare skin where the other hands had tried to pull her back.

Her lungs filled with that sweet summer air. She could breathe again! She gulped down large breaths, her chest heaving, her blood singing with the resurgence of oxygen, but her throat burned as vomit surged up and out onto the path in front of her. Her eyes blinked through the tears that now splashed on the ground and the puddle of vomit below her as she tried to steady her heart's rhythm, to collect herself as quickly as she could so she could fight back.

Wafts of cedar and salt air filled her nose. She knew that scent.

Fynn.

She wiped her mouth, looked up, and there he was, standing over her, eyes scanning the bushes, hair still loose and hanging in his face.

He'd come. Thank Canta, he'd come just in time.

One second, he was in front of her, the next he was a blur of motion and a rustle of leaves in the bush. A moan and a thud echoed behind her, and a few seconds later she regained feeling in her feet, rubbing at them with her hands to circulate the blood again.

He returned to the pathway, with an unconscious man across his shoulder. No, not a man. An aura surrounded him, one that was typical of a witch, but not one she recognized. A hydro most likely or maybe an aero? She couldn't begin to guess based on the magic he had cast.

Fynn thumped the man down on the ground next to her. She flinched when she heard his head hit the stone pathway.

"Do you recognize him?" Fynn's voice lacked any warmth.

Still reeling from both the attack and the fact that Fynn had not only arrived but was currently choosing not to scream at her, Nova tried to steady her breath and study the witch's face. Fynn had delivered a nasty black eye to his right side that distorted his features, but she was certain she had never seen him before. She shook her head, unable to form the words.

"Can you walk?" He offered a hand to help her up.

She took it and stood up to her feet, shaking slightly but steady enough. "Yes." Her heart was finally returning to a normal rhythm.

"Let's go." He heaved the witch over his shoulder with one hand and grabbed Nova's arm with the other, keeping her close.

She didn't even bother trying to resist.

Fynn spoke no other words to her the entire walk home. The male witch was still unconscious and slung over his shoulder, and Fynn's eyes were locked on the road ahead of them. Hanging her head so her gaze trailed the ground beneath her feet, she didn't even try to defend her actions and just remained at his side, silent.

When they reached the apartment building, Fynn glanced up at the sky and signaled to one of the other elven guards. Then he opened the front door and grunted, "In."

Only once they were safely inside the apartment, and she assessed that Esta and Raelyn weren't yet home, did she turn to Fynn and start to apologize. She opened her mouth, but he held up a hand and shook his head.

"Don't. I don't want to hear any of it right now." He laid the hydro on the floor next to the couch. "Go freshen up. Your father will undoubtedly be here soon."

"How—"

He straightened and looked at her with a stare full of anger and...fear? "When I woke up and found you weren't here, I alerted one of the other guards to notify your father straight away. Remember how I said there were others who moved quickly?" After she nodded, he continued. "Go, you probably only have a few more minutes."

Did she really look that bad? She dashed to her bathing room and found that Fynn was right. Despite no lasting harm or pain to her body, she looked like a frightful mess. Her braid had come loose in many places, strands of dark hair framing her face. Her throat had a necklace of red marks encircling it where she had been clutching her throat as she was suffocating. Suffocated—so was the witch an aero? How had he mastered both water and air?

A wielder. The male was a wielder. That's why she hadn't recognized his aura. Was it Blackmore? Nova squeezed her eyes shut and tried to picture the face she'd seen on the posters around town. No, that face was very different from the one Fynn had bloodied up tonight. This wasn't Blackmore.

Then who?

She ran a comb through her hair, rinsed her mouth, and splashed water on her face. That would have to do. On the way out, she grabbed a scarf hanging over the back of the door and loosely wrapped it around her neck, hoping it covered the red scratches well enough.

When she got back to the living room, Fynn was standing over the unconscious witch on the floor, staring at him. He looked her way when she approached, his gaze still unyielding, and said, "Better."

Was this how it would be now? Had she completely lost his trust? She supposed she deserved it, not only slipping out past his notice but also getting herself into trouble. From where she stood now, the idea of escape seemed ridiculous. She should've just stayed in bed with her book and called it a night.

Fynn whipped his head toward the front door, and a heartbeat later, her father and Persy burst in. Father was fuming, the ground beneath him temporarily turning to stone with every step he took, and little rattles shook the floor of the apartment as he boomed, "Explain yourself, Fynn."

Persy showed no signs of emotion at his son being reprimanded by the most powerful of the witch governors. He stood behind her father, with a hardened expression on his own face.

"Sir, I'm—" Fynn began but Nova cut him off. This was entirely her fault after all.

"I'm sorry, Father." She approached her father slowly, reaching out to place a hand on his arm. "I snuck out past him. I camouflaged myself in the back alley and managed to sneak out to the park."

"Oh yes, of that much I am very aware, Nova." He shrugged off her hand, and she backed away. "But what I don't understand is how Fynn let that happen."

Fynn cut in. "I dozed off on the couch, sir. It was a mistake; I shouldn't have let myself do so without ensuring Nova was asleep first."

She looked up at him. His hair had been thrown hastily back up while she was fixing her own, and there were rips in the fabric of his tunic from the bushes he had lunged into. He looked as bad as she felt.

Her father simply glared at Fynn. "We shall discuss repercussions tomorrow. I had expected better from you given your father's commendations, but now I must rethink your position." He turned now to the witch on the floor. "Who do we have here? I don't recognize him."

"Nor do I, sir." Fynn's voice betrayed nothing about his reaction to her father's scolding.

"I suspect he's a wielder, Father," Nova said.

Her father glanced at her, eyebrows raised. "And do I want to know why?"

"He both froze me and tried to draw the air out of my lungs." She tried to sound brave, but the reminder of the feeling of death closing in on her, of being unable to defend herself, lingered and made her voice quiver ever so slightly.

"Water and air. Intriguing." He squatted down next to the male. "You're lucky he chose not to use magic with lasting damage. Fire could have more easily hurt you."

His tone wasn't one of a concerned parent, but rather one of curiosity. As if it wasn't so much that he cared at all for her safety, but rather was unsure why the witch hadn't decided to blast her to smithereens on the spot.

Nova tried to ignore the way her chest sank at his indifference.

The witch started to stir at that moment, but her father casually reached out a hand and laid it over the male's chest. Instantly, the man was petrified, still as a rock, alive but unable to move or speak.

"We will take it from here. I'm sure we will have much to learn from him, especially if he has been in contact with Blackmore." Father stood and turned towards Persy, nodding. Persy nodded back, then strode out of the apartment without a word.

Nova reached for her father's arm again. "How can you be sure he's even working for Blackmore? Maybe this was a coincidence, and I was just in the wrong place at the wrong time."

He shook his head. "I know every wielder in this city. There aren't many of them, and this witch is not one of them. He knows more than we think, and the fact that Blackmore could get an assassin into Arkwood without our knowing is concerning for all, not just our family."

Persy reentered the apartment, with two elves that she recognized from the building guard in tow. Both had dark hair cropped short and were dressed in all black.

"Thank you, Persy." Her father nodded in his guard's direction. Then he turned to Fynn. "You are relieved of your responsibility to Nova for the time being. We will need to have a discussion in the morning and determine if you are truly the best fit to watch my daughter. In the meantime, Daro will look after her."

Father indicated the elf on the right, with a long nose and a look etched on his face like someone was holding a spoiled egg under it. He didn't smile, he just nodded at Father in understanding and then flashed a menacing grin at Nova, who had the sudden urge to run to her bedroom and hide under the sheets until Blackmore was found.

She needed to speak up, to fight for Fynn, so he was not punished for her actions. "But Father, it wasn't his fault. And he saved me—"

"Nova, stop." He turned his deep brown eyes to her with the same look that always terrified her as a child. "That's enough. We will discuss this more in the morning."

Persy gestured for his son, disappointment plastered on his face but there was something else there too. Regret? Panic? "Let's go, Fynn."

Fynn made a move towards his father, casting one side glance at Nova, who met his eyes and tried to send an apology of sincerest proportions through that glance. She had been selfish in her adventure, not even giving a moment's consideration to how Fynn would look if she were caught. Though she'd hardly call him a friend, she had come to respect him over the last few days.

If he caught the apology, he ignored it. Instead, he silently followed his father through the door, leaving her father, Daro, and the other elf in the room with her. Father indicated that the remaining elf should remove the petrified witch from the apartment and then the three of them left without so much as a good-bye.

Alone with Daro, the weight of the evening's events threatened to consume her, and she shoved down the lump forming in her throat.

She had brought this upon herself, but had it been worth it? No. The momentary freedom she'd experienced had not been worth any of this. If she could turn back time, she would go back two hours and stop herself from leaving the apartment. But she couldn't, and she'd have to face the consequences of her actions.

When the weight of it all became more than she could bear, she murmured a quick good night to Daro and tried to slip into her room. But his hand shot out, preventing her door from closing. Another agile elf, moving fast as light.

"It stays open."

Nova didn't try to fight it. She wouldn't win. So instead, she opened the door as wide as it would go, shot Daro a look as if to say *is this good enough?* and then crawled into bed. Exhaustion had overcome her, and she let it swallow her whole.

10

"EXCUSE ME. WHAT HAPPENED?!"

Raelyn had stormed into Nova's room the moment she arrived home last night, causing Nova to stir in her sleep and throw her blanket over her head, but Esta managed to wrangle Raelyn back to her own room. However, the next morning, Esta must have decided Nova deserved her sister's wrath and didn't even bat an eye when Raelyn stomped across the apartment to Nova's room, in nothing but her bra and lacy shorts, curls flattened on one side.

Nova, for her part, expected this and hadn't found the courage to get out of bed yet, even though it was nearly mid-morning. Though her father's reaction had been cold, and her mother hadn't even deigned to show up or voice an opinion via message, Raelyn yelled enough about it for all three of them. And since Nova was feeling very self-critical anyway, she didn't put up a fight.

"You are an idiot!" Raelyn screamed as she picked up one of the extra pillows on Nova's bed and smacked her with it. "You are so lucky Fynn got there in time. You could have *died*."

She was one to talk. Hadn't escape been Raelyn's idea the first time? "Look who's calling the kettle black. If you hadn't—" She'd earned another smack with the pillow.

Nova brushed away the hairs that had been knocked into her face and put a hand up to defend herself against another potential blow, catching a glimpse of the feral rage in Raelyn's eyes as she did.

"It's one thing to run away in broad daylight. But the middle of the night?" Raelyn's chest heaved, but she dropped the pillow to the bed rather than attempt another strike.

"First of all," Nova pushed the covers back and sat up, "it was just after dusk so hardly the middle of the night. And second, I really didn't think much about it. I acted on a whim."

Raelyn groaned and dug her hands into her hair. "Since when does Nova Astor act on a whim? I can't believe you. Honestly."

"I'm sorry, ok? I really am. More than you know."

Nova squeezed her eyes shut but found her vision swarming with the look on Fynn's face when he left the apartment. Her father's harsh words about the elf's now-threatened employment ricocheted through her head. Had she really cost him his job? And not only that, but her father's recommendation? Because certainly her father would ensure that Fynn never found another job as a guard or a warrior again.

She rubbed her eyes and pulled her knees into her chest. Raelyn, whose face was beginning to lose the angry red it had worn just moments ago, sat on the end of the bed next to her feet.

Nova sighed. "Have you heard from Father yet?"

"No." Raelyn's tone was still curt, even if her eyes had gotten softer. "Esta doubts Fynn is coming back."

"It wasn't his fault. I was the careless one." Nova sprang from bed as an idea formed in her head. She needed to speak with her father immediately. "Have the carriage brought around, please. I need to go talk to Father."

Raelyn laughed and patted the bed with her hand. "Sit down. He doesn't want to see you. He already sent word this morning that you're not to leave the apartment or speak to anyone else until he says so."

Nova fell back onto her bed and covered her face with the pillow Raelyn had thrown. What was the point of even getting out of bed now? Maybe she should just stay here until Blackmore was found.

Her bed creaked and shifted as Raelyn's weight moved from it. "Look, Nova, I'm glad you're ok, but don't you dare scare me like that again. We're in this together, remember?" She paused, then Nova felt Raelyn's hand close around hers. "Now, I'm going to make coffee because you definitely look like you need some. Do you know how your new elf takes it?"

Nova muffled a *no* through the pillow. She knew nothing about Daro except that he took his job very seriously. She hadn't slept with the door open since she'd been about five and went through a nightmare phase. Father hadn't had the patience to deal with Nova's midnight hysterics and insisted that she stop being so scared and grow up. Mother would stay just long enough for Nova to calm down and had insisted that keeping the door open would help. It hadn't, but fortunately that phase passed.

As a child, the lack of privacy had been a means to an end, nothing more. But as an adult, it was dehumanizing.

Despite her initial idea to remain in bed, once the smell of Raelyn's coffee reached her, instinct made her follow the scent. Coffee did wonders. Coffee healed all. Especially Raelyn's coffee. One cup. She would have one cup to start the day and see if it helped her feel better.

Esta and Daro were already awake too, seated at the small dining table, piles of food from Mother's initial delivery still stacked behind them. Daro didn't look her way as she poured herself a mug, but Esta gave her a smirk as if to say, *I know what you did, and you deserve what you got.* Nova simply glared back, poured her coffee, and turned to go back to her bedroom, open door and all, when someone knocked on the front door.

She froze, mug half raised in the air, and looked back at the elves. Both stood quickly and assumed their positions, Daro at the door and Esta a few paces behind him as back up. Esta motioned for her to back away out of sight, which she did gladly, backing into the shadow of her bedroom doorway. Then the female nodded to Daro, who opened the door.

Nova nearly dropped her mug when she registered who stood at the threshold. "Fynn!" She took a step toward the door, but quickly stopped herself when she caught the look on his face.

Fynn's blonde bun was pulled a little more tightly than usual, his violet eyes wide but seeming to hide something behind them. He still had all his weapons and his gray guard's uniform, holding his duffel in his left hand and his face—it was completely emotionless.

One of her hands grabbed at the strands of her hair that had fallen over her shoulder and twirled it through her fingers.

Esta spoke first, "What are you doing here." A demand, not a question.

"I've been reinstated." He held out a note to Daro, who took it, read it, and passed it off to Esta.

She scanned the note and looked back up at him with a wicked grin. "Welcome back."

Daro stepped aside for him to enter, then turned to grab a satchel that must have been dropped off while she slept last night. "Good luck. Don't fuck this up again," he said quietly to Fynn, but not so quietly that Nova couldn't hear every word. Daro nodded at Esta, grunted at Nova, and then showed himself out.

Nova's entire being wanted to run and hug Fynn, wanted to apologize profusely, wanted things to go back to how they had been, but given how he had treated her last night and how she had betrayed him, she restrained herself to gauge his reaction first.

He set down his pack in the usual location behind the dining table, next to the food tower and folded cots, and turned to her. "Nova."

Not Al.

Her chest tightened a little bit, like a weight was suddenly pressing on it.

"Get dressed, we're going for a walk."

She nodded slowly, trying to assess his tone. It wasn't as cold as it had been last night, but the warmth he had shown her prior to her stupid escapade was still gone. Her heart sank so much that it took her a moment to register what he had said.

A walk! She was allowed to go outside.

Although surely this was just a way to get her alone, outside of Esta's and Raelyn's range of hearing so that he could reprimand her. She deserved it but she hoped he would also give her a chance to properly apologize.

She changed quickly into leggings and a blue sleeveless tunic, gave her hair a quick comb through and then braided it, and downed the rest of her coffee in two gulps. The red marks around her neck had faded slightly, a subtle reminder of the night's adventure but not a lasting one thank Canta.

Raelyn was sitting at the table with Esta when Nova declared she was ready a few moments later, but she didn't look up other than to give Fynn a nod. "Have fun you two," she called sarcastically from behind them as they exited the apartment.

Neither Nova nor Fynn spoke as they moved down the main stairs and out the front door of the building. Had Daro resumed his post on guard duty outside her building, in the shadows or perhaps on the roof of a neighboring building? Fynn's hand entwined with hers tightly as they made it onto the sidewalk, a death grip she stood no chance of wrangling out of. It was a gesture of force, of authority, so why did it send a shiver up her spine?

Why did his hand, which appeared calloused and firm, feel so *soft* against her skin?

Why were shockwaves running through her body, making her hair stand on end?

She allowed Fynn to lead her but kept her gaze on the ground again, hoping they didn't run into anyone she recognized along the way to wherever they were going, but also so he didn't catch a glimpse at her face, which she was certain betrayed the tempest of emotions swirling inside her. It seemed like it was still early enough on a weekend day that few people were out, which was a blessing.

It took a few blocks but once she allowed her mind to snap back to reality, it became clear where he was taking her: The bench where the attack happened last night. And she wasn't sure she was ready for that. When the outline of the park came into view ahead of her, she started squirming, finally attempting to wrench free from his grasp.

"Can't we have this conversation somewhere else? I'm not ready to go back there." She hated how desperate her plea sounded, how much her voice cracked.

Fynn didn't respond, simply gripped her hand tighter and pulled her a little faster. If he wanted to, he could have gotten them back to that spot in a matter of seconds, but he clearly wanted her to feel the anticipation of slowly approaching the bench. He was doing this on purpose.

She tried again, unsuccessfully, to pull away. "Please, Fynn, I get it, I deserve it, but please don't make me go back there. I'm so sorry, I know

I owe you and I will make it up to you, but not like this. Please." Her skin was starting to crawl, little beads of sweat formed on her brow.

"This isn't for me. This is for you." His eyes remained locked on the path ahead of him.

He didn't speak again, and Nova, truly puzzled by his words, stopped fighting his grip and resumed her normal pace beside him, though her heart thumped so forcefully it filled her ears.

They rounded the corner to the path she had wandered last night. Had it only been last night? Her body seized as she spotted the bench overturned, the broken twigs and leaves that scattered the ground where Fynn had gone into the bush after the attacker.

He dropped her hand, and she immediately mourned its steadying presence. With a single move, he righted the bench, then grabbed her waist and forced her onto it.

She clenched the seat of the bench with her hands and willed her pulse to slow. If she had to do this, she didn't want to show her fear to Fynn, didn't want him to win. But heat was building up inside her, and it wasn't entirely related to the summer's day.

"You should know that the witch who attacked you is dead." He stood in front of her, arms crossed.

Nova stiffened. That was not what she expected to hear. She looked up to meet his gaze. "My father?"

Fynn shook his head. "No, it appears the wielder killed himself during interrogation. Our fathers learned little but were able to glean that he was sent by Blackmore."

She stared at the ground. So close, she had been so close to getting captured or killed. Her body betrayed her and started to tremble. Fynn remained stoic. Maybe he just didn't care. Then the words fell from her mouth. "I'm sorry. I'm so sorry."

Fynn tucked a stray hair behind his pointed ear. "You know, you almost cost me my job. My ability to *ever* find a new job. I was almost disowned by my father."

Again with the cold tone. She would have given anything to go back to how things were only twenty-four hours ago. "I do. I don't know what else to say besides how sorry I am." A single tear escaped onto her cheek as her gaze lowered to her feet. Another betrayal of her body.

"You needed to come back here. To remember, to process, and to allow yourself to move on."

So that was why they'd come to this spot. She had to admit that Fynn was right. Being here, with him, hearing about the fall out of her actions...it was healing in a way. Her heart was slowing, and her body was cooling.

She continued to stare at her feet, digging the toe of her sandal into the dirt. "I understand."

Fynn nodded and then joined her on the bench. She didn't dare meet his eyes, even though she sensed that he was watching her closely.

When he spoke again, his voice calmed. "You will not do that again. It will not end well for either of us. Wherever you go, I go, even if that means you waking me up. That's twice now you've put yourself in danger, twice now you've made me want to—" He paused and exhaled a sharp breath before going on. "Just please, don't do it again. We're a team, ok?

She stole a look over at him, raising an eyebrow. What had he been about to say? Had he been truly worried about her wellbeing, not just for his job? Her pulse quickened at the thought, but she drew a deep breath to slow it. *Don't be ridiculous.*

"I promise."

Fynn nodded and leaned back against the bench. "We will stay until you're ready to go back home."

Nova nodded, and leaned back as well, tilting her head back so her face met the sun that beamed down through the leaves. Tears fell as her chest swelled, and she finally allowed herself to fully experience the trauma from last night, but also to grieve the loss of the innocence she had lived in prior to Blackmore's escape.

11

OVER THE NEXT WEEK, the sisters and their guards settled back into their routines from before the attack, although with slightly more formality. Nova was still walking on eggshells around Fynn, like she was trying to get herself out of a hole she'd dug—or rather, trying not to deepen it. Raelyn seemed to feel that Fynn forcing Nova to go back to the bench was punishment enough for both of them and acted like nothing had happened. But Esta started treating Nova like she wasn't present, ignoring her, looking past her, not even mentioning her name.

"How did I offend her so badly?" she finally asked Fynn one night, when it was just the two of them at the apartment. She had made them both dinner, and now she was drying dishes that Fynn had washed.

Just two hours before, Raelyn and Esta had left for the night market that was held in the park once a week during the summer. Nova still wasn't ready to spend much time in the park, so she had insisted on staying home.

"I'll bring back something sweet for you," Raelyn said as she hugged Nova good-bye. Her curly hair bounced as she skipped out of the apartment without even a glance behind her to see if Esta was there.

Esta had just nodded at Fynn, her eyes passing right over Nova as she turned her gaze toward the door.

It had been the same when the four of them were working on a puzzle yesterday. Nova had found a particularly tricky piece, earning her a high five from Fynn and a round of applause from Raelyn. But Esta? She'd kept her head down, scanning the table for more pieces to insert.

"It's not really you." Fynn handed her the last plate to dry. "She has a general distrust of witches, and I think she feels like you just proved her point. And in the process of that, you made an elf look bad. Many elves don't take kindly to witches doing that. Or humans for that matter. We are a proud race."

Nova's cheeks warmed as she wiped the plate down. "How can I make it up to her?"

Fynn set down the rag he'd been using and turned to her. "Time. Just time. She needs to see you prove yourself trustworthy and an ally of elves."

"An ally of elves? Elves don't need allies. You all are perfectly capable of defending yourselves." She set the plate back in the cupboard, closing the door gently.

Fynn rolled his eyes. "Allies in the sense that you see us as equals."

She turned to face him, leaning against the counter. "But I do. With my whole heart I do. I try to instill that same belief in my students."

"Then it should be easy." Fynn shrugged and walked toward where his cot was stowed behind the couch. "Look, I've known Esta a long time. She will come around."

He began setting up his cot in front of the couch. The cot itself was nothing more than a foldable steel frame with a beige canvas on it, and Fynn was so large that his feet usually hung off the end.

"You know," Nova said, watching him spread a sheet over the cot. "You could just sleep on the couch. It's probably a better size for you."

He stopped what he was doing and looked up at her, a grin lighting up his face. "Now that is something I don't think Esta would come around to."

Nova laughed and pushed herself off the counter so she could lean across the island on her elbows. "Oh? That's very chivalrous of you. Giving up a better bed just so Esta doesn't get jealous."

"You've seen her. You know what she's like when she's angry." He tossed a pillow on his cot. "That's toned-down anger for Esta, too. You don't want to know how she'd react if I angered her."

"Let me guess." She tapped her chin with her index finger, her eyes lowering from Fynn's face down his torso to his waist, ignoring the heat that tickled her cheeks. "She'd whip out one of those blades and shove it right—"

Fynn's booming laugh filled the room, his shoulders shaking as one hand clutched his stomach and the other fidgeted with the waist of his trousers. "Yeah, she'd shove it where it would do the most damage."

The door opened, and Nova nearly jumped. Raelyn sauntered through, a huge grin on her face, her cup clearly having been filled by an evening out. Esta was right behind her, and the look on her face, the furrow of her brows, made Nova certain that she'd overheard their conversation and was not happy about it.

"Welcome back! I'm off to bed." Nova's voice pitched higher than normal as she stepped sideways out of the kitchen and towards her door. But she caught Fynn's eye one last time before she disappeared for the night, the traces of his laugh still etched in them and grinned, hoping Esta didn't see.

Cassie and Bea visited them that week, having heard about the attack and wanting to check in. They were all shocked to hear more about Blackmore and to learn he was ultimately behind the attack.

"I still can't believe that happened, Nova. I'm so glad you're ok," her friend Cassie, a human and fellow teacher, said. She had brought over some homemade scones, a treat Nova usually devoured when she brought them to work. Today was no different. Nova had already eaten three.

They were sitting on the couch together, Raelyn on the floor in front of them with their other friend, Bea, an aero-witch. "Don't worry, Cass," her sister said, wiping crumbs off her chin. "I made sure she learned her lesson."

Nova smirked and flicked her gaze over to Fynn, who was sitting at the dining table with Esta working on a puzzle, the best they could do to give the friends some space in the small apartment. His violet eyes twinkled when they met hers, and the corner of his mouth tipped up in a small, knowing smile.

If anyone had made her learn her lesson, it had been him. But sure, they could let Raelyn think it had been her doing.

A light breeze filled the room as Bea leaned forward, her chocolate brown hair falling in front of her face, and said in a hush, "Lesson or no, I wouldn't mind being saved by your elf, Nova."

Of course. Leave it to Bea to use her wind magic to prevent any sound, any talk of *them*, from being carried toward the elves. As the gossip of the group, it was one of her favorite spells.

Cassie and Raelyn giggled like schoolgirls, and Nova found herself playing with her braid, her heart beating faster, her breaths shallower.

"Wait, Rae," Bea whispered, her hand flying to her mouth. "She's blushing! Is there something going on between them?"

Raelyn leaned forward, lines of laughter still sketched on her pretty face, still reflected in her brown eyes. "No." She paused before adding, "Not yet anyway."

Nova threw a small pillow from the couch at her sister. "Moving on from that—"

"Why? Is Cal jealous?" Cassie nudged Nova with her elbow.

"Cal? No, I haven't even seen him since the weekend before school let out." Nova shook her head. She needed to steer this conversation elsewhere. "Anyway, Cass, that art festival we always go to is coming up. Are you still in?"

Thankfully, the conversation stayed away from talk of Fynn for the rest of the visit, but after Cassie confirmed she still wanted to attend the festival, Nova found her thoughts drifting away from her friends and toward that male elf sitting at her dining table, that knowing smirk plastered on his face, that twinkle still lighting up his violet eyes, like he'd heard the whole conversation despite Bea's spell.

She had to admit there was something between them. The spark in the library. The way he had called her Al. The way her body reacted to holding his hand. Maybe he hadn't felt it, but she could no longer deny it.

Cassie and Bea left after a few hours that only felt like a few minutes. "We can come to you as much as you want. Just send a messenger!" Cassie said as they were leaving. "I'll bring more scones!"

From then on, it got a little less lonely, even if the apartment became more and more crowded. Raelyn, the social butterfly that she was, decided she needed to invite a new person over every day, so the apartment was always buzzing with activity. She kept insisting Nova invite over Cal.

"No, thank you. Cal doesn't need to come here." Nova was lying on the couch, her feet crossed at her ankles, her book open on her lap, wishing Raelyn would stop talking to her and let her read.

Raelyn moved around the island from the kitchen where she'd been—to Nova's surprise—cleaning up after dinner, crossing her arms. "Fine, then at least go meet him somewhere. Fynn can go with you."

Nova glanced across the room at Fynn, certain he had overheard Raelyn's suggestion, but his face gave nothing away as he and Esta performed their nightly blade sharpening ritual at the dining table. The idea of trying to sit through a date with Fynn watching over the entire thing turned her insides into knots.

But if it was a date with *just* Fynn...

She slammed her book shut. There was no point trying to read anymore. "No, he can wait until after Blackmore is caught. Besides, I wasn't very into him anyway, he was just something to do."

The words tumbled out, unfiltered, and her cheeks flushed when Fynn startled. He fumbled his blade but didn't look her way. Raelyn laughed. "Mmhmm ok, Nova."

"You know what I mean. Something to keep me occupied. To take up my time." She was stumbling over her words, trying to save face, as she curled her knees into her chest.

"Keep digging, sis." Raelyn was clearly bemused. She laughed as she walked into her room to get ready for bed.

Cheeks aflame, Nova straightened her legs, pressing her feet into the floor and intending to retreat to her own room, but Fynn cut her off. "Do you need...something to do?"

Esta snorted, then packed up her knives and busied herself with getting her cot set up. But given their cots usually went up side by side next to the couch, she still ended up in the middle of their conversation.

Heart hammering, Nova swallowed and stood. "No, Fynn."

He continued, his tone completely flat, but his eyes wide and playful. "Was he mean to you? Did he hurt you? Do I need to—"

"No, Fynn." She flashed what she hoped was a look of finality his way. This conversation needed to end…now. "He wasn't anything special. It fizzled out. End of story."

Nothing in his tone had suggested jealousy, but she could've sworn she spotted relief flash across his face.

"I'm going to bed," she said, before she could say anything stupid or start to make guesses about what that relief meant.

"Good night, Nova," was all he said back.

12

THEIR MOTHER AND FATHER stopped by once as well. Mother apparently hadn't yet forgiven Nova for her adventure (or really, for potentially putting Raelyn in more danger) and pretended she wasn't there. Though a small piece of her broke each time, she was used to her mother acting this way. On more than one occasion growing up, Mother had completely shut her out in a similar way. Most times, she had no idea what she had done to earn her mother's scorn, and it wasn't until she was a teenager, watching their friends' mothers supporting their every endeavor, that she understood this was not how a mother should treat her children. Since that realization, Nova had decided she didn't need her mother's affection; the release of that weight from her chest had been freeing.

But Father was ready to let bygones be bygones. He had delivered an update on Blackmore ("Still in Noriendar. They spotted two more abandoned camps yesterday.") and even stayed for dinner (a delicious chicken meal he had his penthouse chef prepare and send to them). The visit had lasted longer than Nova expected, and it was nice to have them all together as a family again, even if it meant that Mother wasn't acknowledging her presence and that four elves were crammed into their living room.

Today though, exactly a week after the attack, Nova awoke re-freshed. Today was the day that she planned to meet up with Cassie at the art festival in Arkwood Park, and even though Fynn would be close at hand, she could barely contain her excitement at the idea of a full afternoon outside, a change of scenery, and a change of company. She loved Raelyn but being subjected to her company constantly had taken its toll on her patience.

She was sipping her coffee and nibbling on a croissant at the table next to Fynn and Esta, when a knock came on the door. She moved to answer it, but Esta shot her a look and motioned for her to stay down. Esta and Fynn exchanged a quick glance—what did their elf senses pick up that her own witch senses couldn't? Esta approached the door and opened it a crack.

From her spot at the table, she couldn't see who was at the door, but she could tell no words were exchanged. Esta closed the door again, turning swiftly on her heel to look directly at Nova.

"Barricade this door." The first words Esta had spoken to her all week.

Nova set down her croissant. "Why?"

"Just do it!"

It would never be as good as her father's barricade, but she threw her magic against the door. A faint purple glow surrounded the door as it magically hardened. She would have Raelyn work on it when she woke up.

"What is it?" Fynn's hand reached reflexively for the longsword resting on the wall behind him.

Esta came back to the table holding a small, unfolded scroll. Nova recognized her father's handwriting instantly, though there were only a few sentences on the paper.

"Blackmore's closing in, and we have new information about what he wants." Esta's eyes pierced Nova's. "You."

As the words sank in, Nova's stomach turned to lead, and her hands clammed up around her mug.

"Me?"

"That's what it says." Esta threw the letter at her so she could read it for herself.

New orders: No one is to leave the apartment. Black-more is outside of Noriendar and coming for Nova. Burn this letter.

She turned the paper over, looking for more, but the back side was empty. "That's it? But why?" Words were harder to come by as her mind raced, absorbing the news.

Esta shrugged, but Fynn said, "Everything we know, you know. Maybe Luc will stop by later to explain more." He leaned his sword against the wall, then stood to clean his plate and refill his coffee.

Raelyn's door creaked behind Nova, and she whipped her head around to face her sister, who was emerging from her bedroom. "You'll never guess what Father just sent over."

"Good morning to you too." Raelyn pulled her curls back into a ponytail and made for the kitchen.

Nova stood and shoved the letter—no, not a letter, hardly even a note—in Raelyn's face. "Read this."

Raelyn made a big deal of pouring herself coffee and sweetening it without acknowledging that the note existed. She took a sip, then finally read the words on the paper and almost spit the coffee right back out. "Excuse me, what? Is this because of what happened last week?"

"It seems a very delayed reaction for that. This must be something else." Nova drummed her fingers on the counter. Her pulse was beginning to pick up speed. Whenever Blackmore's name came up, it seemed instead of answers, they were only met with more and more questions. But this? She was the new target? Why?

Raelyn set down her mug and clapped her hand to her mouth. "Maybe he's been after you this whole time and we're just learning. Maybe he decided as Father's eldest, you're the best target to strike the largest chord with him."

Nova faked a laugh, her mind still racing. "Ha. Then he clearly hasn't been doing his homework in Mistfell." Her fingers stopped, and she pressed her palm into the cool stone countertop. "Everyone knows you're Mother and Father's favorite."

Fynn shot Nova a look, but not one of pity. It was more one of compassion. His lips parted for a moment like he wanted to say something, to argue with her logic, but then he quickly closed them and just shook his head.

Raelyn was moving though, pacing back and forth across the kitchen and ignoring what Nova had just implied. "So, you're in danger. But why not leave Arkwood? Would the cottage be safer, further from where you're more likely to be and easier to hide?

And she could be in her happy place too. Her heart immediately started to calm itself. What she wouldn't give to be able to breathe in the salt air and bury her toes in the sand again. There was no better place to get lost in one's thoughts than the beach. No better place to process all these questions.

Fynn jumped in to reply. "I suspect Luc wants to keep Nova close, but also somewhere Blackmore would be instantly recognized. Blackmore can hardly walk down the street here without being spotted.

Adenaport and the cottage are more remote, so it's less likely that he'd be seen before he could make his move."

Raelyn stopped pacing and sipped her coffee. "So instead, we're stuck here."

Nova nodded, resigning herself to that fact.

"All of us?

Another nod. There was no point continuing to daydream about Adenaport.

"For the foreseeable future? With no guests?" Her tone had more bite to it.

Nova's mind snapped back fully to the present, leaving all thoughts of the cottage behind. Why was Raelyn the one upset about this? Nova was the target. Nova was the problem here. "Well technically it doesn't say—"

"It's implied," spat Esta.

"Excuse me while I go vomit, please." And with that Raelyn excused herself to her room. Nova knew better than to follow her. She needed to get out of her own head first.

Esta rolled her eyes. "It's hardly ideal for any of us." She glanced at Fynn. "At least our jobs just got a little bit easier though. Don't have to leave the building."

Fynn didn't reply, but instead looked at Nova, as she shuffled into the living room and collapsed on the couch, her eyes meeting his. She tried to guess what was going on in his head, what message he was trying to convey with that stare but wasn't getting anywhere.

What was it with this male and his ability to send her mind into a spiral just to figure out what he was thinking every time he looked at her? Every time they touched?

It definitely wasn't hatred, like the vibes she got from Esta. There was something more there. Something...sweet.

The image of a teddy bear flashed in her mind again as he sat down next to her.

"You ok? That's a lot to take in."

She exhaled and blinked, letting her gaze settle on a painting of the beach that hung on the wall opposite where she was seated. If she couldn't have the real thing, this would have to do.

"It is," she said, pressing her hands into her thighs. "Why me? What does he want from me? It'd be nice if Father gave us answers for once instead of leaving a trail of more questions."

Fynn paused for a moment before answering. "It could be like Raelyn said. Or it could be—"

"Something else?" But what? She was unremarkable, preferring to keep a low profile. There was nothing special about her that would draw attention.

He looked at her and nodded. "Something else."

Nova leaned forward, resting her head in her hands, her gaze on her thighs. "This means no art festival then?" she asked him in an attempt to distract herself.

"This means no art festival."

"I should write to Cassie. Could you have it delivered for me?" She peeked his way in time to catch a nod.

"Of course."

She scribbled off a quick note to her friend, briefly explaining that she needed to cancel last minute but not explaining why. But before Fynn could take the note to the guards outside to deliver, another messenger arrived. This one had a longer note, written in Mother's hand.

My girls, the fact that Blackmore has escaped Norien-dar is dreadful. Without the elves' wood to contain his powers, there is no telling what he might do, who he might hurt. Not only is it important for you to now stay inside, but for the city to as well. Your father and the governors will be announcing a curfew shortly for all of Arkwood and all social events will be canceled until Blackmore is found. Only those who must seek food or treatment by healers will be able to leave their homes. These are dark times we find ourselves in. Let us hope that he finds himself back in Mistfell soon. Stay safe and smart, my loves.

So, it wasn't just Nova who was locked down after all. All of Arkwood was going into hiding. In all her time living in the city, she had never heard of such a thing, which just proved how fearsome Blackmore, his power, and his research were. She handed the note to Esta and Fynn to read, adding, "The art festival will be canceled, so no need to send that note to Cassie after all."

She snatched the scroll she'd written out of Fynn's hand, ripped it up, and threw it into the ash that remained from burning her father's note. The embers were still hot enough that the scroll fragments caught and burned within seconds. And as they burned, her last hope for freedom, a carefree summer, and now, her future, burned along with it.

13

Tensions were rising in the apartment. While the sun shone outside and the summer sky teased the four occupants, inside the flat was as cold as winter's first frost.

Raelyn hadn't taken the lockdown news well at all, especially when she found out about the city-wide policies. She rarely showed herself outside of her room, which prompted Esta to demand she either leave her door open at times or man up and face the group.

"You will not make an ass of me like your sister did of Fynn," Esta had declared through the closed door, her fists clenched. "If I can't see that you haven't tried to jump out the window—"

"It's three floors down!" Raelyn yelled back.

Nova, sitting on the couch with a book, listened to them spar and frowned. The door was adjacent to the end of the couch, so she rather felt like she was caught in the middle unintentionally.

"And I know damn well you can soften the ground enough so that is not an issue," Esta spat.

Raelyn's door swung open. A hand poked out, bearing an obscenely crude gesture, before disappearing back into the room. But the door remained open.

Esta, for her own part, was holding up decently well. As sassy as ever, she decided that the group would alternate days for cooking and cleaning to keep things fair but also to prevent the place from becoming a sty. With four grown adults in one two-bedroom apartment, that was bound to happen, so although Raelyn grumbled about the rotation, they agreed to it. And it allowed them to finally put a dent in the mountain of food Mother had supplied.

Fynn remained mostly stoic and quiet, his new normal since the attack. He'd either position himself by the window and stare out into the city (was there something, or someone, out there he was looking for?) or he'd be at the dining room table working on one of the puzzles they'd collected over the last few weeks, most recently one that Father had sent over.

Nova was managing well at first, but on the fifth morning of waking up without Raelyn's coffee or the prospect of anything to look forward to during the day, she started to feel depression setting in. Or maybe rage was a better word for it. Whatever it was, it was becoming all-consuming, and she was finding it difficult not to snap at whoever even so much as looked her way. Though she tried and tried to put on a happy face, to work on puzzles with Fynn, or to come up with other fun activities for them to try in the apartment (Learn to bake! Write a novel! Take up painting!), she couldn't stop her emotions from churning.

One of those days, when a summer storm was brewing and the sky outside was darkening though it was only mid-afternoon, Nova found herself working on a puzzle with Fynn at the table, Raelyn beside her with her nose in a book. Esta was on cleaning duty that day and was using the quiet moment to sweep. Raelyn was silently taking it upon herself to magically add little patches of dust and dirt throughout the apartment so that as Esta cleaned, she ended up needing to redo places.

"Stop it," Nova hissed so that Esta wouldn't hear. But apparently Raelyn didn't hear either because she kept going. Nova kicked her under the table instead.

That got her attention. "What?" Raelyn asked, looking up at Nova with her puppy dog eyes again.

"I said, stop it," she hissed again.

Raelyn shrugged, flipping a page in her book. "Don't know what you're talking about."

When Esta cleaned the corner next to the pantry for the third time, Fynn slammed a hand on the table. The puzzle pieces jumped, some falling to the floor. "You need to stop."

Nova looked up to see who he was talking to, assuming it was Esta. But he was looking right at her instead. "Me?"

"And Raelyn." His eyes flicked over to her sister. "I know what you're doing."

She had tried to *stop* Raelyn from spreading the dirt, but it hardly seemed worth it to point that out now. Instead, Nova rolled her eyes and slumped back in her chair with a groan.

Esta dropped the broom on the floor. "You're making it dirty again, aren't you? I knew I had done this area thoroughly enough!" Her face started reddening in anger.

Raelyn set her book down and shrugged, leaning back in the chair. "We needed something to amuse us. Sitting around for days on end unable to leave is boring."

"It's infuriating," Nova added under her breath. Thunder started to rumble in the distance, a low vibration shaking the flat.

Esta stomped over to them and threw her hands on the table, making more puzzle pieces fly. Nova whipped her neck back, stunned, as Esta ground out, "Boring? Infuriating? You think it's just you who feels that way?"

"Theoretically, you and Fynn could leave. Father can send in new guards," Nova pointed out, leaning down to pick up some of the fallen pieces. "We are the ones who have to stay."

"The curfew applies to all citizens of Arkwood. We wouldn't be that much freer out there." Fynn kept his voice steady, but she could see frustration brewing behind his violet eyes, his eyebrows furrowing together.

She smashed the pieces she'd collected onto the table. "But you don't have a mass-murdering, power-hungry, asshole chasing after you, do you?" Here it was, the anger Nova had been suppressing for days finally coming to a head. It felt good, it felt *right* to let it escape.

Maybe it was a good thing Raelyn had catalyzed this confrontation.

Fynn pinched the bridge of his nose between his thumb and forefinger. "That's not the point—"

"We are all in this together." Esta's voice was nearly drowned out by thunder. "The least you and your sister could do is make us feel welcome."

Raelyn jumped out of her seat, her chair falling over backward behind her. "What?!"

"Since the day we got here nearly three weeks ago, we've been outsiders. Hired help," Esta said, her teeth bared. "We aren't just bodyguards though, we are real life, functional beings who are stuck in this same situation. But you two, privileged, spoiled—"

"Esta." Fynn dropped his hand, his eyes blazing at her. Rain was now pouring in earnest outside, splattering the living room windows, and lightning flashing in the distance.

The female elf threw up her hands. "It's true! This job is not turning out to be what I had expected. Maybe I should just leave now with what little dignity I have left."

"Dignity?" Raelyn leaned across the table toward Esta, her hands in fists resting on the surface. "Let's talk about dignity. You coming into my room ten times a day? No privacy. No decency. Like I'm an animal in a cage for someone to ogle at."

"Maybe," Esta leaned forward until she was nose to nose with Raelyn and hovering over Nova, who was unfortunately caught between them, "if both of you slimy bitches hadn't tried to undermine us, we'd be more trusting."

Nova could feel her blood boiling, the thunder outside booming like her heart. She would never end up friends with Esta, but this was more than she expected from the female elf. Her eyes moved to Fynn, who was staring at Esta, open mouthed, as if in disbelief that she was saying these things out loud.

Then again, he'd accused her of taking part in Raelyn's prank when he should have known her better than that by now. Maybe he didn't know Esta as well as he claimed either.

He put a hand on Esta's shoulder and gently pulled her away from Raelyn. "Let's take a breath. I was just trying to get them to stop making the house dirtier. I wasn't trying to cause a bigger issue."

"I'm glad you did." Raelyn straightened and crossed her arms. "Now we know how she really feels. And you know what, she should leave. I'll send a note to Father letting him know she has disrespected us, and we're letting her go."

Esta's mouth thinned as she clenched her fists, and her face turned beet red. "That is hardly how my departure would go. If I'm going anywhere, it's on my terms. Not the whims of a ditzy little geo and her powerless sister."

Though Nova had been called worse in her lifetime, though it was essentially true, hearing those words from Esta's mouth sent her over the edge. Heat spread through every vein in her body at the same time ice filled her lungs, her breaths shallow and quick. Her head began to throb painfully, and she clapped her hands to her temples to staunch the ache, slamming her eyes shut in the process.

She wanted to scream at Esta, tell her that her magic was not a definition of her worth. That there was so much more to her than just a lack of magic. But the pain in her head, the heat in her body, the ice in her lungs, the agony of it all rendered her speechless.

"Nova?"

Was that Raelyn's voice? Was that Raelyn's hand on her back?

The room was spinning. Ringing filled her ears. The ice in her lungs took over the heat in her body, tamping it back until she was almost frozen and her body shook. But then—air, sweet air filled her, and she was lighter than ever. Like she could fly.

Still her head pounded, hard enough that she could think of nothing else but trying to stop the pain.

Someone was screaming. Was it her? The damn ringing in her ears made it so hard to hear. So hard to open her eyes and look for whoever needed help.

Another hand rested on her shoulder, a large one, firmer, trying to ground her. Ground. Sweet earth. The power she was supposed to have harnessed all her life. The power that had betrayed her and left her weak.

No, she was not weak. She would not let herself be weak.

The floor beneath her rumbled and splintered, like it was cracking. No, surely that wasn't happening. She'd never been capable of an earthquake. And Raelyn wouldn't have caused an earthquake inside, would she? But the blood in her head was still thrashing too hard for her to dare open her eyes, so instead she squeezed them tighter and tucked her chin toward her chest.

Thunder sounded from the storm still raging outside, a dull rumble barely perceptible above the cacophony in her head. Then heat filled the room, and the sounds of crackling flames drowned out the ringing and the screaming she was now almost sure was coming from her own icy lungs. Fire? How did a fire start? It was scorching, and more screams filled the room as tendrils of smoke hit her lungs, beginning to thaw them.

This time the screams came from a voice she recognized, a voice that punched her in the gut, a voice she loved.

The hand on her back disappeared but the hand on her shoulder stayed firm.

And still her head pounded. Still, she screamed, vibrations in her throat the only indication it was in fact her that was screaming.

She dug the heels of her palms harder into her temples.

What was happening? Why was it happening? How could she get this goddess-damned pain to go the fuck away?

Just as suddenly as the flames had appeared, they disappeared, and thunder rolled again, louder this time. Trickles of water echoed around the flat, and she could feel moisture seeping into her hair, her clothes, soaking her through.

Rain inside the apartment? Had they left the window open to the storm outside? Well, that wasn't good, it would ruin all the furniture, the floors, the food. If only her head wasn't throbbing so much, if only she could stop screaming, if only she could move her own body, so she could do something about it.

The screams around her stopped but the hand on her shoulder remained.

More thunder—a sound she usually loved—then a breeze swept over her wet skin. It chilled her, cooled her, bringing her back to the present as her body continued to tremble.

The window was closed now, wasn't it? That's why the rain had stopped? But then, how did the breeze get in?

As the breeze tapered off and her heart started to slow, she dared to open her eyes and lift her head. She needed to know what the hell had just happened. To make sure Raelyn was ok.

Slowly the room came back into focus. The pain in her head started to recede. But her body—it couldn't hold her up anymore.

The last things she saw before collapsing to the floor were the tears streaming down the face of a female with curly brown hair, and violet eyes, so close to hers, widened in shock and concern.

14

H ER CLOTHES WERE DRENCHED. From the rain or from her own sweat? And she was back in her own bed. Fynn must have moved her here.

She blinked open her eyes and was met with darkness. It was night. How long had she been out? She could still hear thunder in the distance, but a quick glance out the window showed the rain had stopped so the storm must be on its way out of the city.

What strange circumstances the storm had brought into their apartment. Cracked floor, raging fire, rain, and then wind. How had they been so stupid to leave the window open?

"Oh good, you're awake."

Nova slowly turned her head to look toward the sound of the voice and found Fynn standing at her door, holding a mug. Her mouth watered as wafts of savory broth made their way toward her.

He glanced over his shoulder as he entered the room, then quietly closed the door behind him. She sat up straighter, instantly on guard. They'd never been in her room, alone, with the door closed. And where was Raelyn? Esta?

"Raelyn is asleep. Esta is gone," Fynn said, as if reading her mind. He crossed the room and handed her the mug, then sat at the end of her bed.

"Gone?" Nova wrapped her fingers around the mug, allowing the warmth to soak in.

"Well, she's being seen to by healers." He ran a hand over the quilt on her bed, smoothing it. "She won't be back for a while. It's just the three of us now."

"Healers?" Her eyes grew wide, worry creasing her brow. "What happened?"

Fynn opened his mouth like he wanted to say something, then closed it again before starting over. "She was burned. Pretty severely. I think she'll be ok, but she'll have scars."

"Burned? So that fire was real?" The revelations overwhelmed her, sending her mind into a tailspin. She brought the broth to her mouth, taking a small sip to help clear it. A sigh escaped her. She'd never had anything so delicious. As the warmth of it filled her body, each nerve seemed to twinkle in response, like they were coming alive in a whole new way.

"The fire, the quake, the rain, all of it. All of it was real." He spoke slowly and appeared to be watching her very closely, like he wanted to be prepared for any reaction.

"Is Raelyn ok?" She swung her feet around to get out of bed. "Oh, I bet there's a mess out there to clean up—"

Fynn shook his head and put a hand on her leg to stop her, sending a shiver up her spine that radiated through her whole body. "Raelyn is fine, and there's no mess." She settled back into bed, his hand falling away, leaving a chill behind on her skin. "Whatever magic caused the elements to react also made the damage vanish without a trace—except for Esta's burns. I even scouted around the building and no one else noticed that anything strange happened."

"But...how?"

"I think you know." Fynn caught her gaze and held it.

Nova gulped another sip of broth, then drew in a deep breath. "Me?" It was barely louder than a whisper.

Fynn nodded in reply.

They sat in silence for a few minutes, her head spinning with what he had just confirmed. Fynn was still watching her, but she couldn't look at him. Couldn't look at those eyes filled with what she assumed was pity for the situation she found herself in, with fear for the danger she had put them in. She didn't want to believe that she had caused that.

Finally, she found her voice again. "How? I'm just a geo-witch, and a weak one..."

It was all she could say, and all that she needed to say. Maybe Fynn had the answers, maybe he didn't. But that was ultimately what she needed in this moment: To understand how this could have happened. How she, a geo who could barely dig a hole to plant a flower in the earth, could have cast all four elements in their dining room.

"I can't say for sure." His voice was gentle, calm. "But my guess would be that you're not a geo." He paused and met her eyes. "You're a wielder, Nova."

She just shook her head, pressure building in her lungs and tears filling her eyes as she squeezed them shut. It couldn't be true. It couldn't. There wasn't a way it was possible.

A hand reached for her shoulder. A strong hand, one that had been there earlier.

A jolt of energy shot from her shoulder down her spine, and she didn't think it was from her magic.

"Breathe," he whispered.

She furrowed her brow and looked at Fynn. His eyes were so close to hers she could see the sparkle of violet more distinctly than ever.

"I think your powers are not easily controlled yet. When your emotions run high, your powers will try to escape. Just breathe through it for a minute."

He sounded so earnest—like he truly cared about her, about helping her through this—that she played along and did what he suggested. She breathed in deeply, then exhaled slowly. After a few repetitions, her heart rate slowed, her tears stopped, and the emotions faded to a dull ache.

Fynn smiled and removed his hand. "Mindfulness is its own form of magic. We all learn it at the Academy."

Nova looked at her hands, somehow still holding that mug of broth. "Is it possible to be a wielder if my parents aren't? Magic flows through lineage."

"Straight to the questions now," he said with a smirk. "Ok. But if we need to take breathing pauses, you let me know."

She nodded and sipped more of the broth. Despite being in a mug and not over the stove, it wasn't cooling off. Was this her magic at work already?

Fynn heaved up his legs and crossed them on the bed. "Keep in mind, everything we discuss here will be my own conjecture from the last two hours. I'm not a witch so I won't pretend to know any of your genetics firsthand, but I feel I'm educated enough to make some good guesses."

"I understand."

He cleared his throat. "So, you know how any type of witch can be born of a different type? It's rare, but it does happen." Nova nodded, remembering a student two years ago who was a pyro-witch born to two hydro parents. "I think it's the same with wielders."

Her free hand, though shaky, started to brush through the hair that had fallen over her shoulder and rested on her chest. "Ok, so I'm not crazy. It is possible for my parents to have birthed a wielder. But then why didn't I know until today?"

"Here's where I need you to hear me out. Don't jump to anger until I'm done. Got it?"

She raised an eyebrow but said, "Sure."

Fynn took a deep breath, rubbing his hands on his knees. "I think your parents knew, or at least Luc did, and he has been lying to you, suppressing your powers."

Her head began to throb. *Breathe, Nova, breathe*, she reminded herself. She set the mug on her bedside table, not wanting to risk spilling it. Or boiling it.

"Why would my father do that?" Sure, Father was wary of wielders. That much was obvious given his regulations. But he never outright exiled them. Never did more than just contain what they could legally do.

"Are you sure you want to hear this?" His tone filled with hesitation.

Her fingers laced into her hair and tugged, hard, trying to relieve the pressure building inside. "Just get it out. Please. My world is already upside down."

Fynn just looked at her, as if gauging whether she could really hear what he was about to say. Finally, he inhaled deeply, and said, "Luc's entire political career has been about the containment of wielders. Blackmore was just his first arrest. Much of the legislation your father has put forth has been to stop wielders from gaining too much power. I imagine when he had a daughter born as a wielder, it was an unwelcome shock. How could a man positioned against wielders raise one of his own? He had to either contain your power and hide your abilities or subject you to the same scrutiny and regulation as the other wielders. I imagine he relished the opportunity to practice containment magic on you."

Her body shook, the grip she'd been holding on her hair slackening. Her father had been manipulating her all her life, making her feel like she was worthless, powerless when he was hiding the truth: That she was, in truth, more powerful than him.

Memories flashed through her mind. Moments that seemed inconsequential at the time, but after recent events, may have been...clues.

Like when she was eight, and she'd gotten mad at her parents prohibiting her from going with Raelyn to Cassie's house. Nova had gotten a poor grade on a recent test—a common occurrence in her magic classes—and was grounded. Raelyn wrapped Nova in a hug, attempting to calm her, but then the stove burst into silent flames during the middle of her tantrum. Almost as soon as it had started, it stopped, leaving no traces of char behind. Father claimed it was an issue with the gas line and sent Raelyn away immediately. Nova hadn't had a reason not to believe him. But he'd still been so furious with her, holding her arm with a vicelike grip while he scolded her.

And then there was her thirteenth birthday when she and Raelyn had been walking hand-in-hand just behind their mother on the way to a celebratory dinner. Father had been held up at work, but he so rarely turned up for Nova's birthdays anyway. The sisters had been swinging their arms and gossiping merrily about the new boy in Nova's class when they happened to run into him with his family. Mortified, she'd tried to hide herself behind Raelyn and somehow in the process, her hair had paled. Mother noticed and pulled the two of them away quickly. They went straight home instead of to that dinner, and once Father returned home, he'd scolded her yet again, his hand on her shoulder this time.

Some magic required contact to be reinforced. What if those two instances had been a lapse of the suppression spell, and the scolding had been Father reinforcing it...

Perhaps she should be grateful he chose suppression instead of regulation. At least she had been able to live the life she desired, rather than be subjected to the scrutiny of the governors.

Breathe. Breathe.

But the breathwork wasn't enough this time. The pressure building in her body, the pulse of magic moving through her veins, feeding off her confusion, her desperation, finally broke free, sending a wall of water that mirrored her own tears streaming down her doorway.

Fynn jumped off the bed to stand before she could reel in the magic. She searched inward, locating the channel the magic had escaped from and shutting it off. As suddenly as the waterfall had started, it stopped, leaving the floor...dry.

Her hand flew to her mouth. "I'm so sorry—"

"It's ok, Nova," Fynn said, giving her shoulder a soft squeeze and returning to his seat on the bed. "We'll get this figured out. The best thing you can do now is learn control."

She curled her knees into her chest, shaking his hand off her shoulder as she did. Her forehead connected with her knees; her hands clenched together over her shins. "I can't, Fynn. This is too much. What if I hurt someone? What if I hurt Raelyn?"

His hands broke hers apart as he grabbed one in each of his. She lifted her head, blinking away the tears to meet his gaze.

"You can," he said, his eyes boring into hers.

"You barely know me. How can you possibly say that?" She tried to pull her hands away from his, but he held on tighter.

"I've also been doing nothing but observing you for the last three weeks. I doubt there's anything you can't do once you've set your mind to it. The only thing holding you back is yourself."

His thumbs traced circles on the back of her hands sending waves of calm through her. Her magic, something she now had to get used to feeling within her, seemed to react to his touch. Or maybe it was just the newness of it all, just her body adjusting to this newfound power.

But…maybe he was right. She'd never been one who believed in her own magic, but that was because she hadn't had any. Maybe she could learn to accept this new power.

Maybe this would be the key to surviving Blackmore. To protecting Raelyn from his wrath.

A yawn escaped her mouth, the overwhelming urge to sleep overcoming her like a tidal wave.

Fynn smiled and dropped her hands. "Raelyn added some herbs into the broth that she said would help you sleep tonight." He stood and reached for her now empty mug. "Get some rest. We can discuss more in the morning."

She shivered at the chill that fell over her hands when he removed his own. As quickly as it had come, the wave of calm subsided but was now replaced by a fogginess in her mind. Damn, Raelyn was really good at these brews. "Before you go, does Raelyn know? Esta?"

Fynn, walking toward her door, stopped in his tracks and turned to face her again. "Raelyn and I have…discussed things. She wanted to wait for you to wake up, but I convinced her to take some of her own broth and sleep. She will be anxious to see you in the morning." He paused. "Esta does not know. And for the time being, it may be best if we don't tell anyone outside the three of us."

He was protecting her. He understood that if her father knew what had happened, he would try to contain her magic again or maybe worse. She wasn't sure how she broke through the containment today, and she wasn't sure what she was going to do with this new knowledge. But she didn't want to go back to who she was a few hours ago.

"Get some sleep, Al. We'll talk more in the morning."

He closed her door and in seconds, exhaustion overtook her.

15

"**W**ANNA TALK ABOUT IT?"

Raelyn was lying in bed next to Nova when she awoke the next morning. All remnants of last night's storm had vanished, and the sun was back, shining brightly through her window.

She sighed and rubbed her eyes. "Good morning to you, too."

"Coffee is on your side table."

And sure enough, there was a steaming mug of coffee—Raelyn's coffee! —waiting for her to enjoy. She sat up, snatched the mug, and drank, savoring every bit of the warm brew as it lingered on her tongue. If there was anything she needed to get through this day, it was coffee.

Raelyn was still laying down, an arm tucked behind her head. "How are you feeling?"

Good question. Nova took stock of her body. The coffee spread down her torso as she swallowed and seemed to warm up every bone, but not in the way the fire last night had. In an entirely different way that made her feel more alive, stronger. Her head was clear; her pulse hummed normally.

"Physically, I'm well." Nova paused for another sip, her unfocused gaze settling on her armoire across the room. "Actually, better than I think I've felt in a long time."

"Maybe the suppression spell was suppressing more than just your powers? Or your powers being suppressed kept you from being fully...alive?" Raelyn sat up and crossed her legs, spinning to face Nova.

Nova turned to look at her sister. "Do you believe the theory about Father?"

Raelyn pressed her palms into her knees. The sunlight from the window left half her face in shadow. "He's always been a little...stricter with you—"

"Strict?" Nova's memories flashed back to the same ones as last night. "More like aggressive. I don't remember him ever yelling at you the way he did at me."

"As much as I hate it, you're right. Given how Father has treated you, Fynn's theory makes sense. And," Raelyn drew in a deep breath and sighed, "I honestly don't have any better ideas right now."

She nodded slowly. Raelyn had a point. There really wasn't a better explanation that she could come up with. But that her own father, and likely her mother, had done this to her for her entire life. That they had caused her to spend her whole life avoiding magic, thinking less of herself. It was almost as much to absorb as the presence of the powers themselves.

"Fynn thinks we should keep it quiet, even from Esta."

"I'm inclined to agree with that, too," Raelyn said. "We don't want to risk angering Father right now or drawing more attention to you from Blackmore. And Esta was unconscious long enough that she is unlikely to remember or even comprehend what happened."

Nova sat up straight, spilling a small amount of coffee on her lap. "Blackmore! What if he somehow knows I'm a wielder? What if that's why he is targeting me?" She paused, wiping up the spilled coffee with her hand, not daring to try casting a spell to dry it. "What if that's why Father hid my powers? Maybe Blackmore's research was targeting wielders, and Father didn't want him coming after me?"

"That is a more noble way to look at what Father did. It's certainly a possibility." Raelyn leaned forward and took Nova's free hand in hers. "Regardless, I'm in this with you. Always, sis."

She smiled. "Thanks, Rae."

A light knock on the door interrupted them, and she called for Fynn to enter. He walked in carrying a platter of pancakes, his blonde hair loose around his shoulders. When he set the plate beside the bed, the sweet, buttery aroma coaxed a growl from Nova's stomach. Fynn grinned as he said, "Figured you might enjoy, and *need*, breakfast in bed."

She didn't need to be told twice. She cut up her pancake, then stabbed a few bites with a fork and ate happily, temporarily lightened by both the pancakes and the idea that Father's intentions may have been just after all.

Beside her, Raelyn also devoured her breakfast, while Fynn just watched from the end of the bed. When only a few bites remained, he cleared his throat. "We need to discuss what comes next."

"Whaddaya mean?" Nova asked, mouth full of the delicious pancake.

"You have raw, untamed magic flowing through you that you've never learned to control or use properly. Staying in this apartment is dangerous for all three of us." He said the words delicately, but there was no mistaking the seriousness of his tone.

Nova took a quick sip of coffee, then set the mug back down. "Breathing worked last night...or at least well enough," she added, remembering the waterfall and wincing.

Raelyn seemed to catch on to what Fynn was saying, or perhaps this was also something they had discussed while she was unconscious.

"Breathing will only get you so far. Remember when we were little, and I used to accidentally form holes in the ground whenever I got angry or make flowers sprout throughout the house whenever I was exceptionally happy? I hadn't yet learned how to control my powers. We learned that together as we got older."

"Exactly, we already learned that." Control was the most basic skill that young witchlings were taught in school. Nova had done well in those lessons—granted with very little power, it was easy to do.

Fynn folded his hands in his lap. "This is going to be very different. You thought you had geo magic," he said, confirming what she had realized. "But in reality, you can make your magic do whatever you want it to. You could probably alter your appearance, or burn this building to the ground, or create enough food to feed the poor, or conjure a hurricane to wipe out Adenaport. You have magic at its most raw, its most pure. It's most powerful."

Nova stilled as he spoke, the only sound she could hear the drumming of her own pulse. He was right. She had let all that magic loose in the apartment last night and had hurt someone. The guilt she harbored was bad enough even though it had been Esta. What if it had been Raelyn who had been burned?

What if it had been Fynn?

She couldn't let that happen again.

"So, what do we do? It's not like there are a ton of wielders around I can ask for help."

"Aerdmure." Raelyn spoke it quietly, like it was a curse word. Aerdmure, the witches' equivalent of Besa, tucked into the Worgreth Mountains to the west of the city, where the ancient knowledge of witches' magic was said to be held.

The Astors had visited Aerdmure once as a family when Nova was about ten. She recalled the stunning beauty of the small village, set against the backdrop of the lush mountain range that witches claimed was Canta's birth land. Aerdmure was situated on a hot spring, which was believed to be the source of all witch magic. The priestesses at Canta's temple guarded the hot spring, for it was thought that if it were ever to run dry, so too would witch magic, leaving them as powerless as humans.

Few lived in Aerdmure anymore, aside from the priestesses and a small number of witches that could only be described as purists—geos who truly wanted to live off the land, aeros who believed the open air of the mountains was better for casting spells than polluted city air. But it was still a rite of passage for all witches to visit the temple at least once in their life, and it was also not uncommon for witches to stay for a few months to hone their skills, since Canta's gifts were believed strongest when close to the hot spring.

If Nova could find a priestess or another wielder in Aerdmure to train her, to teach her to control her newfound powers, she could do so away from prying eyes in Arkwood. In the mountains, it would be easier to hide, easier to escape to an unpopulated area to practice. Easier to work around her own father's restrictions on wielders.

But getting there would be impossible. "I can't go to Aerdmure."

"Why not?" Raelyn raised an eyebrow.

"I can't even leave this apartment building. How am I supposed to get all the way to Aerdmure without being spotted and brought back? Father would never let me leave his sight again." Another thought occurred to her. "He'd also realize the suppression spell is broken, that I know what he did to me. No, it's too risky."

Raelyn threw up her hands. "It's riskier to stay here! What if he realizes the spell is broken anyway? There's a good chance he could sense it."

Nova hadn't considered that. Magic left traces. Witches could generally sense when their spells were working by a tug in their core. Once the spell was released, that tug went away. Had this spell been in place so long that Father would forget to check for it? Would he even notice that tug was missing?

"I could take you," Fynn said. They both turned to look at him, Raelyn smiling but Nova gaping.

"No, absolutely not—"

"Yes! That's a great idea!"

"I'm sure we could come up with a plan to sneak you out, and then we could travel together to Aerdmure. I can move pretty swiftly, you know." Fynn grinned, and she resisted the urge to stick out her tongue at his idea of humor.

"We definitely could. And I can find a way to cover for you from our parents, so they don't notice you're missing," Raelyn added, clapping her hands.

"You're both insane. My answer is no." The words came out easily but why did the idea of being alone with Fynn make Nova light-headed? Not to mention the idea of escaping under her father's nose. It would serve him right for how he'd treated her, but still...

Fynn and Raelyn exchanged a knowing, mischievous glance, but it was Raelyn who spoke first. "I really don't know what other choice you have, Nova. Staying here isn't an option. Where else could you go?"

Fynn nodded, adding softly, "If you're worried about Blackmore, I can protect you in Aerdmure just as well as I can here. And we wouldn't be stuck in a tiny apartment for Dalia knows how long. We'd have free range of the mountains and the village."

She closed her eyes and tried to quell the fury rising within her. Letting her magic get out of control right now would only add fuel to the fire for Raelyn and Fynn to continue with this crazy plan.

Breathe. Breathe.

Her eyes fluttered open. "I'm not going. That's my final answer."

But the smile on Fynn's face and the chuckle Raelyn emitted sent her over the edge. Her pulse quickened, and power swelled within her. So much power, too much power. It pushed against her skin, her bones, searching for an escape, begging her to do something—anything. She slammed her eyes shut again, needing to rein it in, needing to *breathe*.

But before she could rein in the power, before the breathwork could calm her magic, it forced its way out of her. Her arms flung wide as it surged out of her hands.

The bed creaked and shifted, then two loud *thuds* ricocheted through the room, like books had been toppled off a shelf. Her eyes flew open. She found Fynn and Raelyn lying on the ground at opposite ends of the room. Fynn's stupid grin spread wider as he rubbed the back of his head and pulled himself upright against the wall, while Raelyn propped herself up on an elbow, her back against the armoire.

Concern and fear masked the physical relief the explosion of magic triggered in Nova's body. She clamped her hand to her mouth and sprang from the bed to check on Raelyn first. "I'm so sorry, are you ok?"

But Raelyn resumed laughing. "If you let yourself get trained, you could defend yourself against Blackmore. Look what you're capable of, Nova!"

Nova wanted to punch her in the arm but resisted, then whirled around at the sound of Fynn also laughing behind her. His laugh was infectious, seeping into her bones and setting off a purr in her heart that made her want to smile.

But she resisted.

Once their laughter died down, Raelyn turned serious. She looked at Nova earnestly with pleading eyes, her hand gripping Nova's arm.

"We're laughing now, Nova, but that could have been so much worse. You could have done so much worse. You need to learn to control this. If not for yourself, then for me."

Nova's shoulders sagged, and her dark hair fell into her face. What Raelyn said was true. She was a danger to not only herself, but to Raelyn, the person she cared most for in the world. If she did anything to harm Raelyn, to truly hurt her, she'd never forgive herself. "I didn't ask for this. For any of this."

Raelyn's grip slid down Nova's arm until it found her hand, their fingers lacing together. Her pulse at last seemed to return to its normal rhythm. "I know. But you aren't alone in this. I'm here. Fynn's here. We want to help you."

This wasn't at all how she imagined her summer would go, let alone her life. She was just Nova, a run of the mill witch with no extraordinary powers leading an ordinary life. No part of her wanted this. No part of her had even dreamed of this.

But you must work with the hand you've been dealt, she reminded herself. A phrase she'd told herself so often growing up as she came to terms with her weakness. Now, it applied even more.

There was no going back to just Nova.

She could do this for Raelyn.

Hell, she could do this for herself. A small part of her, deep down, flickered with a glimmer of excitement.

After a few moments' pause, Nova turned to face Fynn with determination in her eyes. "When do we leave?"

16

E STA WAS DOING WELL with the healers, who had quickly mended the burns to avoid permanent damage, but she needed another day for the magic working on the scar tissue to finish the job. Standard procedure for "cooking-related burns", or so the message Raelyn received had said. She would return to the apartment soon, and it was best Nova and Fynn left before she got back so she wouldn't have time to question or try to stop them.

They agreed that Raelyn would play dumb, acting like Fynn and Nova ran away together while she was sleeping but unaware of where they went or why. They figured it would buy them a little time. Esta was unlikely to admit to their father that Nova was missing without first trying to locate them herself to protect Fynn's reputation, so she'd go along with it for a bit. Raelyn, for her part, planned to divert her parents from visiting the apartment by insisting it was too dangerous for them to leave and assuring them all was well.

But they still needed to determine how exactly she and Fynn were going to escape without the building guards being any the wiser. Once they were out of sight of the building, Fynn was going to carry her and run, using his agility to get them beyond the city walls as quickly as possible. They agreed that under cover of darkness was best, even though Fynn was nearly invisible when running.

The trio spent the rest of the day trying to form a plan. Fynn immediately rejected the camouflage idea that Nova proposed.

"The elves know you can do it, and they know what to look for," Fynn explained.

Raelyn nodded in agreement. "I think it's also too risky for you to try something new in terms of magic while it's still raw and uncontrolled. If you try to go fully invisible, who knows what could happen, or how long it would actually hold. And you wouldn't want to try it on Fynn anyway. But it could still be useful as a backup..."

So, they carried on for a few hours, passing ideas back and forth, but each getting excluded for one reason or another. Finally, as night was falling, they settled on one that all three of them agreed may just work.

Once they ironed out all the details of the plan, Raelyn put her hands on the table and declared, "Well that's it then. We'll do it tomorrow."

"Tomorrow!" exclaimed Nova, looking at Fynn for confirmation that was insane, but he just nodded.

"Esta won't be gone much longer. We need to act quickly."

But things were moving way too fast. She needed more time to...do what, she wasn't sure. Process? Mourn? Explore her new identity? "It's been twenty-four hours since I broke the suppression spell, and I've only just started digesting the extent to which my world is turning upside down. I can't just pick up and leave tomorrow."

"The longer you stay, the more you risk Father finding out. You may be his daughter, but I'm not convinced he will take this well at all. For your own protection, you need to go...and now."

There was no point arguing with Raelyn—she was right. But as much as Nova had hated being sequestered in the apartment over the past few weeks, she would miss her sister, miss the life she was leaving behind. If she stayed, she could pretend that nothing had changed, that she was still a geo with limited abilities and her father was still a man who loved her and cared for her wellbeing. But if she left, she would have to fully embrace her new identity as a wielder, as a witch on the run, and as a daughter who couldn't trust her own parents.

She rubbed her fingers in circles on her temples. *Breathe. Breathe.* This was the right thing to do. She would not be alone. Though she agreed that writing to Raelyn while she was gone would be too risky to attempt, Raelyn would be with her in spirit the whole way. And Fynn would be with her physically, blonde bun, belt of knives, and all. She trusted him with her safety, her security; he'd proven he was worthy of that.

And she couldn't ignore the small part of her that was giddy about the idea of spending time alone with him.

Later that night, Fynn gave the sisters the privacy they needed. They were going to be parted for Canta knew how long, longer than they'd ever been before. Because most of tomorrow would be spent setting up the escape plot, this would be their last chance to spend time together, just the two of them. Fynn stayed in the living room, while Raelyn and Nova curled up on Nova's bed.

"This is crazy, right?" Nova stared at the ceiling, shadows flickering around from the lamp on her bed, from the moonlight trickling in from the window.

"So crazy. But also...kind of cool." Raelyn squeezed Nova's hand.

"Only because it's not happening to you."

"Well, of course." They both laughed and rolled to face each other, Raelyn's brown eyes beaming. "Ramifications about our parents aside, this is huge for you. You aren't powerless like you've always believed yourself to be. And that thrills me."

Nova pulled Raelyn's hand close to her chest. "But at what cost? Is it worth all of this? Being a danger to myself and those around me.

Finding out our parents were hiding this all my life. Having to leave my life here in Arkwood, leave you, and run into hiding."

"There's only one way to find out. You've got to live it first."

Nova closed her eyes, trying to picture what the next few days, weeks, would look like. Best case, things went according to plan, and she made it to Aerdmure, honed her skills, and learned to defend herself against Blackmore. Worst case... "And if we're caught?"

"Father will be livid. But I'll stand by you, you know that." Raelyn tucked a strand of hair behind Nova's ear as her eyes blinked open.

Nova nodded and smiled weakly. One of the best things about being close in age to Raelyn was how close it had brought their relationship over the years. They'd never been apart for longer than a day or two at a time, and deep down, much of her hesitation around leaving for Aerdmure was actually fear of leaving Raelyn, fear of not having her support.

And fear of living without her coffee.

Raelyn squeezed her hand and said quietly, "So what do you think about Fynn?"

"Excuse me?" Nova's voice echoed entirely too loudly. She clapped a hand to her mouth, her cheeks flaming.

Raelyn giggled, the shrill sound of a teenage girl sharing gossip. "Shhhhhh. You know what I mean. He's h-o-t, hot!"

Nova snorted and rolled her eyes. "He's got a great body, I'll give you that, but the personality is a little lacking." *What?* Why did she say that? She didn't really think that at all.

He was kind, sweet, gentle...a teddy bear. Unless provoked. Or betrayed.

Raelyn's eyes widened in surprise. "You think so? I don't."

"He's all yours then." Nova clamped her mouth shut, hoping that her sister wouldn't actually take her up on that...or that Fynn had heard her.

"Oh no, I wouldn't dare take him from you. Have you seen the way he looks at you?" Raelyn winked, and Nova released her hand to punch her lightly in the arm. "Just think about it, ok?"

She rolled her eyes again but nodded, more to appease Raelyn than anything. But inside, butterflies fluttered in her stomach as she remembered the electric feel of his skin brushing hers, the way her hand melded perfectly into his, the way she never seemed to be able to *stop* thinking about him. Heat rushed to her face so she shoved those thoughts away quickly before Raelyn could notice.

Nova usually told her sister everything, and this could be her last opportunity to voice her confusion about her...feelings for Fynn. If she could even call them that. But something held her back, as if saying the words out loud would make them true. She needed to sort them out before she talked to Raelyn about them. Hell, she needed to sort out *herself* before she gave any merit to the idea of starting a relationship.

So instead, she squeezed Raelyn's hand close again. "It's getting late. Will you stay with me tonight?"

"I thought you'd never ask!" Raelyn's smile lit up her face.

She smiled, closed her eyes, and fell asleep almost instantly, Raelyn's hand still locked in hers, visions of a blonde elf entering her dreams.

17

"**I** THINK THAT'S EVERYTHING," Raelyn said, placing one last bar of purple soap on the pile. Nova was adding apples to her pack and looked over. It was actually quite impressive what Raelyn had dug up—Nova had no idea they'd had that much in the flat. The floral scent she loved about her sister began to make perfect sense.

"We should really declutter more," she joked, earning a laugh from Raelyn.

That morning, over coffee and croissants, Fynn, Nova, and Raelyn had reviewed the plan. Once they were clear that everyone knew their part forward and backward, they set to work with preparations.

Nova packed backpacks for both herself and Fynn. She darted around the flat trying to find items that would help with their journey while not weighing them down: clothes, food, blankets, dishware. The Astors were not a camping family, so the supplies were meager, but she was proud of what she'd been able to dig up. She silently thanked her mother for sending the massive pile of food, since most of it was easily transportable.

Fynn sharpened his weapons: knives, daggers, and his longsword. He insisted this needed to be done, though he had still been sharpening them nightly and hadn't had opportunities to use any of them, thank Canta.

And Raelyn, after jotting a quick note and handing it to the guard out front of the building to deliver, collected every bottle of perfume or scented soap she could find in the apartment and piled them on the kitchen counter.

Now that the last soap sat atop the pile and her pack was full, the reality of their departure was starting to set in for Nova.

This was real. She was leaving.

They ate a quick dinner mostly in silence, then cleaned up and sat on the couch to wait. Her nerves were a tangle of energy as she twisted her hair through her fingers, and she assumed that Fynn and Raelyn were experiencing the same. Then, just as the sun was going down, a knock sounded at the door.

"Miss Astor, your flowers have arrived."

The elf on the other side of the door was one she recognized from the outside guard rotation. Tonight, dressed in all black, he must have been assigned to the front door and was therefore in charge of delivering messages, both incoming and outgoing.

Raelyn clapped her hands. "Oh wonderful. Esta will be so pleased when she gets home. Let me help you get them."

She started to follow the elf downstairs but managed to sneak in a squeeze of Nova's arm as she walked by. Once the door closed behind her, Nova and Fynn sprang into action, moving quickly to cover themselves with the various scents that Raelyn had dug up. She sprayed a perfume all over herself, head to toe, and then handed the bottle off to Fynn to do the same. They repeated this until they had gone through every bottle and then started to stuff the soap in their pockets.

"Ready?" She looked up at Fynn. They both wore black: Her, black leggings and a short-sleeved tunic; him, black leather pants and a black shirt, with a black hood to cover his hair. The short sleeves of the shirt seemed almost too small for his muscled arms, fitting tightly around his biceps.

Nova wanted to pinch herself for noticing.

Fynn brought an arm to his nose. "I've never smelled so...feminine."

Now was not the time to laugh, but she couldn't help it. It bubbled up from her chest, bursting out of her before she could contain it. "We'll find a way to get you back to your normal musk once we clear the wall." She could almost smell his cedar and salt air scent as she thought about it. It was enough to be slightly dizzying.

"Good," he responded, violet eyes twinkling. "Then yes, I'm ready,"

She quickly braided her hair, and they snuck out the front door of the apartment. From down the hall, she could hear Raelyn's voice echoing up the staircase, talking more loudly than perhaps was necessary. "Yes, we are thrilled to have her back. Such an unfortunate accident with the stove. These flowers are all her favorite, and I know she'll feel so much better once she gets home and sees them!"

Nova motioned for Fynn to follow her quickly as they made their way in the opposite direction to the back staircase. She quietly opened the door, and they swiftly slipped into the stairwell. Skin prickling with goosebumps, she sent up prayers to the goddesses: part one complete and still undetected. They went down one flight of stairs and exited the floor below their flat, then headed for the main staircase down the hall. Checking that no one was coming up or going down, they quickly descended to the ground floor and tucked themselves away into the shadows under the staircase.

Wordlessly, Nova started doing the one bit of magic she could still rely on: camouflage. Though it wouldn't work for the full escape, she forced herself to concentrate hard enough, to control herself well enough, to attempt the small amount of camouflage they needed to get outside. As she was finishing up camouflaging Fynn (something she never could have done before the suppression spell had been broken), Raelyn and the delivery man's voices drifted down the staircase.

"One more load, don't you think?" her sister said, again more loudly than necessary.

The man, a human, grunted in the affirmative. She caught Fynn's eye, and they nodded at each other. Once Raelyn and the delivery man went back upstairs, it was their chance.

They waited and watched as Raelyn and the human loaded up their arms with vases and arrangements of every kind of flower imaginable. Then they headed back upstairs, and Fynn was gone, a breeze against her back the only sign he had once been there.

A large racket boomed through the back alley, and she watched from the shadows as the guards out front exchanged glances and then ran for the back. Though there'd still be elven guards on the roof, Fynn had been confident he could complete the next part of the plan without their notice. The front door guards though...they had needed to go.

A hand touched the small of her back. "Now or never, Al," Fynn whispered in her ear, a shiver racing down her spine. He scooped her up and ran both of them out of the building and into the delivery man's carriage. An old tarp was lying across the bottom, and Nova found herself under it, next to Fynn, laying against the bottom of the carriage, before she even had a chance to catch her breath.

Fynn had moved them both so fast that under the cover of night it would be near impossible to see them, and her camouflage worked to disguise them even further. She only hoped that what he had done to cause such a commotion behind the building had summoned all the guards, including the ones on the roof, so that no one was there to potentially spot them as they had moved under the tarp...or smell them.

Because elves had the ability to discern scents from great distances. Would the elven guards detect the scent of a witch and an elf leaving with the delivery man? Or had the perfumes and soaps done enough to mask their scent and leave just the scent of flowers behind? A now familiar sensation filled her body—heart pounding, head throbbing, and the pit of her stomach falling away.

Her magic was feeding on her fear.

She looked over at Fynn under the tarp, her eyes watering slightly while her hands trembled. He simply furrowed his brow in return, but then his hand grabbed hers and squeezed. *Breathe, breathe*, she could almost hear him whispering.

She swallowed and closed her eyes, slowing her breath. Her body started to still.

She'd just quelled her magic fully when Raelyn's excessively loud voice sounded from outside the carriage, and it took all Nova's willpower not to jump in surprise. "Thanks again! Appreciate the help with unloading. The Astor family will pay it forward."

Nova could almost picture her wide grin and her curls bouncing as she talked. A pang of homesickness racked her gut already. Oh, how she was going to miss her sister!

The carriage creaked and sank slightly as the delivery man climbed into his seat. Then with a lurch the carriage pulled away, and they were off. It was working, it was actually working!

But they weren't out of the woods yet. Fynn had informed them that elves could see great distances even in the dark and could smell almost as far. So, they had agreed that they needed to put at least ten minutes of distance between them and the apartment before they made their move to escape the back of the carriage. And to remain as still as possible in the meantime to avoid attracting attention.

Though she had no idea on which road they traveled, they had selected this florist specifically because of his location in the city. He would be traveling in the same direction they wanted to go, thereby giving them a solid head start. And since Esta wasn't actually due to return until tomorrow morning, they had at least twelve hours to move before she got back to the apartment and noticed they were missing. Raelyn was hoping to be able to hold her off for longer. But given they weren't supposed to leave the apartment at all, it wasn't a guarantee. Fynn had even left her a note with a brief and not entirely accurate explanation of their absence. Even still, they couldn't be sure it would be enough to set her off their trail.

The carriage jostled over the cobblestone streets. Arkwood was quieter than usual for a summer night, likely due to the curfew, and a melancholy air sat over the city. Now that they were on their way, the desperation that had overwhelmed her the last few days had been replaced by excitement and anxiousness. Excitement to learn her new power and explore her strengths. But anxiousness about what it could mean for her family, and what it meant for Blackmore targeting her.

As they rolled to a stop at the next intersection, Fynn squeezed her hand. She locked eyes with him and nodded; she was ready.

In a flash, Nova found herself yet again in Fynn's arms, sliding out of the back of the carriage, and then the city was a blur as he carried her, running down the city streets. Her camouflage was still intact for both of them. No one was going to see them as he sprinted for the edge of the city.

Held in his arms with her head against his chest, she savored the sense of security that accompanied Fynn's presence, something that had been foreign to her since Blackmore's escape. His heart was beating, though certainly not as fast as she would have expected for someone running as fast as he was, and his grip on her was firm yet gentle. She tucked her head into his chest and gave into the peace, even if just for a moment.

Tears found their way out of her eyes, more from the wind hitting her face with immense force than from emotion. Despite the warmth of the night, the wind brushing her bare skin was chilly, and she hoped they'd get to the wall soon. Then again, she enjoyed the proximity to Fynn—his cedar and sea breeze scent somehow making its way to her through the perfumes and soaps—and she embraced the sparks on her skin where he touched her, knowing it was only temporary until he set her down again.

Arkwood was surrounded by a long, thick stone wall that was built around the time that the governors took control. Now that Astria was at peace, it was more decorative and historic than anything. Since the original intent had been to keep invaders out of Arkwood, there weren't many gates along the wall. Fynn and Raelyn had studied the map yesterday and selected which gate was best for their escape: The Lesser Western Gate. It was a small one, almost entirely abandoned, with no guards stationed there normally. There was a small chance it was manned now, to prevent Blackmore from using it as a weak point and slipping into the city, but more than likely the gate had simply been sealed magically.

Their plan was not to exit through the gate anyway, but for Fynn to run up and over the wall.

When Nova first found out Fynn could do that, she had laughed. "Centuries ago, witches and humans built those walls to protect against elves and here it turns out they can scale them easily?"

Fynn had winked. "Only certain, special elves."

"I can see the wall ahead. Less than a minute out," whispered Fynn, bringing her back to the present where she still hunkered against his chest.

She had been clamping her eyes shut against the wind but managed to open them enough to see the enchanted lamps glowing atop the wall in the distance. The fact that he could run there in less than a minute...how could witches claim they were the only race with magic?

Once they reached the base of the wall, she pulled at the magic anchoring the camouflage around them and found it still taut. She wasn't used to her spells lasting this long but was thrilled to see it working.

Fynn set her down and scaled to the top by himself, giving a quick glance in either direction. "Clear," he said as he landed back down beside her.

He knelt so she could climb onto his back. She looped her legs around his torso, arms around his neck. "Let me know if I'm holding on too tight."

"You're not." And with that he scaled back up the wall and onto the parapet at the top.

He was about to retreat down the wall to the wilderness on the other side, when Nova caught a glimpse of the cityscape behind them. She pressed a hand flat against his chest. "Hold on, stop."

Nova jumped off his back and turned to look back at Arkwood. The city was beautiful—buildings of all sizes, architectures from multiple eras, light twinkling through the windows from candles, lamps, and hearths. They didn't have long, but she wanted one last moment to take it all in.

"I've never seen the city like this. It's stunning," she whispered.

Fynn stood just behind her, hand at her back. It was a sweet gesture, though she reminded herself it was likely just so he could quickly grab her if any sign of danger appeared. "The greatest city in Astria. Maybe in the world."

She whipped her head toward him and placed her hand over her heart. "You, an elf, prefer Arkwood to Besa? Say it isn't so!"

He grinned back. "It's the truth. Besa is far too cold for my tastes. It can be our little secret." He held her gaze—for a moment too long—then turned his head to face the other direction.

Beyond the wall was darkness. Not many villages existed outside of Astria's major cities: Arkwood, Besa, Adenaport, and Aerdmure. But there were some small ones out there on the fringe—close enough to benefit from what the city had to offer, yet remote enough to be away from the crowds. Most of these villages were quaint, existing primarily as an escape from the cities and a respite for those passing between them. But some were considered a bit more feral. After living outside of civilization for so long, they had turned wild and cursed those who wandered into their paths. Those were the ones they wanted to avoid, though doing so was easier said than done since they were usually nomadic, not easy to pinpoint on a map.

Fynn pointed out to the horizon, where the tree line appeared. "We'll camp there tonight, just beyond the trees. I'll need to scout in the morning to see which direction is safe to head in, but if we stay right along the border, we should be fine tonight."

Nova nodded in understanding.

"Ready?" He looked down at her, extending his hand.

She nodded again and climbed on his back, that scent of his poking through the perfumes, soothing her nerves just as well as her breathing exercises did.

"Let's go."

18

THE FIRST NIGHT IN Astria's wilderness was uneventful. They set up camp at the edge of the woods as planned, but Nova slept fitfully, the stillness and the quiet in the air such a vast difference from the bustle of city noises that usually lulled her to sleep. And she didn't dare risk her magic to soften the ground in case something went awry and attracted attention.

To make matters worse, without much time to prepare, they hadn't been able to procure the best of supplies, so whatever she had been able to find in the apartment had to be enough. Fynn had emptied out his pack while she had dug up an old backpack from her own schooling days. She had filled each bag with a single blanket, choosing to rely on the summer heat to keep them warm, two spare changes of clothes, a few pieces of dishware, and food that wouldn't perish quickly without Raelyn's spell—apples, nuts, hard cheeses, smoked and dried meat, the last of the bread from her mother's latest bakery delivery. They would rely on foraging and Fynn's trapping skills to get the rest.

But a tent—that was laughable. There definitely hadn't been one of those in the flat. So they'd been forced to sleep without shelter, just the canopy overhead and a blanket each for warmth.

The sound of birds chirping drew her from sleep in the morning, the warmth from the sun drawing a smile to her lips. She slowly opened her eyes, and immediately found Fynn where he knelt, coaxing a fire to life. Watching him only helped to widen her smile, despite the circumstances that brought them to this wood.

"Morning," she said as she sat up, rubbing her eyes.

He looked her way, and a sparkle crossed his eyes. "Morning. I was going to try to have the coffee ready for you, but since you're up, maybe you could start on that so I can scout?" He paused, his gaze drifting toward the ground. "I didn't want to leave you before you woke up."

"If there's one thing I feel I can help out with on this journey, it's the coffee." She walked over next to him and took the small pot of water.

While she attempted to brew some of the coffee Raelyn had packed for them over the tiny fire, Fynn climbed up the nearest tree and darted along the canopy like a squirrel, checking the surroundings and looking for an easy route.

She sat back on her blanket and sipped the mug. Not bad considering the circumstances. The coffee was settling into her bloodstream, fueling her desire to start their trek. She had nearly finished the mug when she heard a rustle of tree branches, her heart stopping and spine stiffening as she froze, fear flooding her veins. But then Fynn landed in front of her, nearly knocking her off her seat and sending her heart thundering with a shower of leaves.

"Fynn, what the hell! I nearly spilled my coffee!"

Fynn chuckled as he helped her right herself and sat down next to her. "We can't have that. I'm not sure I can be alone with you all day if you haven't had at least one full cup."

She rolled her eyes. "Thank the goddess it was nearly gone." Downing the last sip, she turned back to him. "Find anything?"

"Nothing within a few miles except for birds and squirrels." He paused to breathe in deeply, his chest still heaving slightly from exertion. "And there's a trail leading due west about half a mile north of here. It looks well-worn enough that we can follow it for a while but not so well-worn that we'd encounter anyone else."

"Sounds like we found our way then. I'll clean up while you fuel up." She handed him the mug of coffee she'd prepared for him. He gulped it down quickly and tossed the mug back to her.

She quickly rinsed out the pot and mugs with a small amount of water from her water skin, Fynn stamped out the fire, and they both packed up. Nova put her pack over her shoulders and redid her braid.

They were about to set off when she stopped. "Wait. Fynn, come here."

He raised his eyebrows but approached her slowly. "Yes?"

"We'll be out in the sun all day. I can protect your skin from burning, if you'd like? It's something I've been able to do for as long as I can remember, like the camouflage, so it shouldn't be too dangerous."

To her surprise, he didn't hesitate. "Sure. Thank you."

She ran her hands over his arms, not quite touching, but close enough to feel the heat from his skin. Magic rushed to her fingertips in a familiar way, leaving an invisible trace over his skin.

"There." She withdrew her hands and smiled at him. "That should do it."

"Thank you," he said, looking straight into her eyes.

Her skin prickled, and not from the spell she now wove over her own skin. She broke his gaze before the heat rushed up to her cheeks.

"No problem."

She dug into her pack for two apples, tossed one to Fynn, and they set off.

The journey would have gone much quicker if Fynn just continued to carry her, but they had already discussed why that wasn't feasible. Agility drained Fynn. He had saved up his energy all day yesterday to get them to the wall and then to the tree line as fast as he did. If he carried them both for a week straight, it would break him.

No, it was better if they went on foot, at a normal pace, so he could save his strength, and she hers, in case a situation arose where they needed that strength and full power. Though what she could do with this new power, she still wasn't sure. Would she burn the forest around them to ash just as easily as she could defend them? Given her current lack of control, hopefully she wouldn't need to find out just yet.

They made good distance the first day. She and Fynn chatted easily while the lush trees, fully covered in deep green leaves at this point in the summer, and the squirrels that jumped between them kept their eyes occupied and their spirits high. Even though she always called herself a city girl, she did harbor a fondness for the outdoors, largely attributed to the Astors' time spent at the seaside cottage. Though they'd never camped growing up, she did enjoy hikes: the chirping of crickets, the tweeting of birds, the rustle of underbrush from the scurrying of small mammals.

However, none of that was distracting enough to stop the pain steadily growing in her feet.

As the sun was beginning to set, Fynn suggested they set up camp about a quarter mile off the trail. Because it was so warm, they didn't need a fire overnight, which was a blessing. It would have drawn attention directly to their location.

Nova pulled out a dinner of smoked fish and bread for each of them, which they devoured quickly. Their tired bodies probably needed more sustenance than what they were getting, but Fynn hadn't been able to forage or trap anything, so they had to make do. And hope they could find more food soon.

She set about getting the blankets ready while Fynn followed the distant sound of a creek—far enough away that only he could hear it—to refill their water skins.

He returned moments later as she was settling onto her blanket.

"How are you feeling, Al?"

She winced as she removed her boots. "I really wish I had taken the time to break these in before I decided to walk in them nonstop for a week." She rubbed the sole of her right foot with her thumbs, trying to massage out the knot she could feel forming in the muscle.

Fynn took a swig of water then crouched in front of her. "May I?" He reached his hands out toward her foot.

"May you what? Touch my feet?" She raised an eyebrow at him.

He grinned, settling himself down with his legs crossed. "Yes. I can help with that, make sure you can walk tomorrow."

She paused a moment, considering, but then placed her foot in his lap. His hands gripped it firmly, much more firmly than she had been able to herself and began to knead at the muscles. The stroking of his thumbs up, down, around in circles on the arch of her foot felt heavenly. Her head fell back and her eyes drifted closed as he worked away all the knots, all the pain.

And that little spark from his touch certainly wasn't hurting things either.

"Where did you learn to do this?" Her voice came out breathy.

"The Academy." His hands continued to work as he spoke, moving down toward her heel and ankle. "It's not part of the official curriculum, but we go through enough physical training that we all practiced massage on each other."

"Tell me more about the Academy? It's so mysterious."

He didn't answer right away, as if thinking of where to begin, what he could reveal. "One of the first things they teach us is wilderness survival. And by teach, I mean they blindfold us, set us loose in Noriendar Forest, and tell us to find our way back to the castle."

She pulled her head up to look at him. "You're kidding."

He shook his head, a loose strand of blonde hair falling across his forehead and signaled for her to switch feet. She folded her right under her and stretched out her left, eagerly anticipating the relief ahead. "It's how they weed out the elves who shouldn't be there. About a quarter of those who are accepted fail out after that challenge. Noriendar is full of danger. Traps, creatures, poisonous fruits, you name it."

"So, what you're saying is, this journey is a walk in the park?" Her lips twisted into a grin.

He laughed, his eyes crinkling at the corners. "No, Al. What I'm saying is, you've already made it farther than most of those who drop out."

It was an odd compliment, but Nova's chest swelled nonetheless.

"You started calling me Al again." She'd noticed it a few times since the suppression spell broke but hadn't called him out on it.

"Would you prefer I didn't?" His eyebrows raised, but his tone was earnest.

She shrugged. "I used to hate it, but it turns out that I missed it."

His violet eyes caught her green ones, and they both smiled. She held his gaze a moment longer than was truly comfortable, finding herself trapped in those eyes that were glimmering with...something. But then, Fynn released her foot and stood up. "Get some sleep. I'll do a quick scout before I turn in."

The second day of their journey passed in much the same way as the first, except that around midday they got caught in a rainstorm. The drops started out slowly at first, the canopy of the trees blocking them out, but the downpour picked up quickly.

They were thoroughly drenched when Nova decided enough was enough. "Can we find somewhere to take cover?" she called above the sound of the rain.

Fynn's shirt was plastered to his body, causing her heart to skip a beat when he turned around, and she caught sight of the chiseled muscles protruding through the fabric.

The heat coming off her skin could've turned the rain to steam.

"Good idea," he called back. "We can eat lunch and wait it out."

He quickly scouted out a rock formation that would provide enough shelter and led her toward it, mud tracking up their legs as they ran.

"I can probably dry us off with magic," she said as they sat and made themselves comfortable. Pools of water were already forming on the ground underneath them.

"How confident do you feel about that right now?" He looked at her earnestly, not at all scared.

She pursed her lips. "Honestly, not very. Forget I mentioned it."

"If you want to try, go ahead." He held out an arm.

"No, I don't. Let's just eat." She rummaged through her bag for something, anything to eat, to distract her from the fact that she had just willingly admitted she had no confidence in her abilities.

Whether he sensed her discomfort or he agreed, he didn't push the issue further.

They ate their lunch in silence, the rush of the rain slowing to a trickle before stopping altogether.

"Ready to go? We have some ground to make up." Fynn said, breaking the silence.

She stood then held out a hand to help him up. "Lead the way."

19

O N THE THIRD DAY they ran into their first bit of excitement.

"Excitement?" Fynn had asked when Nova said as much. "If this is exciting, you really need to get out more." His words were whispered as they peaked out from behind a boulder. Perched as they were at the top of a small valley, they could make out the camp of a nomadic tribe directly across the way. The settlement was bordered on the other side by a creek.

She punched his arm playfully. "I get out plenty, just not since I met you."

She scanned the group and didn't see any elves among them. They were not in danger of their scent being detected in the wind, or their footsteps being heard.

There were ten to fifteen huts erected within the settlement and just as many family units moving throughout them. Children were chasing each other and playing closest to the tree line, while men and women alike were preparing food: skinning small mammals, chopping fruits and vegetables, stirring a stew that simmered by the fire. It was a peaceful, happy sight, one that was hard to stop watching. But they needed to move—spears and swords would not be the first thing to hit them if the nomads caught wind that someone was upon them: Magic would be their first line of attack.

As they stole away from the scene and back toward the trail, she said, "Very clever of them to position between a mountain and a river. Seems easily defendable yet also full of resources."

Fynn laughed, a bellowing laugh that nearly doubled him over. "Wait till we get closer to the Worgreth Mountains, then you'll see what a real mountain is. And that was a creek, maybe a stream. You really don't get out much."

She ignored the jab. "What do you suppose they were? Geos? Pyros? That fire was impressive." Her mind wandered back toward the nomads.

"Did you notice some were human?" Fynn stopped momentarily to turn and face her. To avoid colliding with him, she stopped abruptly just in front of him, nearly close enough to feel his breath.

"Really?" She took a small step back from him but held his stare. How had she missed the lack of auras around some of the nomads?

Fynn nodded. "I'd say half and half."

"Living together harmoniously and in such close quarters? Willingly?"

Though Astria claimed that the governors helped promote equality among all the citizens, it had been Nova's experience that generally elves, witches, and humans didn't interact closely for long periods of time. There were exceptions of course, and even some married couples were interracial. But seeing a group of them living as they had in the settlement was entirely new to her. True equality. Depending on each other, needing each other, respecting each other. She suddenly understood why someone might choose to live on the fringes of society like the nomads did.

"It's interesting, isn't it?" said Fynn, smiling at her.

"Yes, it is," she replied, her thoughts still lingering on what she had just witnessed.

They didn't see another tribe for two more days, but when they did, they stayed out of sight and out of earshot, lingering only long enough to marvel at each settlement's existence. There were elves present this time, which meant they needed to stay even further away, but they still managed to get the impression of a thriving, inclusive tribe.

The trails got steeper and steeper as they entered the Worgreth Mountains. Their pace slowed and sweat poured down their bodies, but Nova pushed through the fatigue and pain warring within her. Her body had started to ache more and more each day, soreness from so much hiking, stiffness from sleeping on the ground. She was sure Fynn was feeling the same. But they didn't speak of it. They just pushed through.

"Fynn," she called to him, her eyes following the trail up and up and up. He turned to look at her, but she needed another moment to catch her breath before continuing. "You were right. That wasn't a mountain...before."

He laughed and grabbed her hand to pull her along. "Told you."

On the morning before they were due to arrive in Aerdmure, Nova jerked awake to a hand clamping over her mouth. She startled and almost screamed, but stilled quickly when her eyes saw Fynn's, staring at her with a fiery blaze. He moved a finger to his lips. Her gaze fell on the blade poised in his other hand, her heart pounding in response, a second before her ears picked up the rustling of brush and chatter of voices. They sounded distant, but too close for comfort and getting nearer by the second.

So quietly she almost couldn't hear him, Fynn whispered in her ear, "Pack up as quickly and quietly as you can, then hide behind that boulder and wait for me." She nodded and moved, grabbing blankets and dishware off the ground and shoving them into their two packs. With a final glance at Fynn, whose face bore that same untamed expression he'd worn when he rescued her from the attack in the park, she ran, each footstep as light as she could muster, over to the boulder he had indicated. She squatted down in an alcove that had eroded onto its southern side, doing her best to hide.

From where she was hiding, she could see nothing but could hear almost everything. First, the footsteps stomped even closer, then the voices stopped altogether. When the footsteps slowed, then stopped, Nova had to assume they reached Fynn.

"What are you doing out here?" came a burly voice that was harsh enough to shake Nova to the bones.

Fynn didn't respond immediately, but finally his deep voice filtered through her ears. "Just passing through."

Laughter rang out, at least three distinct voices. So three men total, she noted. If only she could determine their race, what kind of magical threat they posed...

"Well now, let's see. You've passed into our territory without per-mission and armed to the teeth. I can't allow a threat to just *pass through*."

Fynn did not respond so the burly voice, presumably the leader, continued.

"But maybe we can let you pass...for a price." He paused for dra-matic effect. "Your sword. An elf-made sword would look nice in my collection. And maybe a dagger or two for my friends here."

Nova choked down a laugh. There was no way Fynn would part with the sword. Though she hadn't yet seen him use it (thank Canta), she imagined his Academy training made him a force to be reckoned with. Certainly, one that could handle a few nomads.

"And if I politely decline?"

More laughter from the group.

"Normally we don't let trespassers decline. But I'm feeling generous, and I like your style. A duel. You and me. No, let's make it interesting. You and all of us. If you can get us all to yield, you may pass freely."

Again, no response from Fynn.

Nova tugged on her braid and weighed the options. She didn't like the idea of Fynn fighting a group of men of unknown race on his own. She couldn't stomach the idea of seeing him hurt, but also if something happened to him, she had no one else. But perhaps he *was* skilled enough to take them on alone, especially if they were human, with no magical abilities. Offering to assist him when she had untrained magic and no idea how to use a blade might put herself in danger while also wounding his pride.

The hiss of a sword unsheathing echoed through the trees and Fynn's voice quietly said, "I accept."

Metal on metal clanged, sending birds flying from the canopy overhead. She fidgeted with her braid, still trying to decide what to do as her pulse started to race. Nothing but the sounds of grunts and metal filled the air, though some cheers rang out from the rest of the group. But without seeing anything, she couldn't tell what kind of shape Fynn was in or if he was outmatched.

At Fynn's first groan of pain, all her hesitation was pushed aside. She had no weapons, but she had her magic, and though untamed, she was sure she could easily knock down the nomads long enough for Fynn to chase them away—at least assuming he wasn't too injured.

Closing her eyes and balling her hands into fists, she willed her magic to pool together in the pit of her belly. It swirled and spiraled, filling her veins, her mind, until the sounds of the duel died away, and her ears filled with nothing but her own heartbeat. She had summoned all she could safely summon for now.

Fynn's next cry brought her back to the present. She quickly darted around the edge of the boulder, rushing toward where Fynn was battling a large man in burlap clothing with a scraggly beard. The man looked up at her, his mouth forming a smile as his eyes widened, but before he could change his target, she shot the well of magic she'd drawn out in front of her. Raw energy pulsed around them. With a whoosh and a bang, it tore through the small clearing, making the trees rustle and one or two of them fall completely. Scrapes and thuds of trees and branches filled the air, along with a roar from Fynn. Dust and dirt kicked up, blocking everything else from view.

The magic took so much from her. Her heart was hammering, and her breath was ragged, but she fought for control. *Breathe, breathe.*

As the dust settled and she caught her breath, she was able to finally take in the scene around her.

Three men lay scattered along the ground. They were all dressed in brown and green burlap and carried both swords and bows. Nova guessed they ranged in age from late teens to her father's age. But all of them were equally unmoving, the only sign of life the rise and fall of their chests.

Fynn was standing to her left about ten feet away, breathing hard. His lips thinned while his eyes stayed firmly shut, his fists clenched around the blades in each hand. White-blonde hair had tumbled from his bun and hung around his face. A small gash was dripping blood down his right arm. At the sight of it, she had the urge to run straight over and heal it, something she had never attempted but suddenly seemed second nature. But the growl he emitted stopped her from moving.

"I told you," he ground out, turning to face her, his eyes now open and blazing with fury, "to stay hidden."

His voice was full of the coldness it had been the night he had saved her from the attack in the park. She couldn't understand why.

Now they were even. They had each saved the other once.

"I couldn't just let you get hurt," she tried to explain, but he cut her off.

"I had it under control." He stormed over to her until he was right in front of her. "I've handled much worse than these three idiots. I'd have had them down in another five minutes."

She tried to reach for his arm. "You're bleeding, Fynn. All I heard was you cry out in pain, and I imagined so much worse." Her voice caught in her throat. A lump formed there, and she tried to swallow it down, tried to prevent the regret, the rage, the guilt she was feeling boil up and take over her magic.

Why was he so angry?

"You're not supposed to be doing magic now. You could have hurt both of us. I had it under control," he repeated through his clenched teeth. He sheathed his sword, turning away.

She reached for him again, but he yanked his arm out of her grasp. "Please, Fynn, let me heal your wound."

"Your magic is uncontrolled. I don't know how you managed to strike all of them, but I'm not letting you take a risk with my sword arm."

A stab to the gut. He didn't trust her.

She supposed she hadn't necessarily earned that trust, at least as far as her powers were concerned. But from the way Fynn had looked at her and the tone of his voice, this seemed to run so much deeper than just distrust of her magic. His pride had taken a direct hit. She hadn't allowed him the chance to prove his worth as a guard, as a warrior. But did he really think that her way wasn't easier? Didn't it give him the chance to save his strength for their last day of the trek to Aerdmure?

The sadness that had coursed through her at his rebuff turned to anger. "Well, I'm sorry I didn't let you have your fun with these men, but I intentionally cast a spell that would not harm either you or me. Isn't that what wielders do? We create our own magic and will it to our desires? I built up a spell and told it not to harm you. And it seems, despite me having no prior training, that it listened. So, if anything, I think I've demonstrated the beginnings of control. But if you'd prefer to walk the rest of the way with your arm open and bleeding, fine by me."

She returned to the boulder to grab the packs, then threw Fynn's down at his feet and started down the trail toward Aerdmure. Fynn's near-silent footsteps approached behind her, and she braced herself either for a telling off for wandering off alone or for his apology. But she received neither. Instead, the pair walked in silence, camped in silence, and didn't speak until, a whole day later, they found themselves approaching a temple that looked exactly as Nova remembered it from nearly fifteen years ago.

Canta's temple.

They'd made it.

20

N OVA BEHELD CANTA'S TEMPLE, made entirely of granite and nestled partially into the side of the mountain, and finally started to feel a sense of excitement for her next steps. She'd made it! Plus, she'd already begun to feel more comfortable, more in control of her powers, just from the run in with the nomads. Surely it would not be long until she could go back home, able to properly defend herself against Blackmore and deal with her father. And maybe at that point, Fynn could leave too. She couldn't stand this silent treatment from the brooding male, who stood just behind her.

She took a step toward the temple at the same moment the massive oak door opened, and a priestess stepped out. The priestess' gray wispy hair was barely covered by the hood of her blue robes, and the wrinkles on her face betrayed her age, but gave her a look of beauty and wisdom. She smiled at them as she approached.

"Nova Astor. Welcome back to Aerdmure." Her voice, though as silky as the fabric of her robes, was not meek as her age might suggest.

Nova tensed. She had not expected a personalized welcome. No one was supposed to know she was even coming. Had Father already found out? Had he alerted the priestesses? "How do you know who I am?"

The priestess' smile widened, and her brown eyes twinkled. "Canta herself alerted us of your arrival. Told us to ready the village and our best wielder for you."

Nova narrowed her eyes, her blood pounding in her ears. If the priestesses knew she had been coming, it was possible that others did, too. That her father did. That Blackmore did. Who else had the goddess informed?

And why was the goddess suddenly even interested in her?

She stole a look at Fynn to see his reaction, but his face remained stoic and expressionless. Apparently, she would get nothing from him.

The priestess reached out for her hand and spoke kindly. "Don't worry. You are safe here. We only want to help you. My name is Silvana, and I am the high priestess here. My sisters are all inside going about their daily tasks, but I would welcome the opportunity to show you around our village and where you will be staying."

"Who else knew I was coming?" She winced at the sharp tone that dripped from her voice, hoping that the priestess was not offended. "Why is Canta involved?"

Silvana patted her hand. "No one outside this village, my dear. As I said, you are safe here. And who knows the whims of our goddesses? I've been a priestess for half a century, and not even I can begin to guess at her motivations." She gestured with her free arm toward the center of the village and a magnificent stone fountain, which stood in front of the temple. "Come. You are safe. But perhaps showing you will make you feel more at ease."

Nova looked at Silvana, then back at Fynn, whose hand was gripping his sword tightly, his eyes, finally meeting hers, having softened slightly. He tucked his chin down in a nod.

The way he stared at her, like he was ready to pounce on anyone who even looked at her the wrong way, instantly settled her heart.

They needed to have a conversation tonight about what had happened yesterday, but she exhaled a sigh of relief knowing those violet eyes may have stopped holding anger in them.

She met the priestess step for step as they wandered through the small village, Fynn staying close behind her. Aerdmure's center was filled with log cabins of all shapes and sizes; inns and taverns lined the main square surrounding the fountain, and dirt roads zig-zagged out from the square like spokes on a wheel, following the slope of the mountain. More wooden structures were built straight into the side of the mountain along the winding paths. Houses, maybe, or shops.

Witches of all types, of all ages, were out and about at their daily tasks: shopping, learning, eating, catching up with friends. Trees lining the paths offered copious shade against the summer sun, which despite being higher in elevation was still fiercely warm. Today, though, was the perfect day to be outdoors, and based on the number of witches wandering Aerdmure, Nova was not the only one who thought so.

Silvana led them down the largest of the roads, directly opposite the temple. "This is where our guilds are housed. Each type of witch has its own guild house where they work together to hone their craft or explore new ways in which to work Canta's gift."

The healers had an open-air hut with many beds and chairs visible, some with patients laying on them as healers went about their work. The geos built a large structure from bricks of mud, with windows made from the most beautiful stained-glass Nova had ever seen. A group of hydros emerged from the stream that ran adjacent to the village, and Silvana explained that their guild house was built under the waterfall just upstream. The aeros had another open-air structure, with nothing inside it, as if all they needed was a place to shield themselves from the rain and the sun.

The only structure that looked out of place was the one built by the pyros: Made entirely of steel, it looked like it had been transplanted from Arkwood.

"So the pyros can't burn it down easily in the event of an accident," Silvana said with a grin.

"What about the wielders?" Nova asked, scanning the road for a structure that Silvana had yet to identify.

Silvana pointed up the mountain, and Nova's eyes traced a rocky path up its steep slope to a massive stone building built into the side of the cliff. "Up there."

A few wielders moved in and out of the structure and a few sat atop it, seemingly working on a spell to build a pyre without using their hands. Amazing, that there were so many here. There were so few in Arkwood that she'd never met one before, but then again, her father's regulations on wielders may have also pushed them out of the city.

"Is that where I will stay?" She turned her focus back to Silvana. Out of the corner of her eye, she could see Fynn, hand on his sword, watching the wielders, a bit of awe written on his face.

Silvana shook her head. "We have special lodging for you and your guard. I have to admit, some of the residents and scholars here were not pleased that an elf would be staying with us. It took some convincing from myself and my sisters to calm them down. But one concession we had to make was to keep you both lodged in a private dwelling away from the guild houses."

Nova could have sworn a snort escaped Fynn, but his face remained unchanged.

"That will be fine," she replied. Though the prejudice was anything *but* fine. Would Fynn face more of that here?

"I imagine you are both weary from your journey and in need of some rest." Silvana folded her hands in front of her skirts. "I will show you to your dwelling and have dinner sent your way. No need to worry about cooking tonight, I'm sure you're both exhausted. Tomorrow, I will introduce you to your tutor, but I dare say you'll want as much of your strength for the first lesson as possible, so there is no reason to start today."

And with that, Silvana led them back towards the fountain and the temple, then turned down a small dirt path on her right, leading them for another ten minutes to a small log cabin on the outskirts of the village. It had glass windows and lamps lined along the front porch, lit in anticipation of their arrival by an ever-lasting flame charm since the gas lines that pyros maintained in Arkwood didn't reach this remote location. Inside was just a single room. There was a small kitchen off to the left, a small dining table and couch in the middle, and a double bed along the right wall in between two of the windows.

Next to the armoire in the back of the cabin was a door that stood open to a bathing chamber. Nova tested the faucet and relief washed over her when water surged through the pipes. Maybe there weren't gas lines out here, but at least the hydros took care of the water lines.

"You'll find clothes for both of you already in the armoire," Silvana waved a delicate hand at the large cabinet along the back wall. "Nothing exquisite, but plenty of good options for your training."

"Thank you so much." Nova returned to the main room. "This is all so unexpected, and I don't know how I will repay you."

Silvana shook her hands in front of her. "We do not accept payment for Canta's work. We only hope you will remember Aerdmure and her people kindly in your future endeavors." She turned to leave, then stopped and doubled back. "One more thing to help keep you and your guard at ease. I know you have a vested interest in the escape of Kael Blackmore. Rest assured that we have the village on high alert and have raised some preliminary enchantments to protect those living here, as well as steady communications with the priestesses around Astria. Should anything change, I will inform you." With that she bowed and backed out of the cabin, leaving Fynn and Nova alone.

21

The priestess' words *had* put Nova at ease. Perhaps having Canta looking out for her wasn't so bad. She may have just arrived, but she already felt safer, more at peace than she had in Arkwood.

She turned back to Fynn, who was laying his pack on the floor next to the sofa.

"I'll take the couch."

The first words Fynn had spoken since she robbed him of the chance to duel with the nomads. How long was he going to hold this grudge? She watched him warily as he turned to the kitchen for a glass of water.

She would confront him. She would. She just needed to work up the courage. Confrontation had never been her strong suit.

She set her pack down on the bed and decided to peek into the armoire. Inside were five of the same black tunics and five of the same black leggings. But when she reached out to feel them, the fabric was not at all what she expected. No, rather than standard cotton or leather, these were made of a fabric she had never worn. It was cool to the touch and thin, something that would feel quite nice to wear on the hot summer days ahead.

"It's probably moisture wicking, so you don't have to worry about sweat."

She whipped her head around and found Fynn holding his glass, leaning against the counter, watching her. The hair on the nape of her neck raised.

"We had some at the Academy for summer. It's treated by highly trained hydros to absorb and repel moisture. Very expensive and hard to find, not many hydros know the art of it anymore."

She was dying to ask how it was that he always seemed to know more about her race than she did, but instead she took the opportunity to ask a more pressing question.

"Are we speaking again? Because I'm over the silent treatment." She closed the armoire door and turned to face him, crossing her arms over her chest as he moved toward the couch.

He plopped down, water sloshing out of his glass and onto his lap. He wiped it away without even a glance. "Depends. Are you done trying to do my job for me?"

She stepped forward, reaching for his arm. "Let me look at your wound."

"It's fine." Fynn held out his arm to show her that not even a scar remained. "Elves heal quickly. It's little more than a memory now."

How had she forgotten that fact? Of course elves healed fast. She saw it often enough with her students that she never should have worried about his wound.

Then again, there was something about Fynn that drove all common sense right out of her mind.

"Ok, look, I'm sorry I didn't give you a chance to act the hero. I'll work on my damsel in distress act while I'm here, too." Sarcasm dripped from her voice.

Fynn stilled, his eyelids dropping to his glass where his finger traced the rim, and Nova immediately sensed she had gone too far. Before she could take back what she said, he spoke again. "It's not that I wanted to 'act the hero'. More so that I have a history of not being able to protect the people I...care about."

He...cared about her? In what way? Like a brother cared about a sister? Like a friend cared about a friend? Like a lover cared about...She shook her head and turned back to the armoire, trying to tuck loose strands back into her braid as she racked her brain for a way to change the subject.

"Moisture wicking, you say. Interesting. I'm surprised I've never heard of it before."

If Fynn sensed the change in her tone, the way her voice came out an octave higher than it had a moment before, he didn't let on. Nor did he remark on her swift departure from the resolution of their feud. "You've always stayed within the city, where the aeros of the world have ample supply of cool air to beat the summer heat."

She couldn't argue that point. Even at the cottage, the air indoors was always exactly the right temperature, whether summer or winter. Father paid aeros well for it, too.

Orange and pink sunbeams streamed through one of the windows near the bed as the sun started to set outside. Now that dusk was setting in, her bones and muscles screamed in exhaustion. A week of grueling hiking, combined with a smaller diet than she was used to, meant her body was feeling the toll. Not to mention, that bed looked awfully inviting.

"Eat first." Fynn must have caught her staring at the bed. She rolled her eyes, but her growling stomach betrayed her. "Then you can sleep."

Right on time, a knock on the door sounded. Fynn opened it and took the food from the priestess on the other side. He closed the door behind him and set down the tray of food.

Saliva filled her mouth at the sight, at the smell of the freshly prepared platter.

A whole chicken, grilled to perfection, sat atop the largest plate, surrounded by freshly cooked vegetables of all kinds: squash, asparagus, carrots, eggplant. A curried rice sat in the small bowl next to the plate.

Fynn divvied up the chicken, vegetables, and rice onto plates for each of them, and they devoured the food, mostly in silence. Nova wasn't sure if the chef at the cottage could prepare chicken this well.

When their plates had nearly emptied, she looked up at Fynn, drawing in a deep breath of courage. "I really am sorry for interfering. I should have trusted you could handle those nomads easily, but I heard you in pain and...worry won out."

He set down his fork and met her gaze. "And I'm sorry for how I reacted. There are things in my past that can make it difficult for me to..." His voice trailed off as his eyes cast down.

She reached over and laid her hand on his. "It's ok. We all have a past, Fynn."

He turned his palm over underneath hers and squeezed. His lips parted into a weak smile, weak but powerful enough to lighten Nova's spirits and her heart.

"Friends?" she asked.

"Friends."

They sat a moment in silence, before Nova pulled her hand back. "Well, if we are friends, I suppose I should learn a little more about you."

Fynn chuckled, leaning back in his chair. "I guess there isn't much to know."

"I don't think that's true." She started ticking facts off on her fingers. "A handsome, tall, muscular elf, who graduated from the Academy and was assigned to guard a daughter of one of the most influential families in Astria? One who can also run the fastest foot race ever recorded? Is that really all there is?"

Fynn laughed again, and Nova's stomach somersaulted at the sound, at the fact that she had provoked that sound, that joy. "Well, when you put it that way, how could I resist answering any question a beautiful, smart, powerful daughter of one of the most influential families in Astria asks me?"

She looked down as her cheeks flamed. No one had ever called her beautiful before. Her mind went entirely blank for a moment before she collected herself and said, "Tell me about your family."

"Starting off with a strong one." He paused, as if hoping she might retract but when she didn't, he cleared his throat and went on. "Well, you know my father. Not much else to say about him since I wouldn't call him affectionate. We've had our disagreements in the past. But my mother...Elves live longer lifespans than humans or witches—maybe we make it to our one hundred fifties rather than our seventies—but we aren't immortal. About fifteen years ago, a group of drunk witches went on a rampage through our neighborhood in Arkwood. My mother was the only one home at the time." His eyes closed. "They think an aero suffocated her."

Nova gasped, her fork clattering onto her plate. "What?" She thought back to his earlier words, about not being able to protect those he cared about. His mother—that must have been to whom he was referring.

He flickered his eyes open and began pushing chicken bones around his plate. "Oh yes. You probably didn't hear about it. Much of that kind of news is suppressed by the governors, and I suppose you were young at that time anyway. But prejudice is out there still, and aeros are known for being violent toward elves, particularly in the northern neighborhoods of Arkwood where my parents lived."

Her father was responsible for censoring the papers? Had she really been so naive to believe that all three races lived in peace? The more time she spent with Fynn, admittedly the most time she had spent with an elf outside of her classroom, she realized it simply wasn't true.

"Fynn, I'm so sorry." She watched him until his eyes drifted up to meet hers and then held his gaze for a moment. "That must have been awful to live through."

Fynn loosened the tie holding his hair back and ran a hand through the long strands. "It was a long time ago."

"But you must have been so young." Nova brought the last bite of rice to her mouth.

"How old do you think I am?" He raised an eyebrow, his hand falling back to the table.

She lowered her fork, gently this time, and tilted her head to the side, contemplating as she chewed. "Not a day older than thirty."

"A compliment I will accept." He raised his glass to her in a toast. "But I am nearly fifty."

Her mouth fell open. "You're twice my age?"

Fynn nodded and laughed. "Like I said, elves have longer lifespans, so we don't age as quickly as witches or humans. I started at the Academy when I was twelve and graduated eight years later. I go back every five years for certification to make sure I haven't lost my skills."

She massaged her temples as the age gap between the two of them set in. "This is going to take me a moment to get used to."

Fynn laughed again, the sound pouring directly into her heart. After nearly an entire day of silence, it filled her with a joy that had eluded her since she'd left Raelyn.

"Well, while you're digesting that...I have one sibling, an older sister named Aury, who serves as a captain of the Astrian Navy. I haven't seen her in nearly ten years, but we write to each other occasionally."

"Does she have the same abilities as you? Super speed, super strength, and all that?"

He shook his head, strands of blonde hair waving in front of his face. "No, not all elves have powers or abilities other than heightened senses."

"Ah." She took a sip of her water. "So you really are a super special elf. On top of tall, muscular, and handsome."

"I suppose so." He shrugged but Nova could tell by the smug look on his face that he was again pleased by the compliment.

The idea that Fynn had already lived so much life, had already been through so much, was slowly sinking in. She wanted to know more—wanted to know it all. A million questions swirled through her mind, and she had no idea which to pick first. But before she could decide, she blurted out, "Have you ever been in love?"

Her cheeks flamed with heat as regret sat heavy on her chest. But it was too late to take it back now. She rearranged her face to erase the embarrassment and replace it with false confidence.

And besides, there was a part of her, not so deep down, that was dying to know.

Fynn leaned back in his chair, his lips tilting upward just slightly. "Jumping right into it, are we?"

She shrugged, maintaining eye contact. "Sorry, you don't have to answer—"

"I have." He paused and met her gaze. Those violet eyes were hiding something from her—something mischievous, something fun—but at that moment, she was too distracted to guess what it was. "Once. About twenty years ago."

"Another elf?"

"Human actually."

Her mouth fell open. Elves and witches sometimes paired up, as did witches and humans. But elves and humans? That was a new one for her. "What happened?"

He sighed and tucked his hair behind his ears. "I couldn't save her."

The air left her, sucked right out of her lungs. Another instance where he couldn't protect someone. While it didn't necessarily give him justification for his behavior after the nomads, at least she was starting to understand why he felt so strongly about being able to protect her. "From what?" she asked softly.

He looked up at the ceiling but not before she caught the raw emotion in his eyes.

"We were together for five years, five amazing years. She was constantly targeted by witches of all kinds for being with me, but she didn't care. And I protected her from as much of it as I could." He paused for a breath. "We were living closer to Adenaport at the time, but I wanted to go home after my mother died to help my father get their affairs in order, and she insisted on coming with me. On the journey there, at one of the inns we stopped for the night, she was murdered while we slept. Some coward came into our room and slit her throat. I awoke to the shutters slamming shut as the asshole escaped, but it was too late."

Nova's mouth dropped open. Whatever she expected him to say when she asked that question, this wasn't it. So much tragedy in a short time. It was too much, far too much for any one person to bear. "I'm...so sorry."

"It's been fifteen years since I lost two people I loved in one week. Around that time, Aury decided to spend more time at sea than on land. I suppose I just figured it was better to live life alone at that point." He looked away, but not before Nova caught the tear slipping down his cheek. Fifteen years later and the emotions were still so present, so real. He wiped the tear with one hand, the other rested next to his plate. Her body moved of its own accord as she reached out and grabbed his hand.

"You're not alone."

Fynn looked back toward her and smiled but pulled his hand away. "Ok, how about an easy one."

Fair. He had earned an easy one. She looked around the room for inspiration. "Um, how about...your favorite color?"

"Green."

Her eyes—her *green* eyes—turned back to his. Her heart skipped a beat under his gaze, and again, her mind spun until she finally spit out another question.

"Favorite place you've traveled?"

"Nothing beats Adenaport beaches in the summer."

"I agree! Maybe we can visit my family's cottage after our stay here." Nova grinned, the knots that had formed in the pit of her stomach as he told her his story starting to loosen when she caught his smile widening, too.

They continued to pass the rest of the evening in the same way, with Nova jumping in to give her answers to each question as well. She didn't dare broach a deeper topic again, and Fynn didn't either.

When her body finally gave in to the exhaustion, she bid him good night and slid under the sheets, replays of everything he had just told her swimming through her mind.

Nova had greatly enjoyed Fynn's company tonight, in a way she hadn't yet experienced. They had gotten close before the attack in the park, but this was different. This was not just friendliness brought on by close quarters. This was friendliness for the sake of...being friends.

So why did she find herself wanting even more?

22

SUNLIGHT DRAGGED NOVA FROM sleep, while birds tweeted lazily outside. She rolled to her side but immediately tensed as her skin registered the caress of the soft sheets and the downy feel of the pillow, both so unfamiliar to her. Whose bed was she in? Where the hell was she and why? And was that...Raelyn's coffee she smelled?

She sat up and rubbed the sleep from her eyes, peering across the room toward the kitchen.

Right, she was in the Aerdmure cabin.

Fynn was standing over a carafe of fresh coffee with his back to her. His shirt was off, and his hair was loose, falling to his shoulders. A grin spread across her face and her stomach did a somersault. The tension that had consumed her a moment before disappeared, replaced by something much more...exhilarating.

He turned to face her, and a smile broke out across his own face. "Hey there, sleepy. I can't promise this is good as Raelyn's but it's the last of what she gave us, and I guarantee it tastes better than what we made on our way here." He brought her a mug of the steaming coffee. One whiff of the scent and she was transported back to the Arkwood apartment and mornings with her sister.

The warmth of the mug spread through her hands as she held it. "Thank you."

"Figured you'll need all the energy you can get today. Breakfast was dropped off as well." Fynn waved a hand at the table, which had a platter of eggs and sausage on it, as well as some fruit.

"I'll get to that. Coffee first." She took a sip and savored every delectable drop that hit her tongue. A pang of sadness gripped her heart as her thoughts drifted to Raelyn. Esta would be with her by now. Were they able to keep the secret of her escape this long? Or was Father on his way here now? She had a renewed vigor to learn as much as she could while she was here...and fast.

She finished her mug and drank a second with her breakfast, then changed into one of the new outfits from the armoire while Fynn sat on the front porch to give her privacy. The leggings and tunic fit perfectly and were surprisingly flattering. The material was light and cool on her skin, despite it being the deepest black. She slid on her boots, ignoring the protest from her feet, and joined Fynn on the porch.

Silvana was approaching the cabin with another witch at her side, her turquoise robes billowing as she walked. They were still too far to make out many details of the witch's appearance, but as they got closer, Nova noted the male's short dark hair, the same shade as her own, dark eyes that slanted up slightly at the outer corners, and his clothes, which seemed to be a male version of her own outfit. He wore a smirk on his face, and she distrusted him immediately, which was odd, because had they met back in Arkwood, she might have found him attractive. He seemed to be about a decade older than herself, maybe a little less.

"Good morning," greeted Silvana, smiling broadly. "I trust the cabin treated you well last night?"

"Very much, thank you," said Nova. Fynn nodded in agreement, rising from his chair.

"Great. Today you will start the training that Canta has asked of you. Jax will be your instructor while you are here in Aerdmure. He's one of our most skilled wielders and one of our most accomplished instructors, as well." She stood aside so the male, Jax, could step forward.

"Welcome, Nova. Silvana has already briefed me on your situation. I understand you need to learn how to use your wielder powers." He looked only at her when he spoke, pretending that Fynn was not even there. She glanced at Fynn, who shook his head slightly, almost imperceptibly. But she understood what it meant: He wasn't a fan already.

"Yes, and Fynn is here to protect me from...threats." She wasn't sure how much he knew about Blackmore targeting not only the Astor family, but Nova in particular.

"Mmmm. Yes, elves make good bodyguards." His mouth pressed into a thin line as he eyed Fynn.

So that was how it would be. Jax thought himself better than Fynn. Probably thought himself better than anyone who wasn't a wielder.

Jax straightened and continued. "We'll have our first lesson today in the clearing just beyond the village. It's best to be away from others in the beginning to avoid harming anyone or anything. Follow me."

She and Fynn fell into step behind Jax, waving farewell to Silvana as they went. The elf gave her a look that said *we will discuss this later*, and she nodded in return. Jax seemed overly confident, almost arrogant, but first impressions could prove incorrect.

The clearing was about a fifteen-minute walk from the cabin. A swath of land the size of the entire village of Aerdmure had been cleared of trees, perhaps accidentally through witches in training, but more likely intentionally to provide an area for training as Jax said. It appeared to be leveled magically as well, as the clearing was entirely flat while the rest of the topography was mountainous. The lack of tree cover should have made the direct sunlight almost unbearable, even at this early hour. But it seemed the clothing really was as good as Fynn said, as Nova stayed surprisingly cool.

Jax stopped in the middle and turned to face the pair. "The elf can wait at the tree line." He placed his arms on his hips and waited.

Nova ignored the jab, already over how often prejudice had reared its ugly head since they'd arrived. "No. Where I go, *Fynn* goes." She crossed her arms, trying to display confidence she didn't actually feel. She'd be much more at ease if Fynn were close.

Fynn's hand brushed her elbow, but she kept her eyes fixed on Jax.

Jax pointed to the tree line. "It's better for you if he's not close by. No distractions."

This conversation was going nowhere, and Fynn's impeccable hearing would mean he was only a call away. So, she looked at him, stared directly into his midnight eyes, and nodded. He bowed his head at her.

"I can be here in a second if you need me," he whispered, his hand still on her elbow. "Make sure you protect your skin."

She nodded, her heart fluttering at his concern, his thoughtfulness, and quickly cast the protection spell. Then Fynn turned and made for the trees.

Jax started pacing in front of her. She stood with her arms crossed at her chest, eyebrows raised in a challenge. Sure, she wanted to—needed to—learn, but did it have to be from this guy? He was giving off asshole vibes from the start.

"Wielders are gifted with the most wonderful powers from Canta," he started. "Our magic supposedly comes directly from Canta's line. The raw magic we harness is different from the elemental powers—stronger—and yet we are not without our own limitations." He stopped pacing for a moment. "We can change our appearance, but we can't manipulate time. We can create objects from nothing, but only for short periods. Wielders were the first to dabble in dark magic, though our ancestors quickly learned the errors of their ways and abandoned the practices. We are truly a league above the rest of the witches and as such, it is our duty to learn to harness those powers and use them for the good of Astria."

Nova blinked. "For the good of Astria? I didn't realize this was going to get political."

Jax shrugged and continued his pacing. "Your father made it political when he restricted what we are allowed to do. Besides, isn't magic at its core political? Who can get the most power? Who can subject others to fear and intimidation?"

She decided to ignore the comment about her father, knowing that would get them nowhere right now. Besides, he'd suppressed her powers for her whole life, hadn't he? No, he wasn't someone she wanted to spend time thinking about right now.

Hands on her hips, she replied, "I thought power was about earning the respect of your people and helping to ensure they could lead a better, more prosperous life than without you there."

He stopped pacing and smiled. "Ah, the idealist. Ok, point taken, let's leave politics out of this. Tell me, what have you been able to accomplish with your powers so far, in the last week or so that you've been made aware that you have them?"

She recounted the events in the apartment from when the suppression spell initially broke, as well as the spell she had wielded against the nomads. She threw in at the end that she had always believed she was a geo and had found that her geo abilities had been amplified since the suppression spell ended. But she left out the shame and embarrassment she harbored internally for most of her life about her lack of powers.

"Knock me to the ground," Jax said, interrupting her monologue.

"What?" She started, her body going rigid.

No other reaction about her abilities, just a command.

He held his hand out at his side, palms facing her. "Knock me over. Go for it."

She summoned up her power as she had with the nomads, feeling it start to swirl in her core, and lurched her body forward, hands outstretched. An invisible force pressed into Jax, and he leaned backward slightly. Just as quickly, he righted himself again.

The forcefield of power she emitted left her feeling a sense of...was that relief? Had the power she hadn't risked using built up in her so much that she *needed* to let it out?

"Not bad. And a good start for defending yourself. Ok, let's move on."

And so they continued for the next two hours, Jax spitting out a seemingly dissonant set of commands at Nova and her attempting to fulfill them. She very easily made the ground tremble (which caused her to squeal in pride) but had a harder time starting a fire and calling on the wind to strengthen it.

She could feel the exhaustion seep into her body, her magic draining with each use. Her hair was starting to fall out of her braid onto her face, sticking to the sweat that beaded there, and she needed longer to catch her breath in between commands. "Can we take a break?" she panted.

"Already?"

Asshole. She was right about that part at least.

"You heard her. Give her a break," Fynn called, appearing at her side without so much as a whisper of wind. True to his word, he had stayed at the wood line but hadn't taken his eyes off them the entire time.

"One hour," Jax capitulated.

Fynn held out his hand to her. She took it willingly so he could scoop her up. He ran them both back to the cabin, where a lunch of bread, cheese, and apples was waiting for them. She toweled off the remaining sweat and helped herself to a large glass of water.

"I think we should ask Silvana for a new instructor," Fynn said, biting into one of the apples.

Nova shook her head, helping herself to cheese. "No, he's the best for a reason. I have to see this through."

He raised an eyebrow. "Are you sure?"

She nodded, resisting the urge to roll her eyes only because she now understood where his protectiveness stemmed from. "Yes, Fynn."

"Ok, but say the word and I'll make it happen." He tore off a chunk of bread and ate it in one bite.

They returned to the clearing exactly an hour later and found Jax standing in the same spot. The afternoon sun was now scorching beyond belief, so she asked if they could practice with water. Anything to cool them off.

"Fine. Make it rain." Jax crossed his arms and tapped his foot.

Manipulating the weather was an incredibly advanced skill. Most hydros could fill a water jug but not bring in a rainstorm, making this an absolutely crazy thing to attempt on her first day. Yet she tried. And when nothing happened, when not a drop of rain fell from the sky, she tried not to let the disappointment show in her face though her heart was sinking.

Jax smirked. How could she already hate a smirk in a matter of hours? "Can we go back to my way now?"

She scowled and clenched her fists. But before she could protest, Jax was spewing out more commands.

Another two hours passed, with Fynn on the sidelines again and her energy now fully depleted. She was drenched in sweat again despite the cooling clothing, and all she wanted was to jump in the stream back in the village to cool off and clean up. She wasn't entirely sure what she learned today or what she was supposed to have gotten out of it, and when she asked as much, Jax just laughed.

"Today was about endurance more than anything. Now I understand your limits, as well as where your strengths lie. Tomorrow we can start with more interesting spells."

Nova furrowed her brow. "What's that mean?"

"Wielders don't just have the ability to use elemental magic, like other witches. We can literally do anything, with very few limitations, like I mentioned earlier. I can teach you how to enter someone's mind, how to avoid being overheard by even an elf, how to relocate objects from one place to another, and how to make yourself or other objects invisible. And that's just a start." He reached his arms above his head, his gaze following for a moment. "Your imagination is the limit, your creativity will be your guide, and your needs at any given time will inspire you."

"You make it sound almost—" she thought for a moment, searching for the right word "—exotic."

Jax laughed, his hand clutching his abdomen. If she hadn't been subjected to his insanity over the last couple of hours, she may have found that endearing. "Of course. Many do believe that we are exotic in a sense. We don't conform, we aren't predictable. Every wielder is different from the rest."

She crossed her arms again. "And you? What makes you unique?"

"That's for another day, if you're lucky."

Apparently, Jax had blocked out Fynn's ability to hear the afternoon session, but had woven the spell so expertly, he hadn't even realized it until Nova started rehashing all she had learned. Much to her amusement, Fynn then proceeded to spend the evening slamming cabinet doors, accidentally knocking over chairs, and stomping around the cabin.

A glass fell out of his hand and shattered. With a wave of her hand, Nova attempted to fix the glass, but found she was still too worn out, so she swept up the mess instead. "Fynn, do we need to take a pause for that breathing trick you taught me? Jax played a joke on you, that's it."

"He's an arrogant prick. I don't like the way he's treating you," he said, after righting the chair he had just uprooted when he stood too quickly.

"And you sound like one of the reasons elves and witches apparently don't get along."

Fynn scoffed, leaning on the back of the couch. "I don't have a problem with witches in general. It's him I don't like, not his abilities."

She couldn't really disagree. Dumping the broken shards into the waste bin, she said, "Look, I'll have a word with him tomorrow to make sure he doesn't do that again. Maybe you could try to be the bigger man and be nice to him?"

"I'll play nice if he plays nice." He crossed his arms, his biceps pushing against the seams of his shirt.

Nova had to look away before she found herself distracted. She busied herself with cleaning the dishes from dinner, accepting that might be as good a compromise as she'd get. "I did enjoy getting to do magic though. Real magic, you know? It felt...beautiful. I've never felt so strong, so capable. I mean, I know I didn't do much, but even what I did do was invigorating."

"Al?"

Nova turned to look at him, her hands in the sink. He was still leaning on the couch, but the worry lines had disappeared from his face. They'd been replaced by a softness she hadn't seen on him before.

"If I get to hear you talk about magic like that more often, I will happily put up with Jax as long as we have to." His eyes twinkled like the night sky during a new moon.

She had to turn back to the sink again before he caught the redness creeping up her face.

23

"MAKE A STICK APPEAR out of thin air?" Nova stared at Jax, one eyebrow raised.

Jax nodded. "Unless there is something else you'd prefer to start with."

She was back at the clearing with him the next morning. He'd met them at the cabin at the same time as yesterday and led them back here. But as promised, she set some boundaries before they started.

"No jokes today, Jax," Nova had said as they'd entered the clearing. "Fynn needs to be able to hear us if he's going to stand at the trees."

Jax had laughed. "Someone's got a stick up their ass."

Fynn had reached for a dagger, but she'd put a hand on his arm to stop him, still looking at Jax. "No spells. I mean it."

Jax had simply shrugged, but nodded, acquiescing.

Fynn now stood back at the tree line while Jax was coaching her on non-elemental magic, such as conjuring objects. The problem was, he hadn't yet told her *how* to do it and here he was, expecting her to whip a stick out of nowhere.

"A stick is fine, but a little more explanation of how to do it would be great."

Jax clicked his tongue. "Sassy again today. Alright, hold out your hand, either one is fine." She held out her right hand like she was holding a platter. "Now close your eyes and find the magic living in your core. Once you find it, visualize a stick, any kind of stick, and will it to appear."

She closed her eyes and did as he instructed, trying to focus on the stick and not on the warmth of his stare. She formed a stick in her mind, a simple small one about a foot long with two small branches forking off one end but couldn't get enough of a grasp on it with her magic to conjure it.

"Focus, Nova," Jax whispered.

She slowly peeked one eye open and found Jax's eyes looking straight at her. Squeezing her eye shut again, trying to force him out of her mind, she turned her concentration back to the stick and gave it all she could, summoning as much magic from her core as possible, because the sooner she made the stick appear, the sooner he would back off.

A moment passed—how many moments she wasn't sure—and then a weight fell into her open hand. Her eyelids flew open.

There it was, a stick, the exact one she had pictured in her mind, sitting in the palm of her hand. She had done it! She glanced over toward where Fynn, eager to share her success, and found him applauding and smiling. From this distance, she couldn't tell precisely, but it looked like his face was beaming with pride.

"Good." The corner of Jax's mouth ticked up into a momentary smile. "Now make it hover."

Jax had her do all sorts of things with that stick: make it spin, slam it into the ground, break it in two, and mend it. Each command he asked of her, she excelled at, whether because of her determination to show him she wasn't weak or because it pulled from her geo roots. Whatever the reasoning, it gave her a renewed confidence in her abilities and in her prospects. At the end of today's session, which had a shorter lunch break because Nova insisted that they bring their lunches with them and eat quickly in the clearing, she could have walked on air, elated at her progress, and couldn't even find it in her to be snarky to Jax.

Fynn praised her on the walk back to the cabin. Well, he walked. She was practically skipping. "You're doing great. I'm really impressed with how quickly you've picked it all up."

She twirled and smiled from ear to ear. "Thanks, Fynn."

She wanted to bask in this feeling forever, this feeling she had never experienced. Before this trip to Aerdmure, she'd always been a mediocre witch, one with very few and very weak powers, one who preferred not to even use her powers if she didn't have to. But now—*now* she could take on the world. She could defend herself, protect herself, and also believe in herself, in her magic. Add to that the fact that she was completely on her own now, no longer under the shadow of her father or avoiding Raelyn's disguised pity. She'd never been so free, and she never wanted this feeling to end.

She was still riding the high after dinner, and the summer sun hadn't yet set. So, after they cleaned up from their meal, Nova suggested they explore.

"Explore?" Fynn set his now-cleaned plate on the shelf above the sink and turned to look at her, his eyebrows raised. "Sounds mischievous."

She shrugged. "I just thought it'd be nice to get out for a walk. See what's around, maybe catch the sunset."

The lines on Fynn's brow disappeared as a soft smile spread across his face. "I'm just thrilled I got invited this time." She punched his arm, not missing the laugh that escaped him in response.

Their cabin was surrounded by tall trees, a mix of deciduous and evergreen, with a few indistinct trails leading away from it. One of those pathways led to the village and another to the clearing. But tonight, Nova decided to lead Fynn down one at the rear of the cabin. This trail was rockier than the other two, with more tree roots poking up from the ground as well. Clearly it hadn't been used as often as the others.

"We should try to be back by dark." Fynn kept his voice low as he walked behind her. There wasn't enough room on the trail for them to go side by side. "Just in case."

Of course. Just in case Blackmore was around. It had been so easy to forget about the murderer currently hunting her while her mind had been occupied with learning and wielding magic, but his threat was still real, still present.

She pushed a low tree branch away from her face, summoning false bravado for her reply. "Or...we could stay out and if we run into Blackmore, I could try out my new skills."

Fynn chuckled as he ducked under the same branch. "I said you were doing well, but it's only been two days, Al. Let's not push our luck just yet." He paused to draw in a breath. "I want to see what else you can learn, before we have to put anything to the test."

They walked in silence for a few moments. Nova took in the scenery around her: the evening glow of the sun casting a golden haze on the trees around them, the occasional *who* of an owl waking up for a night of adventures, the hum of crickets signaling the end of another day. It was so...peaceful out here. Despite all the upheaval in her life right now, nature just...went on. Just continued in its cycle of life.

She was lost in her thoughts, when Fynn's hand grabbed hers. Her heart raced: Had he heard something?

"What is it?" she whispered, stepping back closer to him, her eyes searching wildly around them.

He must have sensed her fear, because he squeezed her hand. "Look over there."

Nova turned back to him, then her gaze followed his outstretched arm to where he pointed. And she gasped.

They were standing just feet away from a ledge of rock on the mountainside that overlooked the range beyond. There was a small gap in the trees around the ledge, with just enough room on the rock for two people to sit or stand. And the view—it was breathtaking. The perfect vantage for watching the sunset in the west, with swirls of pink and orange already filling the sky and casting long shadows along the other mountains in sight. The sky was clear, not a cloud in sight. It was as close to perfection as Nova had ever seen.

"Want to sit for a moment?" Fynn's hand was still in hers as he looked down at her.

She met his gaze, the lowlight from the sun reflecting through the sparkle in his eyes. "Yes, please."

He led her onto the ledge, helping her step over some of the bumpier parts of the rock, until they reached a large flat section right at the end. Their hands separated as they sat, and Nova immediately mourned the loss of his touch as if she'd lost a part of herself. Where had that feeling come from? It must have just been an effect of the sunset, of this gorgeous view.

"I've never seen anything like this," she said, more to distract herself from the chill in her hand than anything else. She crossed her legs underneath her and leaned back onto her hands.

"Nor have I." Fynn assumed a similar seated position next to her, his gaze still fixed outward. "I haven't had much reason to spend a lot of time in the Worgreth Mountains, but I think I may need to find reasons in the future."

"Bring me back with you." Her voice was breathy and soft, carried away in the gentle breeze so quickly that she wasn't even sure he had heard it. Maybe it would have been better if he hadn't. Her cheeks burned, and she was grateful for the dimness of the light around them. Perhaps he wouldn't notice.

But his response only made them burn hotter.

"I can't imagine being here with anyone but you, Nova."

Out of the corner of her eye, she caught him turning to look at her, but she kept her eyes locked straight ahead on the glowing mountains. This conversation was getting into dangerous territory. So dangerous he'd even used her name instead of calling her Al. But try as she might, she couldn't find another topic to switch the conversation to.

Why did her brain just refuse to work around Fynn?

Instead, she let the majesty of the sunset guide her deeper. "How do you suppose this all ends?"

"All of what?" He shifted his seat, so his legs were now outstretched in front of him, crossed at the ankles.

Nova waved her hand around and finally turned to look at him again. "All of this. Blackmore, my training, facing my father. I feel like I'm living my life one day, one moment, at a time. But what comes next?"

Fynn didn't answer immediately. He turned his head and leaned his chin against his right shoulder, his violet eyes reflecting the light from the sunset as they met hers. "I think it could end in a number of ways, but the more important question is: how do you want it to end?"

His stare was so heavy that her mind started buzzing. She turned her gaze back toward the mountains and the sun, collecting her thoughts. "I think...I don't want to go back to how my life was before. I picked teaching as a profession because I wanted to make an impact, but maybe now...maybe I can make an impact in a different way."

"Do you want to know what I think?"

She nodded but kept her gaze forward, the heat from his gaze crawling up her neck.

"Hear me out." He cleared his throat. "I think you don't even let the best parts of yourself shine—" she turned to protest but he held out a hand to stop her "—I think you hide behind a façade of feeling weak and powerless, but inside you are fiercely protective of those you love, willing to do whatever it takes to ensure their safety. I think you haven't yet realized the entirety of your powers because you hid that part of yourself away for so long and told yourself over and over that you are next to nothing. But that's what Luc made you into, not who you are. I think, when you finally accept that you are a wielder, and a damn good one from what I've seen the last two days, that there will be no stopping you. You can do whatever you want."

Nova's breath caught at his words. His tone was not unkind, rather he delivered the words gently. But the way they hit her, square in the chest, like they were shot out of an arrow aiming straight for her heart...he was right. She needed to move past her old insecurities to fully explore and develop her powers and become who she was meant to be.

Too bad that was much easier said than done.

"I hope one day I can be as strong as you see me, Fynn." She sighed and turned back to face the sun that was now halfway over the peaks up the mountains. The outline of the moon was now faintly twinkling above. "I'm not quite there yet."

"It will come." He pulled his legs back in, crossing them. "Do you think I walked into the Academy on my first day as confident as I am now?"

Nova whipped her head back to look at him and laughed when she caught the grin on his face. "I've seen enough twelve-year-old boys from every race to know there is a certain kind of confidence they all have."

He pitched his head back and laughed from the pit of his stomach. "Alright, fair enough." His laughter died away before he spoke again. "What I meant was, you will get there. It takes time and effort. Not just the physical effort of training, but also the mental effort of changing your view of yourself."

"That's definitely the harder part," she mumbled as she looked down at her legs. A lock of hair fell from her braid, and she let it hang there, covering her face.

His fingertips grazed the back of her arm, shooting tingles up her arm and down her spine. The way her body reacted to his touch, the way she had shivered...had he noticed? Goddess, she hoped not.

"Whatever I can do to help," he said, returning his hand to the ground behind him. "I'm here."

She pushed the loose dark strand behind her ear and leaned forward, catching her braid in her hand. She undid the tie holding the braid together and started winding the ends of her hair between her fingers.

"You do that a lot."

Her hand dropped as she narrowed her eyes at him. "Do what?"

He pointed to her hair, which was still halfway braided. "You play with your hair a lot. It seems like you do it mostly when you're nervous...or scared."

He had noticed something like that? Something she didn't even realize she'd been doing? Though of course he was right, now that she thought about it. She'd always done that—it was probably why she'd always kept her hair long.

When she didn't respond right away, his face fell slightly and he turned back to face the sunset, which was darkening further, the sky now purple and blue. "Sorry, I shouldn't have said anything."

"No." She reached out and touched his arm. "You're right. I was just surprised that you noticed."

He looked back at her, his violet eyes piercing straight into her, into her soul. "Of course I noticed."

Her heart hammered so fast in her chest that she was sure he could hear it. And the sweat forming on her palms...that wasn't just from the summer heat. She quickly dropped her hand from his arm and offered him a weak smile, hoping it masked the turmoil going on inside of her right now.

With a brush of her palms on her leggings, she stood. "It's getting dark. We should probably head back, right?"

Fynn looked at her but remained seated for another moment, as if there was more he wanted to say, as if he hadn't wanted that conversation to end.

Truthfully, a part of Nova hadn't wanted it to end either. But they were moving into uncharted territory, into new waters that she wasn't sure she was ready for. What if she was interpreting his words, his actions incorrectly? No, it was better if they tried to keep things as they were. If she focused on her training, on learning to protect herself.

Finally, Fynn hoisted himself up from the ledge. "You're right. Let's get back."

Nova led them back off the ledge, then moved aside so Fynn could lead the way to their cabin, her mind too absorbed with thoughts of *him* to focus on navigating.

24

FOR THE NEXT WEEK, Nova continued to progress with her powers, the feeling of freedom building within her. As it grew, so did her confidence, which in turn helped her magic bloom; it was a beautiful cycle. Jax had her conjure up more and more complex objects, such as boots with a specific number of lace holes or watches with specific designs on the face and do more and more things with those objects. She continued to excel at all his tasks. Even he remarked on how impressive her progress was.

She'd never been so proud or so excited to do magic.

For the first time in her life, she actually wanted to learn spells.

But today, her eighth day in Aerdmure, was her first day off. It was Canta's Festival Day, the witches' most celebrated holiday of the year, which happened to fall on the summer solstice. The summer's longest day was a gift from Canta, an opportunity for witches to harness the world's power more than they could on any other day.

Silvana and the other priestesses had been planning a special celebration for that evening, one of many similar events that would be happening throughout Astria. Nova and Raelyn typically visited the festival closest to the penthouse because they had grown up going to it, but all the celebrations were essentially the same: an evening of revelry, fireworks, music, dancing, and, of course, offerings to Canta herself.

The celebrations in Aerdmure would start at dusk, which meant that she and Fynn had the whole day to themselves.

They ate a quick breakfast, then decided to explore the village. The villagers were out and about in greater numbers than usual, most undertaking preparations for the festival. The population of Aerdmure swelled during Canta's festival because witches from all over Astria traveled here to celebrate. Most of the visitors were witches who lived as nomads or in smaller towns where their own celebrations wouldn't be held. But there were those even from Arkwood who held fast to the belief that it was only right to celebrate Canta in Aerdmure, where her hot spring flowed and her primary temple remained.

And despite the looming threat of Blackmore, despite the extra security measures in place to protect those attending the festival, the party would go on.

As they meandered around watching the busy villagers at work, Nova spotted Jax huddled at a picnic table with a few other male witches clinking tankards of ale. She had to roll her eyes. Leave it to Jax to start the party before the party actually started.

At that moment, his gaze fell on her, so he smiled and raised his glass in acknowledgement. She managed a small smile back, but Fynn pretended not to see him. Despite her gratitude towards Jax for helping her reach this new level of her powers, she was still on edge around him. And Fynn certainly hadn't shown signs of benevolence his way yet, either.

"I hear your lessons are going well," a silky, kind voice said behind her.

Nova turned toward the sound to see Silvana approaching them. The priestess tilted her head in the other wielder's direction.

"Yes, very well," Nova replied.

Silvana smiled and adjusted her hood, which had fallen back slightly to expose more of her gray hair. "Jax is not necessarily the easiest to get along with, but he is powerful, and he's also altruistic enough to enjoy teaching others."

Altruistic would not have been Nova's first choice of word to describe Jax, but regardless, the comment turned her stomach to lead. She knew, after all, how difficult it could be to teach, how easy it was to want to quit when your students showed any kind of disrespect or disregard for your authority. Perhaps she hadn't been the worst kind of student, but she also certainly hadn't been the easiest student for Jax.

Guilt seeped into her veins.

But Silvana's next statement dragged her back to the present. "There is nothing new to report on Blackmore. I realized I hadn't seen you all week, but I promise if there had been any noteworthy news, I'd have sought you out to deliver the message right away."

In all of the activity of the last week, Nova had nearly forgotten that she was being targeted by a mass murderer—that she was ultimately learning how to defend herself against him if he found her. Her stomach knotted as fear and worry returned to her in waves, but a hand pressed into her back, her magic pulsing its way through her body to meet it. *Fynn.*

She nodded back at the priestess. "Thank you, I appreciate that."

Silvana brushed her hands on her skirts. "Now, if you both aren't busy, would you be interested in seeing the hot spring?"

Nova looked at Fynn who raised his eyebrows. Even elves, though they had their own goddess, Dalia, knew the lore of the hot spring and generally respected its sanctity. There probably weren't many who could say they had seen it.

She turned back to the priestess and clapped her hands in front of her chest. "Silvana, that would be lovely."

"Wonderful. Follow me." She turned and strode towards the temple.

Fynn fell into step beside Nova, as they followed Silvana around the fountain. They had to dodge villagers as they went, some carrying streamers to hang up around the fountain and others carrying materials to set up booths for food and drinks. One male witch carrying a large plank of wood nearly knocked Nova to the ground, but Fynn caught her arm and held her steady.

"Apologies, miss," the male said as he scurried away.

They reached the steps to the temple, and Silvana stopped, turning back to face Nova and Fynn. "I'd like to give a brief history of the temple if you don't mind humoring me."

"Of course." Nova dropped her hands at her side, one brushing Fynn's—briefly, but enough to feel that spark. She forced her attention fully on the priestess despite the tug of her magic trying to pull it elsewhere.

"As you're probably aware, this temple has been standing since long before the governors took over, but the exact date of its erection is unknown," Silvana began. The high priestess spoke with such care and grace, more so than she usually did. "We priestesses believe that the initial structure was likely a small hut made from wood, and that over the years more and more witches built on until it became the stone structure you see today.

"Canta is one of three sister-goddesses, the other two being Dalia of the elves—" she smiled at Fynn "—and Terra of the humans. They oversee everything that happens in Astria, from who is granted what powers and abilities to who gets to rule. It is believed by some that they even developed the structure of the governors and gave the idea to those whom they wanted to be elected first.

"Though they are sisters, they don't always get along, and that is why each sister developed her own city, her own stronghold. Dalia created Besa, Terra established Adenaport, and Canta settled here. The hot spring was where she was able to begin wielding her magic as it covered every earthen element: water for the hydros is obvious, as well as heat for the pyros. But the hot spring comes from the earth itself, powering the geos and the bubbles within the spring power the aeros."

"What about wielders?" Nova asked.

Silvana chuckled and held Nova's gaze. "We aren't quite sure, but the current theory is that wielders are descended from Canta herself in some way or are her chosen blessed." She paused to draw in a breath and continue. "We priestesses guard the temple and the hot spring in Canta's name, protecting it from harm, but also from those who might seek to use its powers or its knowledge for...unsavory ends. We are often called to the charge at very young ages and come here to learn from the elder priestesses. But we also serve as the unofficial hosts of Aerdmure, welcoming all who travel here or who look to move here for study. Some choose to stay here after they are ordained, while others seek positions at some of the smaller temples around Astria."Nova pictured the temple nearest her flat in Arkwood. It was certainly smaller, but also more modern, made out of steel instead of stone. There were always a few priestesses lingering around the temple, their robes matching those that Silvana wore.

"Now if you'll follow me in, you'll first see Canta's likeness. The statue was created by a talented geo-witch sculptor five hundred years ago after the previous statue was vandalized. We ask that you maintain silence out of respect while inside the main hall of the temple; however, once we pass through to the cellar on the way down to the hot spring, you may resume conversation."

Nova and Fynn nodded in understanding, then followed Silvana up the steps and into the main hall.

The hall was massive, containing columns covered in glittering gold and shining silver, a marble tile floor that was so clean Nova could almost see her reflection in it, and a towering, vaulted ceiling covered with ornate paintings of stories from witch lore. She recognized some of the stories that her mother had told her in her youth, ones that she and Raelyn had adored and asked for again and again.

In the center of the otherwise empty hall stood a massive stone sculpture of Canta, standing with her left hand on a staff, her right at her hip, and her long hair blowing in an imaginary wind. She had been beautiful, or at least history remembered her so. The sheer size of the statue made her demeanor powerful and imposing even if the stories Nova had heard about her described her as a softer deity. Not weak, by any means, but kind. Caring.

Nova stood in awe of the statue of the goddess who had gifted her with wielding powers. Though she was not a particularly religious person, she had a newfound appreciation for Canta, who was for some reason now looking out for her. Every fiber of her being willed her to bow and pay homage to this goddess, this creator of all witch magic. So, she gave in and found herself kneeling on the marble floor. The sundress she had chosen to wear today pooled around her, and the stone of the floor was cool against her bare knees. She closed her eyes to offer a silent prayer to Canta, thanking her for her protection and guidance.

When she was finished, she opened her eyes and found Silvana smiling and kneeling next to her. Fynn was lurking in the shadow of one of the columns to their left. Silvana held her finger up to her lips in a reminder to be silent, then summoned Nova to follow her down the hall. She stood and followed, Fynn not far behind.

Once they arrived at a small antechamber and left the statue hall behind, Silvana turned back to address her.

"It's truly a surreal experience for those who are visiting for the first time, or the first time in a while."

Nova's voice came out as barely a whisper. "I don't remember being this taken when I visited as a child."

"You are not alone in that. Much of our appreciation for our goddesses comes as we learn to appreciate life's gifts." Silvana drew a breath and extended her arm toward an archway to their right. "Come, it's time to show you the hot spring."

The high priestess led them down a winding staircase that seemed to last forever, leading them further and further into the mountain upon which the temple was built. Nova's head spun, her body unsteady by the time they reached the bottom landing. She paused a moment, her hand on the wall to collect herself. A hand rested on her back.

"You ok?" Fynn asked.

She nodded, swallowed, and continued on until at last they reached the bottom.

Torches lit the hall in front of them, which was nothing more than a tunnel, dirt underfoot and stone arching overhead. The hall felt calm, *safe*, despite the chilled stale air and eerie shadows dancing across the walls in the torchlight. Silvana led them further, then stopped in front of an ancient wooden door.

"I'll wait for you both out here. Please take your time." And with that Silvana motioned with her hand for Nova and Fynn to open the door.

25

Nova reached a hand for the brass door handle in front of her. The door stuck at her first push, but she summoned a small bit of magic to give her strength, and then it pushed open with ease. She silently congratulated herself for both pulling off such a spell and for doing it quickly, as if it were second nature.

"Saw that," Fynn's deep voice whispered in her ear.

She giggled as she stepped through the doorway and looked over her shoulder to whisper back, "I don't know what you're talking about."

When she turned back to take in the cavern, she froze, and her mouth dropped open in awe, a small gasp all that escaped. She was only vaguely aware of Fynn stepping beside her, closing the door, and pressing his hand again to her back.

The cavern was glowing. No, *glistening*. The ceiling seemed to be alive with stars, twinkling as they lit up the room. It was just like the night sky—she even recognized some of her favorite constellations among the stars that weren't stars. She was so engrossed in the light, that she didn't even behold the spring itself until Fynn's voice again drifted into her ear: "Look down."

When she moved her gaze downward, the sound of a bubbling brook filled her ears. Except it was no ordinary brook. This sound was musical, like the bubbles and the water had been chorused into a beautiful rhythm to entertain her and Fynn. The melody filled the whole chamber—how had she missed it when she first entered the cavern? How had the lights, the stars, caught her attention first?

In the middle of the cavern was the spring itself. It was more the size of a pool, with light tendrils of steam coming off the water, just enough to create a hazy effect. The bubbles were coming up in various places throughout the pool, indicating where the heat from Canta's fires were coming through to warm it.

And the smell—the smell that filled the air reminded her of visits to the spa in Adenaport. A mixture of lavender and eucalyptus. All her worries, her cares, her stress floated away, like they had been carried up and out of the cavern by the bubbles themselves.

"This is...enchanting," she whispered, taking it all in.

Fynn's hands squeezed her hips lightly as he said, "I dare you to jump in."

She turned to face him, his hands falling away and hers taking their place at her hips. "Excuse me?"

"You heard me. I dare you to jump in. Imagine how refreshing it will feel against the cool of this cavern." He looked around dreamily, but Nova sensed it was an act to get her to comply with his dare.

"I don't think we're allowed—"

He put a finger to her lips. "If we weren't allowed, don't you think Silvana would have said so?"

He had a point there. She pushed his hand away, ignoring the tingle left behind on her lips. "Ok, but you first."

Fynn laughed. "I doubt Canta will appreciate an elf entering her pool before a witch does, particularly a witch that she has lately been watching out for."

Another valid point. "But I didn't bring a bathing costume."

"I'll turn around." He grinned as he turned to face the door from which they had entered.

She stood, mouth agape, for a moment, debating what to do. She could either decide not to swim and they could leave this cavern, or she could strip down, go for a swim, and see where it led her. Part of her was dying to jump in, to see if it would change her, cleanse her, or transform her in any way, like some of the tales claimed. And that same part of her also wanted to see Fynn without his shirt on again. They'd come to know each other so well since arriving in Aerdmure, and she couldn't deny that she found herself attracted to him.

But a second part of her fought that urge. It was silly to act on impulse. She was here to pay respects, not to play around. She should honor the sanctity of the temple and the spring and leave...immediately.

She bit her lip momentarily before releasing it, drawing in a deep breath to calm the insecurity that her magic was trying to feed on.

With a glance over toward Fynn, his back still towards her, she made her decision. A moment later, her dress was on the floor, and she was down to just her undergarments. With one more look at Fynn to ensure he wasn't looking (although, would it really have been so bad if he was?), she waded into the pool.

The warmth greeted her first. Even though the water only reached her ankles, its heat spread quickly throughout her entire body, inviting her in deeper. With each step she took, her body softened, her mind opened, and her breath steadied. Once she reached waist deep, she dove into the pool and fully immersed herself.

When she came up for air, Fynn turned around to look at her. Treading water, she called, "Come in, the water's fine!"

He grinned that silly little grin that she was coming to love and started pulling off his own clothes. Nova couldn't help but stare.

His body was a maze of hardened muscles and faint scars. He'd seen combat—or maybe the Academy was just that brutal. Whatever the reason, they suited him. Maybe she'd ask about them later.

He caught her eye with a wicked grin, and she gasped, turning away. *Caught.* As she scolded herself for being so foolish, a splash of water doused her, and something tugged on her ankle. She squealed, but all that came out were bubbles as she was pulled under.

She surfaced and found him floating next to her. "That was rude!" She summoned a wave his way, forcing him to roll over many times and come up coughing out a small amount of water.

"Oh? Not quite as rude as watching someone undress." He grinned as he swam toward her again, then scooped her up and threw her—gently of course—across the pool.

Nova pushed her hair out of her face when she resurfaced. "It was your idea to get in. Not my fault you also...."

"Also...what?" One of his eyebrows raised abnormally high, a mischievous grin on his face.

Her cheeks flamed, but fortunately her voice didn't betray her embarrassment at being caught ogling his body. "My lips are sealed."

She ducked before he could get her this time, the echo of his laugh hitting her ears just as she disappeared under the water.

Back and forth they played, laughing so hard they were gasping for air most of the time and completely losing track of time. When was the last time she had been so carefree, or that she had had this much fun with a male?

The attraction that had grown all week was starting to come peak, but she wasn't sure what to do with it. He seemed to be just as attracted to her, but he had been hired to guard her, to be close to her.

Then again, they'd run away together so there was a good chance Fynn would never see a coin of the wages he was owed from the last two weeks. And yet...he was still here.

Nova tipped her head back to float on her back, watching the witch lights twinkling above her. "This reminds me of swimming in the sea at Adenaport."

She couldn't see him from where she floated but could hear his response. "The water there is so crystal clear." Water rippled around her before he continued. "It's like watching the stars from the beach."

She lifted her head momentarily to find him also floating on his back. With a smile, she laid her head back down. "I love visiting the beach at night. It's so...serene. Like it was meant for soul-searching and deep conversations. Raelyn and I would spend hours there as teenagers, discussing the latest drama or gossip."

"I can only imagine the drama and gossip you and your sister could stir up."

She straightened and sent another wave his way. His laugh sputtered as the water overtook him.

"This may surprise you," she said, treading closer toward him, "but Raelyn was often more the subject of the drama and gossip than I was."

"You know what," he said, meeting her gaze. Mischief. His eyes were full of it. "That doesn't surprise me one—" he took one stroke closer to her "—damn—" he took another stroke "—bit."

Fynn scooped her up to throw her again, holding her over his head, when a cough echoed through the chamber from the other side of the wooden door. He lowered her, pulling her into his chest.

Nova's eyes met his. She had never been so close to those eyes that sparkled like the stars in the midnight sky, and she couldn't help but notice the twinkle of the lights in the cavern dancing in their purple undertones. The urge to kiss him burned in her heart, like a fire had been lit within her, fueled by the spark of his touch, but instead she said, "Guess we should go."

But Fynn didn't move, not right away. He held her gaze for a moment longer than was truly called for, and Nova thought—*hoped*—he might kiss her. But then, he grinned mischievously and dropped her from his arms straight back into the water.

Playfulness. Mischief. But is that all it was? Maybe she was reading too much into things. Maybe she was only imagining the desire she thought she'd seen mirrored in his eyes.

26

T HEY DIDN'T SPEAK ABOUT the swim in the hot spring for the rest of the day.

Nova had produced a light breeze to dry them off quickly, then they had followed Silvana back down the hall, up the winding stairs, and out of the temple. She worried that the priestess would have found their behavior inappropriate or disrespectful, but Silvana had said nothing and simply smiled at them as they exited the spring's cavern.

Maybe she had borne witness to such activities in the past. Maybe it was even commonplace.

They returned to the cabin to bathe and get ready for the evening festivities. Earlier this week, Nova had procured a new dress for the evening from one of the shops in the village, though shop may have been a generous term. Cart may have been more appropriate. But in the end, it didn't matter. She had clearly made the dressmaker's day when she offered to pay almost double what she expected the witch would have asked. Aerdmure had already given her so much. The least she could do was repay the favor in kind.

While Fynn was bathing, she slipped on the dress, which was short, falling only to mid-thigh and had thin straps, perfect for a sultry, summer night. The material was light, the color a deep maroon rose.

It hung low across her breasts but fit nicely around her curves, as if magically designed to fit the wearer perfectly.

She wore her long black hair down, something she rarely did, because tonight she wanted to let loose, and her hair was just the beginning. She ran a brush through it—she wanted it as straight and as silky as possible, though in the humidity the effort was probably futile. Then she slipped on sandals she had also picked up in town and rubbed a bit of kohl on her eyelashes. There hadn't been a mirror in the cabin until today, when she had managed to conjure up a small one for this occasion. Though she couldn't see the entire ensemble, she hoped it would have the effect she was going for...that Fynn would notice.

He emerged from the bathing room fully clothed in his leather pants and loose navy blue shirt. His white-blonde hair was still damp and hanging freely as he ran a hand through it. Her heart nearly stopped at the sight.

The blue contrasted his skin and hair beautifully and was a stark difference from his usual gray, black, or white. He'd left the lace of string at the top undone and *extremely* loose, so the muscles on his chest were visible.

She swallowed and tried to find something witty to say but words failed her. So instead, she turned away and grabbed her hairbrush again, running it through the tresses that had been brushed thoroughly already.

"You look beautiful," Fynn said.

Beautiful. There was that word again.

Her heart stopped as she processed what he just said. Sweat pooled on her palms, so she set down the brush before it could slip out. She hoped to Canta, and maybe Dalia too, that he couldn't somehow smell her emotions or read her thoughts.

She turned back to face him and blinked.

"Thank you!" Her voice came out as high pitched as a hormonal twelve-year-old talking to their school crush.

Fynn released a small laugh and reached for her hand. "Come on, Al. Let's go have some fun."

The festival was just getting underway when they reached the village. Surrounding the fountain were food carts, bar carts, and others carrying magical trinkets of all kinds. Twinkling lanterns were hung as if by invisible string all around the square, casting a golden glow on everything their light touched.

A ten-piece band was playing music on a stage near the temple steps, its acoustics amplified by a spell put together by either a wielder or an aero. Nova recognized the song the brass and woodwind musicians were currently performing—a lively tune that had been quite popular just a few years ago—and couldn't help swaying along with the beat. There weren't many witches dancing on the makeshift dance floor in front of the stage, but after a few rounds of drinks, the numbers would surely grow.

Nova gestured to the bar cart closest to them and when Fynn nodded, she bought a glass of wine for each of them.

"Witch wine," she explained, handing him his glass. "Proceed with caution."

"I've dabbled in it before. I think I know my limits." Fynn winked.

Sure he does, Nova thought with a smile.

They circled the various carts, buying food from every single one, then made their way to a picnic table to enjoy their feast. Despite the awkwardness of the afternoon, conversation came easily tonight, though maybe that was the drink's doing.

But when Jax sat down next to her, the mood at the table shifted noticeably, despite the drunken grin plastered on his face.

"Glad you both could make it!" Jax said, clinking glasses with her. Fynn did not offer his up for the same. "Staying for the fireworks? They're my favorite part."

She nodded. "Planning to. Fireworks generally aren't huge in Arkwood because of the dense population. Too much could go wrong."

"Did I tell you I grew up in Arkwood?" Jax took a swig while Nova shook her head. "Yep, the southernmost part of the city. City life wasn't for me though, too many people watching out for wielders. I got out as soon as I turned eighteen."

"I can see why you choose to settle here. Aerdmure has been nothing but lovely to us since we arrived. And I used to be an 'Arkwood or bust' kind of girl." She finished her wine, then glanced at Fynn, trying to silently beg him to join the conversation and play nice, but he was looking up at the stars. She was on her own.

"I'm glad you're enjoying your stay," Jax said. "Aerdmure is a special place." His eyes drifted back over to another table where a group of male witches were sitting and chatting spiritedly.

"Are those your friends?" Nova asked. Fynn looked at her, then followed her gaze over to the other witches.

Jax nodded. "One wielder, and the other two are hydros." He took a long pull of his beer.

"I think I'd like to meet the other wielders here." She could feel Fynn's eyes boring into her, warning her. But it wasn't as if she could lay low here. Everyone knew who she was. Everyone seemed to know why she was here, too.

But Jax didn't answer right away. Instead, his gaze lingered on his friends, his finger tapping absentmindedly on his glass.

Fynn took the opportunity to voice his opinion. "I think we should focus on training, Nova. That's what we are here for, not to make friends."

"I'd like to get to know other wielders too, Fynn. There aren't many back in Arkwood, so really the only one I know is Jax—"

"I can introduce you," Jax said, his eyes meeting Fynn's and hardening. "Don't worry, mate. She's not our type." He took another swig of his beer, then winked.

What did he mean by that? Not our type? Fynn seemed to understand better than she did, because his eyes widened, and his face softened just slightly. She turned to Jax and opened her mouth to speak, but he stood up and slapped a hand on the table lightly. "I'll introduce you another time. Enjoy the festival and don't stay up too late. See you in the clearing at nine tomorrow." With another clap of his hand on the table he left.

Nova tried to decide what to say as she looked between Fynn, whose expression had turned smug, and Jax as he walked away. There were two ways she could go with this conversation, but she decided to go with the one that was irking her more. "What's wrong with me meeting more wielders, Fynn?"

His face fell as he met her gaze. "Nothing, Nova, I just think you should focus on your training for now. Blackmore is still out there so learning how to defend—"

"Aren't you here to help defend me?" She raised an eyebrow at him, letting the witch wine coursing through her veins take over. "I don't see the issue with making a few more friends. Maybe I can even learn from them, too."

Fynn sipped the last of his wine and looked like he wanted to say something. Maybe apologize? But the ease that had befallen them just minutes ago seemed to have evaporated. Needing a moment to clear her mind, she offered to refill their drinks, leaving Fynn alone at the table.

When she sat back down, placing the full glasses in front of them, Fynn reached over and took her hand. "I'm sorry. I overstepped and shouldn't have said anything. You have every right to meet more wielders if you want to."

Tiny pulses were shooting up her arm from his touch. She lifted her gaze from where their hands connected to his face, noting the depth of the emotion in his eyes. He meant it; there was no mistaking that.

She sighed. "Jax clearly gets under your skin. Is there any way you can try to work through that?"

"Yes," he said so quickly Nova nearly spit out the wine she had just sipped. "I can work on that."

Well, that had been easier than she expected.

They shifted back into the same easy conversation from before Jax's interruption, Nova sharing some of her favorite memories from prior festivals before she asked him about Dalia's.

"Are they celebrated in the same way?" She'd never personally been to one, though her parents had made appearances at a few. From what she'd heard, they were a little more...demure.

"Not at all," Fynn said with a laugh. "They're more about connecting with nature: bonfires, hikes, meditations in the forest. Those kinds of things." He paused for a sip of his wine. "Definitely no booze at Dalia's festivals."

Fascinating. With her new appreciation for the outdoors top of mind, she made a mental note to try to attend one someday. "Wonder what my dad would say about you drinking on the job." She'd tried to say it in jest but could immediately tell it had come out all wrong.

Fynn looked at her, those violet eyes darkening. "Is that what you think of me, Al?"

She gulped. How could she save this? "No, of course not. I was just jok—"

"Do you think I'm still only here because I'm getting paid to be?" His face remained neutral, but a flash of something like disappointment shone through his eyes.

She set down her glass slowly. Did she have it all wrong? She regretted wearing her hair down because she was getting incredibly warm.

"Surely you know that I stopped caring about the money weeks ago. That I'm pretty sure I'll never see a penny of the money 'owed' me since we left Arkwood."

Did he say *weeks*?

"What?"

"Why do you think I fought so hard to come back after...after the attack in the park?" He stumbled over the words enough for her to almost lose her train of thought—almost.

She shrugged. "You wanted to save your reputation?"

"No, Al. I wanted to be the one to protect you. And I didn't trust anyone else to do it." He finished his wine, pushing the empty glass to the edge of the table and then met her gaze. "I'd make the same decision again and again."

Her heart was beating out of her chest. Was he saying what she thought he was saying?

Was he saying what she hoped he was saying?

She fumbled around for the right words, the right response but found nothing. Here he was, alluding to the things she had wanted to hear, but she was clamming up and unable to respond.

"Dance with me?" The words tumbled out of her so quickly she didn't even realize she had been thinking them.

She wanted to smack herself—what kind of response was that?—but Fynn smiled weakly and nodded, offering his hand. She caught his eye for a moment, then she took his hand, loving the way his grip felt in hers, and followed him to the dance floor, where more witches had since gathered as the night had fallen.

The band was playing a lively song, one that Nova didn't recognize but that she liked. Fynn immediately gave her a twirl as they entered the throng of dancers, the skirt of her dress billowing out slightly, and she laughed out loud at the joy coursing through her body. The music flowed through her, guiding her in such a way that she could have sworn magic was entwined in the notes.

Alive—this is what it meant to be alive!

This was how people were meant to live! Not cooped up in apartments, not hiding from outlaws who may have a personal vendetta against them for some reason that wasn't entirely clear. And really, what was the reason Blackmore had escaped? Still, no one had explained the purpose of his research.

No. She shook Blackmore out of her head. She shook her father out of her head. This was her night, hers and Fynn's. Nothing would ruin it.

The band switched to a ballad, and Fynn raised his eyebrows at her. She batted her lashes and extended her right hand. He took it with his left, bowed and then reached for her waist with his right.

His touch on her waist, through the thin fabric of her dress, sent a chill down her spine. He held her close, close enough that she could smell his familiar sea breeze and cedar scent. Close enough that she could rest her head on his chest if she wanted to—and she did want to. She laid it there gently. His heart thumped in her ear, beating nearly as quickly as her own.

"Nova?" Fynn whispered into her hair. The sound of her name in his voice was as intoxicating as the witch wine coursing through her veins. She slowly moved her head to meet his gaze, his eyes somehow more purple than ever, a deep amethyst that glittered in the light of the lanterns surrounding the festival.

"Is it alright if I kiss you?"

Ever the gentleman he was. She smiled despite herself.

"I wish you would."

The way her body trembled when his lips met hers, the way her legs wanted to collapse as she breathed him in, the way his arms tightened around her and held her steady. It was all perfect. Magical even.

The kiss was unlike any she had ever experienced. It both weakened and strengthened her. It both made their surroundings more distant and more vibrant. It filled her with enough power to create a true earthquake, one more powerful than even her father's, but also stopped time and silenced the world around them.

And if that wasn't enough, there were fireworks. No, she nearly gasped, there really *were* fireworks. The festival's fireworks were going off all around them, and they held their kiss through them, her tongue searching for his, her arms around his neck.

Fynn pulled away slightly, his forehead still resting on hers. "Nova—"

She silenced him with her lips, pressing them back against his. She didn't want him to say anything to ruin the moment. She just wanted them to have this moment, this magic, and tomorrow they could go back to how it was before.

But for tonight, she wanted this. She wanted *him*.

Fireworks continued to shoot off around them, pyros hard at work making them into a variety of colors, sizes, and shapes. But Nova didn't bother paying attention.

Fynn's right hand moved up into her hair, his left still firm on the small of her back. He pulled her closer, their bodies molding into one. There were no longer any guesses about what each of them wanted.

She could feel it pressed against her, could feel his want, his *need*, as she simultaneously felt the strong desire stirring within herself.

The things she wanted to do next weren't appropriate to do in public.

Unable to deny herself any longer, she grabbed his hand off her back and pulled away, her eyes wide and her lips slightly parted into a seductive grin. Slowly she backed away, pulling him with her, and once they were off the dance floor, she turned and walked more quickly towards the cabin, still pulling him along behind her. His laughter, her favorite noise in the world, filled the air, drowning out the sound of the fireworks and the band until it became the only thing she could hear. She could have flown in that very moment if she wanted to.

But as they approached the cabin, Fynn pulled her to a stop. He looped his arm around her midsection pulling her to the side of the path and closer to him.

"Why did you stop?" she asked, burying her face in his chest, inhaling his intoxicating scent.

But he didn't answer. Instead, he placed a finger under her chin and tilted her head up to look at him. Those eyes, which had previously been sparkling with joy, were now dark. His forehead wrinkled as his brows knit together. In the next breath, his finger left her chin and pressed to her lips before he spun her around to face the cabin.

A light in the dark made her pause. Had they left a lamp on? No, it had been daylight when they'd left.

But there. On the rocking chairs out front. Someone was sitting on the front porch. From the distance and in the dark, she couldn't tell exactly who it was, but it appeared large and male. Jax?

Then another male exited the cabin and joined him on the porch. This male was familiar, but not a witch. She could see the silhouette of pointed ears when he turned to face the male in the chair.

Her hand gripped Fynn's and squeezed. She leaned back against him, her body shivering in response as realization hit her like a sobering tidal wave. She wanted to go back in time, back to the festival, and stay there. But now that these two visitors waited for them at the cabin, she couldn't. Even if her body still wanted Fynn right now, her brain, her stupid brain, would never give her that moment back.

Of all the nights for her father and Persy to show up, of course it would be this one.

Goddess fucking damn it.

27

EVEN THOUGH NOVA SUSPECTED this would happen eventually, a part of her had hoped that it wouldn't. Why did they have to show up on this night? Her heart dropped into her stomach, which had turned to lead, and a lump rose in her throat. She swallowed it down because no, she would not cry. She would not give her father that satisfaction.

The realization that this man, her father, who had suppressed her magic for her entire life, who had convinced her she was powerless, was now here in Aerdmure, just a few feet away, hit her like a ton of bricks. Her blood boiled, her magic stirring excitedly, sensing that release was near.

Fynn, ever the empath, squeezed her waist and repeated their mantra, "Breathe, breathe."

But she didn't want to breathe right now. She wanted her power to build up. She wanted to unleash it on her father, to show him what she was capable of, despite his best efforts.

She pushed Fynn's arm away and stomped out of the shadows of the tree line, into the clearing in front of the cabin, exposing herself. Fynn's light footsteps followed behind her, but he didn't try to stop her.

"What the hell are you doing here?" she ground out as they approached.

Father and Persy had been conversing, but their heads whipped around towards her voice. Persy straightened and put one hand on his sword. Father grinned, a smile that as a child might have warmed Nova's heart, but now, as an adult who was aware of his betrayal, she wanted nothing more than to slap that grin off his face.

"Ah, Nova. I've been so worried."

She stopped short of the cabin porch and put her hands on her hips. His face had no signs of actual worry on it, no look of relief in his eyes that he had found his daughter. She hadn't necessarily expected it—even before she found out about the suppression spell, he was never overly affectionate towards her—but her heart still sank; part of her had hoped that he had legitimately been worried.

"Hello, Father." Her intent had been to sound cold and emotionless, but a slight wobble in her voice betrayed her.

Persy held his stance behind her father as the governor rose from his seat. But the elder elf's eyes had been trained on Fynn since the moment he looked up. Nova could feel Fynn tensing beside her, his hand moving slowly to his sword.

Father waved his hand toward the door. "Come in, let's chat about how to get you home."

She shook her head, summoning every last drop of courage she had. "I don't remember inviting you to our home, nor do I have any intention of going back to Arkwood right now, especially with you."

He laughed. "Our *home*? I was under the impression the priestesses were letting you squat here for free."

She swallowed hard as Fynn moved slightly next to her. His elbow grazed hers, her resolve hardening further at his touch. "I know what you did, Father."

He shook his head. "The suppression spell? That's not what you think it is."

"Does it even matter? You hid part of my identity for my entire life!" She took steps toward the porch and clenched her fists. The magic within her was almost squealing with joy, and she was glad she'd had a week's worth of training to learn to control it. "You made me feel inadequate. You mocked me for not being a good enough witch. You have never loved me."

His face continued to show no emotion, that rotten smile not faltering one bit. "Now, now, Nova, calm down, we don't want anyone getting hurt."

That line alone nearly sent her over the edge, but she managed to reign the power back in. *Breathe, breathe,* she could almost hear Fynn whispering behind her. Her hands warmed as she squeezed them tighter.

"What do you want from me, *Luc*?" she spat.

He didn't even flinch at the use of his given name. "Blackmore has been sighted in the Worgreth Mountains. We suspect he is on his way here because he has found out that you are now here."

The news should have stunned her, especially since Silvana had just told her this morning that there was no new update on Blackmore. How had he learned of this news and traveled to her so fast when Silvana hadn't heard it yet?

But instead, it rolled off her like a wave, the fury building in her like a buffer against the fear. Where two weeks ago those words would have terrified her, made her feel small and weak, now she easily summoned the boldness to retort: "Tell me more about that. Explain to me why he's after me, and me alone."

Luc—she could no longer think of him as her father—met her stare. "If you must know, he knew you were a wielder when you were born. He was performing experiments on wielders and since you were a wielder born to a geo family, he was particularly interested in experimenting on you."

Her breath caught in her chest as he spoke. Finally, the truth, or at least she hoped it was. "How did he know?"

Luc paused, and she could almost see the gears turning in his head. "His wife, Wynna, was a healer, and was your mother's midwife for your birth. They were also...friendly."

Blackmore's wife was the midwife who helped Mother deliver her? That meant the Blackmores had been close to the Astor family. Much closer than just governor and subject. Wynna would have been with Raella for at least the preceding nine months before her birth, and potentially while Mother was pregnant with Raelyn too.

"Wynna sensed it when you were born," Luc continued. "She told us immediately of course—she was a well-respected healer outside of her research work. But she also told Blackmore later that day. They wanted a baby besides their own for their experiments, and they must have falsely believed that because of Wynna and Raella's relationship, we would be willing to subject you to it."

Heart pounding, Nova released her fists and shifted her weight. "While I appreciate you finally telling me the truth, you must know that coming here would be fruitless. I'm not going back to Arkwood."

Luc shrugged, not letting his disappointment show, if there was in fact any disappointment left within him. "Fine. Then your security detail comes back with me. If you think you are above my guidance and protection, then you can take your life into your own hands."

No, not Fynn! She couldn't do this without Fynn. Regardless of how well she was learning to control her magic, she did not want to be out here alone if Blackmore did find her. And what about their kiss—what about their growing relationship? There was so much more she wanted to explore with him, feelings that she hadn't had a chance to fully delve into or voice yet. She was certain her heart would break if Fynn left. Luc had done many things to her, but she would *not* let him break her heart.

She balled her fists again. "Fynn stays."

A hand lightly landed on her low back, and she exhaled a sigh, some of the tension in her body releasing. Fynn, reassuring her that he would in fact stay if she wished it.

This time it was Persy who responded. "Let's go, son. I have my own words for you when we get back to the city."

"I said," Nova repeated, her voice stronger, louder this time, "Fynn stays."

"Don't be ridiculous, Nova." Luc rolled his eyes.

Magic roared within her, and a blast of solid air fell between the four of them, separating her and Fynn from Luc and Persy. She looked down at her hands, fully splayed, the power coming from her core all that was holding the wall steady.

She'd made a shield between them.

Somehow, she made a shield large and powerful enough that it almost knocked their fathers to the ground. Fynn squeezed her shoulder in reassurance. "You've got this. I'm not going anywhere."

She nodded in reply, her ears buzzing with the sound of an invisible wind holding the shield in place.

Luc stood up. "I see you have been practicing well," he called over the noise. He snapped his fingers.

The sound of a tree cracking, falling, could just barely be heard over the wind. Arms looped around Nova's waist, and she was moving—so fast. Rolling backward, away from the house. When she came to a stop, resting in Fynn's arms, she saw what Luc had done. He'd felled a tree. Felled it where they had just been standing.

Her chest was heaving, her breaths shallow, as she stood, Fynn coming to stand next to her. "What the hell, Luc?" she shouted.

"You've been practicing well, but your reflexes are still slow." He began to descend the stairs toward them, stepping over the tree in his path. "I expect next time we meet, your reflexes will be faster. Your elf might not always be there to protect you."

White hot anger ripped through her body, forcing itself out of her as raw power blasted into Luc. He stumbled backward, nearly landing on the tree behind him, and when he stood again, he touched his nose, where blood was beginning to drip.

Nova drew in a deep breath and stared at her hands. She'd attacked her father. What had she done?

Luc wiped the blood and scoffed, then waved for Persy to follow him. "Well, *daughter*, enjoy your playtime. You know where to find me when you realize you need more protection. I'll be waiting for your apology back in Arkwood." He stormed off toward the woods, in the opposite direction of the town.

Persy was right on his heels. "Come, Fynn."

But Fynn shook his head and crossed his arms. "I'm not coming. My place is here. With Nova."

Persy was glaring at Fynn, eyes narrowed and top lip snarling. "I've done all I can to help you, son." And with that, he walked off into the trees after Luc.

Nova stood there, attempting to calm her breath, longer than was probably necessary, but she didn't want to risk Luc or Persy making a last-minute return to the cabin and not being in control of her emotions. Finally, it seemed safe, so she dropped her shoulders and drew in a deep breath. Part of her wanted nothing more than to collapse on the ground right then and there, but she clenched her fists and straightened her back. She would *not* appear weak right now.

She and Fynn had just given up everything they had so she could continue to learn how to use her powers. Family, security—all of it was gone in a moment. To her, it made perfect sense, but for Fynn to do the same? Even after the evening they had shared at the festival, even though she wanted him too, how could Fynn just turn away from his duty, from his father like that—for her?

She took Fynn's hand and led him into the cabin. She poured them both a glass of water, and they fell into the chairs around the dining table.

Fynn opened his mouth to speak first, but she raised her hand to stop him. "Why, Fynn, why did you do that?"

Fynn looked at her, the same way he'd looked at her before he'd kissed her. "Because you wanted me to stay. Because I wanted to stay. With you. As long as you'll have me, I'll be here. With you. *For* you."

Her heart fluttered. His words were touching, even more so than the actions behind them. She reached for his hand, their fingers intertwining. "You realize this means we are completely on our own now?"

He sipped from his water glass. "I don't see how this changes anything. We've been on our own since we left Arkwood."

He had a point. They *had* been completely on their own since then, and things had been fine. The news about Blackmore being in Worgreth wasn't great, she had to admit that, but she had Fynn and the rest of Aerdmure to protect her. And she was learning how to protect herself pretty damn well, too.

"You're right. It doesn't change anything." She took a sip of water and looked into his violet eyes. Something had been nagging at her. Something she needed to talk through. "Do you think what my fa—Luc—said about why he suppressed my magic is true?"

He pulled his hand back from hers and scratched his chin. "Some of it fits. But what I don't understand is, if he was just trying to protect you from Blackmore, why would he leave the spell for your entire life? Why did he attack us—you—now?"

His words gave voice to her exact thoughts. If Luc had just been trying to protect her from Blackmore, there would have been no need to continue the suppression spell once he was locked up. Luc could easily have removed the spell at that point and let her live as she was meant to.

And then there was the fact that he had just toppled a tree on her. To test her, he claimed, but there were so many other ways he could have tested her that wouldn't have resulted in her getting injured.

"That's what I'm wondering too. Regardless of the suppression spell, he just tried to harm me. To harm us. I don't understand why." She hated the way her voice shook, hated the way that even after everything that had come to light, everything Luc had done to her, she still craved his approval.

Fynn leaned over and wiped a stray tear off her cheek. His thumb lingered on her cheek for a moment before his hand joined with hers, and they fell into a comfortable silence.

"Thank you," Nova said after a few minutes, her magic now settled inside her.

She didn't need to clarify for what. He understood.

"Always." His use of the vow she and Raelyn saved for each other sent a pang of homesickness for her sister shooting toward her heart.

He didn't use it lightly. He meant it.

The mood from the festival had been broken, and she didn't dare make a move to continue where they had left off before finding their fathers. But when Fynn sat on the couch and started to arrange the pillows for sleep, she cleared her throat and reached out a hand. They exchanged no words, but he stood and placed his hand in hers, his grip warm and strong. She had no further intentions of anything romantic tonight, but she wanted—*needed*—him close.

By the time they both finally drifted off to sleep, it was side by side, not touching except for their intertwined hands.

28

"**W**HAT CHANGED IN YOU? Your magic is stronger than ever, and you seem to be mastering each new task with more ease than two days ago."

Nova looked up from her sandwich at lunch the next day to find Jax watching her, his head cocked to one side.

She'd been ready and waiting when Jax had arrived at the cabin to start training earlier that morning. She and Fynn had risen early despite their late night, and she had not been able to sit still in the two hours she had to wait for Jax to arrive. The events of the previous night had spurred the desire to keep going, to learn more, to work harder.

But now, she wasn't sure how much to divulge. Though Jax had proved a good instructor, and she didn't dislike him as much as she had initially, she still didn't fully trust him. So, she decided on a blend of the truth, leaving out that Blackmore was believed to be after her specifically. "My father showed up last night. Apparently, Blackmore has been sighted in the Worgreth Mountains, and he wanted me to come back to Arkwood for my safety."

Jax froze, a reaction she had not anticipated. His eyes darted between hers as if searching for a lie in the words.

"What's wrong?" she asked.

"Blackmore is in Worgreth?" He rubbed the sweat off his forehead.

Nova nodded. "That's what he said, and I doubt he'd lie about that." Or would he? Now she wasn't so sure.

Jax shook his head. "That news has not made it into town. We need to warn everyone. There are more defenses that we can use to protect the town against someone like Blackmore."

"I can warn Silvana when we head back for lunch. I'd also love to help with those defenses."

"We need to warn her now. Let's call it for the day." But Jax looked distracted, like he spoke the words reflexively without truly comprehending what she had asked. His eyes drifted around the clearing.

But he was right. It was better to warn Silvana sooner than later. Honestly, she should've gone straight to Silvana last night, but she'd been so...caught up in everything that had happened between the festival and Luc's visit. "Ok, let's go." She waved over to Fynn to come join them. "Hey," she said, trying to bring Jax's attention back to her while they waited for Fynn to walk over. "Do you think I could learn or create a sort of hiding spell?"

Jax's eyes met hers again, his brow furrowing. "What?"

"I don't know." She shrugged and shielded her eyes from the sun to look up at him. "Something to cloak me or keep someone from finding me."

"Why?"

She again decided that a half-truth was better than the full. "To keep my father from finding me again?"

Jax smiled at first, then laughed. "That bad, huh? Sure, that would be some difficult magic, but as wielders we have the ability to create whatever we want, so perhaps we can work on it together."

Fynn joined them, then they took the path toward the village. Nova relayed to him what she and Jax had discussed, both about Blackmore and about the hiding spell. He eyed her with what could only be suspicion, as if sensing her true intentions with the spell and doubting its ability to work, but he didn't say anything in front of Jax.

Silvana, whose eyes had widened when Nova described Blackmore's latest location, didn't appear to panic. If anything, she seemed more disappointed that Luc hadn't warned her directly while he was in Aerdmure, which now that she thought about it, did seem very odd. Almost like Luc had wanted the town to remain vulnerable. If it had just been to her own detriment, she might have understood, but for him, as a governor, to be so furious with her that he risked the safety of all Aerdmure seemed very out of character.

"We will ready the full defenses and ensure that our scouts are on high alert," Silvana assured her, waving away Nova's offer for help.

And sure enough, after the day's training was completed, there was a different aura around the town. Witches moved around quickly, speaking in hushed voices. The guild houses were empty as the witches set about performing their various protection spells, and messengers ran about proclaiming a new curfew in effect for all. No one should be out after dark.

She and Fynn picked up dinner and ales from their favorite tavern in town and returned home quickly, Fynn's steady breath and their footsteps the only sounds, though maybe his elf ears picked up something more. Once back in the cabin, he barricaded the door and asked her to place a spell on the windows and the door to seal them. Her old insecurities intruded into her mind again as she performed the spells so typical of geo-witches, but they were easy to push aside today.

Fynn again slept in the bed with her that night. Neither of them said a word about it to the other, but the unspoken agreement to share the space—but not touch—continued to hang in the air. She enjoyed the security, the comfort that enveloped her when he was close, within arm's reach, and she could breathe in the comforting scent of him as she fell asleep.

They hadn't so much as hugged or held hands since last night. The air between them wasn't necessarily awkward, but it was certainly charged with emotions other than lust: fear and anticipation being the main two. Her heart was tugging her in one direction—to try to reach out through those emotions to Fynn, to bring them back to where they had left off last night, but stupid thoughts of self-doubt crept in and shut her down.

It was just the witch wine.

But he wanted to stay!

You only want him because of the proximity.

But he's incredibly attractive and just as kind!

You don't actually need a male for protection. You're strong and powerful on your own.

But isn't it better to not be lonely?

Those voices repeated over and over again in her head until she finally drifted off to sleep.

Two days later, there was still no sign or news of Blackmore, but the town didn't lower any of its defenses. Jax tried to put a pause on Nova's lessons, since the clearing left them vulnerable, but she just insisted that Fynn be allowed to join them in the clearing and not near the tree line to provide more immediate support if needed. Jax acquiesced, finally, but also brought along one of the temple guards with him to make it even. It was clear that even after a week and a half, Jax still didn't have a high opinion of Fynn.

She had started on the cloaking spell yesterday but didn't get very far. It was the first time she had attempted to create her own spell, and Jax had told her it may take some practice to get it right, not to mention that she selected a very difficult one for her first. When she had asked him what his first wielded spell had been, he just smirked and told her *that* was a story for another day, his favorite answer to her questions.

Each time she asked if he had news of Blackmore or pondered his location, Jax's body would straighten, and he would try to switch the conversation to a different topic. It struck her as odd that he did so, because why would discussing Blackmore make him *that* nervous or fearful? She understood that Blackmore's reputation preceded him and was strong enough to elicit fear, but Jax didn't strike her as the type of witch who feared anything. When she'd mentioned it to Fynn at dinner last night, he had shrugged.

"I've felt all along he was hiding something. This just confirms it."

Nova rolled her eyes in response.

That afternoon, after a quick lunch eaten in the clearing to avoid having to walk back and forth too much, Nova was working on her cloaking spell, but her mind had wandered to Blackmore.

"What do you think his research was about?" she asked no one in particular, partly to gauge Jax's reaction, but also partly because she couldn't get the mystery of it all out of her mind. What had been so significant that it was worth destroying his lab, his partners, his family, and his life for?

As she suspected, Jax stiffened and looked away. She caught Fynn's eye and jerked her head in Jax's direction. Fynn moved his gaze over to Jax and nodded slightly.

"The elves do have some lore about the research, though I'm not sure how much of it is truth," he said, still watching Jax.

Nova stopped working on her spell and flipped her long black braid over her shoulder, her mouth dropping open. Fynn had never mentioned this, but then again, had she ever asked? Had they really never discussed Blackmore's research until just now?

"Back to work, No—" Jax started, his gaze finally back on her, but she raised a hand to cut him off.

"Fynn, tell me more."

"That's not why we—"

"Shut it, Jax." She rounded on him. "Or maybe you could start by telling me why you never want to discuss Blackmore, and prefer to act like he doesn't even exist?"

Jax clenched his fists. "Maybe you start by telling me why you're so captivated by a murderer?"

She crossed her arms and debated how much more to tell him. She could feel Fynn's glare on her, warning her not to say much, but honestly, why did it matter? Why couldn't she tell Jax the truth about Blackmore?

She was tired of the secrets. Tired of hiding.

Her arms fell to her sides as she sighed. "My father believes that Blackmore is targeting our family."

Fynn groaned loudly, pinching the bridge of his nose, and Jax's eyes went wild. "Why?"

"He has a vendetta against my father for putting him into Mistfell in the first place," she explained with a shrug. "Father believes that he would attack me, my sister, or my mother in order to get the worst type of revenge on him." She left out Blackmore's specifically targeting her since she wasn't sure she had a good explanation for it anyway.

"And that's why the elf is with you." She could see the gears spinning in Jax's head, putting all the pieces together.

It was Fynn who answered, his arms now crossed. "Originally, yes. But I was technically fired after the festival."

"So now you're just in it for the sex?"

She whipped her head back to Jax and opened her mouth to scream at him, her magic tapping at her skin, begging to be freed. But a glance from Fynn, a glimpse of his subtle shake of his head, and she willed it back under control.

Breathe, breathe.

"I'm just saying," Jax continued, his tone judgmental, "I wasn't the only one who saw you two at the festival."

"I stayed with Nova because she wanted me to." Fynn looked Jax up and down. "And because there was no way in hell I was leaving her protection up to you."

Nova groaned and hung her head in her hands. These two were going to give her a migraine. What happened to Fynn trying to make nice with Jax?

"Nova has proven to me that she is capable of protecting herself. She's advancing in her wielding faster than I could have hoped. But I suppose it isn't my call to make," Jax said, crossing his arms and shooting a daring glare at Fynn.

Her magic danced internally at the compliment hidden in his remark, but she quickly shut it down. She'd had enough of their bickering.

Fynn scowled, but before he could spit out another retort, she said, "Alright, Jax. Your turn." It came out louder than she'd intended but seemed to have the desired effect.

Jax turned to look at her, and his shoulders sagged ever so slightly. "It seems we may be in the same boat." When she raised her eyebrows at him, he continued, "My mother and her twin brother were two of Blackmore's partners in the lab."

29

"**O**H MY GODDESS." Nova clapped a hand to her mouth, and even Fynn stilled, his face softening, and his hands dropped by his sides.

"My father died five years ago," Jax said, slowly starting to pace back and forth in the grass. "But I grew up hearing about Blackmore. My father strongly believed he had unfinished business."

"Did your father know Blackmore?"

Jax nodded solemnly, his eyes trained on the ground. "Apparently he had always thought highly of both Kael and his wife, Wynna. He said at first he couldn't believe the stories about Kael's rampage. They had been friends, and he knew that as a team they were very close to their final discovery. The way my father put it, the research team had become like family to one another."

"Did he tell you what the research was about?" Nova pressed, attempting to be gentle despite the excitement building in her. Maybe Jax could help them figure this out!

Fynn leaned in, while Jax made sure that the other guard they had brought from the temple was still out of ear shot before continuing. "My father died believing that he had been deceived about the nature of the research. He didn't tell me what he believed it had been, because he felt foolish believing for so long that my mother, Margot, had been pure of heart. He saw her betrayal about the content of the research to be just as bad as what the research was believed to be in the end."

Nova leaned in, glancing between Fynn and Jax, who had stopped pacing now. "Bad enough that the governors covered it all up so no one else would get the same idea."

"Exactly. But since my father was questioned incessantly about it, and eventually sworn to secrecy, he knew what the truth was. And I was old enough to put the puzzle pieces together." He paused for a breath and then continued. "They were conducting research on how to remove magic from the world and give all that power to a select few."

Her hand flew to her mouth again. Remove magic? She'd never heard of such a thing.

Fynn remained stoic, unexpressive, but said, "And the assumption is that Blackmore, your mother, and the rest of the team would be the ones to take over? Overthrow the governors and become the rulers of a powerless Astria?"

Jax just nodded, the sun casting his face in shadow.

"Is that even possible?" Nova asked, her voice breathy.

"According to my father, it was. Blackmore made the final discovery and decided he wanted to take all the power for himself. So he destroyed the lab, destroyed his family, and destroyed his partners—my mother."

"Jax, I'm so sorry." She started to reach for him, but he turned and looked away.

"Did your father have any idea if Blackmore still maintained his power when he was apprehended?" Nova had to marvel at Fynn keeping a clear head and looking straight for the facts, the knowledge, that they would need to stay as safe as possible. Meanwhile, her mind was a puddle of mud she couldn't wade through. "Assuming he stole their magic before he murdered them, he would have more magic than anyone else in Astria and if he still has it, it will make him even more dangerous."

"That I don't know," Jax replied, shaking his head. "I was eight when she died, and Father stopped talking much about it once I turned nine. I didn't even bother asking him many of the questions I started having as I got older."

Nova summoned all her strength to avoid collapsing to her knees. The story was worse than she could have feared, and to meet the child of one of Blackmore's victims—to hear his story and how he had been affected by the tragedy—was almost as painful as learning about the nature of Blackmore's research and his potential for greater power. She was suddenly very glad that Fynn had stayed, regardless of his reasons, and even more grateful that Jax had opened up to her. Perhaps together they could protect each other. Perhaps this was what they had needed in order to finally trust each other fully.

She drew in a deep breath and reached out a hand. "Jax, I promise you; we will avenge your mother. We will find Blackmore, and together we can destroy him."

"Nova," Fynn shook his head, his hand resting on the hilt of his sword. "Stop."

Jax also looked bewildered, the sunlight hitting his green eyes in just the right way to make them appear crazed. "He's right. You can't be serious."

"I am." Her voice steadied, strengthened as she spoke. "I am going to train harder than ever with you, and we will build a spell together, a spell to take him down or at least contain him until he can be taken back to Mistfell. I believe that we can do it."

Jax and Fynn exchanged a look, but she stood firm, hands on her hips and head tilted slightly.

"You truly believe this, don't you?" Jax asked.

"And don't try changing her mind. Trust me. I've learned that lesson the hard way," Fynn said through clenched teeth.

She smiled and reached out her hand again.

This time, Jax took it and shook. "You're on, Astor. Rest up tonight. Tomorrow, we start."

Fynn didn't waste a moment once they got back to the cabin before he started questioning her, just as she anticipated.

"Are you sure about this, Al? Are you sure we can partner with him? Are you really naive enough to take on Blackmore with only Jax as back up?"

Maybe it was the word naive, maybe it was the insinuation that she wasn't powerful enough to do it. But her blood boiled as he questioned her.

She turned to face him, squaring off her shoulders. "I don't know, Fynn, maybe I am. But after hearing Jax's story, after hearing Margot's story, I'll be damned if I'm going to sit by and do nothing."

"I get that, I do. But do you want to throw yourself in his path like bait?"

"I never said anything of the sort." She walked to the sink and poured herself a glass of water then turned to face him. Fynn was standing behind the couch, resting against the back of it. "Do you want to tell me now what the elf lore about Blackmore's research is? And why you never mentioned it before?""First of all," he unlatched his belt from his waist and dropped it on the couch, "you never asked, and Esta and I were told not to discuss it with you initially."

"Initially?"

He stared her dead in the eye. "We weren't supposed to even be friendly with you. And you see how that turned out."

She rolled her eyes. "The lore, Fynn."

He cleared his throat. "The elves shared stories about his research that track with what Jax shared. Blackmore had intentions to make himself powerful and dismantle the governors."

Nova sipped her water and pondered the information. Nothing new, but there had been so much new today already that she was grateful for that. She wasn't sure how much more she could process.

Before she could reply, he crossed his arms and met her gaze again with those midnight eyes that made her heart jump. "Can we go back to coming up with a new plan that doesn't involve jeopardizing your well-being?"

Enough. She'd had enough of him being protective. Enough of him thinking her incapable of defending herself. Not long ago, she thought the same of herself, but since coming to Aerdmure, her entire perception had changed. A change driven initially by his belief in her.

She set down her glass and crossed her arms. "Why do you care anyway? Nothing is holding you here anymore. You can go whenever you want if you don't agree with my choices."

He dropped his head and put a hand up to his temple. "You really don't know? You really can't see it?"

See what? "The exit is over there." She pointed to the front door. "Feel free to show yourself out."

"Is that what you really want?" His gaze collided with hers again.

Nova paused. Was it? She could barely think over the sounds of her heart hammering, her pulse beating furiously.

No, of course not. She already knew she couldn't—wouldn't—let him go.

"Tell me one more time to leave, Al, and I will. But first I need you to hear me out." He stood up straight and approached her, taking her hands in his. His touch sent chills up her arms, his violet stare sparked lightning in her heart as he held her gaze.

Her resolve, already weak, shattered instantly.

"Before you send me away, I need you to know that the moment I hear you are in danger or the moment I hear that you need help, I will come running. I will be there, and I will destroy anyone who dares to harm you."

He had to feel her heart pounding in her chest as it threatened to jump straight out. He paused long enough for a breath then continued.

"The other night, at Canta's festival, that was truly special to me. That was something I had been hoping for, *craving*, for a while. Something I had been holding back since the night you were attacked in the park. When I realized that your safety, your happiness meant everything to me. I couldn't stand the thought of someone else being your protector, of not being able to help when you needed me.

"So know this. You have every right to send me away. You are stronger than you know, and I know you don't need me or Jax or anyone else to protect you, not anymore. But I don't want to be just your protector. And I will spend every moment apart from you agonizing about whether you are safe. Whether you're happy."

His dark eyes glittered with a hint of amethyst as he spoke, his hands in hers gripping tightly. Nova entwined her fingers with his without breaking his gaze and knew in that moment that she wasn't sending Fynn anywhere. She didn't want this elf out of her sight. Together they would face what was coming.

"Then stay with me, damn it."

She leaned in, pressing her lips to his, this time with more gentleness than at the festival, when the witch wine had been roaring in her veins. And he responded in kind.

They both took their time, exploring each other with their hands, his moving up her back, one onto her neck, and hers snaking under his arms, gripping his large shoulders from behind. Just like the other night, strength and magic surged through her body at his touch, his kiss.

Almost like his touch gave her more power, if that was possible. And that power begged for release.

She sent a small surge of magic out of her fingertips and into his spine. He groaned through his lips, still pressed against hers, and she smiled. He moved his hands to her waist and hoisted her up onto the countertop, not breaking his contact with her lips as he did so. Her hands found their way under his shirt to his abs, hard as rocks against her palms, but when she tried to remove his shirt, he stopped her and pushed her hands away.

Her gaze met his, but she couldn't read what those intoxicating eyes were trying to say.

"What's wrong?" she asked, her breath heavy, her chest rising more with every inhale.

Fynn shook his head and pressed his forehead to hers, pulling her hands, now clasped in his again, to his chest between them. "Nothing. But you deserve more than this."

"Stop degrading yourself."

He laughed. "That's not what I meant. We are going to do this right. We are going to take this slow."

Her heart fluttered as his words sank in. The corners of her mouth tilted upward, almost involuntarily, and she wrapped her arms around his neck to draw him in. "Fynn Voss, where have you been hiding all my life?"

He nuzzled her neck. "Is that my invitation to stay?"

Nova nodded and kissed him again, this time savoring every moment, every feeling, every twinkle of magic that burned through her when their lips connected. This moment—this was the kind of joy, the kind of passion, she had hoped to find, but never, not in a million lifetimes, thought she could achieve given her lack of powers, her undesirability.

But Fynn claimed he had been drawn to her since before she had cracked the suppression spell. The more she reflected on it—the more she inhaled his familiar cedar and salt air scent and relished the feeling of his body pressed against hers—she realized that she had been drawn to him from the beginning, too.

30

S OMEONE WAS KNOCKING ON the cabin door.

Shit. Jax was here.

Nova had awoken nestled in Fynn's arms, their silent pact about not touching in bed broken. The events of last night had come crashing back into her, and her mouth had spread into a wide grin.

That smile remained plastered to her face the whole time they ate breakfast, and Fynn stayed close by her all morning, like he couldn't bear to be more than an arm's reach from her. The thought made her giddy, like one of those teenagers that strolled through Arkwood Park with their first love.

They'd been so lost in their reverie that they'd completely lost track of time.

Nova rushed to the door, her loose hair falling around her face as she pulled it open.

"Running late today?" Jax raised an eyebrow. "You're usually waiting for me on the porch." He glanced between them, her standing in the doorway holding the door open with her hair a mess and Fynn directly behind her, bun tousled and one hand on her waist. A look of realization crossed Jax's face, his mouth forming an O.

Nova pulled Fynn out the door and shut it behind them. "Don't worry, Jax. Nothing will compromise our new mission." And without another word, she gathered her black hair over her shoulder, began to wind the strands into a braid, and set off toward the clearing, leaving Fynn and Jax to follow her.

She smiled to herself as she slowed so they could catch up to her, playing through the events of the prior evening in her mind. How well she had slept curled in Fynn's arms all night. How her body responded to being tucked into his. She'd have thought all the muscle on him would have made him miserable to cuddle with, but she couldn't have been more wrong. And she already looked forward to being back there with him tonight. Back where she seemed to fit perfectly.

How could she have believed he remained with her for any reason *other* than her? It now seemed ridiculous that she had ever doubted him, that she had believed he stayed only out of duty, and not because he genuinely felt *something* toward her. He may not have used the word love yet, but she didn't mind—she wasn't sure she was ready for that anyway. But his actions and the words he *did* say spoke loudly enough. He was here for *her*, and he was here to stay.

She was smitten, there was no other word for it. She'd never had feelings this strongly for a male, of any race. The butterflies in her stomach, the way her heart raced when his laugh flooded her ears, the lightning that shot through her body at his touch, and the way her power surged when he kissed her...all of it pointed to something bigger than she had ever experienced, and all of it made her want to be better. To do more.

Which meant that Blackmore needed to be dealt with. And soon

When they reached the clearing, Nova turned to face Jax and Fynn, who were just a few paces behind her. Fynn had fixed his bun, his blonde hair now pulled back taut, and Jax stood with his hands clasped behind his back, his mouth tilted up on one side.

"We've got work to do," she said. "All of us."

Jax shook his head, but the smile remained. "I thought you were the one who needed to train, Nova."

She stared him down. "Not anymore."

"Student becomes the teacher now?" He winked, his green eyes sparkling in the sun. "Are you sure you're up for it?"

"Yes, we're a team," she said. "The only way we can defeat Blackmore is together. We need to outsmart him. We need to be fast, both physically and mentally."

She started pacing back and forth in front of them, her best imitation of Jax. Fynn was eyeing her with a bemused expression, his violet eyes glistening with what could have been pride.

"Fynn, you're the best at agility. We'll start with you giving us some drills to work on before the sun gets too hot. Then after lunch we can focus on wielding and creating new spells. I'm still most interested in a cloaking spell."

"As you wish," Fynn said with a smirk and a bow.

He didn't go easy on them that morning. First, they had to run sprints up and down the clearing, running a few yards in one direction then turning heel and running back in the other on his whistle. Then he had them trying to dodge his attacks, which neither of them did successfully. Fynn was just too damn fast and though he didn't dare harm her, Jax was certainly going to end up with a black eye tomorrow if he didn't see a healer soon. Last, he guided them through some of his training exercises—pushups, crunches, lunges—all the things that made her certain she wasn't going to be able to move tomorrow.

They devoured a quick lunch of packed sandwiches and then returned to wielding. Fynn couldn't participate but stayed close to offer encouragement and suggestions as she and Jax started to work on the cloaking spell.

Nova wanted it to ward against Blackmore only, so that no one within the spell's grasp could be detected by Blackmore: hidden from sight, sound, and smell. They could still go about their regular business and not be invisible to the rest of the world around them.

"That's way too difficult to start with, Nova," Jax said. "What if we start with a generic invisibility spell, or a sound muffling spell?"

She shook her head. "No, we don't have time for generic. We need to focus on what is actually going to help us, and that's creating a spell to ward against only Blackmore."

Jax turned to Fynn for back up, but the elf just shrugged and grinned, acknowledging that she was too stubborn to be persuaded.

There wasn't a good way for them to really practice the spell since Blackmore wasn't near them, so Jax managed to convince her to start with a spell to ward against himself so that he could tell her where the weaknesses were. She started with warding from sight, making herself invisible to only Jax.

Pooling her magic in her core, she closed her eyes and allowed it to spread toward her fingertips and then out, willing it to take the form of an invisible wall that surrounded her. The spell was immensely complex and difficult for her to hold very long but by the end of the day, she managed to do it for a full minute, though she almost collapsed with the exhaustion of the spell combined with the exercises from the morning.

Jax tutted. "I told you this was too difficult."

Nova groaned from where she kneeled on the grass as Fynn approached her. He looked at Jax, and the corners of his mouth twitched upwards. "The more you goad her on, the more likely she is to persist."

"Oh, of that I am certain." Jax smiled, a provocative twinkle in his eyes. "Let's pick back up here tomorrow. Recover our strength tonight."

She agreed, her body telling her she'd had enough even if her mind wanted her to keep going. But between the morning's workout and the afternoon's wielding, she was completely zapped and collapsed as soon as she returned to the cottage. Not even the dinner Fynn prepared could get her out of bed. She woke just enough to eat the plate he brought to her, then returned to sleep, staying put until the sun rose.

After breakfast the next day, she was subjected to more of the same. As expected, each movement she made ached, her muscles screaming in protest at the agony she'd made them endure. But she didn't complain when Fynn guided them through another set of exercises in the morning or when she and Jax worked on the spell in the afternoon. She managed to hold the invisibility spell for five minutes this time and declared that she was ready to add on sound to the spell.

Jax rolled his eyes in response. "Tomorrow. You're making excellent progress, but you need to rest up. The last thing I want to deal with is you burning out."

Resting did nothing for her healing or her recovery. If anything, her muscles screamed louder. She tried her best to keep up with Fynn's exercises the next day but had to adjust more than usual as sweat dripped down her body, and her muscles refused to do what she willed them to do. Thankfully it seemed Jax was also struggling today, so she didn't feel like a complete weakling.

When they finally moved onto the spell, Nova decided to start with sound and sight. Jax tried to persuade her that focusing on sound and then adding it to the invisibility she already had would be easier, but she again argued they didn't have time to do things the easy way. Blackmore could show up at any point, could be watching them now.

Throwing up his hands, Jax admitted that he couldn't argue with that point, so she proceeded with the spell, focusing like never before.

Her invisibility flickered as she worked on adding a sound block in as well. Jax kept pointing out the holes in her wards, showing her where to tighten up and where to focus her magic.

Nova already felt like the invisibility spell was getting easier to hold, even after just three days. She didn't have to focus as much of her mental capacity on holding that ward around her as she worked on blocking out all sounds. Magic pulled from every part of her: core, arms, legs, head, draining her almost entirely. When she couldn't hold another moment, but it was too early to call it quits for the day, she thought of a last-ditch effort and beckoned Fynn over to her.

"Kiss me," she whispered to him, so Jax wouldn't hear.

He started but appeared pleased. "I mean, ok, happily, but why?"

"To test a theory."

She threw up the wards ensuring that Jax couldn't see her, or Fynn for that matter, and then leaned in for Fynn's kiss. Exactly as she had thought, as she had hoped, a new surge of magic flooded her overworked body when his soft lips brushed hers, and she knew, even without opening her eyes or listening for Jax that she had succeeded in blocking out all sight and sound of both her and Fynn.

Not only that though; it was *easy*. With Fynn next to her, with Fynn touching her, kissing her, her magic had no limits, no bounds. She could hold on to this spell forever.

When she pulled away from the elf, the spell held for a few moments then flickered out, and the exhaustion crept in on her again. As the invisible barrier separating Jax from them disappeared, the other wielder came into view, staring at her, mouth agape. She released the spell, drawing in a huge breath of air as she did, the sun heating her cheeks.

"How did you do that?" Jax looked completely flummoxed and rubbed his hand through his cropped dark hair.

"I was testing a theory. My magic feels...different when Fynn is close." She reached for and gripped Fynn's hand, giving it a squeeze.

Magic swirled in her core again.

"It surges? Amplifies? Incredible." Jax's tone was totally awestruck, and his eyes widened, almost enough to see the gears turning in his brain. This connection between her and Fynn must be something unique. She assumed it was something related to hormones or pheromones or just general romantic feelings, but for Jax to be so taken aback—what could that mean?

She caught Fynn's eye briefly but didn't say anything.

"Well, that will certainly be useful. And it gives me something to think about as we move forward." Jax took a look at his watch. "I know it's a little earlier than usual, but let's call it for today and meet again tomorrow."

And without another word, he turned on his heels and left the clearing, not waiting for Fynn and Nova to follow him.

31

H E WAS HALF AN hour late and Nova was about to send out a search party.

Jax was never late. He was always exactly on time, like he had counted exactly how many minutes it would take to walk from his cabin to theirs and timed his departure perfectly. But today he hadn't shown up, nor had he sent word that there was a change in plans. So instead of heading out to the clearing, she and Fynn found themselves trudging back to the village to find Jax.

Once they reached the temple, Nova stopped in her tracks, staring around the village square. She didn't know where Jax lived. Or did he even live here? Was he just bunking somewhere? She had no idea how to find him.

The tavern wasn't yet open, but the temple was so she entered and asked a priestess where she could find Silvana. She was directed to the second floor of the temple, where Silvana was sorting through old scrolls in what appeared to be a library.

The priestess looked up when they entered. "Ah, hello, Nova. Fynn. I'm surprised to see you here. Isn't this usually your time with Jax?"

"He didn't show up this morning. Do you know where we could find him?" Nova tried to keep her gaze on the priestess but found it drifting over the shelves of scrolls and texts, the paper and parchment so yellowed and worn that they must have been hundreds of years old. What histories, what knowledge lay in these texts?

Silvana's brow furrowed slightly, but she pointed them in the right direction, toward a small cabin near the wielder's guild. It was further away than it had seemed last time, but given that Aerdmure was small, it didn't take more than five minutes to walk there.

The cabin appeared empty; there was no movement detectable inside and no one walking around outside. Maybe they had passed Jax on their way over here? But Fynn gave a booming knock on the door and received the sound of a crash and a yelp in return.

Nova looked at Fynn, the pit of her stomach falling away. What had happened to Jax?

With one kick Fynn had the door off its hinges, exposing the interior of a cabin identical to theirs.

The source of the sounds became immediately evident, for rising off the floor was Jax, apparently recovering from being startled off the couch and landing on the coffee table, which must have been strewn with books. The floor was a mess of broken wood from the table and books haphazardly laying around the floor.

Jax looked at them, wiping a bit of dust and wood splinters off his arms. "What the hell, elf? Couldn't have been a little more delicate?"

"Delicate is not something people usually associate with me," Fynn said sharply, stooping to pick up the books. Jax made to stop him, but Nova reached for one too and started flipping through it.

Instead of the printed words she expected, it was filled with handwritten notes and entries, the scrawl a beautiful, flowing cursive that suggested the writer was female.

These weren't books at all, but journals.

"I'll take that." Jax grabbed the tomes from Fynn and reached for hers.

But Nova turned away and continued to flip through the pages. A strange sensation shot its way up her arms: not electric like Fynn's touch, more like a soft embrace. "Whose are these?"

Jax exhaled loudly. "My mother's. My dad saved these; they were the only thing of hers he couldn't bear to get rid of after she died. I think he thought he might find the answers to her death in these pages, but to my knowledge he never actually got up the nerve to read them."

"So you decided to read them." She spun back to meet his gaze.

A nod. "Something about the bond you and Fynn shared made me think of my parents, and of the bond my mother shared with her twin brother. That's when I remembered I even had these. I stayed up all night reading through them and must have slept late. I'm sorry."

"Nothing to be sorry for," she said, her eyes drifting back down toward the book she was holding. "We just got worried when you didn't show this morning."

Jax started to collect the journals and stack them on the table that he had quickly repaired with a wave of his hand. The door returned to its frame with another wave.

"Did you find anything in them?" Fynn asked, picking one off the floor and adding it to the stack.

Nova was still mesmerized by the book in her hand and the feeling in her arms when she held it. She had no intentions to part with it that easily.

"No, nothing." Jax grabbed his water skin from the dining table. "Alright let's go. We can still get in an hour of exercises—"

"No," Nova said quietly, staring at the book that was sending tremors down her spine.

"Excuse me?"

Fynn crossed his arms. "She said no."

"I'm aware of what she said, elf."

Floorboards creaked as Fynn moved toward Nova, then his hand landed lightly on her elbow. "What's wrong, Al?"

Without lifting her eyes from the journal in her hand, she said, "This journal is calling to me."

His hand grasped her more firmly, his thumb rubbing circles on the soft skin of her forearm. The gesture steadied her. "What do you mean?"

"When I picked it up, I felt…I don't know. A singing in my blood, like my magic was celebrating that I found this journal." She paused and looked at Jax. "Did you read this one?" She held the cover up to him, where the dates Margot had written on the front were visible.

He looked at the cover and shook his head. "No, I must have fallen asleep before I got that far."

Nova turned the book over, reading the dates on the spine for the first time herself. "This one spans the time frame when I was born."

"Could it mention Blackmore finding out you were a wielder? Maybe your magic recognizes a reference to yourself?" Fynn suggested.

"That could be it." She straightened and walked over to the couch, sitting down with the journal in her lap. "Three of us can get through these faster than one. I say we cancel our training for today and focus on these."

Jax put his hands out in protest. "Nova, that's not productive. We need to be out there working on your spell—"

She cut him off. "Something tells me that this is what I need to be doing today. Training can wait. These journals may hold the answers we need to understand Blackmore."

Fynn picked up one of the journals. "I think you might just be trying to get out of training, but—" he plopped on the couch next to her "—I'm in."

Hanging his head and groaning, Jax gave in. "And just like that the priorities have flipped. Fine. You start. I'm going to shower."

Without so much as a glance of farewell from either of them, Jax turned and left the room.

Nova's hands trembled as she pulled open the front cover of the journal in her hands and started to read. The first few pages seemed inconsequential, the kinds of entries that one might read and assume this was nothing more than a journal of Jax's life as a child. Margot had detailed everything from what he wore that day to what he thought of the meal she cooked. Instantly, she understood why Jax had protested their reading these. It must have been hard for him to not only read his mother's handwriting, but to have all these memories of her flooding back into him. He had been old enough to remember her when she died, but how many of those memories had faded over the years, until nothing was left?

But after a few pages of entries on Jax, the focus of Margot's writing turned more intriguing.

> *Today I went to the lab for the first time in a week. We were finally given authorization from the governors to resume work, and we were all so thrilled. Kael led us off with a toast to celebrate, a toast to what we hope will be a brighter, more equitable future for ourselves, but especially for the next generation of magic bearers.*

Still no details on the subject of the research, but from the way it was written, Nova had a hard time believing that Margot was referring to a way to remove magic from the world. She flipped a few more pages and continued.

We finally got to meet Baby Blackmore today! She's just as charming as Wynna and Kael had described: a tiny tuft of hair on her head, a grip tighter than one can imagine a baby of her size could have, and already a deliciously charming smile. Jax was smitten with her, so much so that I had to drag him away by the arm and was subjected to questions about why he can't have a younger sibling. Wynna and Kael are the most doting parents, too. For all his toughness in the lab and for all his ruthlessness in managing the governors, Kael is clearly wrapped around his daughter's finger. I can already tell that he will do anything for her, which is probably why he has a renewed vigor in his research of late.

Nova shook her head. Something wasn't adding up. The way Margot was describing Blackmore as a father—how could that kind of man turn around and kill his wife and baby just weeks later?

Kael thinks we are getting close! Wynna said he's been spending extra time at the lab recently, which is hard for her with the baby. She seems to understand, though I can tell she wishes she was there, too. He's always been a bit obsessive. And if we're getting this close to the final discovery, it makes sense that he's delving further into the research. When I was at the lab earlier today, he seemed to be in good spirits. I didn't notice anything off about him, and he was genuinely excited to show me the

*latest. I daren't write more about it here in case prying
eyes read this and word gets out before it's fully ready.
Kael would kill me! But soon...soon the world will know
what we've been working on and oh, I can't wait to see
the difference it will make!*

The word "kill" jolted her. Of course, it could just be a turn of
phrase. Margot wrote like she knew Blackmore intimately, maybe they
had been colleagues and perhaps even friends longer than just on this
one research project. By "kill", she likely just meant that he would be
angry with her. But given how events had unfolded, the word made
her spine straighten.

"Find anything yet, Al?"

Fynn's voice nearly startled her out of her seat. She had completely
forgotten she was sitting in Jax's cabin, that Fynn was right next to her.
Her mind had been completely absorbed in Margot's world.

She cleared her throat and collected herself. "Potentially. Nothing
concrete, but some interesting tidbits into Blackmore's character."

"My entries are from much earlier in her life it seems. Jax wasn't
even born yet. But she still speaks about Blackmore, like they studied
together along with her brother, Hendl." Fynn flipped through a few
pages as if looking for something but then stopped and closed the
book. "He just seems like a good person, at least according to Margot."

She nodded. "That's how she portrays him at the end too. A little
obsessive about his work, but overall, a kind person and a happy father.
Nothing to suggest that he could do what he did."

Fynn stopped and rubbed his hand on his forehead. "What if...what
if we all have it wrong? What if Blackmore is innocent, and he's
escaped to set the record straight? What if the governors—Luc—have
the story all wrong?"

A flash of heat ran through her body—her magic, encouraging her to agree with Fynn. They had no evidence yet to support that, and may never find any, but something about the theory rang true. Something about it felt right.

"Honestly, I wouldn't have wanted to think the worst of my father, but after everything that has come to light in the last few weeks, you may be right." She drew in a deep breath as Fynn squeezed her hand, that now-familiar tingle of magic from his touch crawling up her arm. "I'm getting close to the end of this journal, which must be her last. Let me keep reading and see if I find anything."

She returned her attention to the book, opening it back to where she left off, an entry dated just a week before the day that would be her last.

Benedict thinks we may be going too far. He told me so today, though I doubt he has had a chance to voice this to Kael or my brother yet. He thinks Kael wants to use this discovery, if we even finalize it, for his own personal gain, but I assured him he couldn't be more wrong. Kael doesn't have a selfish bone in his body. Everything he does is for his family, for the good of Astria as a whole. Not even just for the good of witches, but for the good of all races. He's always said so, and in the fifteen years I've known him, his actions have confirmed it. Benedict didn't seem to believe me, though he didn't say anything more.

Benedict...why was that name familiar? Nova tried to place it but came up blank, so she flipped the page and continued, feeling like she was getting to something good.

> *Kael told us today that he thinks he knows the last piece to our puzzle, the last clue that will prove our theory correct. Hendl wanted to stay with Kael tonight to finish the research, but Kael insisted on being alone. Wynna almost seemed relieved. I know she is just as excited about this finding and has been working hard on it like the rest of us, but I also know the exhaustion of raising a baby while Kael spends so much time in the lab is taking its toll on her. Maybe she thinks that once this is done, once our theory is proven, that he will go back to normal, whatever that is. But I think this is just the beginning. If we finish this, Kael will want to spread it far and wide, taking it not just to the governors but to the people too, so that we can all live together harmoniously, with whatever level of magical power we desire.*

She flipped the page at the end of the entry, but the last half of the journal was completely blank. The last entry must have been the day before Blackmore finished his research and took down the entire lab. Tears welled in her eyes and her heart sank. This woman, who wrote so fondly about her son, about the people around her, didn't deserve to die the way she did.

But what did that last line mean: *With whatever level of magical power we desire.* She nudged Fynn and ran her finger under the line to show him.

"What do you think?"

He was quiet for a moment, then closed the journal in his lap. At that very moment, Jax reemerged from the bathing room, in a new set of clothes like the ones he typically wore to training. But training was the last thing on Nova's mind.

Fynn cleared his throat, not acknowledging Jax yet. "It sounds to me like they were working on something that would let us choose the level of magical power we have."

"That's how I read it too."

Jax's mouth dropped open, and he stalked over to them. "What?"

She turned the book in his direction, tapping the last line with her finger. "Do you interpret that differently?"

He was silent for a moment, reading, then said, "No. But that's impossible. Magic and powers are part of our genetics. Manipulating that would be like changing our skin color or our height. It can't be done."

"Healers can modify genetic patterns when someone is born with a genetic disease." Nova closed the journal and set it on the table with the others. "I had a student a few years ago who underwent treatment for a blood clotting disorder that he inherited from his mother, who was a carrier. Healers were able to change his genes to delete the bad gene that caused the disease. Perhaps Blackmore and your mother viewed it more in that light?"

Jax shook his head. "The ethics of it though. Did they think that through?"

"The governors have ethics committees that review all research proposals. It must have passed their scrutiny before they began." Why was she defending Blackmore and his research team now? She wasn't entirely sure where she stood on the matter.

Fynn held up his hands. "This is just a theory. Let's not get too worked up about it just yet."

"But the only way we can prove this theory is to talk to Blackmore. And I'm sure as hell not waiting around for that." Jax scratched his chin, his eyes narrowed.

"I'm not so sure that's true." Nova opened the journal again and flipped to the second to last entry. "Look, your mother mentioned Benedict here. At first that name rang a bell, and I think it's because my father mentioned him as the team member who ultimately turned him in to the governors."

"So?"

Fynn growled at Jax's tone, but Nova put a hand on his knee and lightly squeezed.

"So, Benedict wasn't killed. For all we know he is still alive and knows the truth."

"Then why hasn't he come forward?" Jax asked, his tone still hostile. "Why would he let the governors cover up Blackmore's intentions?"

Nova paused for a moment, considering. "Maybe he truly did feel betrayed. Maybe he believed that Blackmore was in it for the wrong reasons in the end. Your mother said he expressed doubts. He probably felt like he got in too deep and then bailed right before the end."

"Nova, you're not making any sense." Jax started to pace the room, waving his hands as he spoke. "Blackmore killed my mother, my uncle, and his entire family because of the research they did. He took their powers and killed them. But now you're saying that the research was actually to unlock a gene that would allow anyone to have whatever level of magic they wanted?"

She nodded. "That's our guess."

"Then couldn't Blackmore have still done just that, changed his own genes and built enough power to kill everyone?" He stopped his pacing and turned to face Nova and Fynn on the couch.

She looked at Fynn, whose gaze held firm, not giving her any hint of what was going on in that beautiful head of his. Turning back to Jax, she said, "I suppose that is plausible."

"The only way we would know is to talk to Blackmore, or to Benedict."

She nodded and stayed quiet, pondering the difficulty of this situation. Finding Blackmore was potentially a death sentence. But they didn't even know Benedict's last name so looking for him would be a long shot, too. Besides, would he even want to talk?

"This is ridiculous. Can we just get back to training?" Jax had resumed pacing the room, arms crossed and gaze burning holes in the ground.

Something was wrong. She's crossed a line with Jax, and she hadn't realized it until just now. Until his body language gave it away. Digging into his mother's journals, discussing how she may have died—well, who was the asshole now?

"Jax, I'm sorry." She stood and reached for him, Fynn standing behind her like a bodyguard. Which, she supposed, he was. "It's your mother. We should have been more respectful."

The wielder pulled away from her hand. "It's fine, I'd just prefer to keep to the original plan. My instructions were to train you, not to catch Blackmore."

"You're right." Nova reached behind her for Fynn's hand and started leading him out of the cabin. "We'll meet you at the clearing in half an hour."

Fynn closed the door behind them as they stepped onto the front porch but after a few paces down the path back to town, he pulled tightly on her arm to stop her. "Al, are you ok?"

Was she? Had what she read in Margot's journal really changed anything? Blackmore was still on the loose. He was still searching for her for reasons still unbeknownst to her, and she had still been lied to by her father about her powers. Did the reasoning behind the research, the reason behind Blackmore's actions, really matter? For some reason, a small part, deep in the pit of her belly, had decided to give him the benefit of the doubt and that small part is what she wrestled with now.

"I'm really not sure, Fynn. It's mostly just that I'm confused and not sure what truly matters. But Jax is right, I'm here to learn to use my wielder skills, and that's what I need to focus on."

Despite telling herself that, training that day went miserably. Apparently, neither she nor Jax were in the mood to work on her cloaking spell, and after two hours with no real progress to show for it, Fynn intervened and told them they both needed the rest of the day off. Jax stomped off in a huff, not bothering to walk back toward the village with them like he usually did, but instead making his way in the opposite direction to goddess knows where. She watched him for a moment, debating whether to go after him, but took Fynn's advice about rest and followed him back toward their cabin.

The truth was her body was depleted. And not just her muscles, but her brain, her *soul* as well. While in Aerdmure, she had mostly been able to escape the mental load that Blackmore's escape had placed on her. Even her father's visit and his alarming news hadn't really shaken her fully—or at least the revelation of Fynn's feelings for her had overshadowed the visit. But those journals, the handwritten accounts of Blackmore's motives and behaviors in the last weeks of his freedom, had melted the walls she hadn't even realized she'd put up since discovering she was a wielder. She'd been so focused in the last three weeks on getting to Aerdmure, using her powers, and—she had to admit it—getting close to Fynn, that she had blocked out the larger fears about Blackmore. Until today.

They walked back to the cabin in silence, but Fynn kept a tight grip on her hand, reassuring her of his presence beside her. He was right of course. Rest and a clearing of the mind—that was what both she and Jax needed tonight. Tomorrow she would awaken refreshed and reinvigorated to work towards their goal.

No sooner had she resolved as much did she spy a figure on their porch in the distance. Her heart hammered in her chest, and she groaned. Why the hell was Luc here again?

But then an elbow nudged hers. She looked up at Fynn and her body softened: He was smiling, his elf eyesight making out what she couldn't.

She turned back to the cabin, blinking her eyes to try to see more clearly. The figure on their porch was shorter than Luc, with wider hips. A female. And not just any female, but one with short, curly hair that was unmistakable, even from this distance. Dropping Fynn's hand, she broke into a run desperate to get to the female, desperate to be reunited, calling with a cracking voice as she ran:

"Rae!"

32

"**T**ELL ME *EVERYTHING*."

Raelyn didn't waste time getting right to the point.

Fynn had managed to herd them, squealing and hugging, inside the cabin and poured them each a glass of wine. He was currently preparing a small snack plate for them, and despite being caught up in Raelyn's unexpected presence, Nova noted the gesture with a genuine smile.

She was sitting on the couch with Raelyn, both of them cross-legged facing each other, barely an inch of space between their knees. She was still marveling at the fact that Raelyn was here and safe. Raelyn looked the same as she had just a few weeks ago when they had parted ways but had what appeared to be a renewed energy in her eyes, like there was something she was bursting to tell Nova and was waiting for the right opportunity to do so.

Esta had come too, of course. The female elf was waiting inside the cabin, a small, faint scar on her right temple the only noticeable remnant of the burns she had suffered at Nova's hand. She didn't so much as acknowledge Nova's presence, giving only Fynn a nod, when they entered the cabin.

Guilt burned at Nova's insides. She made a mental note to apologize to Esta at the first opportunity.

For now, it was only Raelyn that Nova cared to speak with.

"It took us about a week to reach Aerdmure, a relatively uneventful week except for one brief run in with nomads," she began.

Raelyn clasped her hands to her mouth and glanced between Nova and Fynn, who was setting the snack plate down on the coffee table.

"Nova took care of them for us," Fynn said, with a wink. A wink that told Nova so much, considering how, at the time, he hadn't spoken to her for nearly two days after she'd "taken care of them".

She blushed. "Yes, I suppose it was my first real test at wielding. But anyway, we made it here and started training with another wielder named Jax the next day. Raelyn, you'll never guess but Jax is—"

"Training!" Raelyn clapped her hands together. "What have you learned? What can you do now?"

So, Nova dove into an explanation of the different spells and skills she had learned with Jax over the last three and a half weeks, stopping short of telling her about the cloaking spell and their new training regimen just yet. Raelyn responded with awe, her large brown eyes like orbs the whole time, pride in Nova shining through them like a beam of light. Nova usually preferred to stay out of the spotlight, keep attention away from herself, but she allowed herself to bask in Raelyn's reactions and couldn't resist spilling some of the more grandiose accomplishments.

"But then, as I'm sure you know Father showed up." Her shoulders tensed when she reached this point in the tale.

Raelyn nodded solemnly, her expression hardening instantly. "Yes. He told me after the fact. That was when I knew I needed to come be with you. I have something important to share that might help with Blackmore, and if he's close, it's important you know now."

Nova frowned, doing some mental math to figure out the time-frame for when they would have had to leave Arkwood to be here today. Fynn, one step ahead of her, sat on the edge of the bed and asked, "How did you get here so fast?"

Esta cleared her throat and leaned against the armoire. "When you leave with permission, you travel in comfort. Governor Astor was more than willing to hire us a carriage."

Her stomach turned to stone. Luc had begged her to come home, yet he willingly let Raelyn wander closer to the threat? It made no sense.

"How did you convince him to let you come?" She picked up a piece of cheese from the snack plate and let it melt on her tongue.

"I'm not ashamed to say that I begged," Raelyn answered, but after Nova rolled her eyes, she continued. "Ok, so it was more of an argument. But he let slip that Mother didn't know about the suppression spell, and I threatened to tell her if he didn't let me come. For good measure, he made me promise to convince you to come home, too."

Magic nearly burst forth from Nova, but she reined it in just before it escaped. To think that Luc had the nerve to hide all of this from his wife, that he could send Raelyn into danger for what he knew would be a wasted effort. "He put you in danger for no reason. I'm not—"

"I know, Nova, I know," Raelyn said, putting her hands up in defeat, and Esta shook her head, casting her eyes on the floor. "Esta and I agreed on the way over here that it was futile to try to convince you, but that we could actually be stronger together in whatever lies ahead."

Esta was in this with Raelyn? She had helped her sister deceive their father into letting them come to Aerdmure?

Maybe there was more to this elf than she gave her credit for.

This time Fynn spoke, addressing Esta. "I'm grateful that you are here and that you have been able to forgive the past to help us."

Esta softened slightly and shrugged. "Once Raelyn explained everything to me—about how Governor Astor had suppressed Nova's magic, about how she was wielder—I started seeing things a little...differently."

Raelyn grinned and puffed out her chest.

"I am truly sorry." Nova said, pivoting her head to look toward Esta. "I hope you know it was not intended, and I have worked so hard on control the past few weeks that I don't think you have to worry about it happening again."

"Can we just move on to the news that Raelyn is dying to share?" said Esta, brushing off her apology like it hadn't happened. A small vise clenched at Nova's heart, but she glanced at Fynn, who shook his head ever so slightly, and decided to leave it.

Raelyn clapped her hands. "Yes! Nova, do you remember when Father told us about Blackmore the first time, he mentioned that one of Blackmore's former colleagues turned him in to the governors and that was how they caught him before he could do more damage?"

Nova nodded. "Benedict."

"Exactly. Well, it turns out he lives not far from here. Esta and I managed to track him down, and we want to go visit him." Raelyn appeared to be waiting for a reaction, like she'd just delivered the gift of the century.

"How on earth did you figure that out?" Nova asked, looking between her sister and Esta. As impressive as it was, it meant that Raelyn had convinced Esta to let her leave the apartment, to defy a direct command from Luc.

Raelyn's shoulders slumped, clearly disappointed she didn't receive the reaction she'd anticipated. But before she could response, Esta chimed in. "The annals."

The annals? The records of lineages and histories of all Astrian families that were housed in the Atrium? Luc and the other governors had decided to stop maintaining them a while ago, so most people forgot they even existed. "How did you get to the annals when you were supposed to be on lockdown?" Fynn asked, clearly as perplexed as Nova.

At that question, Raelyn perked up again, her eyes twinkling with pride. "I forged a note from Father summoning me to the Atrium to see him. The guards at the flat bought it, as did the guards at the Atrium. Once we were in, it was easy to sneak around."

"The annals may not have been updated for years," Esta continued, "but they did have Benedict's last known location."

Nova shook her head. "So, for all we know, he could've moved ten times by now."

"It's possible," Raelyn said. "But it's the best we have to go off of."

Pieces were coming together so quickly that Nova's mind could barely keep up. Benedict wasn't far from Aerdmure. Benedict had betrayed Blackmore. Blackmore was heading for Aerdmure. Was he actually coming for revenge on Benedict and not for Nova herself at all?

Fynn moved toward her and laid a hand on her shoulder, leaving her wondering, not for the first time, if he could sense her thoughts. Or more likely, could scent her emotions.

Raelyn's gaze rested on Fynn's hand, her eyes narrowing, and she opened her mouth to speak but Nova cut her off.

"What if Blackmore also knows and is going for him? Wouldn't visiting him be dangerous?"

"Well, yes," Raelyn said. "That is a risk, but how else are we going to find out the truth about the research they were conducting? Father won't tell us, and if our own lives are in danger, I feel like we deserve to know more. The public deserves to know more."

"You want to find out the truth about the research and then expose it to the world?" Nova's hand shook as she spoke. "After all that the governors did to hush it up and make sure no one else could follow in their footsteps or pick up where Blackmore left off?"

Raelyn bit her lip, brown eyes wide, while Esta moved to stand behind her, hands clenched at her waist.

"Sorry." Nova looked down, pressing her palms into her forehead. "I want to find Benedict, too, it's just that knowing his location is a little worrisome."

She stopped and looked up to Fynn for help.

"We've met the son of another one of Blackmore's colleagues. He has her old journals, and we spent the morning reading through them," he explained.

"Oh, my goodness! Was there anything in them?" Raelyn asked.

Fynn shook his head. "Nothing substantial. Mostly things that lead to more questions, but there were a few remarks about Blackmore's character and the nature of the research that led us to believe that Luc's story may not be entirely accurate."

"Which is why we want to find Benedict," Nova concluded. Then she looked back at Fynn again. "I think Jax needs to come with us."

"Jax? Is that the son?" Esta clarified.

She nodded. "And my trainer as well. He's a very powerful wielder so not only does he have a personal interest in meeting Benedict, but he could also serve as another source of defense against Blackmore." She met Raelyn's brown eyes. "Can we sleep on this and discuss it tomorrow?"

"Of course. I didn't expect us to leave tonight. And I know I just put this on you without warning." Raelyn reached for her hand. "Maybe we need some alone time."

Nova exhaled deeply, but then smiled and nodded, folding her fingers in between her sister's. An instant wave of peace washed over her.

"Esta?" Fynn jerked his head toward the porch. "Meet me outside?"

"Gladly," Esta answered. "We have some things to catch up on, too." She eyed him with a look of disbelief that Nova assumed was related to what she sensed going on between her and Fynn, though Nova hoped it wasn't that at all.

Fynn gave her shoulder another squeeze then followed Esta out onto the porch, the door squeaking lightly behind him as he closed it. Nova involuntarily exhaled a sigh at the sight of him walking away as the power that had coursed through her veins at his touch slowly dissipated.

"Oh, you are smitten."

She looked at Raelyn, who was eyeing her with the widest smile on her face. "Is it that obvious?"

"I mean." Raelyn drew out the word like it had six syllables instead of one. "I thought I saw something brewing there back in Arkwood, but damn, it's so obvious now. Did you sleep with him yet?"

"Rae!" Nova tried to suppress the blush forming on her face, but it was impossible. Her pale skin always betrayed her when heat flamed to her face.

Raelyn threw her head back and laughed. "Seriously though! Alone in this tiny little cabin, with only one bed? Spill, sis."

Nova grabbed a piece of cheese off the plate and chewed it to buy herself some time. Raelyn tapped her finger on her chin and kept her gaze firmly fixed on Nova.

"No," she finally responded. "We have not had sex yet. He said he wanted to wait until the time was right and take it slow."

"Dear goddess, he is a saint!" Raelyn threw her body back onto the arm of the couch dramatically. "But he's a good kisser?"

Butterflies fluttered in her stomach as each of their kisses flashed across her mind, but especially the one in the clearing, where her magic had surged, and any spell seemed possible. "Have you ever heard of witches' magic increasing when touched by someone?"

Raelyn sat back up, her face rearranged from the look of a hopeless romantic to the look of a perplexed school child. "Tell me more."

She explained about how when Fynn kissed her, her power multiplied; when he held her hand, her self-doubt disappeared; when he laid a hand on her back, it was like he was transferring some of his power into her core. But he didn't have power like she did, no elves did, so it didn't make any sense.

Brown curls bounced as Raelyn shook her head. "I've never heard of anything like that. But it sounds like the two of you have a truly special connection."

A moment of silence fell between them while they pondered the situation. Nova nibbled another piece of cheese and sipped her wine.

Raelyn snapped her fingers. "You know who might know?"

"Blackmore?"

Raelyn nodded.

"That occurred to me, too. If he was researching the source of power or something along those lines, maybe he came across something in his research that could explain it. Or maybe he has seen it before."

"Another reason to find Benedict." Raelyn sipped her own wine as her words sank in.

Nova draped her right elbow on the back of the couch and leaned her head against her hand. "I know you're right. And I know we need answers."

"I'm open to other suggestions as to how to get those, too." Raelyn waved her wine glass around as she spoke. "Any less dangerous ideas you have, I'm all ears."

"The truth is—" Nova pulled her hair over her shoulder and started tying knots in the loose strands "—that I was already thinking about trying to find Benedict. It's just that knowing that Blackmore may be heading for the same place now makes it seem more dangerous."

Raelyn took Nova's left hand in hers. "It sounds to me like you haven't yet accepted that you aren't powerless anymore. But it also sounds like you've come further than we could have imagined while you've been here. You've already wielded your own spells!" She drew a breath. "I haven't even seen your magic at work yet, but I can tell you that I feel less scared about going to find Benedict because I know you'll be there too. You and your remarkable power can protect us. I know it."

Nova squeezed her sister's hand, grateful for her support, grateful for their bond. "You have a lot more faith in me than I do in myself."

"I always have, sis."

They looked at each other, a smile spreading across Raelyn's face and a small grin starting to tug at the corners of her own mouth. Raelyn squeezed her hand again, a single tear slipping down her own cheek.

"Thank you, for always believing in me, Rae."

"So, you'll come with me? We're in this together?"

"Always." Nova paused, allowing the mayhem whirling in her mind to settle until one thought, one glorious thought, jumped to the forefront. "But I'm going to need about ten cups of your coffee before we do anything."

Raelyn's laugh filled the room, filled Nova's heart too, as magic streamed through her blood.

33

A FAMILIAR SCENT WAFTED Nova's way.

Something earthy. Something comforting and rejuvenating. Something that transported her back to the Arkwood flat.

Once her brain registered what it was and why it was engulfing her, her eyes popped open, and she sat up in bed. Fynn yawned and rolled to his back, the arm that had been strewn across her falling off in the process. "What's wrong?" he muttered, peeking open an eye.

"Absolutely nothing." A grin spread across her face.

For in the kitchen was Raelyn, her beautiful sister, preparing coffee, and there was nothing more in the world that she would have asked for at that moment.

She leapt out of the bed and over to the dining table, while Raelyn laughed and pulled out four mugs. "Good morning, sis."

"You better not be sharing that first pot." Nova pulled one of the chairs out and sat, her feet tapping on the floor excitedly. "I need all of it to make up for my recent drought."

Raelyn set the largest mug filled to the brim in front of her. "How about that to start? I promise I'll make as much as you want."

She sipped it and allowed its warmth to trace every vein in her body, sighing with pleasure as she savored each drop.

Raelyn laughed again then poured a cup for Fynn, who had trudged over from the bed as well. Her eyes remained locked on the mug she was holding, not so much as glancing at the bare chest of the elf, but she gave Nova the subtlest of winks after setting down his mug for him.

So she *had* seen shirtless Fynn.

Raelyn leaned against the counter and picked up her own mug. "Nova, how did you survive without my coffee?"

"Barely," Fynn ground out, voice still scratchy from sleep. He took a moment to redo his bun, which had become disheveled. The muscles in his chest flexed provocatively when he moved his arms, and Nova's resolve to "go slow" nearly crumpled.

Had Raelyn not been present, she may have pulled him back to bed then and there.

Regretfully pushing those thoughts, those *impulses*, aside, she returned her focus to her sister. "The stash you gave us lasted a little over a week. Then I bought some from the geo's guild here and made do with it. But it wasn't nearly as good." She took another delectable sip. "Maybe you should quit teaching and open a coffee shop. Why haven't we ever considered that before?"

Raelyn shrugged, taking a sip from her mug. "We didn't think outside of the box much until Blackmore's escape forced us to."

"Well cheers to that. There's one thing to be thankful for in this whole mess." Nova lifted her mug to toast, drained the rest, and stood to get herself a refill.

"I think there's plenty more than just that to be thankful for." Fynn's eyes met hers when he said the words. His eyes were always expressive, but she had never seen them as affectionate as they were right now. Was he referring to meeting her, to their finding each other? *That* was certainly an upside to Blackmore's escape.

She sat back down, reached across the table, and gave his hand a squeeze. "You're right, Fynn."

Raelyn stuck her finger down her throat and mocked gagging. "Disgustingly cute."

She and Esta had stayed for dinner last night, enough for them to come up with a preliminary plan for finding Benedict. Then the two of them had left for the inn in town. The one bed in the cabin was clearly not going to be enough for all four of them. When Raelyn insisted, with a wink, that they not intrude any further, Nova didn't argue. She was just happy to have her sister close again.

She didn't see Esta around the cabin this morning, but she could sit here next to her sister, a warm mug of fresh coffee between her hands, forever.

"Where's Esta?" Fynn asked, leaning back in his chair.

Raelyn's gaze flicked toward the porch. "Outside. She didn't seem keen on coming in while you both were sleeping. Told me to come grab her once you were decent."

Fynn burst out laughing, while Nova's cheeks flamed again, taking a sip of coffee to hide the redness that betrayed her.

"What did you guys talk about last night?" Raelyn asked, looking at Fynn. "She's been in a mood since you came back in from the porch. She won't tell me a thing!"

Fynn shrugged. "Mostly she berated me for leaving her alone with you with no explanation. But she berated me for Nova a little bit, too."

Nova choked on her coffee and Raelyn burst into giggles. "Seriously?"

"Yep. Said she could smell our scents intermingled a little too much and couldn't believe I'd fall for...what were her words? An ungrateful, uncontrollable minx?"

Raelyn doubled over in laughter, her brown curls falling into her face. Nova giggled too as she caught Fynn's eye. He smiled at her in a way that made her skin break out in goosebumps and her heart start to race. Could his elf ears hear the way her heart reacted to him? Oh goddess, she had never considered that. But if Esta could detect what was going on just based on scent, then surely...

"I'll let her know you're presentable," Raelyn said between bursts of laughter. She stood, carrying her mug, and walked to the door where she poked her head out.

Fynn reached over and took Nova's hand, giving it a squeeze and rubbing his thumb along her palm.

"Did you sleep ok?"

She nodded. "Considering that my mind was spinning last night, yes, I did."

He leaned forward and kissed her temple as Esta and Raelyn walked in, Esta wearing a scowl that must just be part of her resting face.

"When do we leave," the female elf said. Not a question, just a statement. Typical.

"Jax should be here within the hour," Nova said. "And even once he's onboard, it doesn't feel right to me to go anywhere without speaking to Silvana first, at the very least to let her know where we are going."

Raelyn clapped her hands together. "Perfect. So we have an hour to finalize the plan and get everything packed."

She pulled out a map from the sack she must have brought with her this morning and spread it out on the table. They had already noted where they believed Benedict was residing, in a cabin about a day and a half's journey by foot north of Aerdmure. If they left today, they could be there tomorrow afternoon and have time to be in and back out by sundown, a fact that Fynn insisted on. He wasn't willing to risk being anywhere near Benedict in the dark, in case Blackmore was lurking around. He and Esta had far-reaching eyesight during the day, but at night, he explained, they'd have to rely on their ears.

As Raelyn, Esta, and Fynn reviewed the route they would take, Nova set about collecting the gear they had come to Aerdmure with: packs, dishware, blankets—they were in for at least two nights of camping again. It had seemed so long ago now, another lifetime, that she and Fynn had trekked here, her terrified of using any bit of her magic, him reserved but kind. She smiled at the memories of their shared moments setting up camps, running through the rain, and spying on the nomad tribes they had come across. At the time, she wouldn't have dared use the word fun to describe what they were doing, but looking back on it now, now that she and Fynn had started-ed...whatever it was they had started, she had only fond memories. Those little moments, at least before the nomad attack, had shown her who Fynn was, even if he didn't say much about himself. His actions on that journey spoke volumes.

Because they hadn't used those supplies since they arrived, most of the items had been kept together, so collecting them again didn't take long. She decided to take an extra tunic and pair of black leggings, loving their versatility and the reminder of Aerdmure they provided. But other than that, she left everything else they had accumulated over the course of their stay here. The plan was just to be gone for a few nights and then to return to finish her training and spell work with Jax.

A knock on the cabin door brought her out of her thoughts and back to the present. "Jax." She dropped her and Fynn's packs on the bed and approached the door.

Sure enough, the short-haired wielder was standing on her porch, wearing his usual training outfit, his arms crossed over his chest, his green eyes narrowed.

"You're not ready," he said, devoid of emotion and stern.

It stung a little bit that he had reverted back to his old ways around her. Since they started on their mission to build a cloaking spell and he had revealed his lineage, a certain camaraderie had developed between them, certainly enough for him to let her read his mother's journals. But today, from just that one sentence, she could tell he was back to how he'd been: arrogant, demanding, and removed.

"Change of plans," Nova responded, matching his tone, and moving to the side so he could see past her into the cabin's interior, where Raelyn, Esta, and Fynn were visible.

Jax raised an eyebrow.

"Come in, and we'll tell you everything. We need you to make this work."

She showed him into the cabin and closed the door behind him. "Esta and Raelyn, meet Jax, my trainer. Jax, this is my sister, Raelyn and her guard, Esta."

Esta scowled at being addressed as such, but Raelyn bounded forward excitedly, appearing to go for a hug, but given Jax's look of horror, stopped a foot or two away and shook his hand instead. "Thank you so much for all the help you've given my sister!"

"What's going on?" Jax asked, looking directly at Fynn.

Fynn raised his hands defensively. "This is all their idea." He waved a hand at Raelyn and Nova. "But in their defense, I do think it's a good one and that you should hear them out."

Jax stood there, stiff as a board, as if unable to make heads or tails of the situation. "Alright, then. Let's hear it."

Nova jumped in. She knew she had limited time to convince him. "Raelyn knows where Benedict is, and we came up with a plan to find him and learn the truth."

She could tell that whatever he expected her to say, that was not it. His dark eyes widened, pupils dilating, and his mouth almost dropped open, but he slammed it shut again, his mouth thinning.

"Where is he?"

"A day and a half north of here—" she started.

"Are you crazy?" His hands flew to his head in disbelief. "That's probably where Blackmore is headed. If Benedict heard the same rumors we did, he's most likely long gone into hiding again by now."

Raelyn held up a hand. "We considered both of those options. Yes, it's possible that Blackmore is there or headed there, but that's why it's more important that we get there first, and with as much power as possible."

"Hence, why we need you." Nova added the compliment to boost his ego and, hopefully, soften him up.

"Right," Raelyn continued. "And even if Benedict is gone, it's possible his cabin has documents or clues we could look through to learn more or find out where he went."

"Either way, it's worth a visit just to be sure." Nova kept her eyes locked on Jax, trying to get a read on his thoughts.

Raelyn nodded vigorously, while Esta stood stoically behind her, unemotional as always. Fynn moved toward Nova, his hand gripping her waist lightly in support.

"You're going to let them do this?" Jax asked him, man to man. "I thought your whole job was to keep Nova from doing ridiculous things like this."

Fynn narrowed his eyes at the dig. "From what I've learned of these two, ridiculous things seem to find *them*." He shrugged. "They'll do it with or without us. I'd just rather it be with us."

Jax turned to face the door, running his hand through his cropped hair. Nova's mind raced trying to come up with more ways to convince him, more ways to persuade him to come, because she could tell he was leaning toward leaving and shutting the door firmly in their faces.

"Jax." She drew in a breath. "Jax, think about your mother. Think about clearing her name, finding out the truth. Isn't that all you've ever wanted?"

"I thought I knew the truth until yesterday, when you poked around and started questioning things." He turned back to look at her, sadness burning through his gaze and piercing her soul. Her heart shattered for him, for the boy who lost his mother way too soon, who grew up believing that she had been betrayed by her colleague, whose father could never speak about the tragedy or allow Jax to process his grief either.

"You don't have to come. We can do this without you." She paused, trying to gauge Jax's reaction. "But we don't *want* to do it without you."

She watched him closely, following his gaze as he surveyed their unlikely crew coming together to uncover truths and fight for justice. Raelyn was grinning wildly, hands on her hips. Esta was standing in the kitchen area, unsmiling but eyes fierce, belt of blades tied in its usual spot around her waist. Fynn was at Nova's back, a hand still pressing lightly on her waist. And then Jax's gaze met her own. She stared at him with such ferocity that he quickly cast his eyes downwards toward his boots.

His answer came out quietly, but still loud enough for all to hear. "Ok, fine. I'm in."

Raelyn jumped and clapped her hands excitedly, curls bouncing into her face. Nova grinned at Jax, who she'd come to respect like a brother. "Thank you, Jax."

"First, I need to know the plan. I know these mountains better than any of you, so you better be open to some suggestions."

Raelyn tapped the map on the table. "Come, I'll explain it all to you while Nova and Fynn visit the temple."

Jax whirled his head toward Nova. "Suddenly feeling religious?"

"No," she replied, shaking her head, her long dark hair swishing in its ponytail down her back. "But I do feel like we owe it to Silvana to let her know what we are up to."

"Suit yourself." Jax moved towards the map on the table and turned his back on her and Fynn while Raelyn dove into the finer details of the plan.

"Let's go, Al." Fynn took her hand and with a quick wave to the other three, they departed the cabin and started the short hike to the village.

34

I T WAS A BEAUTIFUL summer morning: birds were chirping in the canopy of trees that lined the trail and squirrels were darting along the brush, in search of breakfast. This village, these mountains were truly beautiful in the mid-morning glow, and Nova wasn't sure how she hadn't noticed it on any of the other mornings. What was it about potentially facing danger that led one to fully appreciate one's surroundings?

She must have voiced the thought aloud, because she was jolted back to the present moment by Fynn's laugh, that intoxicating sound that swelled her heart more and more every day.

"Al, don't be such a downer about this. Sure, it's crazy, but it's a good plan, and you don't need to doubt yourself anymore. You are stronger than you realize."

She looked up at him. "I'm not used to that. I've spent twenty-five years of my life thinking I was nearly powerless, so much so that I never did magic so I wouldn't have to face the ridicule. I can't just shut down that self-doubt overnight. And besides, I've only been training for a little over three weeks. That's hardly enough to consider myself a powerful wielder."

Fynn stopped in his tracks and turned to face her, grabbing her other hand and spinning her to face him. "Nova Astor, you are brave, kind, and beautiful. And you *are* a powerful witch. I've been watching you since we arrived, and I am so proud of how quickly you have managed to learn what you have. How much you've taken in, how much you have grown. Never let that self-doubt overtake you again, and if it does, tell me. I'll chase it away for you." His grin looked handsome in the golden rays filtering through the trees.

Her magic started to swirl in her core, building itself up, so she turned to her breath. A deep inhale and a long exhale as she held Fynn's steady gaze. It helped, but her magic still clamored to pour out of her. She squeezed his hands and allowed some of the heat building within her to transfer into him, watching his expression as she did.

His eyes widened at the sensation, first glancing down at her hands and then back to her eyes. "How are you doing that?" he asked, his expression softening.

She shrugged and reeled in her magic again. "I'm not sure, but it felt right. And thank you for saying all those things, Fynn. I needed to hear them."

He placed a light kiss on her forehead.

They continued on to the temple and found Silvana standing on the steps out front. A look of amusement was visible on her face.

"Silvana," Nova said, approaching the aging witch. "Good morning! I'm so glad we were able to find you. We're about to leave Aerdmure, just for a few days, but we'll be back. We didn't want you to worry."

Silvana nodded, smiling. "Yes, I know. This may surprise you, but I am very aware of all that has happened with you and Jax over the last few weeks. And you and Fynn as well, I might add." Her eyes twinkled.

Nova felt heat rising to her cheeks but quickly reined it in. "Then you understand why we have to do what we are about to do."

"Understand, no. But appreciate, yes. And I will not try to stop you. But should you fail to return, I will alert your father."

"Thank you, Silvana. You have been so kind and gracious to us since we arrived." Nova dipped her chin out of respect for the priestess

"I hope to continue to be so when you return. Good luck." She smiled again and nodded at them, then retreated into the temple.

Nova glanced at Fynn to signal their return to the cabin when Silvana's voice rang out again.

"Nova?"

She turned to look at the priestess, who was standing halfway up the temple steps, twisting at the waist to look back at them. The priestesses' eyes were clouded over, and when she spoke again, her voice was harsher than usual.

"This is the beginning. The point of no return. Our children will right the way." Silvana turned back around and resumed her journey into the temple.

The hair on Nova's arms raised. *What the hell was that?*

One of Fynn's hands drifted to his sword, the other wrapped around Nova's waist, pulling her closer. "I don't think that was Silvana speaking," he whispered, his eyes still marking the temple door as it closed behind the priestess.

Nova looked up at him, noting the lines on his brow. He was just as confused as she was. "Who then?" Only one possibility occurred to her. "Canta?"

He nodded, finally moving his gaze to meet hers. "That's my assumption."

"Do we tell the others?" She turned to face him, his hand falling away from her waist, but reaching for her hand.

"No." He shook his head. "Without knowing what it means, there's not much we can do."

"What did she mean by 'our children'?"

"No idea." Fynn took a step back, pulling her with him. "Let's get back. We need to get a move on if we're going to cover enough ground today. We can discuss whatever that was when we return. Maybe even ask Silvana herself."

He was right. They had a mission, and it was time to focus. They'd be back in a matter of days. Whatever Silvana—or Canta—had meant by those statements...it could wait.

They returned to the cabin where the rest of their team was waiting. Jax now appeared to be in better spirits, announcing that he was going to return to his cabin to pack a few necessities and then return in half an hour so they could embark on their journey. After he left, Raelyn explained that he had seemed impressed by their plan but did offer some good suggestions for areas to avoid on the way there. His detours may add an hour to two to their overall journey but would put them out of harm's way of nomadic tribes or areas known to be frequented by other worrisome creatures.

"Creatures?" Nova asked. Of course she had heard the stories, fairy tales really, about the beasts and monsters said to lurk in the Worgreth Mountains. Even Noriendar's forest had its own set of legends about what hid within its depths. But to think that some of those could be true, that these creatures could pose as much a threat to their journey as Blackmore could...

"Yes, Nova, creatures," Esta replied. "They aren't just from children's stories. There are wards around Aerdmure that protect the village and its inhabitants, but once we leave the sanctuary of the village, we are at the mercy of the locals, and not all of them are as hospitable as the priestesses."

"But it will be fine!" Raelyn said quickly, folding up the map that lay on the table. "That's what Jax was able to help us avoid. How did it go with Silvana?"

She noted her sister's abrupt attempt to change the conversation and decided to follow Raelyn's lead rather than dwell on potential unknown threats in the mountains. "Fine. She seemed to already know what we were planning and said if anything goes wrong, she'll alert Father."

"Those priestesses," Raelyn tutted. "Canta can't keep any secrets from them it seems."

Nova opened her mouth, tempted to divulge the strange warning that Silvana had given them but a wide-eyed glance from Fynn made her pause and bite her lip instead.

When Jax returned promptly, as promised, Nova finished locking up the cabin and joined Fynn, Raelyn, and Esta on the porch. Raelyn, sitting on the same chair that Luc had occupied not long ago, had opened her arms for Nova to come join her on her lap, and Jax found them in an embrace, Nova savoring Raelyn's familiar floral scent and presence.

Raelyn was here. This was home.

"Are we ready? Or are we cuddling?" he asked. His tone was stern as usual, but she looked up to a smile on his face.

"Oh, give us another moment. That was the longest we'd ever been separated!" Raelyn exclaimed, tightening her hold on Nova one more time.

Esta stood and went to stand with Jax. "We really should get going, so we can make as much progress as possible before nightfall."

Fynn held out a hand to help Nova off Raelyn's lap. She accepted it and allowed herself to transfer into his arms, just for a moment, so she could right herself and find her footing.

These two standing closest to her—Fynn and Raelyn—were the two people she cared for most in the world, and there was no doubt that they reciprocated the sentiment. Raelyn, her steadfast, courageous, and deeply passionate sister, had stuck by her through all the hard times growing up as Nova was relentlessly mocked for her inabilities. Had found ways to make her feel special and loved despite it all.

And Fynn. New to her world, but honestly, it seemed as if he'd always been there, too. Though they hadn't expressed their feelings toward each other with words, she could feel in her bones that this was more than just a casual relationship. That was what she had conveyed through her magic this morning on the way to the temple. And the way her magic danced when he touched her...he had to feel it, too.

These were the two she could trust more than anyone. The two who would stand by her side through whatever came next.

Her heart soared with strength and adoration.

She squeezed Fynn's hand, took a moment to calm her breath and then descended the steps off the porch to approach Jax.

"After you, sir," she said, hand outstretched in the direction of their next adventure.

35

"**W**ELL, IF THAT'S NOT the best dinner I've ever eaten over a campfire, then I don't know what is." Raelyn smacked her lips as she threw the last of her scraped-clean bones into the woods behind her.

Nova laughed. Raelyn, to her knowledge, hadn't ever eaten over a campfire prior to her journey to Aerdmure, and even then, since she was traveling under their father's protection and stopping at taverns and inns, she certainly hadn't been roughing it as much as she would be tonight.

Jax had trapped a few rabbits, and Esta had cooked them over a fire that Nova conjured. Jax had seemed impressed by her ability to start and control the small fire, giving her a rare, genuine smile as a reward. Fynn had scavenged for some berries and made a sweet sauce that they rubbed over the rabbit meat so that it crystallized as it cooked, creating a truly delicious meal for them to eat.

"Don't get used to it. Fynn and I didn't eat like this on our travels." She was sitting next to Fynn on a log they had rolled next to the small fire. With a wink in his direction, she nudged him with her elbow playfully.

"Only because I was terrified of letting you anywhere near a fire," Fynn threw back at her, knocking her knee with his.

The journey so far had been as uneventful as they could have hoped. Aside from the rabbits, squirrels, and mosquitoes, they had encountered no other creatures or threats. Jax announced he was pleased with their progress, and they should set up camp.

"There's still a few hours of daylight," Esta said, glancing up at the still blue, though darkening sky through the trees. "Shouldn't we try to keep going?"

Jax poured a splash of water from his skin over his hands to wash them. "We've made good time. Let's take advantage of that and get some rest." He glanced over at Raelyn as he spoke.

"Yeah, yeah, I'm the slow poke." She started taking off her boots. "My feet are killing me though, so I won't say no to calling it a day."

Nova glanced at Fynn, waiting for him to offer the same massage he had for her. But he didn't even look her sister's way. That offer must only be reserved for...certain people.

She'd be sore again tomorrow, despite all the training she had been through with Fynn and Jax. The journey from Arkwood to Aerdmure had been fairly flat until they reached the base of the Worgreth Mountains on that last day. But this time, they were traversing the mountains the entire way, and there was a lot more uphill hiking. Raelyn used tiny bits of magic here and there to try to level out the terrain as best she could, but Nova's legs were already throbbing from her training. There was no way they'd get better after just one night's sleep.

Throughout the trek she had found herself glancing over at Raelyn more than anyone else to ensure she was ok. She recognized that Raelyn had not endured the physical training that Nova had and was therefore more likely to be winded by this journey. But although her sister's eyelids hung lower and her shoulders sagged—both from physical and magical exertion—Raelyn never spoke a word about it and carried on bravely and stubbornly with the rest. She had suppressed the urge to play protective older sister, like she needed to watch out for Raelyn and ensure she didn't overexert herself. It was a short journey, but not necessarily an easy one.

When she pulled Raelyn aside to ask her how she was faring while the others worked on setting up camp, Raelyn shrugged her off, focusing instead on getting her blanket out of her pack. "I'm fine, Nova. I appreciate your concern, but I'm not fragile."

Nova dropped it but vowed to continue watching Raelyn tomorrow.

Raelyn might have appeared physically tired, but she was in just as good of spirits as ever, deciding to regale the crew with a ghost story around the small remains of the fire they'd cooked over. No one had a knack for imagination and storytelling like Raelyn; it was part of what made her such a remarkable teacher to the youngest citizens of Arkwood.

"The little girl looked out over the ocean," she said, her voice dreamy and light, drifting around the campsite with the breeze, "expecting to see her father's ship coming home, but instead what did she see emerging from the tide? The ghost ship!"

An owl hooted nearby at the same moment that dust kicked up around them, part of Raelyn's dramatic flair. Nova jumped, her hand reaching for Fynn's thigh. He laughed softly and wrapped his arm around her, pulling her close. His cedar and sea breeze scent enveloped her, calming her nerves as she nestled in.

The dust settled, bringing Raelyn back into view as she continued. "The ghost ship approached the shore and wave after wave of ghost soldiers poured onto the beach. The little girl screamed, running as fast as she could back to her home, hoping her mother would know what to do. But before she could reach the house, the captain of the ghost fleet grabbed her by the arm—"

"Ghosts can't grab," Jax said. He was laying on the ground, propped up on his elbows and his gaze was focused on the trees around them, surveying the growing darkness for threats.

"It's a story, Jax," Raelyn said, shaking her head. "Anything goes in a story."

He exhaled audibly but didn't shift his gaze. "Sorry, go on."

Nova fell back into the thrall of the story, leaning into Fynn's embrace the whole time, his thumb rubbing circles into the small bit of skin between her shirt and the waist of her leggings. Her magic purred.

Esta hadn't moved or spoken a word during Raelyn's tale. She was sitting on Fynn's other side, and the only word that could accurately describe her was enraptured. Her focus was so trained on Raelyn that at the conclusion of the story, when Fynn reached behind Esta and squeezed her lower back, she jumped nearly ten feet in the air.

"What the hell was that for?" Esta cried, her eyes full of savage rage.

Fynn's booming laugh filled the space they had claimed in the woods. "You looked so intense, like you needed to be brought back to reality."

Was Nova having fun? It had been weeks since she could truly just enjoy herself. Sure, training in Aerdmure had been freeing and left her feeling more in control of her own destiny. But it had also been hard work. This little adventure with this little crew of unlikely members—it was her first real fun in so long. She leaned her head onto Fynn's shoulder and smiled, taking in those seated around the fire with her.

"You ok?" Fynn whispered into her hair.

She nodded. "More than ok. Just savoring the moment, this one moment where it seems like nothing is wrong in the world."

He kissed her head and squeezed her hand.

Raelyn helped to soften the ground, so the area was flatter and more suitable for sleeping. Nova asked to see how it was done, because she could probably now do it herself, and sure enough, after just one failed attempt, she made a small space of softer ground just like her sister had. Raelyn, delighted, had clapped and cheered, but Nova waved the praise away. She had forgotten that Raelyn still hadn't seen the full extent of her new powers and that doing any magic, especially a geo spell, was big news to her.

Despite the happiness of the day, Nova slept fitfully that night. Her mind would not stop replaying visions of what could happen tomorrow: the good, the bad, and the ugly. Some moments she was too hot, others she pulled her blanket back up over her body, huddling her knees into her chest for more warmth or tucking herself closer to Fynn, who draped an arm over her waist, his hand pressing lightly into her stomach.

But she must have eventually fallen asleep because the sunlight was now peeking through her eyelids, and the others were shuffling around the campsite.

They ate a quick breakfast and then packed up their gear. Jax managed to clean up the camp with a wave of his hand, making it appear as though they had never been there at all: no footprints, no food remains, no ashes from the fire.

"In case Blackmore is around. We don't want him following us," he explained.

Though the journey today was technically shorter than yesterday, it was more tumultuous. Benedict had apparently chosen a cabin far out of reach intentionally, so the path (if one could even call it that) leading to it was narrow and steep. Fynn and Esta were the only ones, due to their elven genetics, that did not need to stop for a break or two on the journey up, though they willingly obliged whenever one of the three witches asked for one.

On the last of such stops, Nova was redoing her braid while Raelyn sipped from her water skin and the elves scouted up ahead. Jax looked at the map. "Not much further. I'd say we can make it there without another stop."

Raelyn capped her skin. "Great, let's get to it!"

She stepped back up the path and went to find Esta and Fynn. Jax glanced over at Nova, who was working on the ribbon to hold her braid in place.

"Is she always this chipper?" He looked resigned, like he was already sick of dealing with her, as he folded up the map and put it back in his pack.

"Yep, that's Rae for you. Hopelessly optimistic. Honestly, all of her emotions are exaggerated." She looked up the path to where her sister was hiking just out of earshot up the path. Raelyn had always been that way, for as long as Nova could remember. It made for some very good times, but it also made the bad times seem abysmal.

Jax squinted slightly against the afternoon sun as he slid his pack back over his shoulders. "It's a little bit aggravating."

Nova shrugged and hiked past him as she said, "Not everyone is a grump, Jax. You get used to it."

Finally, after another hour of walking under the sun's midday heat, they spotted a small clearing up ahead with a cabin resting on it. The cabin was haphazardly built and seemed to be held together by magic. It looked like it had started out with one central room, but Benedict had expanded it over the years and didn't bother to design the expansions uniformly. It was still small, maybe just three or four rooms, but it did at least appear well maintained.

Though, she supposed, if Benedict had been hiding from the world for the last twenty-five years, tending to his house was probably one of the most stimulating things he could do.

Twigs snapped under footsteps behind her, then Fynn whispered in her ear, "Are you ready, Al?"

She sucked in a deep breath and nodded, but words got stuck in her throat. Her braid found its way into her fingers again.

"I'm here with you. We're all here." He gave her arm a squeeze and then stepped back half a step, giving her room to breathe and control her emotions.

Inhale. Exhale. Breathe. Breathe.

It did little to stop the nerves currently attacking her insides.

They had all agreed that Nova would do most of the talking and questioning, with Jax serving as her back-up given his relationship to one of Benedict's partners. But while she had spent the last two days preparing herself mentally for this, standing here now was a totally different story. Her knees shook and her mind turned foggy, pushing out the questions she had been forming in her mind as they'd been hiking.

This could be it.

This could be the missing link to the puzzle of what Blackmore and Margot had been up to, why Blackmore was targeting her specifically.

It was exhilarating but terrifying all at the same time.

A warming sensation tingled on her skin in the area Fynn had just touched, raising the hairs on her arm. Her magic reminding her that she was not alone. That Fynn was also here. That his presence, and Raelyn's presence, made her feel stronger.

Her mind started to clear again, and her throat opened to whisper the words: "Let's go."

Fynn and Raelyn followed her closely to the front door, Jax and Esta falling slightly behind them. The door itself was solid wood and intricately carved, but not with any pattern that she had ever seen. Instead, it seemed to be glyphs or runes of an ancient language long forgotten and strewn about in no real order. Either it was done for artistic flair or Benedict had slowly been losing his mind out here in the mountains by himself. They were about to find out which.

She drew in another deep breath as she raised her fist to the door and knocked three times. She waited, listening intently for sounds of anything on the other side but hearing nothing.

Without warning, the door swung wide open and a male with thick graying hair, a salt and pepper beard, and a scrawny body that seemed as though it had been malnourished for several years, stood in front of them.

He glanced around wildly, his mouth dropping open and his eyes churning in panic. He may not have seen this many people at once in many years. Nova immediately regretted the size of their group. Perhaps they should have reevaluated their approach, so they did not come across as intimidating.

But it was on her that the male's eyes came to rest. To her that he spoke his first scratchy words.

"You shouldn't be here."

36

"**E**XCUSE ME?"

Nova struggled to find other words. Benedict's greeting, if one could call it a greeting, had taken her so aback that all niceties flew out the window, and she forgot to even say hello.

Then again, he hadn't said hello either.

"No. You shouldn't be here," Benedict repeated, his voice shakier with each word spoken.

She drew a sharp inhale, disregarding that statement for now, and pushed forward with their original plan. "Hi, Benedict, I'm Nova, and this is my sister Raelyn, and our friends, Jax, Fynn, and Esta. We came from Aerdmure and have a few questions for you about the research you conducted with Kael Blackmore."

Something dark flashed in Benedict's eyes, and he made to close the door. "No, no, I don't know anything."

No way was he getting out of this that easily.

She reached out to grab the door handle. "Please, sir, we just want to know the truth. If there's a chance something about the publicized story could be wrong—"

"Nothing is wrong. I gave my testimony decades ago."

"Margot was my mother," Jax said from a few paces behind, his voice, unlike hers or Benedict's, demanding and assured.

Benedict stopped moving and left the door partially open while he stared at the wielder, wide-eyed. "Jax?" he whispered.

Jax nodded. His body remained tense, but Nova saw the resolve in his eyes flicker for a moment as Benedict drank in the sight of him, a man who had been just a boy the last time Benedict had seen or heard of him. Though Jax had already told Nova that he couldn't remember ever meeting Benedict personally, his mother would have spoken about him to her colleagues. Benedict would have known about him.

The older male continued to stare while Jax held his gaze, green eyes meeting grey, and the tension that had settled on the group upon approaching the cabin slowly started to settle. Benedict's face softened slightly, and he finally spoke again.

"I am sorry for what happened to your mother. She was always so kind to me." Then he stood aside at the doorway. "Please, come in."

His voice was still shaky, and his hand wobbled a bit as he guided them into what could be called a dining room but was really just a room with a table in its center. The table was flanked by only two chairs, both of which were covered in peeling paint, but there was a small couch with stuffing sticking out of it in multiple places along the wall behind it. She and Raelyn took seats on the couch, avoiding sitting on the myriad of stains, while Jax went for the table, sliding in opposite Benedict, but angling the wobbly chair in a way that allowed Nova full view of Benedict too. Esta and Fynn took up positions by the doorway, each with a hand on one of their blades, eyes trained on the witches in front of them, and ready to intervene if needed while also watching, and probably listening, out the window for Blackmore.

"I suppose I should offer you tea. It's been so long since I have entertained." Benedict attempted to rise from his chair.

"Please, don't worry about that." Nova raised her hand to stop him. "We just want to talk to you, and then we'll be on our way."

Benedict nodded slowly, giving her that same strange stare he had given her when he opened the door, then switched to shaking his head and looking down at his wrinkled and feeble hands. Raelyn nudged Nova with her elbow and gestured around the room, then at Benedict and mouthed the word "Crazy."

For along the wooden walls of the cabin were more etchings of the same runes on the door, like Benedict had chosen those as his decoration instead of artwork. It seemed there wasn't an empty space on any of the dark walls or ceiling, and there were even some places where Benedict had simply chosen to draw some runes over top of others.

What did they mean?

Dust had accumulated on most surfaces as well, and the entire cabin reeked of must and mold, so much so that Esta's nose had yet to unwrinkle. Books were haphazardly strewn all over the place: the floor, the side of the couch, the table. Some open to pages, some with ripped off covers, some neatly piled. Why hadn't Nova expected this of someone who had lived alone for so long? It was deeply saddening, and her heart gave a sudden lurch for the old man. This poor male had been forced into this existence, withering away, by her own father.

Was that what he meant by "You shouldn't be here?" Had he somehow recognized her and Raelyn as Luc's daughters and had no desire to interact with them, let alone be reminded of Luc Astor? Though they weren't easily recognizable or celebrities by any means, it wasn't uncommon for their faces to end up in the newsprints supporting Luc at various events. It was possible one of those newsprints had made it out here.

Raelyn nudged her again, bringing her back to the present, as her gaze snapped back to the center of the room, to Jax, who was staring at her, waiting for her to start asking questions.

She cleared her throat and began again. "Mr. Benedict, we—my sister and I—have been put under guard—" she indicated the elves in the doorway "—since Blackmore's escape from Mistfell. Our father—Luc Astor, that is—believes Blackmore is seeking revenge on our family for what Father did to him, and, for reasons we don't understand, is targeting me in particular."

She paused as her words sunk in, gauging Benedict's reaction. But he had none, just stared blankly at her as she continued.

"Um, so—I met Jax at Aerdmure where he has been helping me hone my wielder skills. When I learned that he was Margot's son, we looked through her old journals together, and it raised some questions about the nature of the research your team was working on. So, we wanted to come and find you, the only person who would know the full truth besides Blackmore himself, to see what you can tell us. So that we can fully protect ourselves against him. So that we know what we are up against."

Benedict continued to stare at her, like he had somehow slipped into a trance and not grasped a word she said. She flicked her eyes toward Jax who shrugged.

Finally, after a long moment of silence that left her ready to bolt up off the couch and straight for the door, Benedict spoke. "You have nothing to fear from Blackmore."

Not only was that not an answer, not what Nova was hoping to learn, but she also couldn't fathom what he meant. "I'm sorry, but why not?"

"You have nothing to fear from Blackmore, and you shouldn't be here." A single tear slid down his right cheek and stuck in his beard.

Something wasn't right. Her skin crawled and goosebumps formed on her flesh. Every cell in her body wanted her to get out, to leave.

Raelyn had been right; this man was crazy. They had wasted time coming here and put themselves in greater danger out in the open. They needed to return to Aerdmure and focus again on her magic and her cloaking spell.

This had been a fool's errand.

But when she stood to leave, Jax caught her hand and forced her back down.

She opened her mouth to protest, but he swiveled his gaze back to Benedict and spoke before she could.

"Benedict, help me understand," he said to the older man, who moved his now watering eyes from her and on to Jax. "Why shouldn't we be here? If we aren't to be afraid of Blackmore like we've been told, that would mean he didn't commit those murders. That he didn't try to steal power from others."

"Is that what you've all been told?" Benedict whispered slowly.

Nova wiped the sweat pooling on her hands on her leggings while Jax continued. "No, we deduced that last bit—that Blackmore stole magic from you, my mother, my uncle, and others. That he was planning to use the research you conducted together to continue stealing magic—and become the most powerful witch in history."

Benedict hung his head low and drummed his fingers on the table.

Nova, her bones still itching to leave but her mind fighting them with the craving for answers, added, "But Margot's journals led us to believe another thing. That the original intent was more...benevolent."

Again, Benedict remained quiet for a moment, but this time no one else spoke, allowing him the space to process what they had told him. It couldn't have been easy to be confronted with their questions twenty-five years after the fact, when he had probably spent most of that time trying to forget it ever happened.

Finally, his whispering, quivering voice filled the room again. "It was."

A hand grabbed hers—Raelyn—and squeezed. Fynn shifted his weight ever so slightly, floorboards creaking under his feet.

"It *was* more benevolent?" Jax prodded, his chair squeaking as he leaned forward.

Benedict nodded, his gray eyes casting toward the ceiling. "When Blackmore recruited me, he spoke only of equality. Of wanting to build a better world for future generations."

His eyes turned and bore into hers, as if he was trying to say something to her wordlessly.

"You are a wielder?" he asked her.

She flipped her dark braid over her shoulder to lay across her chest and started winding it in her free hand. "I am." She kept her gaze on Benedict but could feel Fynn's eyes locked on her.

"It's starting to make sense." Benedict spoke so quietly that she almost didn't catch it. But Jax, sitting closer to him, raised his eyebrows, and Fynn exchanged a glance with Esta.

"What is?" Nova responded, as calmly as she could muster despite the heat rising in her body.

But Benedict didn't answer and instead continued his explanation. "I met Kael shortly after I had completed my studies and determined I wanted to go into research. He was an up-and-coming name that many of us in the research field wanted to get to know. I believe at that point he had already partnered up with your mother—" he looked at Jax "—and uncle, her twin brother."

Benedict was starting to sound stronger as he spoke about the past, the words flowing more easily. A dreamy, misty look spread about his face.

Nova's magic tapped gently at her skin, trying to escape, reminding her to breathe. Once she exhaled, those taps faded away.

"It was luck, really, that brought me to him. I stumbled into the same bar he was in one night. Him and his wife. They were celebrating the success of receiving endorsement and funding for a new study from the governors. I overheard enough of their celebrations to get the gist of what they were planning and decided that if I wanted in, that was my chance.

"So I approached them, said my piece. And Kael immediately stretched out his hand to shake mine and welcomed me to the team. He asked me to sit with them and ordered me a drink. Then he regaled me with his dreams of equality, of a peaceful world, of a world where anyone could have magic."

Jax coughed. "I'm sorry, anyone?"

"Well, yes." Benedict leaned back in his chair, his hands pressing into his thighs. "That was the intention. To unlock the genetics of magic and unleash it for all to access."

A hush fell over the room. Benedict looked among his guests, and smiled, bemused, when they all looked so taken aback.

It was unheard of for anyone to question the lineages of magic. Or to want to open the source of magic for anyone to take advantage of its power. True, humans had always had a bit of a complex about their lack of magic, but in general they were content. Not since the days before the governors, over five hundred years ago, had there been issues with humans feeling defenseless against witches and elves. Not even wielders had threatened to take over since then.

The governors promoted harmony and unity. Allowing all to access magic would undoubtedly lead to some trying to garner it all for themselves. It would destroy any current semblance of peace. Why would they have allowed this type of research to be performed?

Her head was still reeling when her sister squeezed her hand again.

"But sir," Raelyn said finally. "If magic was unlocked, if magic went unchecked, wouldn't that mean the end of harmony as we know it? Sure, everyone could have equal power, but at what cost?"

Benedict looked at his hands, now curled together on the table in front of him and nodded slowly. "That's what I started to realize after I worked with him for a few months. The closer he got to figuring out the genetic code of magic, the more power hungry he became. The less he seemed to care about equality anymore.

"That's why I had to turn him in. I just wish I had done it sooner. Before he destroyed everything." He looked back at Jax, sadness and guilt pouring out of his eyes. "I'm so sorry I couldn't save your mother. She was one of the best witches I had ever met. Strong and stubborn; tough, but also incredibly kind. And she spoke very fondly of you."

Silence fell over the room, and Nova watched Jax's reaction. An invisible tether around her stomach tried to pull her toward him, urged her to place a reassuring hand on his shoulder, but Raelyn's hand squeezed hers again, and she remained still.

After a moment that stretched to eternity, Jax responded. "Thank you."

"And for what it's worth," the graying man continued, "I do not think she knew what she was getting into. I do not think she deserved to die disgraced, that your father deserved the shame. None of us knew what Kael was capable of, not even Wynna."

"What kind of person could kill his own wife, his own child?" Raelyn's eyes glistened with tears.

Benedict looked at Raelyn and furrowed his brow, then shifted his gaze to Nova. "I'm not sure."

She broke his stare to glance at Fynn, trying to convey a message that she'd had enough, had learned enough, and wanted to leave.

But his gaze was elsewhere.

Both Fynn and Esta had stiffened, their heads now turned sharply toward the front door.

37

"I HEARD IT, TOO," Fynn said to the female elf. "You go."

Esta glanced back at him, nodded, and left the house, a small click as the door closed behind her the only sound emitted.

"What is it?" Nova asked him, her voice shaking slightly. Magic swirled inside her as her heart started to race. Something wasn't right.

"Something, or someone, is moving around outside. Could be just an animal, could be a creature, or it could be—"

"Blackmore." She released a large exhale.

Benedict rose so quickly his chair fell to the ground with a clatter, earning him a disapproving glance from Fynn, whose attention was clearly still on any sign of movement or struggle outside.

"Kael is...here?" Benedict started scurrying around the room, mumbling to himself and biting at his fingernails.

Jax stared at him, eyes wide. "I thought you said we have nothing to fear from Blackmore."

Without stopping or looking at them, Benedict replied, "You do not. I do."

Of course. He was the one who turned Blackmore in after all. Had Benedict not turned him in to the governors, those who died would probably still be here today. Of course Benedict would be fearful of Blackmore's retribution.

But that still didn't explain why the rest of them had nothing to fear.

Fynn straightened again, whipping his head back toward the window. "Something's not right out there. It sounds like Esta's in trouble."

Jax stood. "I'll go, you stay here with Nova and Raelyn. I've got a bone to pick with Blackmore anyway."

Fynn nodded and stepped aside as Jax dashed out of the cabin without another word or even a glance back.

Raelyn's hand shook in Nova's. Fear flashed across Raelyn's eyes when their gazes collided, Raelyn squeezing her hand so tight that her knuckles were turning white. "Is it...really him?"

Benedict continued to rummage around, looking for something. Fynn approached the sisters, but his gaze remained on the man. "Do you have any wards or protection spells on this house?"

No reply. Benedict continued flipping over books, tossing trinkets, plates, cups, aside as he continued his search.

Nova closed her eyes and stretched out her magic slowly, carefully, attempting to locate any traces of spells in the house. But there was nothing.

She opened her eyes again and looked up at Fynn. "I don't sense any. I could try to cast some?"

Fynn shook his head, eyes not leaving Benedict as he spoke. "It's probably too late. And I don't want you to wear yourself out yet." Louder and towards Benedict, he said, "Benedict, I can't imagine you lived here alone all this time without some kind of protection spells. We need to know what we are up against."

But Nova really couldn't sense any spells or any traces of magic at all. There was no hum in her ears, no stickiness in the air. Nothing but stillness.

Something clicked in her head.

The runes covering the walls, while from an ancient magical language, were not something witches had used in recent memory. But they *had* been used by some who wanted to perform magic despite a lack of given powers...

And Benedict's desire to join the research. Was it just because he too had a deep-rooted passion for equality? Or could it have been something else...something more selfish?

"You're a human." Nova stared at Benedict flatly, her head tilting slightly to one side.

How had she not realized it? How had they missed his lack of aura? They'd been blinded by their mission, blinded by his proximity to Aerdmure. Blinded by assumptions.

Raelyn gasped beside her with a little yelp. Benedict stopped moving and turned to face them, his eyes crazed.

"These runes, they're your attempt at magic. Your attempt to summon any ancient power to your aid. You wanted to join Blackmore's research because you wanted magic for yourself." Nova cast a stern look his way, this time narrowing her eyes.

There was nothing wrong with being human and wanting magic. Of course, that was what Blackmore's research was all about—so anyone who wanted magic could find a way to use it. But it did mean that they were here, completely unprotected by any magical wards or spells.

And that she now had no idea whether she could trust Benedict's side of the story at all.

"And I almost had it." He wrung his hands and started slowly approaching them. "All I wanted was for the governors to take Kael away at the right moment but not to destroy his work. *I* wanted it. *I* wanted to use the success of his research myself, but I would never have let anyone else have it. Do you know how dangerous it could have been, letting power like that out in the world? How ethically and morally wrong it would be? But he destroyed his discovery before I could use it, before I could become a wielder myself."

Raelyn trembled as she leaned against Nova's side. Nova needed to get her sister out of here and back to safety. They had learned enough, and now they needed to get back to Aerdmure, or maybe even Arkwood.

Nova jumped to her feet, dragging Raelyn with her. She could feel Benedict's eyes on her as she said, "Fynn, we have to go. I think I can cloak myself and Raelyn, if you can carry both of us away from here quickly."

Benedict, now just paces away, cast his wild eyes among the three of them, mouth agape like he was struggling for air. "You...you can't leave me alone here with him."

"We can," Fynn said, "and we will. You are the one that got yourself into this mess." He reached out a hand to Nova and started to guide her and Raelyn toward the doorway. Raelyn was sobbing in earnest now, enough that she could barely support herself and was clinging to Nova's arm. "Is there a back door we can use?"

The graying man fell to his knees, his voice barely a whisper now. "Please, you don't understand. He will not harm you. He only wants me. You are safe."

"I don't see how we can trust you," Nova said, struggling to support most of Raelyn's weight as they moved, floorboards creaking under their weight. "You could be saying that to use us as scapegoats to buy yourself time to escape again."

"He'll kill me." Benedict's hands came together in front of his chest. "Please. Please, Allie."

She froze. What had he called her? Allie? No one had ever called her that in her life. Fynn was the only one who even called her Al.

Raelyn's whimper snapped her awareness back to the room.

"We have to go." She tore her eyes from Benedict's and moved toward Fynn, who was scanning the entrance hall, looking for another way out other than the front door. He pulled her and Raelyn away towards the back, leaving Benedict behind, wailing at them.

All at once, a deafening roar filled her ears and heat blasted her with such a force that she was knocked off her feet, losing her grip on Raelyn in the process. Magic erupted from her, but in what form, she could not determine. Her vision blurred, dust and smoke swirling around her, and her ears rang, making it impossible to try to find her sister's hand again. Strong arms scooped her up, and then a warm breeze and the humid outside air tickled her skin.

She drew in a sharp breath, trying to rid her lungs of the smoke, and caught a whiff of cedar, of the sea air.

Fynn.

Her vision started to clear. She looked up at the elf who was carrying her away from what was now the wreckage of the house. Over his shoulder she could see the roof partially blown off and flames licking the right side of the structure. The side where they had just been with Benedict.

"Rae—" she started to scream, her voice hoarse as her ears still rang.

Fynn kept running, flashes of trees all she could see around them as he carried her away from the house, from Raelyn. "I'm going back for her. But first I need to get you safe."

Nova looked over his shoulder toward the house, now so distant she couldn't even see the flames. Every bone in her body wanted to run back into the wreckage to find Raelyn. "Stop, please, I'm fine. Go back now!"

She fought against him, trying to writhe free of his hold on her. But his grip was too strong, so she resorted to pounding her fist on his chest as she continued to beg him to stop, to turn back.

"Be quiet!" Fynn demanded, his eyes trained ahead, surveying and scouting. "Your safety is my number one priority. I'm going to drop you a mile away, and I want you to use that spell you've been working on as best as you can until I return."

"That's too far! It'll take too long!" She pounded his chest in protest again, tears now streaming down her face, but he ignored it. He didn't even look at her.

But within moments, he was setting her down near a large boulder that would serve as a hiding spot and a marker to help him find her again. The house was out of sight this far in the woods. Not even the smell of the smoke reached her here.

"Do your cloaking spell, Al." Fynn stood in front of her, his hands gripping hers. "Please."

She would have rather run back up the mountain to the house to find their friends, but Fynn wouldn't leave, wouldn't go save Raelyn, until she cloaked herself. So, she quieted her breath, closed her eyes despite the tears still flooding them, and willed her magic to do what she had been practicing, allowing only Fynn to see her.

"Good. Thank you." Fynn gave her a quick kiss on the forehead. "Stay here until I get back and, please for the love of Dalia, Al, don't do anything stupid. I'll be back soon. I promise."

With a turn on his heel, he was gone, dashing back to the house in search of Raelyn.

Would there be anything left to find? Why had she let herself get separated? Why hadn't she held onto Raelyn tighter?

For several minutes, she paced back and forth in a small swatch of ground near the boulder, only stopping when she found herself ankle deep in a trench she had accidentally worn into the ground thanks to her emotionally responsive magic. Grumbling, she sat down instead, pulling her knees to her chest and laying her head down on them.

More minutes passed. Sweat trickled down her back. Shouldn't Fynn have been back by now? It shouldn't have taken him this long to run back, find Raelyn and return. Had he stopped to find Esta and Jax, too? Had he been hurt?

Losing him when she'd only just found him—that thought alone was enough to break her.

It took every ounce of control she could muster not to let her magic escape through the emotions swimming through her body.

They had been foolish to come, just as she had feared. And what had they learned? Their suspicions about the research based on Margot's journals had been confirmed, but Benedict had made it sound like Blackmore was still responsible for the death and destruction. Even if Blackmore's initial intentions had been benign, something must have happened to turn him power hungry in the end. Or perhaps he had just been good at hiding his intentions all along...

But could they even trust Benedict after learning his side of the story?

A branch snapped nearby, and Nova lifted her head, heart pounding but body remaining absolutely still.

"Al?"

Fynn.

She leapt up and dashed around the boulder, dropping her cloaking spell as soon as her eyes found him.

He was alone.

Nova stood as still as death, her gaze piercing his red rimmed eyes. "Where is Raelyn?" A whisper, a plea.

"I'm so sorry, Al." His voice wavered as he approached her, pulling her numb, stiff body to his. "He took her. Blackmore took her and jumped."

The tears from Nova's eyes were a torrent, blurring the world as she started chanting "no, no, no," gripping Fynn's shirt tightly. When her legs gave way, Fynn slid to the ground with her, holding her there while she sobbed, never loosening his embrace, never letting her go. His lips grazed against her hair.

This time, as her emotions threatened to drown her, Nova didn't try to contain her power. As she sobbed against his chest, the earth rumbled around them.

38

NOVA COULDN'T FEEL ANYTHING other than the wetness streaking down her cheeks and the firm body she pressed herself harder against.

Raelyn was gone.

Fynn's arms encircled her and remained there for a few moments, then he pulled away slightly, leaving one hand on her arm, tipping her head up to face his with the other. "Al, we will find her. Jax and Esta are back at the house."

"They're ok?" she managed to choke out.

The earth underfoot started to still.

"Yes. They confirmed that it was Blackmore, and they believe that he is heading to the old lab. Jax and Esta are currently trying to force the lab's location out of Benedict." He paused for a moment. "Honestly, I've never seen Esta so charged. She seems like she's genuinely grown to care for Raelyn."

She managed a weak smile and brushed a tear from her cheek. "Rae has that effect on people."

Fynn pulled her back in, and she basked in the comfort of his embrace. "Breathe, breathe," he whispered into her hair, her earthquake finally stopping.

She whipped her head up to look at Fynn, something he said fully registering. "Wait, Benedict survived the blast?"

His thumb brushed away the tears on her cheeks. "He's not in great shape. Jax knows a bit of healing and is trying to at least make him comfortable until they can get him elsewhere."

She snorted. "Jax is willing to do that for the man who is responsible for his mother's death?"

"We're going to sit here for a moment," Fynn said, ignoring her question. "Give them time to get what they need, give you time to get control of your magic. Then we'll go back and find them so we can make a game plan together."

Torn between the desire to go back and assist with the interrogation, the desire to move somewhere else to start finding Raelyn, and the desire to collapse to the ground in exhaustion, she just nodded. She didn't have enough willpower to fight against anything Fynn said right now. Her mind was overcome with fear for Raelyn's safety and spinning with the knowledge they had just gained.

But, at least for now, Fynn would be staying with her.

Taking his hand, she led him back towards the boulder, pulling him down to sit beside her, her head leaning on his shoulder, their hands intertwined.

"What is Blackmore going to do to her?" She threw the question out to the world in barely more than a whisper.

Fynn squeezed her hand and drew a deep breath. "I don't know, Al, but Jax and Esta made it sound like he wanted to test out his work."

She lifted her head and looked into his violet eyes, which were full of apprehension. "He wants to use her to test his genetic codes? No—no, no, *no*, he can't. What if something goes wrong? What if she's—"

But her throat closed up around the word, like the air had been completely vacuumed from her lungs. Her body trembled—or was that the ground?

"Just breathe, Al." He wrapped his arm around her back and squeezed, then his hand slid up to her neck and lightly stroked the braid that was now a mess. "I'm not taking you back there until you're certain you're under control. We will find Raelyn, but we—*she*—needs you at full strength right now."

They sat in silence for a moment, quiet tears running down her face, the only sounds around them those of the birds tweeting merrily as the sun was starting its descent. The sky was a blend of breathtaking pinks and blues that, along with the birds, completely contradicted how she was feeling right now.

Then Fynn spoke again, his fingers still in her hair. "Her name was Lena. She was a florist, and we met when she delivered flowers my mother had sent me for my birthday one year."

The woman he had loved. Lena. She didn't move or turn to look at him but gave him the space he needed to voice his story.

"Even though she didn't have any geo abilities, she had a strong connection with nature. She loved exploring, hiking, and camping. Anything she wanted to grow, whether flowers, vegetables, or grasses, would grow and grow well. She had an eye for the artistic too, making her floral arrangements stand out, even in a city where geos typically dominate the market." Pride beamed through his voice. "But she was also kind. She was known to stop her delivery carriage on the side of the road to help any poor soul in need. One time we were out for a walk when she saw a baby bird that had fallen from its nest, still alive. I've never seen anyone move as swiftly and as delicately as she did, scooping it up and placing the baby back in the nest with its siblings."

He paused for a moment, and Nova felt the deep breath he took, his chest expanding under her cheek.

"Elves don't typically marry or mate outside of our race because of our longer lifespans. We could outlive a witch or human partner by decades, and most of us choose not to live with that grief. But I was drawn to Lena—I loved her—so I didn't care about that. Until others started threatening her life for being with an elf.

"We like to think we live in a society where equality prevails, where the three races live in harmony and can do or be anything they want. But in reality, I think we are all incredibly divided. Three governors for each race. Three different cities for each race. Sure, Arkwood houses all three, but even then, neighborhoods tend to lean more towards one race, and there isn't one district that I would call truly integrated.

"I can see the appeal in Blackmore's work, if that's what he truly wanted. To find peace and harmony by removing the main cause of strife between the races. Because that's what magic is. It's a way to keep humans oppressed. It's a way to dominate elves if needed. And don't take this the wrong way, but wielders are among the worst of the lot. Their raw power is limitless and can do virtually anything they want it to.

"I can see why Blackmore wanted to be able to unlock the genetics of magic, to create a way for anyone who wants magic to have it. But I'm also glad he never got to release what he discovered. Because if everyone has limitless power, where does that leave Astria?"

"Destroyed." The words left Nova's lips in a hush, carried away with the passing breeze.

Fynn dropped his lips into her hair again, leaving her with the sensation of her magic's sparkling response to his touch. His fingers trailed down her back, leaving a shiver in their wake.

The rage that had been fueling her magic only moments ago had subsided slightly, her power now more easily subdued.

He continued, "I couldn't protect Lena from her fate, from being with me. She wasn't helpless. No, she could defend herself, but elves are known for being territorial, and it took me years to get over the fact that I couldn't save her in the end."

He gently pushed her off his shoulder and lifted her into his lap, her legs straddling his waist so they were facing each other. His hands wrapped around her hips.

"I don't know what's coming, what finding Blackmore will bring, if he'll still try to release his discovery. But I will try my damnedest to protect you. You make me feel alive in a way that I haven't since Lena. You give me a purpose in life that I haven't felt in years." He paused and drew in a breath. "I can't get enough of you, Al."

Tears were still streaming down her face, but her heart was leaping. She pushed a fallen strand of white-blond hair behind his ear, then put a hand on each of his cheeks, staring into his violet eyes as she responded, "Fynn, I can't get enough of you either."

One of Fynn's hands wove itself into her hair and pulled her closer, until their lips met. Shockwaves of magic coursed through her body, rippling outward from her core, tingling in each extremity. She didn't even try to stop it from leaving her body and entering Fynn's as it crossed over from where her hands were still resting on his face. His body trembled in response.

With this kiss, she was able to momentarily forget about Raelyn, forget about Blackmore and Benedict, forget about the journey that lay ahead. With this kiss, it was just the two of them, these two lost souls who had found each other and helped each other find their way back to themselves.

Fynn drew back first, leaving his hand wrapped in her braid, resting his forehead on hers.

"I want you to know," he said quietly, his breath coming out in pants, "that I believe you are strong, powerful, and fully capable of defending yourself. You have demonstrated that you are in control, that you can wield your magic, and that your confidence is the only thing holding you back."

"Is that why," she whispered, trying to still her heart, to ignore the heat building in her core, "when I feel your touch, when you kiss me, I feel my magic surge in a way that I don't when you aren't near? Because you instill that confidence in me?"

He smiled. "I don't want to give myself that much credit."

She laughed lightly, kissing him quickly, but when she pulled away his face had turned back into a mask of gravity.

"Al, even though I vow to protect you, I do it knowing that you don't *need* my protection. You are more than capable of facing this alone."

Nova buried her face in his neck, taking in the sea breeze and cedar scent that had become her sanctuary. "I'm glad I don't *have* to do this alone."

Fynn's body softened into hers for a brief moment but then he straightened. "Do you feel ready?"

She lifted her head and stood up, and despite the summer air, her body felt slightly chilled as she removed her body from the warmth of his. The sun was nearly set, the sky now a dark orange, and though it was cooler this high up on the mountain, summer stickiness still hung in the air.

"I do."

She reached out a hand, and he took it, pulling himself to stand. Then he scooped her up, and after one more quick kiss on her forehead, he sprinted off toward the cabin.

39

O NCE THEY WERE IN sight of the partially smoldering house, he set her down, still holding her hand tightly. "Stay right behind me."

She didn't dare try to argue.

They stayed back from the cabin but circled the periphery, trying to get a sense of the scene before them. The left side of the cabin was completely blown to shreds, and smoke hung thickly in the air around it. There were no immediate signs of life, but as they approached the front side of the cabin, she started to hear Jax and Esta's voices and exhaled in relief.

They were alive, they were unharmed…and they were bickering.

"It's faster to get back to Aerdmure and arrange transport," Esta was saying.

"You're wrong, we'd lose valuable time doing that. We can get there quicker on foot without needing to backtrack." Jax. His tone was the same as it had been for her lessons: stern and unyielding.

They appeared around a crop of trees: Jax slightly disheveled with a small bruise on his temple but otherwise uninjured, Esta covered in dirt and soot.

Her hands were gesticulating wildly in the air. "We have no more supplies. We can't just traipse off into the land of the nomads without supplies!"

"We'll find them as we go," Jax said, shrugging.

Jax and Esta looked up and spotted Nova and Fynn in front of them. Jax smiled broadly and swept her into a hug, while Esta kept her face steady and spoke to Fynn.

"Benedict caved. I think Jax used some kind of mind trick on him to coax him into speaking, but we know where the lab is now."

"Mind trick?" Nova asked, looking at Jax with an eyebrow raised as he stepped away from her.

"Persuasion. Remember on our first day you asked me what my 'special skill' was?" He winked.

Now that was a skill she wouldn't mind knowing. "Teach me."

"I can try...after we get Raelyn."

Right. How had she already forgotten about her sister? Her mind refocused on the task ahead as she turned to Esta.

"I want to know what happened out there. Did you see Blackmore? Did he recognize Jax?" Nova stepped closer to Fynn again, slipping her hand back into his.

Esta hardened. "We don't have time to explain, we need to move."

Despite the control she'd felt over her magic just moments ago, the ground shook beneath her foot as Nova took one step forward. "I want to know! We all need to know what we are walking into!"

Esta looked to Fynn for support, but he just pulled Nova back, drawing her in closer. "She's right, we all need to be on the same page going into this."

"I, for one, would also like to know what happened before I came to your rescue," Jax goaded, leaning back against a tree.

Esta's eyes narrowed and she crossed her arms. The air stiffened with tension that wrapped around Nova's limbs.

The elf was embarrassed. Whatever had happened to her, she was embarrassed.

"Fine," Esta said through gritted teeth as she kicked the ground with the toe of her boot. "I was able to track him outside the house without detection. He was hiding just a few feet behind the tree line and down the slope a bit, but he was there. I recognized him immediately from his likeness in the newsprints and posters all over Arkwood.

"I tracked him for a bit, certain he wasn't aware of my presence, but I was wrong. He was tracking me, too. After a minute, he threw a spell at me, knocked me flat on my back and stunned me. I couldn't move. Then he approached and started speaking to me."

Nova pictured Esta lying on the ground, defenseless, with Blackmore towering over her, and shuddered.

"What did he say?" Fynn's grip on Nova tightened, his free hand moving toward his longsword.

"That I had what he wanted. And he would stop at nothing to get it."

"Me," Nova whispered.

"Or Raelyn," Jax said. "That's about when I showed up. You must have sensed her being attacked, Fynn. I don't quite have the stealth of an elf, so he sensed my approach and was prepared, blasting spells out left and right in my direction even before he could see me. But I put up my best shield, and it worked. He wasn't able to get any spells through to me.

"It made him quite angry actually. He was rambling about waiting twenty-five years for this, whatever this is, and that he wasn't going to let us stop him getting back to his lab."

"Surely he knows his lab is destroyed?" Nova cut in. "Or that the governors would expect him to go there?"

Jax shrugged. "He's a man acting in desperation, and he knows he's getting close to being caught anyway. Honestly, I'm surprised we haven't seen any signs of governor outposts here around Benedict's cabin. I'd have thought they'd anticipate his arrival." He ran his hand through his cropped hair, looking around nervously.

Now that he pointed that out...it was odd. Almost like the governors had hoped he would finish Benedict off, and then they could track him elsewhere. A shiver raced down Nova's spine.

"Anyway," Jax continued, "I had to drop my shield to get to Esta. While I was freeing her, he tried attacking again—got a good blow to me at one point—" he pointed to the bruise on his temple "—but I got him back. He's powerful, no doubt about that. He wasn't wasting away in Mistfell. But I think I was able to slow him down a bit."

"He still attacked the cabin though?" Nova asked.

Jax's shoulders sagged. "Yes. I had turned away for a moment to get Esta to safety when the cabin exploded. I managed to get out of sight, and I shielded us both, but that meant losing Blackmore. That must be when he took Raelyn because when the dust settled and we approached the cabin again, no one was there except Benedict. It wasn't until Fynn came back, and we heard him shouting her name that we realized what had happened."

"Where is Benedict now?" Fynn asked, his hand slightly loosening in hers.

Jax pointed back toward the remains of the cabin. "Inside, asleep. Once we were done questioning him, I did my best to heal him up and then cast a sleeping charm on him. He won't wake until tomorrow, but he'll be fine. I doubt he'll cause any more trouble.

Esta crossed her arms and hung her head. "I've never felt like such a fool. We should never have let him escape."

"Esta, we're facing magic we haven't seen before. You didn't *let* him escape. He got away, but we can't dwell on that," Fynn said. "We need to focus on finding Raelyn. Where is the lab?"

Jax picked up a pack from the ground near his feet that Nova had somehow missed before. Her pack.

Her jaw dropped. "How did you—"

Handing it over to her, Jax replied, "I found it while I was looking for Raelyn and Blackmore. It's the only one I could find that survived." He looked at her, with a mixture of pride and confusion in his eyes. "In fact, the area where I found it was completely free of any damage from the blast. Did you cast a shield?"

That must have been the magic she'd felt leaving her body when the blast hit. Without even realizing it, she'd reacted instinctively to save herself, and more importantly, Raelyn. The knowledge that Raelyn was likely unharmed by the blast was comforting, even if her disappearance still hung in the air like a storm cloud.

"I guess I did," she said, as she opened the pack and pulled out the map they had studied for the journey here just a few days ago. She held it out so the four of them could huddle around it.

"We are here," Jax said, pointing to the X that Raelyn had drawn marking the location of Benedict's cabin. While Aerdmure was just at the edge of the Worgreth Mountains, their journey to the cabin had brought them deeper into the range.

Esta pointed to a spot of open land in the area between Arkwood and the mountains. "It's around here. Benedict said it was along the river, just a few hours by carriage outside of Arkwood. Close enough for them to commute using magic, but not far enough to be at risk of nomads."

Fynn put both of his hands on his head. "That's practically back to Arkwood. Would he dare risk going that close to the city guard and the governors?"

"If he felt he was close to getting the revenge he desired, then yes," Jax said.

Nova swallowed and tried not to imagine Raelyn at the lab, Raelyn being tortured, Raelyn being experimented on. Her arms sagged. "You don't think he'd try to...modify her powers, do you? Use her as a test case?"

No one spoke as the realization hit them. Though destroyed, the lab could still hold secrets, or at least memories, that might facilitate the renewal of his work. And what better way to exact revenge on Luc than to experiment on one of his daughters?

She stood up straighter, folding the map and shoving it back in her pack. "We have to go. *Now*. Fynn, how fast can you run there?"

It was a sign of how much Fynn understood the gravity of the situation that he didn't even try to object. "That's nearly a week's walk from here. I could probably run there in two days."

Her heart sank as she dropped the pack to the ground. "That's too long."

"What if," Esta began, winding a loose piece of brown hair around her still-tight ponytail, "you and Fynn run back to Aerdmure and find a wielder to jump you there?"

Fynn could easily run back to Aerdmure in a matter of hours. And it was true that in the wielder's guild they may be able to find a witch who could jump with them, the way that Blackmore had jumped with Raelyn. But it was a gamble.

"Ask for Mehta," Jax said, picking the pack back up and looping the straps over Nova's shoulders. "He's an old friend. Trustworthy, and he can do it. Could probably jump with both of you at once."

"What about you two?"

There was no way Fynn could run carrying all three of them, but she didn't like the idea of leaving them behind either.

"We'll be right behind you. I can use wind to help us get down the mountain quickly," Jax explained, "but not as quickly as Fynn. Then we'll find Mehta and meet you there."

Fynn nodded in agreement and looked down at her. She was sure the fear and uncertainty were showing in her eyes, but this was the quickest way to get to Raelyn, to save her. Even if it meant leaving two of their group behind.

"You didn't want to come here without Jax as added protection," she said to Fynn quietly. "Yet you're ok with leaving him behind?"

"Do you remember what I just told you about your own power?" He gripped her chin between his thumb and index finger, holding her gaze to his. "I was wrong to doubt that before we came here. I was blinded by fear."

She drew in a deep breath to settle the magic brewing in her at his touch. This decision was hers to make. The others needed *her* to decide how they would proceed. Outside of the classroom, she'd never been a leader, had never been one to take charge of a group, to be the chief decision maker, but the stakes were so much higher now. Raelyn's wellbeing, her *life*, was on the line, and although Jax, Fynn, or Esta could probably save her all on their own, now—now that she was a wielder, she was the one who had to do it. This was her responsibility, not because she didn't trust them, but because she could never live with herself if she sat back and watched.

Nova turned and faced the group, hardening her gaze and drawing up as much strength as she could muster.

"Ok, let's do it."

40

"**I**'M LOOKING FOR MEHTA. It's urgent."

Nova and Fynn had reached the wielder's guild in darkness. It had to be close to midnight, and the guild was encased in silence, save for the incessant chirping of crickets.

Her voice was breathy, not from physical exertion (Fynn had done all the hard work and was taking a well-deserved rest a few feet down the steep slope), but from exhilaration. Her heart hadn't stopped pounding since she had climbed into Fynn's arms a few hours ago and held on tight while they sprinted back to Aerdmure.

The wielder on the other side of the door raised an eyebrow and paused, looking her up and down, but must have decided she seemed harmless because he eventually stepped out of the guild house, closing the door behind him. His skin and hair were as dark as the night around them, but his blue eyes shone brightly when the moonlight hit them, twinkling like the reflection of the moon on the sea in Adenaport.

"You've got him." His voice was deep. She could almost feel the ground vibrating from his words.

"Thank goodness. I'm Nova, and this is Fynn." She waved her hand lazily over to where Fynn was sitting and watching them. "Jax sent us. He told us you may be able to jump us somewhere."

Mehta laughed, his whole body shaking. Those striking blue eyes met her gaze, and he shook his head, wavy dark hair falling into his face. "Motherfucking Jax."

"Can you help us?" she asked, trying not to be offended by his response. It had to seem weird that two strangers appearing out of nowhere begged for this kind of favor.

"Only because I already owe him a favor." He pushed his hair off his forehead.

"Thank you!" She bounced from foot to foot. "Thank you so much for your help. You have no idea—"

He held up a hand to stop her. "Save it. I don't need you to grovel. It's clearly important to Jax, or he wouldn't have told you I could even do this. It's not something I publicize. People tend to take advantage of wielders who can jump."

She nodded, hardly hearing what he said and only wishing they could go already. She slid her pack to the ground and pulled out the map while Fynn stood up and approached them.

"Is that the elf that's been around town?" Mehta said, as he beheld Fynn up close for the first time. Something about his tone told her exactly where this conversation was going.

Nova straightened. Not this again. She'd never encountered this kind of intolerance of elves in Arkwood, but the wielders in Aerdmure were certainly testing her patience. "Yes. That better not be an issue."

But Mehta still eyed Fynn closely. Their statures were similar: where Jax was more lean, Mehta seemed to match Fynn muscle for muscle and inch for inch. Mehta's eyes drifted down toward the elf's belt but if he was surprised or threatened by the weapons sheathed there, he didn't show it. His face remained unchanged.

"We don't have time for prejudices. Jax trusts Fynn. So let's get to it." She pointed to the spot on the map where they had deduced the remnants of the lab were. "This is where we need to go."

The wielder moved his gaze from Fynn and studied the spot on the map. "That's not an easy jump. If I'm taking both of you, we may need to make a stop or two along the way."

She rolled the map back up and shoved it back in her pack. "How long will it take?"

Mehta looked at her and appeared to finally see the determination on her face. "An hour maybe?"

"Then we leave now." She threw her fiercest stare at the wielder and waited, tapping her foot.

Finally, after what felt like hours but was probably mere seconds, Mehta held out his hand. "Hold on tight."

Nova and Fynn exchanged a glance, then Fynn nodded at her to take Mehta's hand first. She placed hers in the dark hand he offered, taking great pains to suppress the tremble coursing through her body. Fynn then placed his on top of hers and squeezed, both for her own comfort but also for his security in the coming jump.

Nova had never jumped before and didn't know what to expect. Very few witches could do it, only wielders were even able to attempt it, and even fewer could do it while carrying others. What did that mean about Mehta's powers?

But she quickly cast the thought aside and focused instead on maintaining the hold on his hand.

Without warning, Mehta jumped, literally jumped into the air, bringing the two of them with him. The world shot by in a blur as they continued moving, spinning and whipping around in every direction. Unlike when Fynn carried her while running, where she could still feel the steadying presence of the ground and recognize the shapes of whatever they were whizzing past, this time she could see nothing. Could *feel* nothing aside from Fynn and Mehta's hands on hers.

Her lungs constricted, her eyes watered, and her head started to throb, but she held on tight. She didn't even want to guess what would happen if she somehow loosened her grip.

Her stomach lurched into a somersault. Were they descending now? Mehta shouted something that sounded like "Brace!" but she couldn't hear well enough over the rush of the wind. Her feet slammed into something unbearably hard, and her knees buckled, forcing her to lose her grip on Mehta and fall.

The wind had been completely knocked out of her, and her hip ached from the impact. She caught her breath, then raised herself up on her elbows and looked around. They appeared to be in the forest, their surroundings similar to what she and Fynn had hiked through on their way to Aerdmure. The ground was flat again, not sloping and rocky like it was closer to the Worgreth Mountains.

"Are you ok?" Fynn knelt at her side, placing a hand on her cheek. A beam of moonlight snuck through the canopy and illuminated his face.

A quick body scan revealed no major pains other than what would likely be a bruise on her hip tomorrow. She nodded to him. His eyes held hers for a moment, softening, before he looked up at Mehta.

"When can we go again?"

Mehta looked around their landing point and up at the stars barely visible through the canopy, taking in their bearings. "We made it further than I expected. We can either go again in ten minutes and make one more stop or if you give me twenty minutes, I may be able to get you the rest of the way without a stop."

"Twenty," Nova said, digging her thumb into her hip to massage out the sore spot.

Mehta nodded. "Then I need to meditate. It helps me recover my powers more quickly. Do not disturb me."

He sat cross-legged on the ground and placed his hands on his knees. His eyes drifted closed, and his face softened completely, blocking out all sights and sounds around them.

The moon was thankfully bright enough to cast a glow around them, but the canopy of the trees prevented it from illuminating too much. Nova could barely see past their little landing area, but Fynn would be able to see much further.

"I assume you scouted?" she asked him quietly, trying not to distract Mehta.

Fynn nodded, coming to sit a few feet away. "I did a quick scope of the area when we touched down. There's nothing around, or at least nothing awake. And no signs of human, witch, or elf presence either, just wildlife."

"Good." She crossed her legs and scooted closer to where Fynn was seated. "Raelyn's got to be ok, right?"

Fynn took her hands and brought them to his lips. "We will be there soon. We will save her."

Not the words she had been hoping for, but then again what did she expect? Fynn wouldn't promise that Raelyn was fine without being able to know for sure. He wasn't one to give false hope, or to make promises he couldn't keep.

They sat in silence for the rest of the break, though Fynn did offer to help massage out her hip. She gratefully accepted. When Mehta finally stood up and announced he was ready again, Nova stood quickly. She gripped his hand with even more fervor than last time and tensed her body. Now that she had experienced it once, she could better prepare herself for the landing. Fynn placed his hand on hers and nodded to Mehta.

This time the jump didn't seem so intense. The air around them still spun, wind whistling in her ears and making it impossible to see anything, but it seemed to go much quicker. When they landed, her knees buckled again, but not so much that she fell over.

She looked around, and again it seemed like just a wooded area. Surely this wasn't the right spot? There didn't appear to be a building that could have been a lab or even an entrance to an underground tunnel system anywhere.

"I'm sorry," Mehta panted, his hands pressing into his knees. "I couldn't get quite far enough. But the location you want," he pointed off to their left, "is about a hundred yards that way."

Fynn nodded. "I hear the river. We are close, Al."

Nova turned to Mehta and hoped she could pass enough gratitude through her gaze. "Thank you. I truly appreciate it. Now get home and rest up because Jax will be there soon and need to join us here."

"I'm gonna kill that motherfucker," Mehta said, but with a grin on his face. He waved his hand. "You go, I need twenty to rest again before I can jump myself back to Aerdmure."

Fynn reached out for her hand, and she grasped it, giving herself a moment to feel the pulse of magic flowing through her before she took her first step. Though her weary body protested every movement, her magic thrummed in her veins, unconstrained, strong. As long as she could keep her mind sharp as well, she could handle Blackmore.

Was that confidence? Was that what it felt like? To believe you could do something you'd never done?

Fynn led her through the brush and trees, following the sound of the river and showing her where to step so they made as little noise as possible. Nothing seemed amiss around them: the forest was quiet and still.

But Blackmore was lurking somewhere in this area, holding Raelyn captive.

41

THE CRACKLING AND BUBBLING sounds of water sweeping by rocks alerted her to the presence of the river before she could see it, but soon it appeared in front of them. The riverbed was wide enough that there was a significant break in the tree line, allowing the moon to shine down and light up the water, sparkles reflecting off it and onto their faces when they stopped at its edge.

"Now what?" Nova looked around for any signs of life, of Blackmore and Raelyn. Clearly the lab was not in an above ground building, so they must be looking for an underground entrance. But there was nothing around to indicate the presence of anything other than wildlife.

They'd come to the wrong place. Raelyn wasn't anywhere nearby. A lump started to form in her throat as visions of Raelyn—Raelyn tortured, Raelyn dead—flooded her mind. Fynn's hand in hers was the only reason she remained standing.

He squeezed her hand. She shook the images of her sister from her mind and looked up at him, his other hand pointing across the river.

"There."

And sure enough, across from them and down a few yards, was a huge pile of brush, looking like it had recently and hastily been moved.

Next to it was a patch of ground that was obscured in their current view, but looked bare and could easily have been a doorway.

The lump in her throat dissipated, but the visions of Raelyn crept back into her mind, a constant reminder of her goal.

Save her sister.

Without a word, Fynn scooped her up, ready to carry her across the river.

"No, please...let me," she said, and he lowered her back to the ground.

Closing her eyes, she summoned up her magic, calling on those powers that harkened to water. She brought her hands slowly up in front of her until they were shoulder height, and then, feeling the weight of the water and the pressure of the current against her, she pushed her hands outward and opened her eyes.

The river had split in front of them, creating a small, dry, walking path for them to cross the river safely.

"I will never not be blown away by you," Fynn said, with a quick kiss in her hair.

She smiled broadly, lowering her hands, but the water stayed put.

They crossed quickly and then turned back toward the river. She snapped her fingers, and the water collapsed with a splash, flowing back to its normal rhythm.

She expected to feel drained from the use of her magic, but somehow, instead, her body awakened. As if the magic itself made her more alive, more refreshed.

They approached the pile of brush and sure enough, there was a doorway built into the ground just next to it. A shattered padlock lay cast aside in the brush.

Fynn reached for the handle but turned back to her first. "Ready?"

"Open the damn door."

Fynn yanked the door open with such a creak that she was certain their element of surprise was now lost. But as they descended a steep staircase into the tunnel, illuminated by torches that must have been recently lit, it became obvious that any sound they made would be drowned out by the hallway ahead of them.

The tunnel was long and wide, with no signs of doors or rooms on either side for as far as she could see, and lined with debris in the form of rocks, large and small. She and Fynn walked hand in hand down the hallway, mud squelching beneath their shoes. Silent, enchanted flames flickered on the torches casting shadows along the cracked stone walls, and a chill raced up her spine despite the warmth that filled the air.

"We should get in and get out as fast as possible." Fynn's voice was barely audible so as not to attract attention. "If this is the lab that Blackmore destroyed, I don't trust it to not cave in on us."

But there was a dull hum vibrating off Nova's skin, a slight stickiness to the air that caught in her nose and lungs, only noticeable now that she was searching for it. "I sense magic—enchantments—are holding this place together. Probably Blackmore's work? But you're right. We shouldn't linger."

They had made it nearly halfway down the tunnel when Fynn whispered, "I hear someone."

He pointed toward the end, where the tunnel appeared to open into a large chamber lit by more torches. There were a few closed doors flanking the open chamber on either side of the hallway. Her heart leapt. *Raelyn*. She was so close.

She wanted to run, but that would draw attention. Instead, she quickened her pace, checking that her magic was ready if she needed to call on it and trying to remain as quiet as possible as they moved along the corridor. When she reached the end, her heart nearly bursting from her chest, she managed to restrain herself and hide in the shadows along the wall. Fynn, across from her, mimicked her, so they could take in the room around them before entering.

The inside was expansive. The ceiling towered higher than the one in the hallway—they must have gone further underground than Nova realized. Piles of rubble littered the floor, along with broken chairs and tables, some appearing charred and some splintered. Cracks lined the walls of the room as well. Had they always been there or were they a remnant of the destruction that had occurred here? Was this place still safe for them to enter?

And there, off to the left was Raelyn, lying on the ground, appearing to be asleep. Or worse.

But no, her head was propped up on something—a folded up blanket? A backpack? It was too hard to tell from here, but a dead woman wouldn't need a pillow. That had to mean Raelyn was—

Nova gasped and wanted to call out to her sister but hadn't yet seen Blackmore. Before she could go to Raelyn, she needed to find him. She looked over at Fynn and tilted her head in Raelyn's direction. He pointed toward the other side of the room in response.

Leaning forward slightly to see what he was pointing at, she found Blackmore, sitting at an upright but still broken desk, his head hung in his hands. He was either studying something on the desk, or he was somehow sleeping in that awkward position. But his back was to them, so if they did this right, they could have Raelyn out and Blackmore down before he even realized they were there.

She looked back toward Fynn, pointing to him and then to Raelyn, to signal that he should check on her and get her out. Then she pointed to herself and Blackmore, to show that she would handle him. Fynn raised an eyebrow in response, but she shook her head.

She could do this. She could shield all three of them against him.

Her magic came alive inside her, excited for the opportunity to showcase itself.

Fynn nodded and held up three fingers. He lowered one; she drew in a deep breath and tried to settle her nerves. Then he lowered another; she turned her head to focus on her target, her mind made up on what she was going to do. Then he lowered the final one and took off.

Fynn was quiet and stealthy as he moved toward Raelyn. She watched him reach her, place a hand on her back, and then waited for his nod of reassurance.

Raelyn was ok.

Now it was her turn.

She drew in a sharp breath as she took two steps in Blackmore's direction, preparing to cast a spell so that he would neither hear nor see them.

But she didn't make it any further. Blackmore spun quickly in his chair and looked up at her, with green eyes that seemed familiar somehow, but were rimmed with red. A wild look appeared on his tanned and hardened face, but not a look of anger, not one of revenge, not one of retribution or greed. No, this look was one of...relief? Admiration?

She stopped in her tracks, but kept her body tense, magic ready to attack, unsure why she decided to wait and not follow through with her original plan. Something about him, maybe those familiar eyes, maybe that facial expression, maybe the fact that up close he seemed weakened and helpless from all those years in Mistfell, made her pause, taking a moment to see what he would do first. Behind her, she hoped that Fynn was already assessing Raelyn and moving her towards the corridor.

Blackmore opened his mouth to speak, his voice cracking as he said the words that shattered Nova's world.

"It's you. Allie...my daughter."

42

A DEAFENING SILENCE FILLED the room.

Nova heard nothing, not even the sound of her own heartbeat, of her own breath, as she stared into Blackmore's eyes—familiar because they looked like *her* eyes—which were welling with tears. Her mind was spinning at the revelation he had just professed. It couldn't be true, and yet...

Her magic was swirling and spinning within her, as happily as it did when Fynn was next to her. Her magic...the wielder powers that shouldn't have been possible if she had descended from a long line of geos.

But here—here was Blackmore, a wielder himself.

Calling her Allie. The same name that Benedict had used. Benedict had known, that was why he looked at her the way he did. That was why he'd been surprised beyond belief to see her, why he told her she had nothing to fear from Blackmore.

Maybe Blackmore was right. But her heart couldn't accept it.

Finally, she found her voice. "My name is Nova."

Blackmore smiled sheepishly and dug his toes into the ground. "Yes, Alinova. A beautiful name that your mother picked out. But we called you Allie."

She shook her head, finally breaking his stare and casting her eyes briefly at the rocky ceiling high above. "This can't be right. You killed your family; you killed your daughter."

A single tear escaped and slid down Blackmore's cheek, and her heart involuntarily clenched at the sight. Why was she feeling sympathy for this man?

"I did not. But I couldn't protect them either."

"Who *did* kill them then?" Her voice dripped with unintended fury, and she clenched her fists in an attempt to calm herself, to settle her magic. *Breathe, breathe.*

To Blackmore's credit, he seemed unphased by her tone. His eyes met hers again, his expression unchanged. "That's a question we would need to ask the man who stole you from me."

Of course. If Blackmore was her true father, then Luc...Luc and Raella were nothing to her. Kidnappers, if Blackmore's story was in fact true. Was that why Raella had never treated her the same as she had treated Raelyn? Not out of favoritism but because...Nova wasn't her daughter at all? Because she had been thrust upon them, leaving them with a giant secret to harbor? Her physical differences had always set her apart from Raelyn but was it possible that they meant she wasn't *actually* her sister?

Raelyn. Raelyn wasn't her sister. She had no siblings.

This must be the reason why Blackmore had been targeting her specifically. Why Luc had suppressed her powers.

Luc hadn't wanted her to find out that she was different, that she was a wielder, and start questioning her parentage.

Blackmore wanted to find her, not to *harm* her, but so he could see his daughter once again. To reunite with her and see for himself she was alive.

And Luc had hidden her. Had stolen her away and hidden her for decades. Why?

Her mind was spinning, and she put her hands to her temples to try to silence it. Blackmore took a step toward her, right arm outstretched, but she retreated, taking a step back of her own. She wasn't sure she could trust him and didn't want to be near him right now.

Raelyn. That's why she was here, to save her sister—no, just her friend?—and to get back to safety together.

She turned slightly, keeping Blackmore in her periphery but looking for Fynn and Raelyn. Across the room, Raelyn was sitting up with Fynn at her side, drinking from his water skin and otherwise looking unharmed. There was no way Raelyn was aware of what had just transpired between Nova and Blackmore, but she had been around Fynn long enough, had underestimated his hearing enough times to not make that mistake again.

His ears had picked up the whole conversation.

"I promise I did not harm her."

Blackmore's voice was kind, not cruel as she looked his way again. He clasped his hands together in front of him. "I hated that I had to bring her here, hated that you would fear for her, but I knew you would come for her."

"You used her as bait," she said through gritted teeth, turning back to face him.

Blackmore winced. "I suppose. Though as I said, it pained me to do it. I can tell how much you both mean to each other."

"How?"

"We talked, she and I." He tucked his hands into the pockets of his tattered trousers. "Once we got here, I told her everything. She was as surprised as you are but wanted to wait for you to get all the answers to her questions. I wasn't sure how long it would take for you to find us, so I was letting her sleep while we waited."

"Was she hurt in the explosion?" Nova hadn't spotted any injuries on her sister but then again, she hadn't looked closely yet.

"Only cuts and scrapes. You must have done one hell of a job shielding both of you." Pride shone through his eyes. "I healed her as soon as we got here."

But something still didn't make sense. Nova crossed her arms, narrowing her eyes at him. "If what you say is true, why did you cause the explosion? You could have killed us."

"I didn't, I swear on my life." Blackmore held his hands up in resignation.

"Then who—"

He sighed. "My guess is that Benedict had the whole house rigged to blow. He never used to let his paranoia get the best of him, but two and a half decades in isolation will change you..." His voice trailed off, but the words he didn't say hung in the air.

Two and a half decades in Mistfell had changed *him*.

Maybe it had even caused him to go mad enough to blow up a house. "How do I know you're telling the truth, that you didn't just try to kill us?"

His shoulders fell, strands of hair falling into his face. "As a human, he wouldn't have been able to cause the explosion magically. He would've needed an ignition source. Did you see anything that could have been one?"

Benedict's frantic search. He'd started looking for something as soon as Esta had left in search of Blackmore. That must have been what he was looking for. And he must have found it.

She glared at Blackmore for a moment, her resolve still hardened, but her eyes beginning to soften. This man in front of her didn't seem like a ruthless murderer, like a power-hungry monster.

He seemed kind. Compassionate.

"Nova!" Raelyn's voice called from across the room. She broke Blackmore's gaze, slightly more confident that he wouldn't harm her while her back was turned, and ran to Raelyn, kneeling beside her and grabbing her hand. Fynn recapped his water skin.

"Are you alright?" she asked, surveying Raelyn for signs of injury and finding none, just as Blackmore had said.

"I'm fine!" Raelyn said, smiling. "Did he tell you?"

She nodded, looking at Fynn who nodded back at her, confirming he had heard what Blackmore had said.

"There are so many unanswered questions. But also, so many that now have answers." Raelyn tucked her curls behind her ears, her tone dreamlike.

"I know, Rae," Nova said, rubbing her sister's arm. "But right now, we need to get out of here. Get all of us to safety."

"No!" Raelyn straightened her back and moved her arm from Nova's grasp. "No, Nova, we are staying. This man could have hurt me—*killed* me—but instead he healed me from the explosion. He says he's your father. He clearly has a story to tell. We need to hear him out." She paused, then added, "*You* need to hear him out."

Nova looked to Fynn for help, but he shook his head, adding delicately, "I'm with Raelyn on this one. You need to hear his story. You'll always wonder if you don't, and this could be your only chance."

She swallowed, looking between the two of them, the two most important people in her life. Raelyn, who had always been her rock, the one constant she could rely on, always. And Fynn, new but no less important, the one who had helped her grow, who had pushed her to be more, to become what she wanted to be and not what others forced on her.

With a deep inhale, she stood, Raelyn and Fynn joining her. She looked over her shoulder to where Blackmore was waiting, expectantly, hands clasped.

They could leave now and find a way to alert Luc and the other governors to Blackmore's whereabouts, get him sent back to Mistfell or more likely, executed for his escape. She could pretend she had never heard his confession, go back to living in the city, teaching students, and practicing her wielding. Life would go on.

But didn't she owe it to herself to hear the truth? So much of her life had changed over the last few weeks and for what? Just to go back to how she had been before he escaped? If his story was true, then this man, her real father, had risked everything just to see her, just to try to know her. Luc certainly never showed her that kind of fatherly love.

So she approached Blackmore, Fynn and Raelyn not far behind her, and said, "I'd like to hear the rest of your story. But I think I need a drink first."

43

"**W**HERE SHOULD I BEGIN?"

The four of them had settled down on the floor of the room, after searching for four unbroken chairs and coming up empty handed. Blackmore had checked the remnants of what had once been his office and found a bottle of whiskey still there, dusty but corked, hidden in a cupboard built into the stone wall. He found a few dusty glasses in the same cupboard, which Nova quickly cleaned with a wave of her hand. Fynn politely declined a glass, but Raelyn insisted on taking the first sip, nearly spitting it out when it touched her tongue.

"Oh, *hell* no," she had said, taking the bottle in her hands. A faint blue glow had surrounded the bottle and then disappeared, leaving the brown liquid inside looking the same. But the second time she sipped, she smiled. "Much better."

Blackmore had downed his glass and set it down in front of him on the floor. His body was lean, no doubt from the two and a half decades in Mistfell. His eyes were sunken and his hair, like Benedict's, was graying. His shirt and pants were tattered and stained, which Nova found odd. Why couldn't he have just conjured up new clothes each day? Or at the very least mended the ones he was wearing?

"Maybe at the beginning?" she finally replied, setting down her whiskey glass so she could rebraid her hair. Fynn, watching her fingers work, scooted a little closer. "What led you to start your research?"

Blackmore nodded and cast his eyes at each one of them.

"I had always dreamed of a free and harmonious society. The history lessons I had learned in school as a child frightened me and, frankly, disgusted me. I didn't understand how we could live in a society where people were seen as inferior just because they didn't have magic. Magic should not be a way to suppress. It should be a way to enlighten."

His eyes lit up slightly when he spoke, and Nova could tell this was his true passion. Deep down, he really believed in total equality. At his core, he believed that people are inherently good and would use magic to help one another.

"But the genetics of magic weren't well understood. It's long been...not banned, per se, but frowned upon to look into genetics, outside of healers' work. When I met my wife, your mother, Wynna," his eyes twinkled in Nova's direction, "and learned more about what healers know and can do, I realized there may be a way to unlock magic if we study the genetic code."

Her insides twisted as she thought about her birth mother, who even Raella had revered. "What was she like?" Nova asked quietly. She tied off the end of her braid, letting the end fall over her chest, and picked up her glass.

Blackmore looked at her with a small smile. "Another time, Allie. Sorry, *Nova*," he corrected, causing her cheeks to warm. She brought her whiskey to her lips to hide it.

He continued. "As you all know, all research proposals must be approved and funded by the governors. At the time when Wynna and I first started drafting our proposal, we knew the governors would never go for it. They were an older lot, many reaching an age when most would choose to retire, but of course, those in power never like to relinquish it. Over the next two years, while we busied ourselves with other smaller projects, four of those governors either passed on or retired, and a new generation of governors was elected to take their place. One of them being Luc Astor."

"Father," Raelyn whispered.

Blackmore nodded, leaning back and planting his hands on the ground behind him for support. "We had crossed paths before. Wynna and Raella were old school friends and though they had grown apart as they got older, they kept in touch. The four of us got together to celebrate Luc's election, and to announce Wynna's pregnancy, when we decided to socialize our idea. See what he would think of it.

"He was enamored. I could see a spark in his eye at the thought of finding a way to provide magic for the whole population of Astria. He went on about what it could mean for the next generation, hinting that he and Raella were also trying to conceive, something Wynna would later use her healer skills to help Raella with."

This time he smiled at Raelyn, who must have been the outcome of that help.

"Anyway, Luc convinced us the time was right to seek approval from the governors, that he would speak to them and make sure we got at least the minimum votes for approval. We were delighted when just two months later, we were moving into this very lab to begin working, with the three new recruits we had found along the way."

"Margot, Hendl, and Benedict," Nova said.

Blackmore nodded, leaning forward again. "I know you've spoken with Benedict. I'll touch on his betrayal later."

Next to her, Fynn straightened and whipped his head toward the door.

"Did you hear something?" she asked him.

He nodded. "Hopefully just Jax and Esta, but it seems too soon for them to arrive." He stood, squeezing her shoulder on the way up. "I'll go check it out."

Blackmore started at the name and looked up at Fynn. "Jax? Margot's son?"

"Yes." Fynn's hand rested on his sword. "He's been training Nova and was with us at Benedict's cabin."

Blackmore's eyes widened, and he ran a hand down his cheek. Nova quickly jumped in. "He's fine, don't worry. Fynn, bring them here so he can see for himself."

Fynn nodded and turned toward the entrance, his footsteps silent on the dirt floor. When he was out of sight, Blackmore cleared his throat and continued.

"You were born a few months into the research," Blackmore said to her, his eyes watering. "I will never forget that day. How proud I was of Wynna, how elated I was to hear your cry the first time, how I felt an overwhelming surge of magic the first time I held you, like I needed to protect you forever." He paused. "I'm so sorry I wasn't able to."

Unable to come up with anything to say, she just sipped her whiskey, now almost gone, and nodded in reply.

"As you neared your first birthday, we finally got our breakthrough. I regret that I spent so much of those months staying here late," he waved his hands around the space, "running tests and calculations until the wee hours of the morning, rather than spending them with you. Then came the day I told Wynna I thought I had it. We had finally found the genetic sequence in our DNA that our magic derives from, and the codes for each of the six types of magical abilities in witches: geo, pyro, hydro, aero, healer, and wielder.

"I summoned our partners here to the lab to let them know and to celebrate. But Benedict never arrived. Instead, we were accosted by soldiers, insisting that Wynna, Margot, and Hendl were to be executed without a trial and that I was to be taken to Mistfell. They said the governors, the very ones who had approved our study, now deemed it to be heretical and dangerous to society. All knowledge of it had to be eliminated."

His throat caught and his eyes glazed over with a haunted glow. She and Raelyn remained silent and waited for him to collect himself and finish the story.

"They told me they killed you," he whispered to her, his voice cracking. "Wynna lost it, absolutely lost it, and then I lost her, too. I watched all three of them die before me. Margot and Hendl were suffocated. Wynna was—" he choked back a sob "—burned."

Nova gasped and a tear slipped down her cheek. Raelyn's hand grabbed hers, and when she looked over, she found her sister was crying too.

Her mother had met such a horrific end.

"I had nothing left to live for." Blackmore gazed at the floor. "My family was gone. My work was gone. I let them take me without a fight. Let them stick me in a cell and do whatever they wanted to me. I was numb, dead inside." He lifted his gaze to hers. "Until I found reason to believe you were still alive."

Raelyn gasped this time, and Nova's mind whirled. Had he escaped from Mistfell to find her, so that they could be reunited? Not to get revenge on Luc after all, but to see the daughter he had assumed was dead?

"About ten years ago, a new prisoner was brought in, and he was a talker. Liked to run his mouth. Luc had apparently been the one to apprehend him for a string of piracy, so he spent most of his time talking about Luc and the Astor family. He particularly liked to joke about one of Luc's daughters, and if I recall his exact words, he said 'the older one may as well not be a witch.' I think he truly believed she was a disgrace to the Astor family, and he didn't understand—nor did I if I'm being honest—why Luc kept her around and didn't disown her. But he liked to describe her, and knowing Raella and Luc personally, I didn't understand how they had produced a daughter who had long dark hair and green eyes."

Blackmore's green eyes met her own, mirror images reflecting each other. "He didn't last long in the prison and then I largely forgot about the whole thing. Until a year ago, when another prisoner snuck in a newsprint, and it had a family picture of the Astors on the front, with a caption that said 'Luc, Raella and their daughters Raelyn, 23, and Nova, 24, both teachers, attended the opening ceremony together.'

"Before I could even look at your face closely, I was caught off guard by your ages. And your name. Raella had just had a baby the week before I was sent to Mistfell. Wynna had attended the birth. But they didn't name her right away, and I never learned what the name was. But it had been twenty-three years in prison at that point for me, not twenty-four. So where had this older daughter come from?"

Nova stayed close to Raelyn, her heart pounding and her magic demanding an outlet as her emotions tensed.

"When I looked more closely at your face, Nova, I was taken aback. You look just like Wynna. A spitting image. As beautiful as she was in every way." He brushed away a stray tear from his cheek.

"And that's when I realized. Luc hadn't had you killed. For some reason, he had spared your life, had taken you in and paraded you as his own daughter. Who would question a governor? But you were alive. And it gave me renewed life, a new purpose. I needed to see you, to talk to you, to try to make you understand the truth. That's when I started planning my escape."

"Ah, so that's how it went."

A new voice thundered from the doorway to the room, causing Raelyn to jump, spilling the rest of her drink, and Nova to fly to her feet, sparks dancing at her fingertips. But Blackmore just stayed where he was, all color draining from his face when he beheld whoever had spoken.

Nova whipped her head around to the entryway to see the owner of that voice, and her stomach sank through the floor.

Luc.

He had found them and was glaring at them with a smile so wicked that dark magic could have been wrapped up in it. And behind him stood Persy, clutching the arm of a bound and gagged Fynn in his right hand.

"Well, well, well, Kael, isn't this a nice little reunion?"

44

"**F**ATHER!" RAELYN CRIED, BRINGING her hand to her mouth.

Nova's blood was boiling. This man, who had suppressed her power, who had made her believe she was someone she's not...this man was a murderer, a kidnapper, and a liar. If Blackmore' story was true—and the more he told her, the more it filled in the gaps of her own life and recent events, the more she believed it—then Luc was not only *not* her father, but he was also a criminal. An utterly corrupt politician.

And he now had Fynn in his clutches.

"Let Fynn go." Her voice came out with a strength and power she hadn't known she possessed, echoing off the cracked stone walls.

She looked Fynn in the eyes, and he looked back at her with a hardened gaze, as if he didn't want her to do anything stupid in the name of saving him. But she'd be damned if Luc was going to get away with any more destruction on her watch.

She was done being a puppet in someone else's life.

Done standing by on the sidelines, inept and disgraced.

"You know," Luc said, stroking his chin, "I don't think I will. He failed in his job to protect you, failed to listen to his father, his superior, when we found you in Aerdmure, failed to alert us when you found

Benedict or Blackmore. Seems he needs to be brought down a notch or two in Mistfell."

Raelyn whimpered, but Nova used her new-found resolve to stay strong, not letting her face falter or show any sign of weakness. If Fynn was the reason she had become more sure of herself, more powerful, then a threat to his life, one that she could eliminate with these new powers, would *not* take her back to where she had come from: weak and powerless.

For him, she could be strong.

For him, she could fight.

She replied, "I hardly think that those charges warrant a trip to Mistfell."

Luc just laughed. "You forget who makes the rules." He started pacing toward where she and Raelyn were standing. "Now, I'm so sorry to interrupt this *family reunion*, but this one is late for his execution." He turned his gaze directly on Blackmore, who, to his merit, didn't cower or hide in fear, but rose from the ground and stood tall, with his shoulders back, ready to face whatever was thrown at him.

But it was Raelyn who jumped into action, intercepting Luc. "Father, he's innocent. He didn't kill anyone." She grabbed his arm and tried to hold him back.

Luc gazed at her, his lips snarling and his nostrils flaring. He'd never looked at either daughter with that much disgust. This was not a father Nova could defend.

This was not a father she could love.

"Oh, Rae, he's been feeding you his lies already, I see." He patted her hand, then plucked her fingers from his arm. "Don't worry, I'll make sure he pays for trying to rip apart our family."

Nova looked from Blackmore to Luc, from one father to another. The man who had given her life and the man who had raised her.

She felt no deep affection in either direction: Luc had never been the doting father to her that he had been to Raelyn, and the revelation of his suppression spell coupled with the felling of the tree in Aerdmure had just been the final straws for a separation that was a long time coming. And she had only known Blackmore for an hour or two, having spent the last few weeks believing him to be a murderer and a power-hungry monster.

But he was her real father. He had figured out a way to escape Mistfell—something that had never been done—and find her, all to tell her the truth. All just to see her again. He must have known that there was a good chance he would die if caught, possibly before getting to tell her his truth, *her* truth. That he wouldn't get to spend meaningful time with her. But to him, the risk had been worth it. To him, it was enough.

And that was a parental love she had never experienced.

Unconditional.

Selfless.

Pure.

So she stepped in front of Blackmore and faced Luc with her hands on her hips, using every fiber of her being to control and contain her power so her head stayed clear. Raelyn gasped, but Nova didn't break Luc's gaze to check on her. Fynn, just visible over Luc's shoulder, appeared to be smiling through the gag.

"There's only one criminal here tonight." She watched Luc for signs that he was about to use magic. She'd grown up with him, she knew all of them: a curl of his left fingers, a slight tilt of his head to the right. She doubted he'd try an earthquake while they were underground, but there were a multitude of other things he likely *would* try, and she needed to be ready to defend herself and her friends if he did.

She *was* ready.

"You," she continued, "you betrayed your friend and had his partners killed, his wife—my mother—killed, had his lab and his life's work destroyed. You kidnapped me, raised me as if I was your own, but neither you nor Raella loved me. Tell me, why didn't you just let me die? Why would you live with a tangible reminder of what you had done for almost twenty-five years?"

Her magic was building, feeding off her anger, but this time, she didn't have any problem containing it. This time, the wall she built to contain it stayed firm, more easily than it ever had before.

Luc laughed again, the sound ricocheting off the walls of the cavernous room. "If it had been up to me, you would have died. It was Raella who stopped me, told me I couldn't just let a baby die, an innocent. If she'd had her way, you would've been left at an orphanage. But I knew better. I knew that coming from the Blackmore line, you'd be powerful, and I wanted to keep an eye on you. So I brought you home instead.

"Raella was furious. Especially when you grew up to look so much like the friend she had lost. Because she did truly care for Wynna. But she could never love you."

He stopped talking for a moment and began pacing back and forth just a few feet in front of where she and Blackmore stood. She stole a glance at Raelyn and though she expected to see her crying, watching their father mournfully, Raelyn was eyeing him with a disdain equal to what she was feeling.

"That's why you allowed me to come to Aerdmure." Raelyn's voice was deep, angry. Nova had rarely heard such a tone from her before. "You knew Blackmore wasn't actually a threat, that he wouldn't hurt either of us. That I would be fine. But you wanted me to lure Nova back in the open to draw him out."

Luc's gaze drifted between Blackmore and Raelyn. "Well, of course, I couldn't be certain how Mistfell had changed him, but yes, I never actually believed that either of you were in danger from him. I did hope that you'd inspire Nova to do something foolish so I could catch him, and it looks like my plan worked. Here we are."

Nova clenched her fists, furious that she and Raelyn had fallen prey to his manipulation. But she kept her mind clear. She needed to keep him talking. She would have to strike eventually, but she'd be damned if she wasn't going to try to learn as much as she could about her true heritage along the way.

"How did you explain the sudden appearance of a new baby in your family, so soon after Raelyn was born?"

Another one of those vicious smiles. "Raella was worried about that. But I simply didn't say anything publicly. We hadn't yet announced Raelyn's birth so I think once we did—and it was many months later that we finally did announce it, once we had cleaned up this one's mess—" he waved a hand at Blackmore "—I guess the public just believed that we had kept you both secret for almost two years."

"What about the servants? Our grandparents?" Raelyn asked.

"Ah, now we're getting to the good part." Luc stopped pacing and stared directly at Blackmore. "You'll be thrilled to hear your discovery was correct."

Nova turned to look at Blackmore, her real father, over her shoulder. His face turned beet red, his fists clenched as he took one step forward and said, "You monster."

"You thought Benedict was the only one who wanted that power for himself? Ha! I saw the weakness in him immediately and asked him to report to me when you figured it out. Of course I wanted to take advantage of it for myself, but Kael, you have to know that if your discovery made it to the public, it would have resulted in war.

Humans demanding to have magic, witches all wanting to become wielders. Elves too proud to change their powers but also furious that they would now be the weakest race."

Blackmore's eyes sparkled ever so slightly with awe as he continued to stare Luc down. But the next moment, they hardened, and the words he spoke came out drenched in disgust.

"You changed your own power. You made yourself a wielder."

45

Nova, for the second time tonight, was stunned into silence while Raelyn screamed in despair. Fynn started fighting the ties that bound him. Only Persy remained unchanged, expressionless, focusing only on holding tighter to Fynn.

Blackmore's eyes darkened, now full of nothing but fury. "Luc, don't you see how bad this could be? I've had two and a half decades to think about this, about what I discovered, and you're right. It can never be allowed to get out. But for you to—"

Luc let out a low laugh. "Don't worry, don't worry. The secret is safe with me. I saw to the destruction personally, after changing myself, of course."

"You didn't, Father!" Raelyn finally managed to get out, her hand clasping her cheeks.

"I assure you, Rae, that I did." Luc's wicked grin spread wider as he faced his daughter. "How else would I have been able to change the memories of those closest to us? Or cast such a strong suppression spell on this one for as long as I did?" He waved his hand at Nova, her stomach curdling.

Fury boiled her blood. Sparks were flying off her fingertips again, spitting magic she could no longer contain.

But it was Blackmore who spoke first. "You did *what* to my daughter?!"

"He suppressed my magic for years. I didn't realize I was a wielder until a few weeks ago when I finally broke through it," she said, as calmly as she could muster, trying to will her magic back inside of her.

Luc laughed again. "She's always been a weakling. I really didn't have to try hard. She did a lot of the work for me."

Her anger flared again, hot and fiery, and flames shot out towards Luc's feet. Flames from *her* hands. He jumped away in time, but the embers continued to burn, just inches from where his toes had been. Raelyn shrieked, and Nova could have sworn a momentary panic flashed in Luc's eyes, but it disappeared quickly as he regained his composure.

"Learned a few things in Aerdmure, have we?" Luc took another small step back. "But still not able to fully control your emotions yet? It's like I said. *Weak.*"

His hand flew forward, then she was flying backwards, landing with a thud on the hard floor below her, her hip sounding off in pain and a snap coming from her left wrist. It took her a moment to figure out what had happened but then three things occurred at once that made it click for her.

Fynn roared and snapped out of the ties holding him together. He took advantage of the surprise on Persy's face and knocked him out with the hilt of his sword, moving faster than lightning.

Raelyn yelled, "Father, how could you?!"

And Blackmore charged for Luc with a renewed vigor, flinging his hands out in front of him as Luc tried to fight off an invisible force.

Luc had attacked her. Had harmed her.

Nova's eyes were locked on Blackmore and Luc while she completely ignored the pain in her wrist. Blackmore clearly hadn't let the years in Mistfell waste away his powers, but his physical weakness was showing as he tried to keep up with Luc's deflections. Anytime Blackmore shot out a spell, Luc dodged or threw up a shield, but he wasn't able to get out of a defensive position.

A firm hand gripped her shoulder and that scent she'd come to love filled her nose. She managed to pull her eyes away from the sparring long enough to turn toward the body that had knelt next to her.

Fynn.

He was staring at the limp wrist she was cradling next to her torso.

"It's broken. Can you heal it yourself?" he asked. His hair had come loose, and white-blonde strands were hanging in his face. Red marks lined his cheeks where the gag had been digging into them.

She winced as the pain throbbed for a moment before she was able to shut it back down.

Wait, did she shut out the pain using her magic? Was that something she could do? That was convenient.

"I'll wait for Jax to get here," she said, resting her cheek on the hand that still gripped her shoulder. "I've never healed something this bad before and would rather not try on myself."

Fynn's eyes widened, and his voice went quiet. "Jax and Esta."

She gaped at him. "They don't know."

She looked back up around the room.

Luc and Blackmore were still sparring in the middle of the room, neither yielding ground yet but both looking like they had been dealt blows through their shields. Persy was still lying in a heap by the entrance to the room. And Raelyn was kneeling on the floor a few feet away, confusion plastered all over her face. Like she couldn't decide whether to intervene and if so, on whose behalf.

It wasn't lost on Nova that all three of them were coming to terms with their fathers right now.

"If they get here before we have a chance to explain, they might attack the wrong person." She turned her attention back to Fynn and tried to summon as much bravery into her face as she could. "Go find them. Tell them what Blackmore told us. I think you heard enough to know the story. We can fill in the gaps later." The idea of Fynn leaving her side again made her want to collapse, but she had no idea how either Jax or Esta would react, what they would do, if they arrived while Blackmore and Luc were sparring.

Fynn's eyes widened. "Al, I can't just leave you—"

"Please, Fynn." Her good hand found his, lacing their fingers together. "I'd go, but I can't leave Raelyn."

But he shook his head. "We'll figure it out when they get here. I'm staying with you."

Raelyn's shriek brought her back to the fight around her, her face and Fynn's whipping in her sister's direction. Luc had cornered Blackmore, who had his hands up in front of his face, bloodshot eyes and quivering legs betraying how close he was to burning out.

"Please, Father, don't hurt him! You've done enough, stop this madness!" Raelyn stared at Luc with a ferocity Nova had never seen.

"Shut up, Raelyn," Luc called over his shoulder, not moving his gaze from Blackmore. "Blackmore alive, Blackmore with his truths, is a threat to our family, to our position of power."

"You're despicable," Raelyn spat at him, finding her way to her feet again.

Luc whirled towards her. "Excuse me?"

Blackmore lunged, taking advantage of Luc's attention on Raelyn. An icy gust of wind collided with Luc's back, enough to knock him down to his hands and knees. But the spell drained Blackmore, who was already approaching the limits of his power; he couldn't hold it longer than a few moments before the winds died out, leaving his breath ragged. He stumbled backward, finding a table to lean on for support.

Luc coughed and sputtered, then started to right himself when Raelyn spoke again.

"You heard me. You're despicable. An embarrassment of a father." She stepped in front of him and stared him down, her chestnut eyes full of a hatred Nova had not thought Raelyn was capable of.

Nova tried to call out to Raelyn, but her voice caught in her throat as Luc, still kneeling, threw out a hand and then curled his fingers into a fist.

Raelyn started gagging and clutching at her own throat.

No. Luc was *not* going to suffocate her. His treatment of Nova was one thing, but to harm his true daughter? His flesh and blood?

Nova would not stand for it.

She dropped Fynn's hand, stood up, and ran for Raelyn, ignoring Fynn and Blackmore's screams to stop. Holding her left hand close to her body, she skidded to a halt in front of Raelyn, whose lips were turning blue.

"You've done enough harm to this family, Luc."

And she threw every bit of power she could summon, every ounce of strength she had, through her right hand and straight at Luc.

His eyes grew large as the blast of power flung him across the room. He flew right over Blackmore's head, hit one of the overturned, broken tables, and sank behind it.

Once she was sure he wasn't going to reemerge, she turned towards Raelyn, who had knelt to the floor and was panting heavily but, thank Canta, the color returned to her face.

"He...attacked me." Red marks, not unlike the ones Nova had sported after the attack in the park, were starting to surround her neck, like Luc had physically tried to suffocate her with his bare hands. She swept Raelyn into her arms and held her there while she caught her breath. They had both lost a father, and while she may have gained another, Raelyn hadn't.

"Did you..." she sputtered in between gasps, her watery gaze focused on the location where Luc had disappeared.

Nova shook her head. "No, I couldn't. Despite how horrible he is, how awful he's treated us, I don't think I have the heart to kill anyone. I think he's just knocked out."

Blackmore approached and knelt next to them, Fynn just behind him. Nova looked up at them and could see Persy kneeling in the doorway just over Fynn's shoulder, his face a mask of confusion.

"Are you both alright?" Blackmore asked them. His breath was still heavy, and his hands were shaky, but his voice at least sounded strong.

She nodded up at him in response, noting the pain she could see in his eyes. But it wasn't his own physical pain. It was the pain, the fear, the concern of someone who is worried about someone they care for. The pain a parent might feel if their child is in danger. The pain she had suffered watching Raelyn nearly suffocate.

She had never seen a look like that on Luc's face.

Her wrist throbbed, but the ache was dull, her magic still suppressing most of the pain. Perhaps it was aided by adrenaline.

"I never thought he'd..." Persy's voice trailed off from the doorway, shaking his head and standing.

Blackmore turned and gave him a weak smile. "Then I hope we can count on your testimony to help bring the man to justice."

Fynn tensed, his hand grabbing his sword as he looked over his shoulder at his own father. "Yes, this would be the perfect opportunity to redeem yourself, Father."

Persy didn't answer, but instead his eyes wandered the room. His gaze rested on the stack of tables Luc had fallen behind.

"What do we do now?" Raelyn asked, sitting up a little straighter, pulling her knees to her chest.

Nova shook her head. Would they be able to get Blackmore released? His story made sense, especially after hearing Luc's corroboration. And if it were true, then he hadn't committed any crimes, especially the ones he was imprisoned for. Was there a way for him to become a free man? A man she could spend time with?

Could she start a new life with her real father?

And what would happen to Luc? His offenses were capital, but would anyone believe them? Would the other governors truly sentence him to death? What would that mean for Raella, for Raelyn?

Blackmore spoke first, and her heart swelled at his fatherly ability to take charge of the situation. "Well, first we need to get you both to safety. And we need to get a healer to look at you."

"Jax can heal us." Nova looked up at Fynn, who was still standing protectively over her. "They should be here any minute, right?"

As if on cue, his head spun to face his father in the doorway. Persy had turned to look over his shoulder as well, his brow still furrowed in confusion. A moment later, Nova heard footsteps echoing down the corridor.

Jax and Esta appeared, winded and out of breath, but safe and unharmed.

46

"WHAT THE HELL IS going on?"

Jax's voice reverberated off the stone and dirt walls of the former laboratory.

Esta ran straight for Raelyn, with a show of emotion that Nova never imagined possible for her. Her sister was now in the hands of someone else who could protect her, so Nova stood, shakily, and faced Jax, Fynn reaching out a hand to steady her as she did. He pulled her delicately toward Jax.

"Fix it," he said to Jax, pointing at the limp wrist she was still holding.

But Jax was staring over their shoulders at something behind them. Nova turned to look and saw Blackmore, standing now, with his hands clasped in front of him and a weak smile on his face. Her gaze turned back to Jax, who had turned beet red, his fist tightly clenched.

"Why isn't he dead?" Jax spat, his eyes fixed on Blackmore.

She opened her mouth to speak but Fynn beat her to it. "Fix Nova first, then we'll tell you everything."

Jax's arm swung back, like he meant to throw a punch at Fynn, but the elf was faster, gripping Jax's arm in his hand and pushing it away. "Don't you dare."

"You're working with him?" Jax's voice was booming, but slightly fractured. "All this time, you've been working with him? While I was teaching—"

"Jax, stop please," Nova said, moving to stand right in front of him, still clutching her injured wrist to her chest. "It's not what you think. We can explain. We're all on the same side. We all want justice for your mother. You have to trust us."

He paused, his chest heaving under the weight of his anger, but slowing with every exhale. His green eyes moved back and forth among Fynn, Nova, and Blackmore, until finally his shoulders dropped. He tilted his face down to her wrist, not reacting at all to the unnatural angle at which it was bent.

"I'd have thought you capable of healing it yourself." His tone was still tense, but there was a hint of its usual spirit.

She stared him down, reciprocating his tone. "My instructor hasn't yet covered complex healing, and I didn't want to get it wrong."

"Fair enough. I'll talk you through it." Jax's tone softened as he placed his hand lightly on her wrist, his eyes continuing to flick between Nova and Blackmore warily. "I'm using my hand now to scan your bones for the exact break. It doesn't quite allow me to visualize what is going on so much as reflect the damage in my own body. Ah, yes, there it is. Now I'm told this next part can hurt momentarily, but I'm going to focus my magic on that spot with the break. Healing magic is a bit different to summon than the others and can give most wielders trouble, but with practice it can become second nature."

Sure enough, a small surge of energy trickled into her wrist and with a zap of pain that nearly made her yank her hand from his grasp, her bones shifted inside. The pain subsided, then Jax removed his hand, and she swiveled her wrist slowly in both directions.

"Thank you," she breathed in relief.

Jax nodded, then turned to acknowledge Blackmore, his features hardening again. "*You.*"

Blackmore, standing slightly behind her, smiled weakly. "Jax. You're all grown up."

Jax crossed his arms and glared at him. "Someone better start talking."

Nova quickly recounted Blackmore's story for Jax and Esta, letting Blackmore fill in some of the gaps himself. Esta stayed seated on the floor with Raelyn, but her mouth gaped open. Jax paced back and forth across the room as he listened, his arms crossed, gaze cast to the wall across the room.

When she finished, he looked over at Blackmore, his eyes blazing. "So, you had nothing to do with my mother's death."

"No, I respected your mother so much, and your uncle, too, for that matter. I would never have harmed either of them. Margot and Hendl were some of my oldest friends, and I was always in awe of their magical bond. I'm so, so sorry for you and your father. Losing her must have been horrible for you both."

Jax softened, slightly, and Nova exhaled a breath she didn't realize she had been holding. "It's just me now."

Blackmore nodded solemnly and clasped his hands in front of him. "I'm sorry to hear that. But I do want to thank you for teaching my daughter how to use her magic. I owe you so much for that."

My daughter.

The words clattered in her ears. Was she ready to accept that this man was her father? She believed his story, she believed that he was truly innocent, but she'd been harboring feelings of fear and anxiety toward this man for weeks, and those wouldn't go away immediately.

But something about the way he said "my daughter" rang true in her heart, her magic humming almost happily within her. It sounded protective, loving, and proud, a tone that Luc had never once used with her. Comparison between the two was futile—she barely knew Blackmore, after all—but with Luc's future now uncertain, wouldn't she want to give Blackmore a chance, to let him into her life, to find out what a true father is? Didn't he deserve that chance after everything he had been through? Didn't she deserve it just as much?

Jax turned his gaze toward her. "She didn't always make it easy."

"Oh dear," Blackmore said playfully, catching her eye. "You inherited my stubbornness,"

"Where is Astor?" Esta asked, still hunched over Raelyn who had been insisting she was fine and didn't need to be fussed over. "I'll kill him myself for what he's done to Raelyn."

Nova glanced over to the table where Luc was still hidden and unconscious, Esta following her gaze. The female elf stood and stomped across the room, only to be stopped by Persy, who Nova had entirely forgotten was still there.

"Esta." His hand was outstretched, though he was too far away to grab her. "Do not dirty your hands in this. I won't be able to protect you from the ramifications."

Her nose wrinkled in disgust. "That man does not deserve to live. This isn't just witches' business. This is Astria's business. He'll likely kill every one of us here just for knowing the truth."

"He wouldn't—"

"He would." Raelyn spoke, loud and strong. Nova turned to look at her, finding her standing. She reached her hand out to Raelyn, who stepped closer and took it.

"He just tried to kill me, his own flesh and blood, and would have succeeded too if my *sister* hadn't stepped in."

Raelyn looked at Nova with sadness in her eyes. She understood, in the same way that they usually understood each other without words.

Bound by blood or bound by love, they were sisters through and through.

"You're right, Rae, I *am* your sister. What Luc did, who my true father is, doesn't change that." She squeezed Raelyn's hand as Raelyn rested her curly head on Nova's shoulder. "Together, remember?"

Raelyn wrapped her arm around Nova's back.

"See?" Esta ground out at Persy. "The man deserves to die. We have two races represented here who have heard the truth. Six of us, plus Blackmore, who would be willing to give testimony to what happened. That's enough for the other governors." Her face paled. "Unless he's corrupted them."

"What?" Jax exclaimed.

Persy huffed and crossed his arms. "The human governors may be weak enough to be corrupted, but the elvish ones certainly would be smart enough and powerful enough to withstand—"

"I thought the same. Turns out, I was wrong."

Seven heads turned in unison toward the voice.

Luc.

47

H E WAS STANDING NOW, a cut bleeding from the side of his forehead and his clothes dirty and tattered but standing and looking at all of them with a brute hatred that made Nova shake. Raelyn gasped as Nova pulled herself in front of her sister, slipping her hand away from Raelyn's and into Fynn's. She embraced the silent surge of magic from his touch.

"No!" Raelyn's voice stayed steady, strong. "You didn't!"

Luc laughed, a sound that was really starting to grate at Nova's last nerve. "Well, the humans were easy. They've been under my thrall for years. The other two witches went next. And Persy, you're right, the elves did put up a fight. They were more difficult to subdue. But I did finally figure out how to get there. I've been the sole governor for five years now."

"No." Persy's face was a mask of shock, his voice little more than a whisper. Esta, still standing near him, was frozen.

"Based on the looks on your faces," Luc's eyes darted among them, "I'd say I've done my job well. No one suspects the other governors of acting on anyone else's agency, when in reality, every vote, every regulation is my doing."

His wicked laugh hung in the air for a moment until Blackmore spoke. "Luc, how could you do this? Everything the past five hundred years has stood for, everything that our country fought to achieve. You've destroyed it."

"Ridiculous, really, the concept of equality. The concept of nine governors to rule all of Astria. Nine! That is far too many voices in the room. It's a miracle anything ever got done." Luc threw up his hands and paced slowly around the room. "No, Astria was headed in the wrong direction, and it was time for a new regime. Everyone knows that witches are the most powerful race and are therefore meant to rule. I was just getting Astria to a place where that could happen."

"You let your own ambitions take over. Let them blind you to the harm this will cause," Blackmore spat back at him, somehow able to maintain a level of civility while Nova was busy fighting against the tide of fury surging through her.

She glanced up at Fynn, who met her gaze, his violet eyes filled with fear. The memories of Lena, of his mother, must be coming back to him. Elves and humans being targeted by witches simply for the sake of being who they were.

She had seen it herself. Hadn't she and Raelyn been discussing earlier this summer that their students had been getting more and more troublesome in recent years? Her thoughts flew to Addy, to the conversation she'd had with her student all those weeks ago. But it wasn't just at school: There had been an uptick in racial violence, too. And it all lined up with when Luc said he ensnared the last elven governor. He'd been laying the groundwork, slowly planting the seeds for a rebellion among the people. For the witches to rise up and seize control. And it all started with destroying her true father's life and stealing his research.

She would be damned if it went further on her watch.

"This ends here, Luc," she declared. She'd try for a bargain first, though he was unlikely to take it. "Turn yourself in, admit what you've done to both Blackmore and the other governors, and we will keep this out of the press."

Jax whipped his head around to her, wild green eyes colliding with hers. "Nova, what the hell?"

"She knows I'll say no." Luc waved his hand in dismissal of the offer. "And besides, it doesn't matter what happens here tonight. The last part of my plan is already in motion."

What the hell did *that* mean? *What* was in motion?

But before she could give it another thought, the ground started to rumble beneath their feet. Raelyn lost her balance, immediately collapsing to the ground, while Nova fought for her own footing. If Luc was going to cave in this entire cavern, it was time for them to get out.

She put out her hands in surrender, finally releasing Fynn's hand but managing to keep that swirl of power still contained within her. "Ok, ok, can we at least get Raelyn out of here?"

She caught a flash of movement in her periphery and turned in time to see Esta move swiftly towards Raelyn.

The ground rumbled further, and rocks started to fall from the ceiling around them.

"No one leaves," Luc snarled.

But Nova nodded to Esta and began calling darkness to the room to block Esta and Raelyn from view. Esta was able to scoop up Raelyn and get her halfway to the hallway when flames danced along the ends of the room, filling the space with light again. Nova quickly extinguished the flames with water summoned from nowhere while Jax tried to summon more darkness. But lightning pierced the air, shooting bolts of electricity throughout the room.

Fynn's body slammed into her and tackled her to the ground, shielding her from the lightning. More rocks fell from the walls and ceiling, larger ones this time.

The strength she'd mustered to wield her magic dissolved completely into fear.

As Jax's shadows dissipated into whisps and the lightning subsided, Nova glanced past Fynn to see Esta and Raelyn had made it safely into the hallway, but Persy was now missing. Jax had crouched and had his hand over his head as if casting a ward to protect himself from the lightning. Blackmore was still standing, looking unphased.

The growl that Luc emitted upon seeing that three of them had escaped, three who had heard the truth and could use it against him, shook her to her core. Fynn rolled away from her, so they could get back to their feet.

This wasn't over. Fear would not win today.

"No bargains," Jax yelled at Luc as he stood. "This ends here, Astor." He threw out shadows again, this time letting them wrap around Luc like a rope but with a snap of Luc's fingers the shadows turned to water and fell away into a puddle at his feet.

Fynn disappeared then reappeared at Blackmore's side and whispered something to him that she couldn't hear. Blackmore's eyes glanced at her and nodded.

Jax and Luc continued to spar, throwing out magic that she had never seen. Light of all colors was darting across the room, along with flame, water, wind, and rumbles of the earth. The cavern alternated between darkness and light as they continued to wield against each other but neither appeared to have an upper hand. Luc may not have publicly used his wielding powers, but it was clear he had been training them. Jax was holding his own, a true sign of his strength and the depths of his power, but she got the sense he would need help soon.

And she was ready.

"Blackmore is going to jump you out of here," Fynn whispered behind her, halting her just as she was about to intervene.

"Excuse me?" She wasn't about to leave, not when she could help.

His violet eyes pleaded with hers. "Just to get you out to Esta and Raelyn. Jax and I will handle Astor and meet you there."

A quake in the ground nearly knocked her to her feet but she grabbed Fynn's arm to steady herself.

"Handle? What does that mean—" But Blackmore was already grabbing her arm and looking at her pleadingly. "Fynn, no, I can help. I'm staying!"

Jax was continuing to flood Luc with attacks, inadvertently keeping Luc distracted from her and Blackmore trying to escape. He lost his footing for a moment and stumbled, allowing Luc to get one good hit on him. Without even thinking, she sent a gust of wind his way to keep him upright and steady him.

"I'm not leaving you!" She turned her attention back to Fynn, back to those violet eyes that usually felt like coming home, full of warmth and depth like a gateway to his soul, but now looked nothing like those she adored. Now they were fierce, shallow, and feral.

Like they had been after the attack in the park. After the nomads.

They were warrior's eyes now.

She tried to wrangle free of Blackmore's grasp but despite how fragile he appeared, how depleted he had become, his grip was strong. "Fynn!"

Without looking at her, he removed her grip from his arm to unsheathe his sword and nodded at Blackmore. A scream escaped her throat as she was whipped into oblivion, Blackmore's grasp on her arm tightening further. In a matter of seconds, her feet met the hard ground beneath her, and she collapsed down onto it, still screaming.

She threw her fists into the dirt as tears streamed down her face, the weakness and vulnerability that she had so often struggled with, that she had so often fought against, the feeling she thought she had finally overcome, threatening to overtake her.

To his credit, Blackmore didn't try to comfort her, didn't try to soothe her. It would be pointless, and she didn't want him interfering in case her emotions unleashed magic that she couldn't control.

She glanced up and, through the tears clouding her vision, took in the scene around her. She was back in the forest, near the river she had parted just a few hours ago. Raelyn and Esta were sitting on the ground nearby, next to each other, watching her and Blackmore warily. Persy was nowhere to be found.

What was she supposed to do now? Go back down there and fight? What was the endgame anyway? She didn't have it in her to kill Luc, and ultimately isn't that what it would take for his tyranny to stop? If he died, the spells he had cast over the other governors would break. The knowledge of how magic would be unlocked for all would die, with the exception of Blackmore, but it seemed he wasn't a threat to that anymore.

If Luc died, Raelyn would be without a father. How would she handle that? Nova's own emotions swung wildly in each direction when the thought entered her head. As much as she hated what he had done to her—taking her away from her family, having her real mother murdered, suppressing her wielder powers—he had raised her. He and Raella may not have treated her the same as they treated Raelyn, but she never wanted for anything. She had never been abused.

Just not properly loved.

She glanced at Blackmore, who had crouched down and was watching her from a few feet away. He again had a look in his eye that could have moved mountains, could have taken down armies to ensure her safety. Certainly, neither Raella nor Luc had ever looked at her that way.

And then it hit her.

If Luc died, she would still have a family. He had never been her family.

She would still have Raelyn. She would still have Fynn. Hell, she'd even have Jax.

And now she would have Blackmore, too.

Breathe. Breathe.

The tears started to slow, and her breathing steadied as she recited the mantra to herself over and over. Inhales and exhales blended together to mollify her raging magic.

Finally, she collected herself enough to push herself into a seated position, facing Blackmore. She brushed away the wetness that remained on her cheeks and pushed loose strands of her braid behind her ear.

He smiled at her weakly, and she found her heart warming. "You have a good one down there."

"He knows I could have handled it." Hadn't he always been the one to encourage her? To tell her she was strong?

"He knows you are powerful enough, yes. But he also knows your heart is too big to be able to pull off what needs to be done." Blackmore paused and drew a breath. "He knew that to protect your future, you needed to not be there."

Jax and Fynn were going to kill Luc. And they didn't want her to be implicated in his death, because Luc's death is not one they could cover up. Sure, his crimes had been capital, and with a trial he would be executed. But they couldn't risk their story not being believed. Couldn't risk that he wouldn't manipulate the entire trial and turn the tables on them instead.

And if he was dead, the other governors would become disenchanted and might be convinced that Luc's death was just.

He had to die tonight. And Fynn and Jax would be the ones to face the consequences. They were taking that responsibility—that *liability*—on themselves.

Raelyn seemed to grasp what was happening too. "No, no, they can't!" Esta, still sitting next to Raelyn, wrapped an arm around her shoulders.

Nova ran to her side.

"Rae," she said, taking Raelyn's hands in hers and looking at her sister. Because she still *was* her sister, always would be. "Rae, you heard what Luc did. You know what has to be done."

"He's our—"

She shook her head. "He's not who we thought he was. He's a murderer, a kidnapper, he deserves to pay for his crimes. But I'm still here, I'm still your sister. *Nothing* will change that. You are my number one, forever and always."

Raelyn looked at her, her mouth open in disbelief.

"We will get through this. We will be ok."

And she found when she said it, she truly believed it. After a few moments of holding each other, Raelyn's face started to soften. She believed it, too.

48

Nova, Raelyn, Esta, and Blackmore sat in silence, the chirping of birds greeting a new day and the bubbling of the river the only sounds around them.

The sun was just beginning to peek over the horizon, filling the trees around them with a warm orange glow, when Fynn and Jax finally emerged from the cave entrance, just visible from where they sat.

Nova jumped up and ran as fast as her weary legs could carry her to Fynn.

He was alive. He was standing.

She forgot about the fury that had overtaken her when he banished her, every last bit of the anger and pain cast aside by the simple relief that he was here, that he'd returned.

She threw her arms around him, ignoring his wince and held him tightly. He wrapped his arms around her, too, then his lips brushed the top of her head.

"Hey, Al." His voice was feeble but unbroken.

She managed to pull herself away long enough to get a glimpse at him properly. His blonde hair was loose from its bun, falling in front of his face and matted with blood in places. His face was dirty, and there was a gash along his left cheek, answering the question of where the blood in his hair had originated. He was breathing heavily;

between that and the wince, he must have either bruised or broken ribs. But he didn't appear permanently harmed.

She exhaled deeply as relief washed over her. "You're ok."

"Nothing a healer can't fix," he replied.

She reached up and ran a finger along the side of his face, over the gash, allowing her magic to channel through that finger and into his skin, the way Jax had just shown her. The wound healed instantly, until all that was left was a faint scar, one that he would wear proudly like the others he had.

"There." She let her fingers graze his cheek a moment longer than necessary. "I won't touch your ribs though."

He sucked in a breath. "I think they're intact anyway. Just bruised. Another few hours and I'll be good as new."

She turned to Jax, who looked relatively uninjured as well, but drained and pale. And she couldn't blame him. None of them had slept since the night before, when they'd been en route to Benedict's cottage. Had that really only been thirty-six hours ago? It felt like a different lifetime.

"Jax?"

He looked at her, his face cast in shadow by the early morning sun and nodded. "I'm fine. Luc has been taken care of."

Thank goodness Fynn still had his arms around her because, even though this was the necessary outcome and their emergence from the laboratory could only mean one thing, she nearly collapsed when Jax confirmed it. Fynn gripped her tightly and held her to his chest, grimacing against the pain in his abdomen.

Luc hadn't been a good father, but he had still been all she'd had. His death, while necessary, hit her harder than she expected.

The world turned upside down and a wailing sound rang in her ears. A wailing sound from her own mouth. A sound she didn't recognize.

Raelyn's sobs behind her pulled her back to the moment, and she struggled with the urge to go to Raelyn or stay in Fynn's embrace, the only place that felt safe right now. But Fynn whispered, "Go," into her ear, releasing his grasp on her.

Without a second thought, she ran to Raelyn, the sister she had tried desperately to protect but ultimately was unable to shield from this mountain of pain. The two fell into an embrace, allowing the tears to fall while they lamented the destruction of their family, their past, their reality. Nova was vaguely aware from the churning of her magic that Fynn had approached and rested a hand on her shoulder. But no one spoke, no one tried to intervene while they mourned.

"What now?"

Esta had waited until Nova and Raelyn collected themselves, and Blackmore had foraged through their one remaining pack for some food to eat before asking the question they all had been thinking.

They were sitting in a circle, Nova nestled between Raelyn and Fynn, Blackmore directly across from her, flanked by Jax on one side and Esta on the other.

Silence reigned for another moment. Then Fynn straightened and spoke up. "Where is my father?"

Esta shook her head. "Long gone before I got up here."

Jax cursed and slammed a fist into his knee. "That's a variable we are going to need to consider. He could get back to the other governors and spin tales."

"The governors should be of their right minds by now though," Nova said, pulling her braid forward to her chest. "Won't they realize what's happened when suddenly they can't remember the last few years?"

"We can't rely on that. I'll go after him," Fynn said. Her heart clenched as if Fynn had squeezed it with his bare hands and not just his words. "I can catch him if I leave now. He doesn't have my speed."

Jax and Esta nodded in agreement.

But Nova's heart started pounding. "Fynn, no, you're exhausted. We all are. Rest first—"

"There's no time, Al." He wrapped an arm around her, pulling her close enough that she could breathe in his scent. "I've got enough left in me to find him."

"Perhaps I should come with you?" Blackmore suggested, uncrossing his legs as if to stand.

But Fynn shook his head. "Let me get to my father and assess the situation. Then we can regroup and discuss when to share the truth." He hesitated then added, "I think you should stay with Nova for now."

Blackmore's gaze burned into her, but she was too caught up in what Fynn was doing, where he was going—without her, and so soon after everything that had just happened—to respond or to look his way.

"I'll take the group back to Aerdmure," Jax said. "Maybe if we can get the priestesses and the witches there to understand the truth of what happened, we can get ahead of it too. Especially if we have Blackmore with us."

Fynn nodded, then unwound his arm from Nova as he stood. "Al?" He held out a hand to help her up. "Walk with me?"

She stood on shaky, numb legs. She had just moments left with him before he went in the opposite direction. And she had no idea when or if she would see him again. He led her along the river, then back into the trees, so they were just out of sight of the rest of the group.

Time seemed to flow both too quickly and too slowly all at once. Blood was pulsing through her veins so hard she was certain he could hear her heartbeat. It was beating so furiously it had drowned out the sounds of the forest.

"Al." He stopped walking, then grasped her hands in his and held tight. "I want you to continue to train with Jax. And with Blackmore, too. Learn as much as you can. I'm already so proud of what you were able to accomplish down there, how you controlled your emotions, what new magic you summoned. If you continue to train, I know you'll be one of the most powerful witches in Astria."

Maybe it was the blood rushing to her head. Maybe it was adrenaline. Maybe it was the force of her magic building from his touch. But those words brought the anger she'd felt toward him earlier back to the forefront. How dare he leave now after just removing her from the fight?

"You can honestly say that after you had me forcibly removed from a battle where I could have helped? You say you're proud, you say I'm powerful, but when it comes time to let me act on that, to prove it, you don't let me." Tears—somehow she still had tears left—threatened to burst through but she held them back. For now, she could hold them back.

He bristled slightly, his face betraying the hurt she had caused with her words and instantly her stomach turned to knots. She hadn't intended to hurt him, had just wanted him to see her side. "I deserve that. I was more concerned about you witnessing Luc's death, about you having to help—"

She placed a hand on his chest, lightly enough not to hurt his ribs. "Let me worry about that. I know you want to protect me, truly I do, but I need to be able to protect myself. I need you to trust that I can."

"I know, Al." A tear slid down his cheek as he placed his hand over hers on his chest. "And I *do* trust you. I know you can. I'm going to need you to do just that while I'm gone."

He was going to do it. He was really going to leave. "Fynn—" she started, her voice cracking, but he put a finger to her lips to stop her.

"Don't. If you say anything else, you may weaken my resolve to go after my father and not go back to Aerdmure with you. Because right now, I'm really fighting with the need to be with you, to go with you." He drew in a deep breath with a grimace. "But we need to get ahead of this, Al. We need to make sure the governors realize the truth if there's any chance of us getting out of this situation."

He was right. If there was any chance that Blackmore could walk free or that he and Jax could avoid the consequences of killing Luc, they needed to start finding support. People who believed their far-fetched story.

"But you're walking right into the den after—" She couldn't quite get herself to voice what he had done.

"Another good reason for me to get the governors to see the truth about Luc. But I need my father on our side, too. Do you trust me?" His violet eyes, darker than usual right now, beseeched hers, begging her to say yes, to go along with his plan. To make it easier for him to do what needed to be done.

She nodded, trying to fight the pressure of tears that still welled in her eyes. He was right, she knew he was right. And she trusted him with her life. If anyone could help, could make this right, if anyone was as motivated to spread the truth as she was...it was him.

"Then know this." He cupped her face with his hands, his thumbs stroking her cheeks. "I will find you again. We are not done here. I am yours, and I want you to be mine, too. There is no one else for me, and we have so much left to explore. I will come back to you as soon as I can."

She nodded, swallowing the lump in her throat.

He tipped her chin up to meet his gaze. "I will *always* find you. I've been telling you so for weeks."

Her eyebrows knit together. "What do you mean?"

"Al. It isn't just a nickname based on your name. It's an old elvish word." He smiled. "It means forever."

The tears broke free in a torrent, and she pressed her lips to his, winding her hands through his hair and pulling him closer. How could her heart be so full and yet completely shattered at the same time? Every piece of it belonged to this male, this elf who had helped her become who she was meant to be. Who had pushed her and guided her but never made her feel inadequate.

Forever. He'd been calling her his forever for *weeks*!

And now he was leaving her.

He meant it when he said he would find her, she knew that. But there was a good chance the governors and Persy would turn against him—Canta knew Persy wouldn't necessarily protect his own son because he was family. And if they turned on him, he would be executed for killing a governor.

This could be the last time she saw him, the last time she could kiss him, could feel her magic swirling in her body in response to him. The last time her hands could bask in the warmth of his skin.

So, she threw all she had into that kiss. She ran her hands down his back and under his shirt, feeling his skin one last time, her heart pounding as his hand slid from her face to her waist, pulling her closer until her body blended with his. Her lips parted and allowed his tongue in; each time they collided a new spark trickled its way down her spine.

If only this moment could last forever. If only time could stop right here.

He pulled away much too quickly, but she could see the remorse in his eyes as he did. "I need to go."

"I love you." The words tumbled from her mouth, but she meant them. She meant them from the bottom of her heart, the depths of her soul, and she needed him to hear them before he left.

The smile he gave her nearly burst her heart and reached all the way to his amethyst eyes, which sparkled in the early morning sun. "I love you, too, Al. Until all the stars in the sky turn to dust and every drop of water in the ocean runs dry, I will love you." He bit his lower lip, then opened his mouth as if to speak again, but closed it and instead brushed one last kiss across her forehead.

Leaving Nova wondering what he had almost said—and why he hadn't—he turned on his heel and sprinted off to track his father. The heartache, the fury, the *love* from the past few hours overwhelmed her, so much she almost couldn't breathe, and her magic begged for release. She fell to the ground, her kneecaps crying out, one hand clenched at her chest.

At the impact, a cloud of dust kicked up, and the earth rumbled beneath her, a warning of what her magic was threatening to do if she allowed it outside her control. Despite the tears streaming down her face, despite the fact that her heart was left in a million little pieces, despite her entire body wanting to run after Fynn, she snapped her eyes shut so her mind, which had always been her strength, could take over.

Breathe. Breathe.

She knelt there, repeating the mantra to herself over and over, inhaling and exhaling, until finally her body started to unwind. The pressure from her magic finally subsided enough for her to open her eyes and stand.

Had minutes passed by?

Hours?

Time without Fynn, without any idea when she would see him again seemed to freeze and stretch to eternity all at once.

Her footsteps were heavy, and the sun had fully risen by the time she made her way back to the group, brushing the remnants of her tears off her face and rearranging it to appear strong. Brave. That's what she needed it to be, for Raelyn, for her upcoming training. They couldn't know that she was crumbling inside.

Raelyn and Esta were standing with Blackmore and Jax, huddled together. The resolve on Raelyn's face matched the strength Nova herself was trying to exude. Was she putting on a brave face, too?

But there would be time for them to discuss things in Aerdmure. Time for them to rehash, digest, process, and mend all the damage that Luc had caused. Time for them to decide how and when to involve their mother—*no, Raelyn's mother*. Time for them to figure out what was going to happen to Astria now and what role they could play in it.

The path forward couldn't have been less clear, but even if she had no idea when—*if*—she would see Fynn again, she had Raelyn. Her beautiful, funny, steadfast sister, and they'd get through this like they got through everything: together.

"So," she said, stopping a few feet from where the group stood. To her surprise her voice sounded steady, not cracking once as she continued, "Back to Aerdmure?"

They turned to look at her, and a shadow of pain passed over Raelyn's face, almost like she could sense what Nova was covering up, but it was gone so fast that it may have just been a shadow cast from the sun.

"Yes," Jax said. "We'll have to walk until Blackmore is rested enough to jump me back, then I'll get Mehta."

She looked up at the trees, the sunlight now steadily pouring through them and allowed it to hit her skin. The warmth filled her from her toes to the crown of her head, and she smiled. Summer was still her favorite season.

"Then let's get going." She picked her pack up off the ground and slung it across her back.

Jax started off, Esta and Raelyn following him close behind, but Blackmore lingered. She glanced at him and raised an eyebrow.

"You are truly remarkable. Your mother would have been so proud." He paused and looked at the ground. "*I'm* so proud."

The heat from the sun flooded her cheeks. "I'm looking forward to getting to know you...Father."

His mouth dropped open for a moment then turned upward into a smile.

"I would be honored to get to know you, daughter." He gestured his hand out for her to lead the way and fell into step beside her.

She might not be sure what role she was ready for this man, her real father, to play in her life, but it was already clear that he was powerful. And if he was going to be around them, needing their protection until Fynn sorted things out, she might as well learn what she could from him. "Would you be willing to help with my training when we get back to Aerdmure?"

Nova's eyes were fixed on the ground ahead of her, but she could hear the smile in his voice when he replied, "Of course! Nothing would make me happier."

She was surprised at the ease with which the corners of her lips turned up into a grin. Though she'd only come to terms with the truth for a matter of hours, something about this man felt like home, felt right, felt comforting. Like her body, her mind, and her magic understood it had found someone trustworthy, someone she could depend on. Someone like a parent.

Neither spoke as they continued walking up the path, but it didn't feel strange or strained. It was natural, just two witches finding their way in the world together.

She broke the silence with a question.

"Luc mentioned that there was more to his plan. More that was already in motion. Even if Fynn convinces the governors of Luc's crimes, do you think the end of Astria as we know it is coming?"

Blackmore stopped walking and grabbed her arm so that she did as well, her gaze settling onto his.

"No, Allie. I think this might be just the beginning."

EPILOGUE

Meanwhile, at the Atrium...

The darkness had been lingering, waiting for so long. But tonight, something had changed. It felt...alive. For the first time in its existence, it felt alive.

It shifted slightly, pulling against the restraints holding it in place. But how was that possible? The darkness wasn't corporeal, wasn't a thing that could be restrained.

No sooner had the thought crossed the darkness' mind than a body began to take shape. Eyes began to form, to see what was happening within the shadows it was being held in.

Two blinks and its vision focused enough to take in its surroundings. A large study, with a wooden desk as the focal point that was littered with papers and shelves flanking either wall filled with trinkets, instruments, books.

Never mind that the room was cast in shadow, the only light trickling in from the large window above the desk: the moon, nearly finished with its descent toward the horizon. Darkness didn't need light to see.

And darkness didn't need restraints.

Without another thought—how amazing to be able to think! —the darkness ripped itself free from its shackles, pausing momentarily to turn and glance at them. Tiny things, really, those shackles. Amazing that they had held it in place for so long.

But now it was free.

And despite being trapped for its entire existence, despite having no memory of life before this moment...

It knew what it needed to do.

ACKNOWLEDGEMENTS

If you'd have told me a year ago that I would not only have finished this book but *published* it, too, I'd have laughed in your face. What started out as a fun little NaNoWriMo challenge has turned into a whole new adventure for me and fulfilled a dream I never thought I could fulfill: becoming a published author.

First and foremost, I have to thank my husband, Chris, mostly because he's upset he didn't get this book dedicated to him and so I promised I would thank him first. Thank you, babe, for always believing in me, from day one when I said, "I think I want to write a novel." You've known about this dream and my passion for reading for over a decade so it probably didn't surprise you at all. But I was blown away by your support and encouragement. You're the reason this book is getting published. All because you gave me the book on self-publishing for Christmas and helped me find the time (and money) to get it done. I love you so much!

Second, I want to thank my family. Mom and Dad, you instilled a love of reading in me from day one. Even as an adult, some of my favorite things to talk to both of you about are books. Thank you for all the Barnes and Noble visits, book release parties, library trips, and gift cards growing up and to this day. If it weren't for you, I wouldn't be who I am today! Bubby and Alyssa, thanks for always checking in, asking how it was going, offering to share it with friends, and generally being excited!

To my in-laws and Uncle Thom: Thank you for asking me every Sunday for an update over spaghetti, meatballs, and red wine. You have no idea how much that meant to me!

To my beta readers, Sarah, Marianne, Emily, Abigail, Kayla, Casey, Erin, Danielle, and Ashleigh: there's so much of each of you in this book! I hope you enjoy the final version and know that I appreciate every comment, every nugget, every reaction that you left for me. You're all amazing!

To my editor, Kelly: Thank you for sticking by me from the earliest draft to the last. Your guidance has helped me grow so much as a writer and gets me even more excited for what's to come!

To my book club/boom club: You've all been some of my biggest cheerleaders since literally day 1 of writing! Thank you for your undying support, both bookish and non-bookish.

To my Bookstagram and Discord friends: thank you for welcoming me into your platforms with open arms and embracing this story! I can't believe I didn't join sooner, but hey, better late than never!

To Stella the cat: Thanks for keeping me warm while I wrote or edited and for a few typos, too, along the way. I'm pretty sure you're the reason why some of my Instagram followers stick around too, and honestly I can't blame them!

To my kids: You probably won't understand what it was like to write and edit this while you were sleeping, napping, or at daycare, and it'll be years before you read this, but I hope one day you do and it makes you proud! I love you both and have been so inspired by watching you learn, grow, and tackle new challenges every day.

And to you, reader. Thank you for taking a moment (or ten) of your time and from your loaded TBR pile to read my book. It means the world to me.

Leave A Review!

One of the best ways to support an indie author, like me, is to leave us reviews. I would be so grateful for just one more moment of your time to leave a review on your favorite platform or two. *The Wielder's Discovery* is available to review on Goodreads, Storygraph, Amazon, and of course, social media.

About the Author

When not dreaming up new fantasy worlds or teaching her toddlers how to recognize her favorite bookish characters, Meredith can be found curled up with a book or planning adventures with her husband. Though a chemical engineer by day, she's been writing stories for as long as she can remember, most notably finishing her first novel (which will never be published) at the age of 12. After growing up in Virginia, she now lives outside of Philadelphia. Find her on Instagram @meredithkasianauthor to learn more about upcoming releases and to join her newsletter!